EPITAPH FOR THREE WOMEN

JEAN PLAIDY HAS ALSO WRITTEN

EPITAPH FOR
THREE WOMEN

JEAN PLAIDY

G. P. Putnam's Sons, New York

Library of Congress Cataloging in Publication Data

Plaidy, Jean, date.
  Epitaph for three women.

  (Plantagenet saga ; 12)
  Bibliography: p.
  1. Great Britain—History—Henry VI, 1422–1461—
Fiction.   2. Catherine of Valois, queen, consort of
Henry V, King of England, 1401–1437—Fiction.
3. Joan, of Arc, Saint, 1412–1431—Fiction.
4. Eleanor of Gloucester, Duchess, consort of
Humphrey, Duke of Gloucester, 1391–1447—Fiction.
I. Title.   II. Series: Plaidy, Jean, date.
Plantagenet saga ; 12.
PR6015.I3E6   1983   823'.914   82-23175
ISBN 0-399-12782-8

CONTENTS

Part One
KATHERINE OF VALOIS

Part Two
JOAN OF ARC

Part Three
ELEANOR OF GLOUCESTER

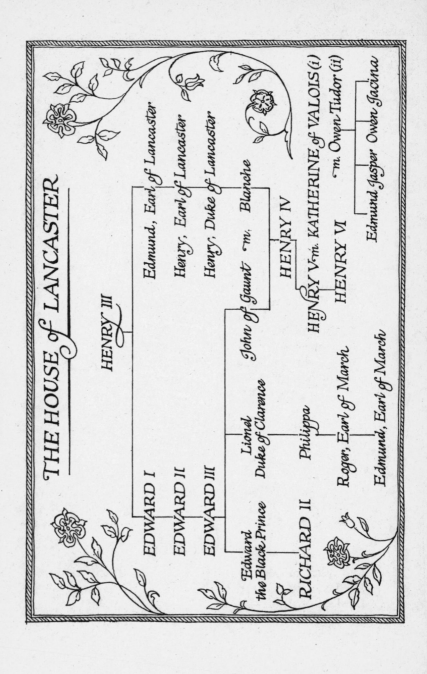

THE HOUSE of LANCASTER

HENRY III
├─ EDWARD I
├─ Edmund, Earl of Lancaster
│   └─ Henry, Earl of Lancaster
│   └─ Henry, Duke of Lancaster
│   └─ Blanche m. John of Gaunt

EDWARD I
└─ EDWARD II
    └─ EDWARD III
        ├─ Edward the Black Prince
        │   └─ RICHARD II
        ├─ Lionel, Duke of Clarence
        │   └─ Philippa
        │   └─ Roger, Earl of March
        │   └─ Edmund, Earl of March
        └─ John of Gaunt m. Blanche
            └─ HENRY IV
                └─ HENRY V m. KATHERINE of VALOIS (i)
                    │   m. Owen Tudor (ii)
                    └─ HENRY VI
                                    └─ Edmund Jasper Owen Jacina

THE PLANTAGENETS

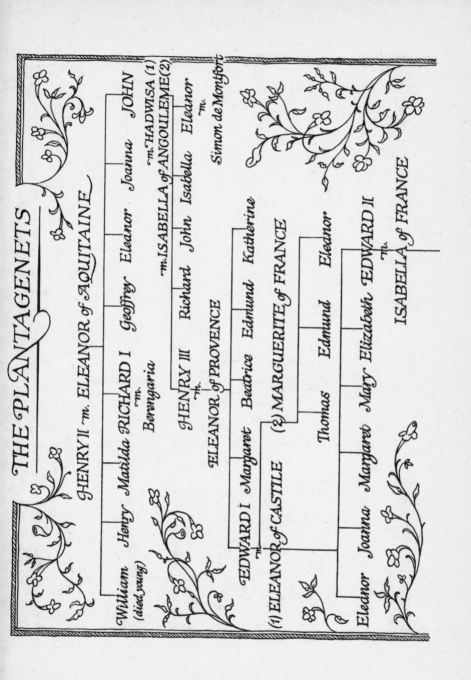

HENRY II m. ELEANOR of AQUITAINE

William (died young) — Henry — Matilda — RICHARD I m. Berengaria — Geoffrey — Eleanor — Joanna — JOHN m. HADWISA (1) m. ISABELLA of ANGOULEME (2)

HENRY III m. ELEANOR of PROVENCE — Richard — John — Isabella — Eleanor m. Simon de Montfort

EDWARD I m. (1) ELEANOR of CASTILE (2) MARGUERITE of FRANCE — Margaret — Beatrice — Edmund — Katherine

Eleanor — Joanna — Margaret — Mary — Elizabeth — EDWARD II m. ISABELLA of FRANCE — Thomas — Edmund — Eleanor

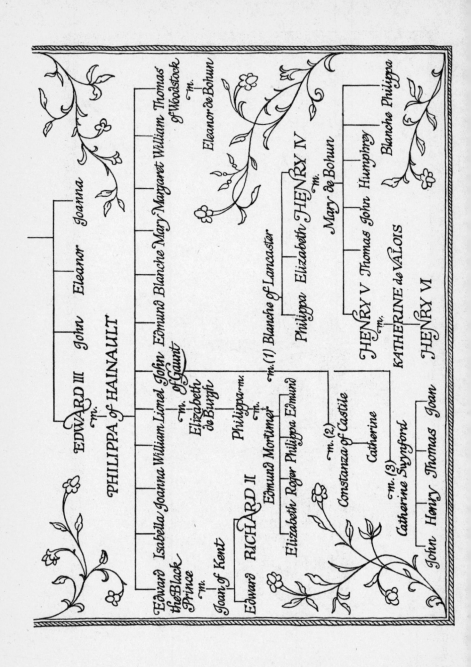

EDWARD III
m.
PHILIPPA of HAINAULT

Edward Isabella Joanna William Lionel John Edmund Blanche Mary Margaret William Thomas
the Black   of Gaunt   of Woodstock
Prince   m.   m.
m.   Elizabeth   Eleanor de Bohun
Joan of Kent   de Burgh

Edward RICHARD II   Philippa m.
                          Edmund Mortimer
                                          m. (1) Blanche of Lancaster
        Elizabeth Roger Philippa Edmund

                          m. (2)
                          Constanza of Castile   Philippa Elizabeth HENRY IV
                                                                           m.
                          Catherine   Mary de Bohun

                          m. (3)
                          Catherine Swynford   HENRY V Thomas John Humphrey
                                                      m.
        John Henry Thomas Joan   KATHERINE de VALOIS   Blanche Philippa

                                                      HENRY VI

John Eleanor Joanna

PART ONE

KATHERINE OF VALOIS

THE WELSH SQUIRE

WHEN her brother-in-law came to tell Katherine that the
King was dead, she could not believe him. Not Henry, not
the mighty conqueror of her country, not the lover, husband
and father of her child.

She stared at him incredulously, shaking her head. 'No,'
she cried. 'No. It cannot be so.'

John, the great Duke of Bedford, who had loved his brother
Henry well and had always declared it was his dearest wish
to serve him with all his might, and had indeed proved that
this was so, now regarded her with melancholy eyes.

'His last thoughts were for you,' he told her. ' "Comfort
my dear wife," he said. "This day she will be the most afflicted creature living." '

She continued to stare at him with disbelieving eyes.

She murmured: 'He was a little sick ... yes ... But
death ... ! Oh no ... not that.'

'He should have rested. He insisted on going to Burgundy's
aid.'

Anger showed in her eyes, momentarily subduing her grief.
All her life had been overshadowed by the conflict between
Burgundy and Orléans. And once again it was Burgundy.

'You knew him as I did,' went on the Duke. 'He would
never rest while there was a battle to be fought.'

She murmured quietly: 'England ... France ... my son
... What shall we do now?'

The Duke laid his hands on her shoulders and drawing
her to him gently kissed her brow.

'It is for God to decide,' he said.

And because he knew there was nothing else he could do to comfort her he called one of her women to him.

'Leave her with her grief,' he said. 'But be prepared. It will be terrible when she realizes what this means.'

*   *   *

So he was dead, the seemingly invincible Harry, the very mention of whose name had struck terror into the French. Since his coming to the throne he had left his dissolute life behind him and had devoted himself to winning the crown of France. He had been tall, handsome, virile, active yet gentle and just in his dealings save when his anger was aroused. Then men compared him with a lion. He was a man who refused to see failure and forever after when men spoke of him they would think of Agincourt, that famous battle into which he led his men with all the fire and confidence of a conqueror so that his tiny army, depleted by sickness, had faced the might of France and won a resounding victory. It had been a more than victorious battle for it heralded the end of the war which had been going on since the days when Edward III decided that he had a claim to France.

And just as the great warrior was about to accept the fruits of his conquest, he had taken to his bed and died.

Katherine might well ask, What now?

She was twenty-one. Not very old but it might be that a childhood fraught with disasters had prepared her in some way for them.

In Windsor Castle in England a nine months old boy was living cared for by his nurses under the control of Henry's brother Humphrey, Duke of Gloucester. That little boy—Henry like his father—was the most important child in England, because on the sudden death of his father he had now become England's King.

Now that she had grown accustomed to the fact that Henry was dead a calmness settled on Katherine. Her brother-in-law John would tell her what to do and she would trust him, as Henry had.

She travelled from Senlis to the Castle of Vincennes where Henry lay and when she looked on the dead body of her husband her calmness deserted her and for the first time since she had heard the news, she wept. It was as though at last she realized what the death of Henry meant, and she was desolate, afraid of the future.

There were so many who wished to talk to her. His body must be taken back to England, they said. There should be no delay. But the Duke of Bedford had ordered that her wishes should be respected in every way.

She wanted to be alone, she said, just for an hour ... alone to think. She ordered that her horse should be saddled; she had a desire for the solitude which the forest could offer.

So they saddled her horse and she rode out into the Bois de Vincennes while at a respectful distance the King's squires waited for her. When she dismounted one of the squires hurried forward to take her horse. She looked at him. He was young, about her own age, tall, dark, with a face which interested her.

She said: 'I have a mind to rest here for a little while. The forest is beautiful at this time of year. Do you agree?'

'It is, my lady,' he replied. He had an accent which she found difficult to understand, but then she was not as proficient in the English language as she would have liked to be. She remembered afresh how Henry had laughed at her delivery of some words. 'I must improve,' she had said demurely. 'No,' he had cried. 'I like it your way, Kate. Don't change. Just stay my little French Kate.'

She wondered if she was going on all her life remembering.

She said: 'Already there are signs of autumn.'

'It's so, my lady,' answered the squire.

'It is sad ... the summer over. The leaves are already changing colour. Soon the branches will be stark and bare.'

A terrible melancholy had come over her. As with my life, she thought. He is gone. Summer is over. The winter is coming on. Then she looked at the squire. He was very young—in the springtime of life one might say.

'How old are you?' she asked impulsively.

He looked surprised as though wondering of what interest his age could possibly be to this Queen.

But he answered promptly: 'I am about to be twenty-one.'

She looked at him and smiled. A moment ago she had been thinking how young he was, with his life before him; and he was just her age.

It was like a revelation. Henry was dead; but she was alive and she was young. She was beautiful; she might be the

widow of Henry the Conqueror but she was also the mother
of Henry the Sixth of England and there was so much left
to her. There was her baby to care for. Her whole life lay
before her. She had lived through terrible hazards in the past;
she would do so again if necessary.

For a few moments her melancholy had lifted. She smiled
dazzingly at the young squire.

'I will return to the castle now,' she said. 'There is much
to be done.'

Obediently he helped her to mount.

'Thank you,' she said. She looked at him steadily. 'You
have a strange way of talking,' she went on in halting English.
'I think you could say the same of me.'

He did not know what to answer and she smiled at him
again.

'Tell me,' she said, 'what is your country? Where do you
come from?'

'I come from Wales, my lady,' he answered.

'Wales. Oh yes, I have heard the King speak of Wales.
Tell me your name.'

'It is Owen Tudor, my lady.'

'Owen Tudor,' she repeated. 'Thank you, Owen Tudor.
You have done well.'

She rode thoughtfully back to the castle. A hope had returned to her. It was strange that it should have happened
during a few moments' conversation with a Welsh squire.

*   *   *

They laid the King's body in a chariot which was to be
drawn by four horses. She had ordered that an effigy should
be made resembling him as near as possible, and that this
should be placed above the coffin and borne across France
to Calais. On the head of the image was set a crown of gold
and brilliant gems and about its shoulders was a purple velvet cloak trimmed with ermine. In the right hand was placed
a sceptre and in the left a golden orb. It was uncanny. As
though Henry had come to life again to observe his funeral
rites.

The Queen had chosen those who would accompany the
cortège to England.

'What do you know of the King's squire, Owen Tudor?'
she asked Bedford.

He had never heard of the man but would discover since he had caught the Queen's interest.

Bedford was clearly wondering why the young squire had done this, and she answered quickly: 'He seemed greatly moved by the King's death. I have a feeling that he was a loyal servant.'

Bedford came back with the information: 'A Welshman of obscure origins. Grandson of Sir Tudor Vychan ap something. These Welsh have unpronounceable names. I gather the father disgraced himself in some way and was outlawed.'

'Don't let us blame the son for his father's sins,' she said.

'Nay, he pleased my brother. He was on the field at Agincourt and so distinguished himself that in spite of his youth he was made squire of the King's body.'

'I had a feeling that he had served the King well.'

'How did he come to your notice?'

' 'Twas nothing. He brought my horse. I spoke to him and I was impressed by his ... feeling for the King.'

'Henry had a way with him,' said Bedford. 'He could bind men to him. It was one of his qualities as a leader. They would have followed him to hell if need be.'

The Queen showed signs of being overcome by emotion and Bedford hastened to discuss further details of the progress to England.

Before they left Katherine gave orders that Esquire Owen Tudor was to be among those who escorted the cavalcade to England.

*   *   *

So they set out and the Queen with her retinue followed the chariot containing the King's corpse, accompanied by all the princes and lords of the King's household and a few of his squires. At Abbeville they paused, where masses were sung for the repose of the King's soul. It was an impressive sight and people waited along the roadside to catch a glimpse of it as it passed. The banners of the saints were held by the Duke of Exeter and the Earl of March and with them was Sir Louis Robsart, the Queen's own knight, among numerous knights and nobles. Four hundred men-at-arms in black armour surrounded the bier; very sombre they looked, as befitted the occasion, their horses barbed black and their lancets held with the points downwards. At dusk, when the torches were lighted and they sang a dismal dirge as they walked, it was even more impressive—a solemn and fearful sight.

In every town through which they passed, masses were sung. They went through Montreuil to Boulogne and then on to Calais where vessels from England were waiting to carry the King's body home.

It was a calm crossing and soon the white cliffs were in sight. Crowds of sorrowing people were waiting on the beaches and when the Queen stepped ashore she was greeted by fifteen bishops, and abbots and priests who were too numerous to be counted.

Katherine looked very young and desolate and won the sympathy of the people. They cheered her fervently. 'Long life to the Queen,' they cried. 'God bless her and our baby King.' She lifted her hand as she passed along in acknowledgement of their feeling for her but she was longing now for the dreary business to be over.

She wanted to be at Windsor, to see her baby, to assure herself of his well-being. She who had lived through the troubled reign of her father knew that she would have to be very careful now.

But for the time being she would go to Windsor. They would not attempt to stop her doing that. First she must see her little son, hold him in her arms. She must never forget that although he was only a baby—and very much like all other babies—he was the King of England. She was apprehensive. To be nine months old and King, surrounded by ambitious men, was a matter to be regarded very seriously; and although the baby sleeping in his cot was unaware of this ... just yet ... understanding would soon come to him.

In the meantime there was his mother to fight for him.

She was deeply moved as the castle came in sight. She had always loved it best of all her homes. To her it represented peace and security and her early life had instilled in her a need for both. The castle, grand and imposing with its Round Tower standing on an artificial mound surrounded by the deep fosse, the strong stone walls and battlemented towers filled her with pleasure as she advanced. She could see the great forest nearby in which she and Henry had hunted together—not often for he had rarely time for such pursuits —but those great oaks had been the background of her first

weeks in England when she had been so happy and young
and innocent enough to believe that life would go on like
that forever.

It was in that castle that her baby had been born and
when she thought of that she felt a qualm of uneasiness for
Henry had expressed the wish that his son should be born
anywhere but at Windsor. Why had the impulse come to
disobey him? She could not be sure, but it had been irresistible.

He had said: 'I do not wish our child to be born at
Windsor.'

'Windsor is a beautiful castle,' she had replied.

'Ah, you love it well and that pleases me. I too have a
fondness for the place.'

'It should be the birthplace of kings,' she had said.

Then he had taken her hands and looked very serious.
'Not for our child, Kate. Not Windsor.'

No more had been said and they had revelled in the
beauties of the forest and returned to the castle and partaken
of the fine buck which they had proudly brought back with
them. And they had laughed and frolicked together while
briefly he forgot to think of war.

And when her time was near she had been at Windsor.
I must leave here, she had told herself. It is the King's wish.
But she delayed leaving and the snow came. There were high
snowdrifts everywhere and ice on the road. 'It is no time for
travelling, my lady,' said her women.

And she was only too ready to agree. Henry would not
wish her to take to the roads now. Who knew what would
happen to a pregnant woman on a journey fraught with the
dangers of winter travel?

It had been just a whim; she had always been one to shrug
aside that which was unpleasant. It had been the only way
to live through a childhood such as hers had been.

So in Windsor Castle her little Henry had been born.

With what joy she had sent messengers to France. How
delighted Henry would be to learn that he had a son. And
when the messenger returned to her she had sent for him
and eagerly had asked: 'How was the King? What said he
to the news that he has a son?'

'My lady,' was the answer, 'first he shouted his delight. He
said it was the happiest moment of his life. And then ...'

'And then?' she had asked. 'What then?'

'He wished to know where the child had been born, my lady.'

'Oh!' Her hand had flown to her throat and she had said quietly: 'And what said he when you told him?'

The messenger had hesitated and she had gone on quickly: 'Tell me.'

'He turned pale. Then he said a strange thing, my lady.'

'Yes, yes?'

' 'Twas something like this:

' "I Henry born at Monmouth
Shall small time reign and much get
But Henry of Windsor shall long reign and lose all."

'Then my lady, he added with great melancholy, "But as God will, so be it." '

For a while she had been uneasy but she refused to be depressed. It was only now and then that she remembered; but as she rode towards Windsor it came into her mind again more forcibly than ever, because the first part of the prophecy had come true. Henry had gained much and reigned such a short time. Henry the Sixth would reign long. Yes, he should; she would cherish him and love him, and see that no harm came to him.

Her brother-in-law Humphrey of Gloucester was riding out to meet her. With him was Henry of Winchester, the baby's great-uncle, who was one of the child's godparents. They were accompanied by a retinue of knights and squires.

The two parties drew up and faced each other. Humphrey of Gloucester rode up to the Queen and taking her hand leaned forward to kiss her cheek. Then she was greeted by Henry of Winchester in like manner.

'Welcome to Windsor, dear sister,' said Humphrey. 'This is a sorry occasion.'

He was handsome like his brothers but already the signs of the profligate life he lived were apparent on his face. He was a man of overwhelming ambition and even at this moment when he genuinely mourned a brother whom he had loved and admired he could not help wondering what advantage to himself could come out of the circumstances.

The Bishop—son of John of Gaunt and Catherine Swynford, beginning life as a bastard and later being legitimized —had always served the crown with loyalty. He was deeply disturbed by the death of the King, for he knew that with a child heir there was certain to be jostling for power and strife between various factions which was no good for any country.

'Bless you, my lady,' he said to the Queen. 'May God guard you.'

Then they rode to Windsor.

First she must go to the royal nurseries.

'You will find him in good health,' Humphrey told her.

The nurses were with him. One held him in her arms and she was crooning a ditty to him while he played with coloured rings.

So unceremoniously had she entered that at first they did not recognize her.

Then someone said: 'The Queen!'

They curtseyed deeply—all but the woman who held the child. Katherine went to her and took the baby.

He stared at her with wondering eyes and suddenly seized the gold chain about her neck and tried to put it into his mouth.

'He seizes everything, my lady. He is so quick and bright ...'

'Henry, Henry,' she said. 'Don't you know me? I am your mother.'

Then she kissed him tenderly and she took him to a window seat and sat down holding him tightly.

'Yes indeed,' she told herself, 'I have much to live for.'

*   *   *

In the apartments of the Duke of Gloucester, he and the Bishop of Winchester faced each other. Humphrey had been trying to avoid the interview for he knew what its nature would be and he had no intention of listening to the advice of the old man.

Who in God's name are these Beauforts? he asked himself. Bastards all of them. They should be grateful that their father thought enough of them to legitimize them and leave it at that. Instead they think they are as royal as I and my brothers are, and have a right to dictate to us what we should do.

Henry Beaufort had always had great influence with King Henry. He had been his tutor at one time and Henry had set great store by the views of his uncle. Before he had died he had named him as one of his son's guardians.

And he wants to dictate to us all, thought Humphrey. Well, he shall find his mistake there.

Humphrey knew that the interview was to concern Jacqueline and he was certainly not going to be told what to do about her, because he had already made up his mind that he was going to marry her.

Humphrey was a man of conflicting characteristics. Dissolute in the extreme, given to frequenting low taverns and consorting with prostitutes, he was yet a lover of the fine arts. He had been most carefully educated at Balliol College and had quickly acquired a love of books which he had never lost. He collected them; and he honoured the men who produced them. When he was twenty he had made a gift of books to Oxford at the time when the library there was being enlarged. A patron of the arts he was respected by those who performed in them and in their circle he became known as the Good Duke Humphrey. It seemed incongruous that one of selfish ambition who indulged in riotous living should earn such a title; but his was a nature of contrasts.

On his accession Henry had made him Chamberlain of England, and he had accompanied his brother to France and had taken part in the battle of Harfleur as well as that of Agincourt. In fact at Agincourt he had come near to losing his life when he had been wounded and thrown to the ground by the Duc D'Alençon. It was Henry the King who with characteristic courage and energy had found time to rescue his brother and save his life.

One must admire and revere Henry, Humphrey had believed; but when Henry was dead, what then? Humphrey was ambitious. A man must look to his own advantage. He had always believed that.

And who would have guessed that Henry would die so young? He was only thirty-five and strong, hale and hearty so it had seemed. And to be carried off by a fever and dysentery! It had happened to others. Soldiering was a profession which took a high toll of those who followed it. But who would have believed at the glory of Agincourt that Agincourt's hero could so soon become a lifeless corpse.

Well, it happened and we must forsooth go on from there, Humphrey told himself.

His elder brother John had had the King's confidence. He had the people's confidence too. There was a quality of honesty in John which appealed to the people. But worthy as he was he had just missed that aura of greatness which Henry had had and which had enabled him to charm all those with whom he came into contact and inspire loyalty and belief in his invincibility. That was true leadership. It is found rarely and Henry undoubtedly had had it. And he, Humphrey? He was no Henry, he knew that. But he was a man who knew how to fight for what he wanted.

While John was in France Humphrey was in control in England. When John returned he would take a step backwards of course. But in the meantime he was in charge and he was not going to be dictated to by Beaufort, Bishop and royal bastard though he might be.

When the Lord Bishop had arrived, the squires had heralded him in with a show of reverence which irritated Humphrey, yet he had to admit that Henry Beaufort had an air of royalty about him. He could never forget he was the son of John of Gaunt and grandson of a King, and was not going to allow anyone else to do so either; and now behind him he had the authority of the Church.

Ambitious—was he not a Beaufort? Handsome—he took after his mother—and dignified. He was reputed to be impetuous and it was true he now and then acted without due thought; and he loved worldly possessions of which it was also said he had amassed a good deal. Whatever his faults he was consistently loyal to the crown. He had lent money to the King for his campaigns in France and none rejoiced more whole-heartedly than he at the success of those campaigns.

It was for this reason that he was now determined to turn Humphrey from a course of which he disapproved.

'The Queen, God help her, will find comfort with her babe,' said the Bishop. 'Poor lady, I doubt she understands the difficulties ahead.'

''Tis a pity he is of such tender years,' said Humphrey.

'A matter which time will remedy.'

Humphrey was a little impatient. The Bishop had not come to him to talk of such an undisputed fact as the King's youth.

Humphrey dismissed the squires and when they were alone and comfortably seated the Bishop put the palms of his hands together as though he were about to pray and looking steadily at Humphrey said: 'I have heard disturbing rumours.'

'My lord Bishop, who has not? Disturbing rumours are as commonplace as the air we breathe.'

'Some are more disturbing than others. My lord, I would ask you this. Is it true that you are contemplating marriage with the Lady Jacqueline?'

'I will confess to a liking for the lady.'

'My lord Duke, I must have a straight answer.'

'*You* must, Bishop? Why so? Is not this a matter between myself and the lady concerned?'

'No, my lord, it is not. It is a matter of deep concern to France and England.'

'You are dramatic.'

'It is a dramatic situation. Have you considered that such a marriage could bring about a breach between England and Burgundy?'

'So?'

'We rely on our allies in France. The late King would have been the first to admit that. So would the Duke of Bedford. I ask you, my lord, have you discussed this matter with the Duke?'

'My lord Bishop, let me tell you this. I will marry where I will, and neither my brother nor the Church shall dictate to me on that matter. I go where my fancy lies.'

'It is to be hoped that your fancy is not to undermine our conquests in France.'

There was a brief silence. Both men were thinking of Jacqueline. Who would have believed, pondered the Bishop, that when Jacqueline of Bavaria had sought refuge at the English Court this would have been the result? She must be now about twenty-one years old. She was personable, though not outstandingly so, and an heiress, if she could regain what she had lost. The Bishop had no doubt that Gloucester's eyes were as firmly fixed on her possessions as on the lady herself. Henry had welcomed her to England and had so favoured her that she had acted as godmother at the christening of young Henry.

Jacqueline was the only daughter of William IV, Count of Hainault, Holland and Zealand as well as being Lord of Friesland.

Jacqueline had been married to John of France, Katherine's brother, who had briefly been Dauphin on the death of his elder brother Louis. Almost immediately John had died and when her father died also Jacqueline became the sovereign of Hainault, Holland and Zealand. With such possessions she was not allowed to remain a widow for long and a second husband was soon found for her. This was John, Duke of Brabant, her own cousin and also cousin to Philip of Burgundy.

Her father's brother, at one time Bishop of Liège, took her possessions from her and made a treaty with her husband, the weak Duke of Brabant.

It was at this stage that she fled to England and threw herself on the mercy of the English King. Henry not only gave her asylum but treated her with the dignity due to her rank and the Spanish antipope Benedict XIII was persuaded to grant her a divorce from the Duke of Brabant.

So here was Jacqueline in England, a member of the Court and a lady who was heiress to great possessions, if they could be won back, and in view of English successes on the continent, Humphrey did not see why they should not. Then he could be not only husband of Jacqueline but the Count of Hainault, Holland and Zealand. A pleasant prospect for a man who could never hope to rule England. His baby nephew and his brother John came before him. He was a man who would seize every opportunity and this had seemed one of them.

The Bishop saw the matter in a different light and that was why he was so uneasy.

'My dear Bishop,' said Humphrey at length, 'you distress yourself unnecessarily.'

'Then you see what the implications of this marriage would be?'

'I see, my lord, that through it I could bring further honour to England.'

'By marrying this lady you would put yourself in conflict with the Duke of Burgundy.'

'I have not the same fear of the noble Duke as you have, Bishop.'

'I fear what it could mean to England if he withdrew his support and ceased to be our ally.'

'An uneasy ally,' murmured Humphrey.

'I agree and therefore to be treated with caution.'

'One can be too cautious in life,' commented Humphrey.

'I know this,' replied the Bishop. 'My Lord Bedford will be as anxious to avoid this marriage as I am and as are all those who wish our country well.'

'I like not your tone. None serves his country better than I.'

'We are not concerned with what you have done in the

past. This is one act which could bring disaster. By such a marriage you would put yourself in competition with Philip of Burgundy for the control of the Netherlands.'

'They are in the hands of the one-time Bishop of Liège at this time.'

'They will not remain there long. Burgundy will see to that. He will press his rights through his cousin of Brabant and, my lord, should this marriage take place I doubt not that you also will turn your thoughts to the lady's lands. Burgundy will not see them pass to you ... any more than you will wish to see them go to him. England cannot afford your quarrel with Burgundy, my lord Duke. That is why I ask you to consider this matter very carefully.'

'Then you have done what you regard as your duty by asking me. Shall we let it rest there, Bishop?'

Arrogant coxcomb, thought the Bishop. Henry would never have allowed this had he lived. Each day one realized more and more what a tragedy it was that Henry had died.

The Bishop rose to his feet rather slowly; his limbs were a little stiff nowadays.

Pompous old fool, thought Humphrey. What right has he to tell me what to do? To hell with him. To hell with Burgundy. Why shouldn't I have Jacqueline ... and Hainault, Holland and Zealand.

*   *   *

Although Katherine found great comfort in the royal nursery she realized that this was a short respite. Soon people would want to see the baby and when the Parliament met she would have to take him to London. She would have to travel through the City holding the baby. Poor child, he would have to get used to being on show. But in the meantime she could be quiet. She could stay in her beloved Windsor; she could be with her baby like any other humble mother; she could ride in the forest although she could never get the solitude she longed for because always she would be accompanied by her attendants. They kept their distance, it was true; they understood her desire to be alone. Once or twice she had caught a glimpse of the Welsh squire. She remembered him with pleasure and she was glad that she had commanded that he be a member of her household. He stood out among the rest. He was not especially handsome but there was an air of innocence about him which she found refreshing. Perhaps, she told herself, it is because as a Welshman he seems different from these English; as I must seem.

She knew little about the Welsh. She vaguely remembered Henry's saying that at one time they had given trouble ... as the Scots had in the past and as the Irish did always.

It was late October when the messengers came from France. She received them immediately in her private apartments and she saw at once that the news they brought was of a melancholy nature.

'My lady,' she was told, 'the King your father has died in Paris.'

She was silent. She could not judge her feelings at that moment. The father whom she had loved and for whom she had so often feared was no more. Poor sad King of France, whose life had been such a burden to him and to others. For a moment she was back in the Hôtel de St Pol, a frightened child listening for strange noises which might come from that part of the mansion which had been set aside for the King. She could remember turning to her elder sister Michelle and burying her face against her to shut out the sounds, and Michelle's stroking her hair and whispering: 'It is all right, Katherine, he can't hurt you. He can't get out. His keepers are with him.'

Then there was another memory, her father emerging from the Hôtel de St Pol, coming to the Louvre, himself again after one of those strange periods, caring for them all, caring for his country and his people.

'His end was ... peaceful?' she asked.

'My lady, when he came back to Paris he was well. He came through the streets and the people cheered him. He was deeply loved.'

She nodded. 'Yes,' she said. 'He was deeply loved. He was a good man when he was free of his affliction.'

'The people knew it, my lady. They were saying that if the King had not suffered his illness the trials which have come to France would never have happened.'

The man stopped abruptly. He remembered suddenly that he was talking to the wife of the Conqueror. She was the enemy now.

She cut in quickly: 'I understand how they feel. They are right. Everything went wrong for France when my father became ill.'

But she was thinking: Nothing would have stopped Henry. He was determined to win the crown of France and none knows more than I that he was a man who would have his way.

'My lady, it would have warmed your heart to see how the people greeted him when he came to Paris. They were under the rule of the English ...' again that fearful pause and again she nodded reassurance ... 'but they shouted for him. "Noel!" they cried. "Noel!" and they seemed to think that because he was well again we should regain our country. And when he died his body lay in state for three days and the people came to see him and to show their respect and their sorrow. My lady, they said of him "Dear Prince, there will never be another as good as thou wert. Accursed be thy death for now thou hast gone there will be nothing for us but wars and trouble." They likened themselves to the children of Israel, my lady, crying out during the captivity in Babylon.'

'It must have been very moving.'

'My lady forgive me. Like many I loved the King your father.'

She said: 'Alas that he should have been so afflicted. And what is happening now in Paris?'

'The Conqueror is there.'

The Conqueror. Her brother-in-law, John of Bedford!

'He has ordered heralds to proclaim Henry of Lancaster King of England and France.'

The baby in the cradle. Her little Henry. Not yet a year old. Such weighty titles for such a little one to bear.

The messenger was nervous. His was an unenviable task. He must proclaim the death of the lady's father when her husband had been the reason for France's downfall and her own child was the usurper King of France.

She understood and her glance and gentle tones reassured him once more that she attached no blame to him because he showed so clearly his loyalty to his own country.

She dismissed him that he might be refreshed after his journey and she went up to the nursery for she felt an irresistible urge to be with her child.

Henry was sleeping peacefully in his cradle. His small hand was clenched about the bed quilt and he was sucking the corner of it. It brought him some sort of odd comfort and he sought it as soon as he was laid in his cradle.

Such a baby. Not yet a year old and already the crown

of England was his and they were trying to force the crown of France on top of that.

She was afraid for him. In that moment she wished that she were the wife of a country gentleman living far away from the events which rocked the country. She imagined herself waking each day to the sound of birdsong and the lowing of cattle. It was absurd. Life was not like that. She tried to imagine the warlike Henry in such circumstances. Battle with conquest had been his life; and it seemed certain that it would be the lot of this little one in the cradle.

Why did men seek to be kings and rulers? What joy did it bring them? It had brought death to Henry and to her poor sad father nothing but unhappiness.

And as she looked down at her sleeping son she thought she saw her father's face.

She began to tremble. It was almost like a revelation. She stared down at the baby. What had come over her? The little face was in repose; the chubby hand clutched the edge of the quilt. He was just a baby ... not in the least like a sad old man.

She was melancholy; she mourned her father; and she was filled with apprehension for the future.

If only Henry had not died, she thought. How different everything would have been. Then she thought that if he had lived, he would have been the one who was proclaimed in Paris, and she would be beside him ... the crowned King and Queen of France. And there would have been those in the crowd who would murmur against them.

No, it seemed that there was little happiness for Kings.

She went to the window and looked out. It was a damp and misty day. Winter would soon be upon them. She thought again of that December day when little Henry had been born in Windsor ... forbidden Windsor, and she caught her breath with sudden terror.

She stared with unseeing eyes at the late wisps of foliage on the oak trees, and suddenly she caught a glimpse of the Welsh squire. He was riding into the courtyard on the way to the stables.

She remembered then that encounter in the forest and she had a desire to see him again.

She said to one of her women: 'That Welsh squire, I would have a word with him.'

The woman looked surprised, but it was easy for Katherine

to overcome awkward situations. She could always fall back on her lack of understanding of the language and the customs of the country.

'I would like to know how he does his duties ...' she went on. 'I would not want to think that I had introduced into my household one who ...'

She floundered and the woman said: 'Do you wish me to make enquiries about him, my lady? If he has done aught to displease you ...'

'No ... no ... I do not know. I will speak to him myself.'

'Yourself, my lady?'

'It is what I mean. Send him to me. I will talk to him in my ante-chamber.'

The woman curtsied and retired to do her bidding, no doubt thinking that the behaviour of the French was sometimes incomprehensible. But the late King had said his wife should be humoured. He did not want her to lose her foreign charm.

He came into the room, rather shyly, surprised as he was naturally to be summoned to the presence of the Queen.

'Ah, Owen Tudor,' she said stumbling a little over his name, 'the squire from Wales.' She smiled for he was beginning to look alarmed. 'There is no need to fear,' she said. 'I remember seeing you in the forest of Vincennes. I commanded then that you should join my household.'

'I thank you, my lady;' said the young man, 'and if I have done aught to displease you ...'

'No, no. You have not displeased. You have pleased ...' He looked even more alarmed and she went on quickly: 'You must understand I have not yet learned well the language. There are times when I say what is not always understood.'

He bowed and waited.

'I just wished to talk to you,' she said. 'We talked before. It was good for me. I was very unhappy then ... I still am unhappy.'

'My lady, you have had a great loss. All England has.'

'And Wales?' she said.

'I have always served the King well, my lady.'

'I know, and now you must serve your new King.'

Her expression clouded. She had remembered what had set her off on this strange impulse.

'Tell me, Owen Tudor,' she said, 'are you like your father ... or perhaps your grandfather?'

'My father was accused of murder, my lady,' said Owen, 'and I should not like that to happen to me. My grandfather was Tudor Vychan ap Gronw and he was a very fine man I have heard.'

'You are proud of your grandfather, Owen Tudor?'

'He received a knighthood at the hands of the great King Edward the Third. My father, Meredydd, was steward to the Bishop of Bangor.'

'And he was the one who was accused of murder. Tell me about that.'

'I know nothing of it, my lady. Families do not talk of these things except to say one of their number was wrongly judged.'

'So you believe there was no murder?'

He lifted his shoulders. 'I do not know, but my father was a hot-tempered man and he was outlawed and forced to live in the mountains. I was born there.'

Owen Tudor stopped, suddenly realizing it was the Queen to whom he was talking in this manner.

'Do you think you are like your father ... or your grandfather?'

'Sons often bear resemblances to their parents, I believe my lady.'

She looked at him blankly for a few moments. Then she said: 'My father was mad.'

He did not know what to reply. He thought this was the strangest interview he had ever known. The Queen looked different from when he had seen her on previous occasions. She looked very young and vulnerable, like a young girl he might have known in the mountains before he had joined the King's army.

She said: 'I have just heard the news that my father is dead.'

She was overwrought. He understood that now. He must listen to her; he must behave as though it were the most natural thing for a Queen to send for a squire and talk to him as though they were two simple country people. He must listen, not talk too much and hope that she would not remember her indiscretion later and blame him for it.

'Oh,' she burst out suddenly, 'you think it is very fine to be the daughter of a King, do you not, eh, Squire Tudor, do you not?'

'It is a very great honour, my lady.'

She laughed a little wildly. 'When I was three,' she said, 'I was put into the Hôtel de St Pol with my brothers and sisters. There were six of us ... Louis, John and Charles were the boys ... and then there were Michelle, Marie and myself, the girls. I was the youngest. Do you know why we were put there ... the children of France? It was because our mother was living at the Louvre with her lover. He was the Duke of Orléans and my father's brother. You are thinking why did my father the King of France allow her to do this ... it was because he was mad, Squire Tudor. They put him away ...' She turned her head and her mouth twisted as though she was going to cry. 'When he was ... well, he was kind and good and by no means weak ... a good King. But then terrible afflictions would come on him. He would rave and storm ...' She stopped and covered her face with her hands.

'My lady ...' began Owen.

She dropped her hands. 'Don't go,' she said. 'Stay. I can talk to you. I wonder why. I like you, Owen Tudor. You are good, I think, and I trust you. You do not know but once before you gave me ... hope. I don't know why it was. Perhaps because you were young ... and innocent in a way ... They have just brought me news of my father's death. My little one is now to be crowned King of France. He is a baby yet. What lies in store for him? You think me strange, Owen Tudor. I am not English ... I am not Welsh. I am French, and I am frightened. I am frightened for my son. I must talk of this ... to someone ... and there is no one.'

'My lady, my wish is to serve you ... now and always ...'

She smiled at him.

'I had heard stories of my father,' she went on. 'His madness came on suddenly. A terrible thing happened when he was young. He loved to masquerade and one day he ordered five of his courtiers to dress up as savages and they went to a ball. They wore tight costumes made of linens and these they covered with resin to which tow was stuck so that they looked like naked hairy men. Someone approached with a lighted torch and suddenly they were all ablaze. They could not remove their costumes, of course, and were burned to death all except the King, for his aunt the Duchess of Berry recognized him and shouting, "Save the King", wrapped her cloak about him. The King was saved but the other five were burned to death. That was the start of his madness. It had been his idea and he blamed himself and for ever after he would have his fits of madness. They took his hunting knife away from him because he tried to kill himself with it. They put him away. He was fed like a dog and for five months no one went near him. He was violent when the moods took him. So they shut him away in the Hôtel de St Pol. We would hear him shouting and throwing himself against the walls of his chamber. We used to shiver and cling together and say: "That is our father the King." '

Owen stood looking at her while she was talking. He wished he knew what to say to comfort her.

'Then,' she went on, 'there was my mother. She was said to be the most beautiful woman in France. She came from Bavaria. When she was present it was impossible not to look at her. All men desired her and she desired many men. My uncle, the Duke of Orléans, was her lover. When my father was in the Hôtel de St Pol he lived with her as King and together they ruled France. They liked it that way but you see there was Burgundy. My father's uncle. He cared for France; he cared even more for Burgundy. Then he died and John the Fearless was the new Duke. Of course it was wrong. But is it ever right to murder? Did your father think so, Owen Tudor, when he was in exile in his mountain home? You see, my mother and her lover were bad for the country. They had put us ... the children of France, into the Hôtel de St Pol and they would not pay for our household for they wanted the money to spend for themselves. So there we were, dirty, hungry and yes ... Owen Tudor ... we were lousy. We, the children of the royal house lived like urchins in the slums of Paris. We had no clothes to wear ... nothing to keep us warm ... no food to eat ... You see something had to happen and it did. The Duke of Burgundy caused the Duke of Orléans to be set on when he returned from supping with my mother and he was left dying in the streets of Paris. We were brought out of our misery. Then I was sent to the convent of Poissy where my sister took the veil. But why do I tell you this? Do you think I am mad ... like my father?'

He went to her on impulse. He took her hand and kissed it. 'No, no, my lady. I think you are good and brave and I will serve you with my life.'

She was sober suddenly. She withdrew her hand sharply.

'You should go now,' she said. 'You have done me much good as you did before.'

She smiled at him and he bowed.

She lifted her hands in a helpless gesture. 'I talked a great deal, did I not? I surprised you. Well, I am French, Squire Tudor, and you are Welsh. We are not like these English, eh?'

She was smiling and he smiled too.

'*Adieu*, Squire Tudor,' she whispered.

She watched him as he went out. She felt better. What nonsense to have thought young Henry would inherit his grandfather's malady. Owen Tudor's father was a murderer and he was the gentlest man in Windsor.

As before her encounter with him had done her good. She was glad she had brought him into the household.

BURGUNDY

FROM a turret window Jacqueline of Bavaria watched for the arrival of Humphrey, Duke of Gloucester. Her hopes rested on him. Jacqueline was a young woman, but she already had had two marriages and was now contemplating a third.

Jacqueline was no fool. She often complained to her maid that her husbands had not so much married her as her possessions.

'How fortunate you are, my girl,' she said, 'to have no possessions. You will know when *you* marry it will have to be for yourself.'

And now Duke Humphrey. She wanted desperately to marry him. Not that she was in love with Humphrey but he was important enough to have a certain charm. Power in men was something which Jacqueline had been brought up to admire and for her it always had been one of the most attractive attributes a man could have. Now it was a necessity for her to have a powerful husband if she were ever going to regain her rights and cease to be an exile living on sufferance in an alien land. That was the hardest part to endure. She who had once been a considerable heiress now to be relying on the bounty of a foreign court.

Marriage to Gloucester would change the position. A King's son—and an ambitious man at that—would give her prestige and if his interest in her was tied up with her estates, well hers for him was in the security and hope which he could bring her.

At first her future had seemed promising enough. To be

married to Dauphin John had been an excellent project with a crown in sight, which as soon as his father Charles VI died would be his. Poor mad old fellow, he had seemed more dead than alive, but there was that harpy Queen Isabeau who would have to be dealt with when John came to the throne. Jacqueline had been sure that she could deal with that situation. But it had never come to that.

John had shortly followed his brother Louis to the grave. Of course many said he had been helped there by his fiendish mother, but the affair was wrapped in mystery and it was certain that Queen Isabeau would extricate herself from such an accusation. She was now becoming friendly with the Duke of Burgundy as the better side to be on.

Well then, after poor Dauphin John was in his grave, Philip of Burgundy himself had thought it would be a good idea to marry her to his cousin—and incidentally her own, for Margaret of Burgundy had been her mother. So she had married another John and from the early days of their marriage she had regretted it. Her husband was a weakling, not what she would have expected to come out of Burgundy and it was not long before her wicked uncle, yet another John known as John the Pitiless, for obvious reasons, was discovering that it was not right that such an inheritance—Hainault, Holland and Zealand—should be in the hands of a woman and that as the brother of the late Count William he had more right to it than the Count's daughter.

What a weak ineffectual husband they had married her to! It was child's play for their wily uncle to wrest the territories from the meek little Duke of Brabant and there she was without her possessions and saddled with a husband she did not want.

Katherine de Valois had meanwhile married Henry of England and when she herself was married to Dauphin John, Katherine had become her sister-in-law. Katherine was a kindly girl, ever ready to give an ear to those in trouble, so she had appealed to Katherine and Katherine and Henry, who was then alive, had made her very welcome in England.

And then she had met Duke Humphrey and from the first they had been drawn together. She knew that when he smiled at her he was really looking at Hainault, Holland and Zealand and when she returned that smile with all the charm she possessed she was seeing a strong and powerful man who could regain her estates for her.

Thus they were attracted and she waited eagerly for his coming.

At length she saw the cavalcade in the distance ... banners flying, lances glistening in the sun. Humphrey always travelled in style and wished it to be remembered that he was the son of a King. She sometimes fancied his insistence on this had come about because his father had not become King until he had deposed Richard the Second. Humphrey and his brothers, the grandsons of John of Gaunt, had not been born in the direct line to kingship.

Never mind. Humphrey was a power in the land and while his elder brother Bedford was in France Humphrey was to all intents and purposes the King of England for that infant in the Windsor nursery need not be considered for years to come.

So she was triumphant as she went down to the courtyard to greet him.

He was a fine figure in his embroidered houppelande buckled in with a glittering belt; his full-blown sleeves followed the newest fashion and his hair was closely cropped, a fashion admired by his brother which no doubt accounted for its being followed so much. His shoes were long and pointed, though not ridiculously so; they matched his hose which were of two blending colours—blue and lavender.

He would have been a very handsome man but for the pouches under his eyes, the clefts at the side of his mouth and a somewhat ravaged complexion. They were the outward signs of the life he was reputed to live and yet there was about him a certain aestheticism. The debauched gentleman was yet a lover of the finer arts. An interesting man with conflicting characteristics, but there was one which overruled all others—ambition.

Jacqueline understood it all; and she would not have had it otherwise.

The servants handed her the goblet. She tasted it smiling —following the old custom which had arisen to assure the arrival that there was no poison in the cup.

Humphrey drank deeply and let his eyes rest on Jacqueline. Fair enough, he thought. She did not drive him to a frenzy of desire. It would take an extraordinary woman to do that nowadays. He had known too many of them. But Jacqueline ... with all her estates, albeit they had to be won back ... would suit him very well.

He passed the goblet to the waiting man-at-arms and leaped from his horse. He took her hand and looked at her searchingly. She smiled. 'I have news,' she said. 'But pray you, my lord, come in. We are prepared for you. We shall do our best to offer you hospitality which shall be worthy of you—though that is impossible, of course.'

'Nay,' he said, 'it is I who must prove myself worthy.'

Pleasant talk which neither of them meant or believed for one moment.

They went into the hall. He could smell the roasting venison and it was good. In fact everything was good. To hell with Burgundy. To hell with Bedford. He was sure that in a very short time, Hainault, Holland and Zealand would be his.

He was in an excellent mood when he sat down to eat. The minstrels played sweet music to his liking and only the finest musicians could please his refined taste.

She had whispered the news to him as they went in to dinner:

'Benedict has annulled my marriage to Brabant.'

'That is good news,' replied Humphrey.

'I hoped you would think so. Is it good enough though?'

Humphrey hesitated for only a few moments. It was not really very good. The man calling himself Benedict XIII was not generally recognized. In some circles he was known as the anti-Pope for since the Great Schism there had been much conflict in papal circles. Benedict XIII was a certain Peter de Luna chosen by French Cardinals and recognized only by Spain and Scotland.

It could often be useful to have these opposing sides for there was always a desire to win the support of people in high places. Oh yes, thought Gloucester, very useful. They would make Benedict's annulment suit them; and on the other hand if at some time they wished to change their minds they could always throw doubts on its validity.

Humphrey's hand closed over hers. 'We'll make it good enough,' he said.

She sat back smiling complacently. It should not be difficult to bring back those excellent lands to where they belonged.

While the musicians played they were already making plans.

'I see no reason why we should delay longer,' said Humphrey.

A serving-maid was filling his goblet. She leaned closer to him; a lock of dark, rather greasy hair fell forward over her hot face; her bodice yawned a little to show an ample bosom. Their eyes met briefly. These greasy sluts appealed to him now and then. I have had a surfeit of fine ladies, he thought.

He followed the swing of her buttocks as she walked away not forgetting to glance over her shoulder at him.

A lusty wench, he thought.

'There will be opposition,' Jacqueline was saying.

'My dear lady, when has opposition deterred me ... or you either for that matter?'

'Rarely, I admit.'

He leaned towards her. 'They will shake their heads in dismay. They will curse us mayhap. Do we care, sweet Jacqueline?'

'Why should I, if you do not?'

He put his hand over hers and held it tightly. 'Then we go ahead, eh ... without delay.'

She was gazing before her, smiling, seeing herself riding back through Hainault, Holland and Zealand, a strong husband beside her.

Humphrey smiled with her, seeing much the same; but the saucy serving-girl crossed his vision again. He was thinking: She will be a girl of some experience.

It was growing late. There was much to be done. They would ride off together tomorrow and the marriage should take place without delay. He retired to the chamber which had been prepared for him and wrapping his bed-robe round himself he sat on his bed thinking of the future. He had dismissed his servants.

He thought of Jacqueline and wondered whether she was expecting him.

Perhaps it would have been a loving gesture. He imagined himself taking her into his arms. 'I could not wait for the ceremony, my love, so great was my need of you.'

No. It would not ring true. Jacqueline was too clever.

There was that other. A certain excitement was rising at the thought of her. It would be easy. He could send one of his servants to find her. They had performed missions like that for him often enough and would do so with discreet efficiency. If he wished it within fifteen minutes he would have the girl in his bed.

He was about to summon his servant. Then he hesitated.

No. Perhaps it would not be wise. His brother John had said to him time and time again, 'You're too impulsive Humphrey. One day that impulsiveness will lead you into trouble.'

Why think of John now? Hardly the time to think of the good elder brother, the noble one, Henry's favourite. John was not going to be overpleased by this marriage with Jacqueline. Yes, even John would lose his calm when he heard of that.

Still, perhaps it would be a mistake to send for the girl. Jacqueline might discover. And if she did ... who knew. He thought he understood Jacqueline but he had had a great deal to do with women, and knowing them well, the one fact he was certain of was that one could never be sure of them.

He, who had lived through so many erotic adventures, could surely spend one night without one. I will, he told himself, for the sake of Hainault, Holland and Zealand.

*   *   *

John, Duke of Bedford, was a very uneasy man. There was scarcely a moment of the day when he did not bitterly regret the passing of his brother Henry. John was the one who had lived more closely in his brother's shadow than any of the others. Henry and he had worked together, trusted each other, understood each other. It was as though part of him had died when Henry went, thought John, and the better part.

Sometimes it seemed to him that there was a blight on the family. Could it have been the result of their father's taking the throne from Richard? There were some who believed such actions could bring a curse on a whole family. Not long after his accession their father, King Henry IV, had died of a loathsome disease. He had never enjoyed the power he had fought so hard to win. In fact John was sure that at times he longed for those days when he had been plain Bolingbroke. Crowns brought fearful responsibilities and it was only such as Henry—born to be King if ever a man was— who could carry them with ease and the certain knowledge of success.

But Henry had died—cut off in his prime. He would never have believed that was possible. In the old days they

had jousted together, played jokes on each other, dreamed of
the future. And how differently it had turned out! There
had been four of them, Henry, Thomas, himself and Humphrey. And now only two of them left. Thomas had died
only a year before Henry. But his death was more understandable because he had been slain in battle.

Henry had loved him dearly. John clearly remembered
the tragedy of Thomas's death.

Henry had made him Captain of Normandy and Lieu-
tenant of France. Poor Thomas, how proud he had been.
But he was impetuous ... always in a hurry. It will be his
downfall, Henry had said; and how right he had been!
If only he had waited; if only he had curbed his impatience.
But Thomas wanted as glorious a victory as Agincourt. Henry
would never have allowed it to happen the way it did—and
consequently it cost poor Thomas his life. The Dauphin's
forces had advanced to Beaufort-en-Vallée and got as far as
Beaugé. When the news was brought to Thomas he was eager
to go into the attack. Henry would have warned him to wait
until he could muster the main force; but being Thomas he
could never wait for anything. So with a few chosen knights
he rode into the attack and was slain.

Poor Thomas, he had yearned so for glory. He wanted to be
as great as Henry. But alas, he was not. The tragedy is,
thought John, that none of us is.

The Earl of Salisbury had recovered Thomas's body from
the battlefield and it had been brought to England and
buried with great pomp at Canterbury, where the English
paid homage to him, believing him to be almost as great
a soldier as his brother.

And after Thomas the big tragedy: the death of Henry.

Only two of us boys left, thought John. Humphrey and
myself.

The thought worried him and he wondered how much he
could rely on Humphrey.

And now the King of France was dead. It was a calamity
although not unexpected. When he had lived Henry had
longed for it, for on the death of the King of France, Henry
was to have been proclaimed that country's king. That would
have been a great and glorious occasion. But now there was
only a baby boy where a strong man should have been. Moreover there was a Dauphin who would now call himself King
of France and the English invaders must inevitably find

themselves surrounded by a hostile people. None understood more than John that a proud people like the French would never submit to a foreign invader and accept a foreigner as their King.

A great deal depended on Burgundy. Henry had always said: 'We need Burgundy.' In fact the downfall of France was in a great measure due to the warring factions in the heart of her country. The long-standing feud between Orléans and Burgundy had weakened France to such an extent that the conquest had been more easily accomplished than it could possibly have been if the French had been united against the common enemy.

Henry had made John aware of the importance of Burgundy. Even on his death bed his thoughts had been of the Duke. He had gripped John's hand and talked to him very earnestly and had said: 'I leave the government of France in your hands, brother. But if Burgundy has a mind to undertake it, leave it to him. Above all things, I tell you to have no dissension with Burgundy. If that should happen—and may God preserve you from it—the affairs of France with which we have progressed so favourably would become bad . . . for us.'

They were words which were engraved on John's mind because he had come to realize the wisdom of them. He was not likely to forget the importance of keeping the peace with Burgundy.

France was in turmoil. While mad Charles had still borne the name of King of France there was a respite. The French could go on believing that a usurper had not taken the throne. But now Charles was dead and action must be taken to bring the French to reality, so after the burial of Charles VI at St Denis, John had no alternative but to have the baby Henry VI declared King of France. This proclamation must take place in Paris and as the time grew nearer the more uneasy John became.

The body of the King of France was taken to St Denis and there with appropriate ceremony laid to rest. The only Prince to attend was John, Duke of Bedford. He had hoped that Burgundy would be there, but clearly Burgundy would have no desire to pay homage to the Duke of Bedford. He could not expect that.

So far so good. The ceremony had progressed without incident. Now came the testing point. He must ride back to Paris and there proclaim his nephew King of France.

He was deeply conscious of the sullen crowds. He knew that any moment they might arise and attack him. He had his guards who would be on the alert for any disturbance, and they had no weapons but he did not underestimate the power of the mob. He thought of Henry and took courage from the fact that he was doing what his brother would have done had he been alive on this day. Before him rode one of his knights carrying a naked sword, which was an emblem of kingly authority. The people of Paris would be aware of that.

He sat his horse very still and silent as the proclamation rang out: 'Long live Henry of Lancaster, King of England and King of France.'

He waited. They could have come against him then. He might be called upon to face the violence of a Paris mob. He was deeply aware of the sullen silence all about him.

No. It was well. They had had enough of fighting. They had starved and suffered; they had lost members of their families; they were a subdued and beaten people. They knew that at this time they dared do nothing but accept Henry of Lancaster as their King.

John believed their English claim was just and true— as Henry had always said and others before him. It came through Isabella who had been wife of Edward the Second, and if the French upheld the Salic Law the English did not. Moreover they had won by conquest. Still they were considered to be usurpers.

The ceremony was over. He had done his duty. As he rode on to the Louvre he heard the rumbling of voices and he knew the silence was over. Henry had been proclaimed but now the discontent would break out. He knew they were talking of Good King Charles, not mad King Charles, the poor ineffectual man, reduced at times by his madness almost to savagery. The man whose rule had brought disaster to France had become a saint.

Was it not always so?

There were dispatches from England waiting for him. He was tired, exhausted by the emotion of his recent experience. But he must read the dispatches. There could be something in them of the utmost importance.

He read and when he came to the news of his brother Humphrey he paused. He felt the blood rush to his face. He could not believe it. He read it twice. Humphrey . . . married to Jacqueline. It was impossible. The woman was married already . . . and to Brabant—a marriage arranged by Burgundy which meant that the wily Duke had his eyes on Hainault, Holland and Zealand. And Humphrey had had the stupidity to marry this woman. He could not have thought of a better way of arousing Burgundy's wrath.

He read on. Benedict had annulled the marriage with Brabant . . .

Benedict. The anti-pope!

Here was disaster. Burgundy would turn against them. They could not afford to make Burgundy an enemy. Burgundy was the most powerful man in France. Henry's all but last words had been a warning about Burgundy. Never act in such a way as to make him your enemy. Why, he had even offered to make Burgundy Regent of France on his death bed and it was because Burgundy had refused that John himself had had to take on that tremendous task.

And now by this foolish marriage Humphrey would soon be involved in a quarrel with Burgundy.

Exhausted as he was by the ordeal through which he had just passed he must think now how best to act. Should he explain to Burgundy, consult with him?

Oh Henry, he thought, had you been living at this day this could never have happened.

*   *   *

Philip, Duke of Burgundy, one of the richest and most powerful men in France, was the son of John the Fearless. At the time of the battle of Agincourt Philip had been nineteen years old, already married to Michelle, who was the daughter of the King of France and had, as a child, shared with Katherine the privations of the Hôtel de St Pol. The greatest regret of Philip's life to this time was that he had not been present at the famous battle which had led to the downfall of France. Duke John had given orders that his son was not to leave the Castle of Aire where he was staying at that time and his governor, on pain of severe penalty, had been warned that no matter how much he protested Philip was to remain there.

Philip had chafed against such orders, but had not known of course how important that battle was going to prove. If he had, he vowed, he would have broken free no matter at what cost, and he would have been there.

And so the flower of the French army had been destroyed by a small opposing force and to her everlasting shame France had been brought to her knees. When he heard of the defeat, Philip wept for three days. He refused all food and those about him feared for his health. For years to come he was to refer to Agincourt as the most grievous time of his life.

As for Duke John, he also was overcome with grief. Two of Philip's uncles, the Duke of Brabant and the Count of Nevers, had perished with much of the nobility of France. But while he mourned, Duke John rejoiced that his son had not been present on that field.

All the same he was ashamed that he himself had not been there and he sent his gauntlet to Henry who was at that time at Calais.

'The Duke of Brabant is dead,' he wrote. 'He is no vassal of France and holds no fief there, but I his brother of Burgundy defy you and send you this gauntlet.'

Henry's reply was characteristic of him.

'I will not accept the gauntlet of so noble and puissant a Prince as the Duke of Burgundy. I am of no account compared with him. If I have had the victory over the nobles of France it is by God's Grace. The death of the Duke of Brabant has caused me great sorrow. Take back your gauntlet. Neither I nor my people caused your brother's death. If you will be at Boulogne on the fifteenth of January next, I will prove by the testimony of prisoners and two of my friends that it was the French who accomplished his destruction.'

This was an astonishing reply, completely lacking in the arrogance of the conqueror. It was a tentative hand of friendship towards the Duke of Burgundy and it had a marked effect on John the Fearless. He recognized in Henry not only a great soldier but a diplomat as well. He compared him with the mad and feeble King of France and thought what a much more worthwhile ally Henry would make. He ignored Henry's invitation, however. Instead he marched to Paris and gave every indication of taking arms against the English; but he was really more concerned in the struggle for power between the Burgundians and the Armagnacs—this last named after the Comte Bernard d'Armagnac who had put himself at the head of the Orléans party.

This struggle had been going on in earnest since the Duke of Orléans, lover of the Queen, had been murdered at the orders of the Duke of Burgundy some years before. The King was inclined to favour the Armagnacs which set Burgundy thinking more and more favourably of Henry. Although there was no open alliance he made it clear that he did not consider Henry without claims and the attitude of Burgundy was a source of continual anxiety to the King of France.

Queen Isabeau, who enjoyed intrigue almost as much as she did amorous adventures, at this time decided that she would support Burgundy against her husband and the Orléanists. The only reason she had been with the Orléanists was because her lover had been the Duc d'Orléans. She found it most exciting to send feelers to Burgundy. She was living close to the King—while he enjoyed one of his lucid periods, and was in possession of information which could be useful to Burgundy. As for Burgundy he was only too delighted to have someone as influential as the Queen working for him against his enemies and encouraged the new friendship.

It was hardly to be expected that this should be undiscovered for long, for the Queen was not the only spy in the palace, and the Count of Armagnac soon learned that valuable information was being passed to Burgundy by none other than Isabeau herself. He took the obvious action of discrediting the Queen and this was not difficult, for the Queen's conduct to say the least was discreditable. Since the murder of Orléans she had had a succession of lovers and the favourite at this time was a certain Louis de Bosredon who was not only her lover but worked with her in getting information to Burgundy.

Armagnac chose the obvious method of revenge. He went to the King and with a show of reluctance implied that not only was Louis de Bosredon the Queen's lover but that he was acting with her in sending information to Burgundy.

Charles's temper was unstable. Although at times he was the mildest of men he could suddenly fly into violent rages. He could not help but be aware of his wife's infidelities. The whole of France had known that the Duc d'Orléans, the King's own brother, had been her lover. Charles knew it too; but from the moment he had set eyes on Isabeau he had thought her the most beautiful creature he had ever seen, and he still did. His mind was often cloudy even during those times when he was considered well enough to live a normal life; and when he heard that his wife was carrying on an intrigue with Louis de Bosredon in the palace itself he flew into a violent rage.

The Queen was amazed when he approached her. He knew her way of life; everyone knew of it, so why express such surprise? But even she quailed at the storm of invective he let loose upon her.

'Charles, Charles,' she murmured, 'you must calm yourself. If you do not they will take you back to St Pol. Louis is a friend ... of yours as well as mine ...'

But for once the King was immune to her wiles.

'You have not heard the last of this,' he shouted; and he called for the arrest of Louis de Bosredon. That somewhat exquisite gentleman, on his way to the Queen to show her a new pair of embroidered gloves he had had made for himself and to ask her if she would care to patronize the excellent embroiderers he had discovered, was astonished to find himself seized and thrown into a dungeon.

The Queen was temporarily distraught, but she soon assured herself that she would bring the King to reason; and then she would take her revenge on that spy Armagnac. She would rouse the Burgundians to such wrath that there would be massacre in Paris.

It was not quite as easy as usual. The King was adamant in his determination to unmask Louis de Bosredon; he threatened to have him put to the question and the idea of his beautiful body being mutilated sent Louis into panic so that he very quickly admitted everything—his relationship with the Queen and his participation in her spying for Burgundy.

The King ordered that forthwith he be sewn up in a leather sack and thrown into the Seine. A sack on which had been embroidered 'Let the King's justice run its course' was brought and the sentence carried out.

This was not all. Isabeau herself was not to go unpunished. She was banished from the Court and sent to Tours. There she was put into the care of guards who were ordered to watch her night and day and make sure that she neither sent out or received correspondence.

Isabeau thrived on intrigue. She was resourceful and now she decided to ally herself completely with the Duke of Burgundy. She was beautiful, she was beguiling; few men could resist her; certainly not members of the guard. Would one of them do her a service? she wondered. She need not have asked. The chosen man was honoured, he would serve her with his life and it might well be with his life if he were discovered, for what she asked of him was that he should take a message from her to the Duke of Burgundy.

John the Fearless laughed aloud when he received the seal she sent him. He liked the message which told him that if he cared to come to fetch her she would go with him.

To have the Queen in his possession, the Queen his ally! That would be greatly in his favour. He did wonder how he would be able to capture her without storming the château. But she was a resourceful lady. She evidently had ideas.

The messenger went back to tell the Queen that by the time she received his message, the Duke of Burgundy would be two leagues from Tours with a company of men.

Isabeau had her plan ready. She told the guards that she wished to go to Mass at the convent of Marmoutier which was outside the city walls. Her guards conferred together. They were not supposed to leave Tours. Isabeau stamped and raged. Did they forget she was the Queen? She asked only to be able to worship. Was that to be denied her? They would be sorry they treated her so ill. She would not always be in this sorry position and she was not one to forget.

The guards conferred together. What harm could the expedition do if she were well guarded?

So they set out but when they came near the church they saw a company of soldiers approaching. The guards were immediately wary.

'My lady,' said their leader, 'we should return. These soldiers could be Burgundians or English.'

At that moment the Captain who was riding at the head of the soldiers galloped up to her.

He came close to Isabeau's horse, took her hand and kissed it.

'I salute you, my lady, on behalf of the Duke of Burgundy.'

'Where is the Duke?' she asked.

'He is close by, my lady.'

'Then arrest these men who believe themselves to be my captors.'

The astonished guards were bewildered; they could not believe that they had been victims of such a simple ruse.

And there was the Duke of Burgundy himself, riding to the Queen, bowing in his saddle, his eyes alight with pleasure and amusement.

'Dear cousin,' cried the Queen, 'you have delivered me from captivity. We are friends. I shall never fail you. I know you to be a loyal servant of my poor misguided lord and all his family and a true protector of a sad war-torn realm.'

It was a great achievement. Burgundy and the Queen were allies. They set up a Court of Justice to replace that in Paris; Burgundy was now the acclaimed enemy of the King and still more inclined to be on friendly terms with the King's enemy.

At the same time there was still no open agreement between Henry and Burgundy but they were moving closer together.

It was not until July of 1418—nearly three years after the battle of Agincourt—that Henry took Rouen. This was the deciding factor and Rouen had held out valiantly realizing that as capital of Normandy if it fell to the English that would put the seal of death on French hopes of victory.

It was a particularly heart-rending siege. The inhabitants sent urgent appeals both to the King and the Duke of Burgundy; they sent out from their city any who were unable to fight and this meant that old men, feeble women and young children were wandering in the districts beyond the city walls, dying of starvation; but the citizens were ruthless. They knew they were going to need all the food they had for those who could defend the city. All through the heat of August to the mists of September and the threat of cold in October the siege continued. December had come with all the bitterness of a hard winter. The citizens of Rouen were at the end of their resistance when a message came from Burgundy bidding them treat with the English for the best terms they could get.

It was desertion. Neither the King of France nor the Duke of Burgundy could or would help them.

Henry had expended men and wealth in the siege and he was angry with the citizens for holding out so long. He ordered that all the men should deliver themselves to him and believing this to be certain death the people of Rouen prepared to set fire to their city.

Henry was amazed at a people who could consider burning themselves to death and he immediately granted pardon to all men except a few whom he would name.

Thus on a cold January day Henry made his entry into the city of Rouen and now was the time for the French to come to terms with the English before they took the whole of France and thus make bargaining out of the question.

It was then that Henry set eyes on Katherine and no sooner had he done so than he greatly desired to marry her. He was first of all the soldier, though, and he was not going to concede too much even for Katherine. He had come for the crown of France and would take nothing else.

He was deeply aware of Burgundy. Eager as he was for the Duke's friendship he was delighted because of the conflict between Burgundy and the King and the Dauphin. He wanted to keep that going.

Burgundy knew too well what was going on in Henry's mind and determined to exploit it to the full. What he wanted was to enlarge his possessions, and he decided he might come to private terms with the English. He might be their ally—even against the French. Why not? The Burgundians were waging battle against the Armagnacs. At the same time he did not want Henry to think he would be a willing ally. He would have to be presented with advantages if he was going to join the English. And how could that be— a Burgundian fighting with the English to take the crown of France from the reigning French house!

At the conference Burgundy was extremely cold to Henry.

Henry did not mind. He understood exactly where Burgundy's thoughts were leading him.

They had refused his terms. They had refused to allow him to see Katherine again.

'We want you to know, cousin,' he said to Burgundy, 'that we will have the King's daughter and all that we have demanded with her. Otherwise we will thrust the King out of his Kingdom, and you too, my lord Duke.'

Burgundy had looked at him cynically and replied: 'You speak as you will, sir. But before thrusting my lord King and myself from the Kingdom you will have to do what will tire you so much that you will be hard put to it to keep your hold on your own island.'

Henry bore the Duke no animosity. Of course he spoke in that manner. Of course he could not hope for an open alliance between them. It was true too that if he must go on fighting in France he would impoverish his own country. At this time he was flushed with victory and his people applauded their great King whose genius had brought him many conquests; but such conquests had to be paid for ... with taxes ... and still worse the blood of his soldiers.

Burgundy was right.

One day, Henry was thinking, he and I shall stand together. He is the only man in France that I would wish to be my ally.

Isabeau took a hand after that. She had made sure that she had charge of her daughter when she had seen that she was to be the best bargaining counter the French could hope for. The King was by then in one of his dark moods and shut away from the country. Very soon after that Katherine and Henry had been married.

Then there happened that incident which made Philip of Burgundy the enemy of the Dauphin of France and turned him towards the English with an enthusiasm which his father had never shown.

It was decided among the followers of the Dauphin that he and the Duke of Burgundy must settle their differences and in order that this should be so there must be a meeting between them.

The country was overrun by the English; there must be an end to this conflict within.

Messengers from the Dauphin came to the Duke to tell him that the Dauphin was now staying close to Montereau and if the Duke would come there the meeting would be arranged. Some of the Duke's friends were against the meeting. It seems so strange they said. Why should you not meet the Dauphin at Court?

The Duke shrugged aside their apprehension and he went ahead with preparations for the meeting. He discussed it with his son Philip who would be pleased to see peace between their House and that of the King for the sake of his wife. He was devoted to Michelle. He had often remarked to his father that the royal princesses seemed of a different calibre when compared with the mad King and his vacillating son.

'I hope you achieve peace, sir,' he said. 'Michelle gets very upset about this conflict. She would be so happy if you were on friendly terms with her brother.'

'Michelle is right,' said Duke John. 'We should be standing together against the English.'

So Duke John had set out for Montereau and there it was agreed that the Duke and the Dauphin should approach each other from either end of the Montereau bridge and each of them should take with him ten men-at-arms.

In the centre of the bridge, the Dauphin and the Duke

came face to face. Duke John doffed his hat and bowed low.

'My lord,' said the Duke, 'it is my duty to serve you first in the land after God. I have come to offer you service.'

'You speak fair words,' replied the Dauphin. 'None, I believe, speaks fair words better. You have long delayed coming to us.'

'Indeed I have,' replied the Duke. 'And now I wonder why we are here, for nothing can be settled save in the presence of your father the King.'

'The King will be content with what I do,' replied the Dauphin. 'There is one point I would take up with you, lord Duke. You are over friendly with our enemies the English and therefore have shown yourself to be lacking in duty to the crown of France.'

'I did what I believe to be my duty,' insisted the Duke.

'You have failed in your duty,' cried the Dauphin.

'That is a lie.'

One of the men on the bridge shouted: 'Vengeance for the death of Orléans.'

The Duke turned and saw the axe a second before it struck him.

'A trap,' he murmured as he sank to the ground. 'Betrayal ...'

They were standing over him, their swords drawn. There were many who wanted to avenge the murder of the Duke of Orléans. It was twelve years since it happened but it had rankled ever since. It had been at the very heart of the hatred of the Orléans faction for that of Burgundy. Now the man who had instigated that murder had become a victim himself.

When the news was brought to Philip he was stunned. His great and powerful father done to death on a bridge after having been lured to a meeting with the Dauphin, and there foully murdered.

He listened to the account of what had happened with black hatred in his heart.

'They stripped him of his garments, my lord,' he was told, 'and planned to throw his body into the river.'

Philip clenched his fists in anger. They should pay for this. Curse the Armagnacs! Curse the Orléanists! Curse the Dauphin!

'They were stopped doing this, my lord Duke,' he was told. 'One of the citizens of Montereau intervened. He put on the Duke's shirt and breeches and took him to the church at Notre Dame.'

'Curse, curse, curse them!' cried the Duke.

The only way in which he could bear his sorrow was by feeding his anger.

Michelle, hearing the messenger leave and realizing that he had brought ill news, went to her husband.

She stared at him in horror and he burst out: 'Your brother has killed my father.'

'No.' Her hand went to her lips. She was trembling.

'He lured him to his death. They were to talk of peace and when my father arrived they fell on him and murdered him.'

'Charles ... not Charles,' she murmured.

'Yes, Charles, our poor ineffectual Dauphin ... All he is fit for is to stab brave men in the back.'

She turned away and buried her face in her hands.

He laid his hand on her shoulders. 'Michelle,' he said, 'I hate your brother. Strange that I should love his sister.'

'But this ...' she said.

He drew her to him and held her tightly. 'Even this ... makes no difference. I despise your father. I hate your brother ... but I love you, Michelle.'

'Then,' she said, 'we can face whatever is coming.'

He nodded. He held her against him that she might not see the desire for revenge in his eyes.

The Dauphin must not be allowed to think that he could treat Burgundy thus. Oh, Burgundy had murdered Orléans, yes. He knew. Burgundy had removed that lecherous cheat who leaped into the Queen's bed as soon as the King was sent to the Hôtel de St Pol, who diverted the King's exchequer into his own coffers, who made no effort to rule though he had been made Regent at the request of the Queen on whom at that time the King doted. It had been an act of service to the state to remove Orléans. Orléans and his mistress the Queen had put the children away in the Hôtel de St Pol where they lived like denizens of the stews of Paris ... his own gentle Michelle, Katherine Queen of England and Marie now in her convent. Oh yes, his father had done his duty to the nation when he had caused Orléans to be removed.

It was different to call the mighty Duke of Burgundy to

a meeting with the Dauphin and there murder him in cold blood.

When Michelle's sister Katherine married the conqueror, when Henry declared that he would be King of France after the death of the mad old King, the new Duke of Burgundy decided that anyone who was the enemy of the Dauphin was his friend.

Thus a closer bond with the English was possible.

Now that King Henry was dead Bedford would proclaim Henry VI King of France and England. It was inevitable and well might the wretched Dauphin seek to raise forces against the English. His skirmishes were laughable. Bedford was a great soldier—not quite what his brother had been, it was true, but formidable. He would not make it too obvious to Bedford that he wished to be his friend.

For instance he did not go to the burial of the late King and the proclamation of the new one. That would have been asking too much of him. He did not wish to be seen taking second place to Bedford. But he admired Bedford; he would be a more staunch ally than that murderous Dauphin, now doubtless calling himself King of France.

*   *   *

Burgundy was surprised one day to find that Bedford had called on him. He glanced from a window and saw the Duke below. He must have arrived most informally. He was talking to someone, and he seemed animated and pleased.

He noticed then that Bedford's companion was Anne. Burgundy studied his sister as though seeing her for the first time. She has a stately air, he thought; and she is comely. It struck him that Bedford seemed to think so too. He was talking to Anne with the utmost respect and somehow gave the impression that he regarded her as a very great lady.

That pleased Burgundy. So he should, of course; but he must not forget that Bedford was a very important man. Many would say the most important in France at this time.

Anne was eighteen. There had been offers for her but their father had always been too occupied with other matters to give them the consideration they deserved. There is time, he used to say; and as Anne showed little enthusiasm for them they had been set aside. He supposed it was now his duty to find a good match for Anne.

He went down to greet Bedford, trying to hide his wariness as he wondered what had brought the Regent to him in this informal manner.

'I have long wished to talk with you,' said Bedford. 'There are several matters of importance which I want to lay before you.'

Anne inclined her head towards Bedford and smiling at him said she would leave him with the Duke.

Bedford's eyes followed her as she disappeared.

'Your sister is a charming and gracious lady,' he said.

'Oh, yes, I agree. It is good of you to come to see me. Have they taken your horse? Have you friends with you? Have they looked after you?'

'Only a party of six. They are in the stables now. I do not imagine my affairs will take long.'

'Then come in. You must refresh yourself.'

'Thank you, my lord.'

'You have come from Paris?'

Bedford nodded.

'You will take wine now. I hope you will dine with us.'

'I will take a little wine. Then I will be off. I want to be on my way before nightfall.'

Wine was brought and looking into his goblet Bedford began: 'I would ask your advice. This country is in a sorry state.'

'The country has fought a bitter war ... and lost,' said Burgundy.

'I sometimes wonder if any country ever truly wins. War brings hardships.'

' 'Twere a pity your brother ... and those before him did not consider this before making war on France.'

'Alas, it was not only the English who were making war in France.'

The Duke nodded gloomily.

'We want to undo the effects of war as quickly as we can. I want to bring prosperity back.'

'You have yet to face the Dauphin who calls himself King Charles VII.' Burgundy's face grew dark when he mentioned the Dauphin's name and Bedford noticed that with pleasure. There was a hatred there which would never pass. Bedford rejoiced in what had happened on Montereau Bridge; it had made Burgundy the Dauphin's enemy for ever and any enemy of the Dauphin must be a potential friend for the English.

'We will deal with him, my lord Duke. He is a nuisance, nothing more. I have no great respect for that young man.'

Burgundy was silent.

'The currency has been greatly debased,' went on Bedford. 'I want to encourage trade. Rouen has been sadly battered.'

'The siege all but destroyed it,' agreed Burgundy.

'Aye, a great and valiant people. My brother had deep respect for the citizens of Rouen.'

'I know it. They would have fired the city rather than surrender it.'

'And he was lenient with them. Like the great conqueror he was he was always merciful in victory.'

'And what would you ask of me?'

'Advice ... and help.'

There was silence. Burgundy was no fool. He knew the reason for this flattering show of deference. Bedford wanted to make sure of his friendship. And yet they respected each other. They must do: Bedford to come here and speak almost humbly; and Burgundy to shed his haughty indifference enough to listen.

'I want to let the people of Rouen know that I plan to revive the woollen trade. I want to make them prosperous again.'

'That is the best way to win their favour, my lord.'

'I thought you would agree. I want your help in doing this. I want you to advise me. You know these French better than I ever can. A prosperous country and an end to strife ... that will be good for Burgundy no less than France.'

'It is true enough.'

'Then to reform the currency, to get the wool trade on its feet again. Then there are the silk weavers of Paris ...'

'You do not talk like a soldier.'

'Nay, it will please me to have done with wars. Would that please you too, my lord? To live in peace and prosperity ... is that not to be preferred to the ravages of war?'

'If it can be achieved with honour, most certainly.'

'I want you to help me achieve it with honour.'

Burgundy was pleased and he made no attempt to disguise the fact.

'You speak good sense ... Regent,' he said, and Bedford felt he was getting on very well.

'There is one other matter,' he said. 'Your sister.'

Burgundy narrowed his eyes and regarded Bedford somewhat sardonically. Now he understood the meaning of this show of friendship.

'I have seen little of her, too little. But it is enough. She impresses me greatly. Perhaps I am a sentimental man. My brother was the same. He took one look at Katherine and was in love with her.'

Burgundy smiled but it was not an unpleasant smile. 'I think, my lord, he was more than a little in love with the crown of France.'

'There you speak truth. But he delighted in Katherine. He said he was the luckiest man on earth because he would have them both ... the crown and Katherine. And let me tell you this, my lord Duke: if the King of France had had no daughter my brother would still have had the crown of France. Nay, he took one look at Katherine and was in love with her. Thus do I feel regarding your fair sister.'

'Like Katherine my sister has much to recommend her.'

'My brother had a crown to offer Katherine. She is Queen of England now and was as soon as she married my brother. I cannot offer your sister a crown, but I can give her almost anything else she might desire.'

'It may be that she will not desire you, my lord. Have you thought of that?'

'Yes, I have,' said Bedford, 'and so great is my esteem for her that I would not have her forced to a marriage if it were distasteful to her.'

'You are a gallant suitor, my lord Regent.'

'She fills my thoughts. My brother was a simple man, and so am I. Perhaps like him I lack the ability to make flowery courtship but my heart is sturdy none the less and my feelings go deep.'

'Then you would take my sister without a great dowry, I daresay.'

Just a moment's hesitation then Bedford said: 'I would not demand what the great House of Burgundy could not give but knowing its wealth and power I doubt it would wish one of its daughters to be sent to her husband like some low-born woman.'

Burgundy began to laugh.

'You have approached my sister?' he asked.

Bedford shook his head, and looked shocked. 'My lord Duke, I am surprised you could suggest I should be capable of such indiscretion.'

'Nay, I did not think you would for I fancy you would not wish to displease me.'

'It is the last thing I would wish.'

Burgundy nodded. It all made sense. Cement friendship with Burgundy. It was the wisest way Bedford could act. His respect for the Regent had always been there; it was growing fast.

And it would be wise. By God's Head, thought Burgundy, if I stood with the English what chance would that miserable little monster who calls himself the King of France have against us?

He would see him humbled. It would be a shock for the silly young fool when he heard that Burgundy's sister was betrothed to Regent Bedford.

'You raise my hopes, my lord Duke,' Bedford was saying.

'Such matters cannot be decided in a moment.'

'Nay, but I see you are prepared to give consideration to this.'

'It would depend on my sister Anne. I know not what she feels about the English.'

'She seemed ready to show friendship to this Englishman.'

Burgundy nodded.

'If you gave your consent,' went on Bedford, 'if we could come to some arrangement agreeable to us both I should be the happiest of men.'

It was clear that Burgundy was not ill pleased with the idea. Now was the time for John to hint at the matter which was the real reason for his seeking this interview with the Duke of Burgundy.

'I have heard disturbing news of my brother Humphrey,' he began.

Burgundy raised his eyebrows. He was clearly surprised by the change in the conversation.

'Oh, forgive me burdening you with these matters. But the lady concerned is a connection of yours ... in a manner of speaking ... and this affair is much on my mind. You know my brother is of a somewhat impetuous nature. It was a source of great anxiety to my brother Henry. Humphrey acts first and then faces the consequences afterwards. They are not always pleasant. To tell the truth he has made a foolish marriage ... or not in truth a marriage ... but it could be awkward. It is the lady in question, you see.'

'What lady is this? Is she of my acquaintance?'

'Well ... she is in truth a kinswoman of yours. I refer to Jacqueline of Bavaria.' The Duke was astounded.

'Married!' he cried. 'Did you say ... married to your brother Humphrey!'

'I did.'

'It's nonsense. She is married to Brabant so how can she be married to your brother Gloucester?'

'It seems there has been some sort of annulment.' Burgundy looked as though he was going to strike his guest. It was clear that he was deeply shocked. John congratulated himself on having put him in a mellow mood before he gave this news.

'Annulment!' cried Burgundy. 'How could that be?'

He had arranged the marriage between his cousin of Brabant and Jacqueline who was also his cousin and he had his eyes on those important territories Hainault, Holland and Zealand. It was not going to be difficult for powerful Burgundy to wrest them from the one-time Bishop of Liège and soon he had thought they would be back where they belonged—ostensibly with Brabant which meant with Burgundy.

Bedford was eager to soothe him. 'It is not a true annulment. Benedict XIII pronounced it.'

Burgundy was relieved.

'Ah, it is no true marriage then,' he said.

'You can understand my anxiety,' said John.

'Your brother clearly has his eyes on her lands. What does he propose to do? To attempt to take them?'

'He will plan that most likely. But whether he will carry it out, who knows. He tires easily of his projects.'

Burgundy was clearly disturbed.

'I shall find some way of dealing with him,' said Bedford. 'I am sure I can rely on your help.'

'You may rest assured that I shall not allow my cousin to be treated in this way. Those lands came to him with his wife.'

''Twas a pity Brabant passed them over so lightly to the old Bishop of Liège.'

'Like your brother he is not always wise.'

They looked earnestly at each other. 'We shall know how to deal with this matter,' said Bedford.

As he rode away he was congratulating himself on his cleverness. He had broken the news of Gloucester's folly to

Burgundy himself, for it would never have done for the Duke to hear of it from another source and he had turned it to good account, he believed. It might even have strengthened the bond between himself and Philip of Burgundy.

A SCOTTISH ROMANCE

LIFE was pleasant at Windsor. Katherine knew that it could not go on like that. She would not be allowed to keep her baby to herself and live apart from ceremony. There had already been one occasion when she had had to take Henry to London for the meeting of the Parliament. So ironical it had seemed to have the King present, arriving in his mother's arms, lying there looking with interest at those around him, laughing suddenly as though he found the proceedings ridiculous and then dropping off to sleep as if he found it after all unworthy of further attention.

How the people had cheered as she had ridden through the streets seated on a kind of moving throne drawn by white horses. Afterwards she had sat with her baby on her knees while the lords came up one by one to salute him, and they all said he had behaved with becoming gravity which was an indication of future wisdom.

But how glad she had been to come back to Windsor!

Two nurses had arrived. The first was Joan Astley and the Parliament had agreed that she should have a salary of forty pounds a year which was about the same as a privy councillor for the nursing of the King of England was a task of the greatest importance. She quickly became devoted to Henry and he took to her at once.

Then there was Dame Alice Butler who was given the same salary as Joan Astley and the same privileges including permission to chastise the royal infant if the need should arise. Katherine was thankful that this infrequently did, for

Henry was a good baby—he rarely cried and he only did so when he was hungry or tired; he was contented and showed an interest in everything around him.

Katherine felt she could safely leave the care of her child with these two women.

Life at Windsor resembled that of a country house. There were not a great many visitors from Court. The Queen had implied that she wished to live quietly for a while as she continued to mourn her husband and her wishes so far had been respected but she feared that life would have to change in time.

One day however James the First of Scotland arrived to take up his residence there. She had heard much of him at Windsor for the castle had been his principal residence for a good many years. At one time he had been lodged in the Tower, and later he had accompanied Henry to France; but at the same time he was the prisoner of England and would remain so until his people paid the ransom required for him.

Katherine had expected a sullen young man. After all it might be expected that he would bear resentment towards a people who held him so long against his will. She was agreeably surprised when they met. He was some seven years older than herself—good-looking, witty, an eager conversationalist and a man who was ready to see more than one side to a question—in fact a very agreeable companion.

There followed delightful sessions when she talked with him, his chaplain Thomas of Myrton and others of his household. In the evenings there would be music and dancing.

He liked to talk with her of the past and contemplate what the future would be. He could remember a little of his native Scotland, though he had left it when he was ten years old and had not been back since.

'Nor shall I go,' he said, 'until they pay the ransom for me.'

They had much in common for they had both lived through strange childhoods. Both had had a father who had suffered from weakness, mentally and physically, although King Robert of Scotland was not mad as Charles VI had been.

James and Katherine agreed that to be born royal was to be born to danger.

They rode together in the great forest of Windsor; they walked in the castle gardens and she told him of those fearful days at the Hôtel de St Pol and he told her of his childhood at Dumfermline and Inverkeithing. His fears had been less horrifying than hers for he had had a strong good mother; but he on the other hand had been in greater danger than she had, for she was only a girl—to be used later as an important bargaining counter it was true but as a child, of little importance.

'It was when my mother died that I was in danger,' he said. 'My elder brother was murdered by my uncle and my father, fearing a like fate for me, decided to send me to France. However the English intercepted the ship in which I was sailing and brought me to the King—your husband's father—and I have been a hostage ever since.'

'You do not seem unhappy,' she commented.

He shrugged his shoulders. 'It happened when I was young. Ten years old. It seemed an adventure then. In a way it has seemed an adventure ever since.'

Of course he had been treated with honour. He was a King even though a captive one. Kings usually respected kings. They never knew when they themselves might be in need of respect. His education had not been neglected; he had excelled in manly sports; he had taken a great pleasure in literature and was writing his own poem which he was calling *The Kingis Quair* and he would read parts of it to Katharine now and then.

One day when they sat talking there were sounds of arrival at the castle and looking out they saw a girl riding at the head of a small band of attendants.

'Visitors,' cried Katherine. It was always pleasing to have visitors providing they were not important men from court who had come to make demands.

'What a strikingly beautiful woman,' said James.

Katherine agreed.

They went down to the courtyard to greet the newcomers. Katherine recognized the young woman at once as Lady Jane Beaufort, the daughter of the Earl of Somerset. Katherine embraced her and then presented her to James.

He bowed low and Katherine was amused to see that he could scarcely take his eyes from Lady Jane.

For the next weeks Jane shared their rides and their talks and she seemed in no hurry to leave the castle.

*   *   *

They were in love. Katherine wished she could help them.

She knew that they wished to be alone but she as the Queen must not allow any act of impropriety in her presence. On one occasion she went riding with them and deliberately lost them. The grooms were surprised to see her return alone and she told them she had lost the party; and they, accustomed to her eccentricities, thought no more of it. Then she wandered out into the gardens and seated herself on a rustic seat sheltered from the castle by bushes.

While she was seated there she heard the sound of footsteps and with mingling surprise and pleasure she saw Owen Tudor coming towards her.

He seemed overcome by embarrassment and she cried out: 'I am pleased to see you, Owen Tudor. Pray sit down beside me. I would talk with you.'

He hesitated. He was always shy when she addressed him. He could not forget the great gulf which divided a Queen from a humble squire.

'You think this is not ... *comme il faut* ... is that so? Not what is right for a Queen. But I do so much that is not right for a Queen. Shall I tell you I have just lost—on purpose—the King of Scotland and the Lady Jane. What do you think of them, Owen Tudor? Are they not a handsome pair? Are they not so beautiful ... and is not it wonderful to be in love as they are?'

Owen was silent, tongue-tied in the presence of his Queen.

'Of course he is a King,' she went on. 'But a King in exile. And she is royal, you know, Owen. Her father is John Beaufort Earl of Somerset, son of John of Gaunt and his last Duchess. She is connected with Richard II through her mother. I do not see why she should not mate with the royal house of Scotland. Do you, Owen?'

'No, my lady.'

She turned to him suddenly. 'In fact, Owen, I do not see why anything should separate those who love. Poor James, he has talked much to me. He had a sad childhood ... just as I did. You should be thankful Owen that you were not born royal. He loved his mother dearly. I think he was a little unsure of his father. Still, his mother was always there to care for him ... until she died. Then his brother was murdered by his wicked uncle. Why is it uncles are so often wicked? It is ambition perhaps and they are usually younger brothers who by removing one person here and another there could come to the throne. I sometimes wonder whether it is not foolish to dream of a crown, Owen. Do you think it brings happiness? Do you, Owen?'

'No, my lady. I think it rarely does.'

'It brought my husband happiness ... I think above everything he loved his crown. Men do, you know, Owen. So that is why those who have no hope of a crown or power are happier than those who have. You should be a happy man, Owen Tudor.'

'I am, my lady. Particularly so to enjoy your favour.'

She laughed. 'You have it, Owen. It shall always be yours.' She looked at him a little archly. 'Unless of course you do aught to lose it.'

'Will all my heart I shall strive to keep it,' he replied.

'With all my heart I trust you will. But what will become of our lover, think you, Owen? I would to God it were in my power to send him back to his kingdom with the bride of his choice.'

'It may well be that his people will raise the ransom and he will go.'

'Oh Owen, how happy you must have been among your Welsh mountains when you were a child!'

'There was always the fear, my lady. Remember my father was in exile.'

'Your father ... yes ... the outlaw accused of murder. We are all the victims of our fathers it seems. How pleasant it is here. I hope I shall stay long at Windsor. It is my favourite place. They will be wanting my son to take on his duties soon, I doubt not. Oh, you smile Owen. He is but a baby. Think of the burden on that little head! A baby ... to wear a crown. They try to force the orb and sceptre into those chubby hands. I tell you, Owen, he will confound them all by trying to eat them.'

She laughed and he joined with her and the sound of their laughter reminded her of the impropriety of sitting in the gardens chatting and laughing with one of her squires. If they were seen ...

She wanted to snap her fingers. What cared she for their rules. She would do as she wished and if she wanted to be with Owen Tudor so would she be.

He was uneasy though, and she remembered suddenly that her conduct could perhaps place him in greater danger than she herself would be.

That sobered her a little.

She rose and gave him her hand. He kissed it and released it quickly.

'Poor Owen,' she murmured, and she realized that he was even more aware of the danger than she was.

Even so she would talk to whomsoever she wished, and at the moment she was sure her conduct had not been observed. It was one of the blessings of living quietly.

She said fervently: 'I want to stay at Windsor for a very long time.'

Then she walked quickly into the castle.

*   *   *

James and Jane were seated in a window-seat. He was reading to her from his *Kingis Quair*.

Katherine walked in softly and sat watching them for a while. There was an aura of happiness about them. How magical to be in love! It had never been quite like that with her and Henry. He had liked her well and she had liked him. This was different. This was not loving because it would be expedient to do so. This was love which crept up unbidden and caught two people and held them. It was the most beautiful thing in the world. She wondered whether it would ever happen to her and something told her that it would.

There was a scratching at the door and Thomas of Myrton entered. It was easy to see that something important had happened.

'Come in, Thomas, and tell us your news. I see you are eager to do so,' said Katherine.

'My ladies, my lord,' said Thomas, 'I am to leave forthwith for Pontefract.'

James had risen. 'Tell us more, Thomas,' he commanded.

'I think this time there will be an agreement. Perhaps, who knows, you may very soon now be back in your own land.'

Jane put out a hand and James took it and held it firmly.

'It would appear that your fellow countrymen are ready to agree to the terms at last.'

'They will pay the ransom then?'

'Oh there is more than the ransom ... sixty thousand marks ...'

'A great deal of money,' said Jane.

'For a King?' asked Katherine.

'All Scottish troops are to be removed from French soil.'

'And they are ready to agree to that?'

'It would seem so, my lord. In any case I shall know more in Pontefract. This may well be an end to your captivity.'

'They will no doubt want to make a marriage for me,' said James. 'Thomas, you must tell them that I have already chosen.'

Thomas nodded. 'I will do that,' he said. 'And my lord, until my return I beg of you do not act rashly. Let us see if we can conclude this matter to the satisfaction of all concerned. I now ask your leave to retire. I have to depart without delay.'

The three of them talked excitedly together.

'I shall not leave without Jane,' declared James.

'I shall not let you,' answered Jane.

Katherine listened eagerly. She asked herself what she would do in the circumstances.

She would snap her fingers at them all. She would marry for love; for seeing these two together and thinking of the lives of her parents and her own brief marriage she had decided that crowns—and even the world itself—were well lost for the sake of love.

*   *   *

There was great excitement at Windsor when the messenger came back from Pontefract. The treaty between the Scots and English had been arranged.

The King of Scotland was to be free—after some twenty years—to return to his land. Sixty thousand marks would be paid for his release in instalments of ten thousand a year and hostages would have to be given to make sure there was no defaulting. All Scottish troops would quit France. That was promised and then the best clause of all: King James must marry an English lady of noble birth.

'There are times,' said Katherine when she heard the terms, 'when it seems Heaven is on our side. There is your English lady, James. I do not think there will be the slightest reluctance on her part.'

It was a glorious ending to a happy romance.

Messengers arrived at Windsor. This time they had dispatches for the Queen.

The King must appear before his Parliament and his

mother should bring him to London without delay.

'Well,' said Katherine, 'I suppose it was too much to hope that we should be left long in peace.'

The summons could not be disobeyed and she and Henry with a great many attendants and much ceremony—which must always accompany the baby wherever he went—set out for London.

It was Saturday night when they reached the inn at Staines where they were to stay the night before they made their entry into London. On the Sunday morning they prepared to leave and crowds came out to watch them.

Henry was in a bad mood. The crowd no longer interested him. He screamed until his face was purple and all feared he would do himself some harm. He tried to throw himself from his mother's arms and behaved in a manner so unlike his usual placid self that it was decided he should be returned to the inn. So the protesting child was taken back and there he lay all through that day in a fractious mood.

On the next day, being a Monday, they set out again. Henry was his old self, smiling, chuckling, showing an interest in all about him.

He will be very pious, prophesied the people. So young and already he shows his disapproval of travelling on a Sunday.

So at this early age Henry had already received his reputation for piety.

On Monday they arrived at Kingston and on Tuesday by degrees to Kennington and on the Wednesday he rode into London, sitting on his mother's lap, and it seemed that all London had come out to see their adorable little King.

At Westminster he attended Parliament and was shown to the assembly there who were well pleased with his progress and it was decided that he should remain in his mother's care for a little longer.

Katherine rested for a while at Eltham Palace and from there went on to her castle of Hertford. It was pleasant to be in her own castle for it had come to her as it had to the Queen of her father-in law and it would go in due course to baby Henry's Queen when he had one, for it had been granted to John of Gaunt and thus had come to this side of the family.

She decided she would spend Christmas there and she sent word to James asking him if he would join her.

'I have already asked Lady Jane Beaufort,' she said. 'I thought you and she might have a good deal to talk about.'

They accepted with grateful thanks.

She also asked that some of her personal guards come to Hertford and she made special mention that among them should be the squire Owen Tudor.

* * *

What a happy day that was in February of the following year when James the First of Scotland married Jane Beaufort, at the church of St Mary Overy in Southwark. Katherine insisted on being present for she felt she had played a prominent part in this romance and was overjoyed that it had worked out as it had. She could never have borne it if the lovers had been separated, but of course they would never have allowed that to happen.

It was a fairy-tale ending and when the decree had been announced that the King of Scotland must marry a noble English lady he had cried: 'Right gladly and I have already chosen.'

There could of course be no objection to marriage with the noble Beauforts ... royal themselves through John of Gaunt if they had made their entry into the world on the wrong side of the blanket. What mattered was that they had been legitimized afterwards and held high posts in the land. Moreover Jane was royal through her mother.

The Earl of Somerset was delighted with his daughter's marriage and her uncle the Bishop of Winchester insisted that the banquet should take place in his palace close to the church.

It was a glorious occasion but nothing was more splendid, Katherine decided, than the happiness on the faces of the bride and groom.

The day after the wedding it was announced that ten thousand marks of the ransom were to be remitted as Jane's dowry and the couple were then free to start their journey to Scotland. At Durham the hostages would have to be delivered into English hands but there seemed to be no difficulty about that.

A few weeks later Katherine said goodbye to her dear friends.

She knew that she was going to be very lonely without

them, and when she rode to Hertford where she had decided
to rest awhile, she selected Owen Tudor to ride beside her.

'I shall miss them sorely,' she told him. 'But right glad I am
to see their happiness. Does it not gladden the heart to see
love like that, Owen Tudor?'

He answered quietly: 'It does, my lady.'

'That it should have turned out so neatly ... that was
what I liked. "You must marry a noble English lady," they
said, and there she is ... already there. How fortunate they
were, Owen; if you can call a man fortunate who has spent
the greater part of his life a prisoner.'

'He is finished with prison now, my lady.'

'Yes, he gains his rightful place on his throne and his love
with him. Do you not think love is the finest thing that can
happen to a man and woman, Owen Tudor?'

'I ... I could not say, my lady.'

'I can ... and I will. It is, Owen Tudor. It *is*!'

Their eyes met and she felt a great happiness creeping
over her.

'They were able to marry,' he said. 'They are fortunate
indeed.'

'The happy ending,' mused the Queen. 'No ... not the
ending ... Marriage is just the beginning. But they are
together ... and whatever may come it can be mastered ...
with a loved one to share it. You think I behave strangely ...
for a Queen?' she added.

'My lady, I think there never was such a Queen as you.'

She turned away. The love affair of James and Jane had
affected her deeply. It had made her see what she never dared
look at closely before.

THE MARRIAGE OF BEDFORD

A VERY important ceremony was taking place in the town of Troyes. John, Duke of Bedford, Regent of France was being married to Anne of Burgundy, sister of the great Duke and such an alliance could not fail to raise speculation not only throughout France but in England as well. The English saw it as a master-stroke. Charles of France saw it as disastrous. The old Duke of Burgundy should never have been murdered on the bridge at Montereau. It was deeds like this which were the start of feuds that could go on through centuries; and France at the moment was in need of all the friends she could get. To have alienated Burgundy in such a way was a major disaster. And not only would France lose Burgundy's friendship: England would gain it.

John himself was filled with complacency. Gloucester's conduct had been enough to alienate Burgundy altogether. He flattered himself that he had warded that off by this brilliant stroke of genius. John was too shrewd not to realize that the Gloucester affair was not over yet. It would be a blow of great proportions if his brother was ever foolish enough to try to regain Hainault, Holland and Zealand. At the moment he was just a threat. Pray God, thought John, that it remains only that until I can stop the mad affair.

John was philosophical. Life had made him so. He realized that in such a hazardous position as he found himself he could take only one step at a time. This he intended to do. And it was a very clever and happy step he was taking now.

He glanced at Anne riding beside him. The ceremony was

over and they were on their way to Paris where the Palace
of the Tournelles had been made ready to receive them. Anne
was young and beautiful; moreover she was good and gentle,
even greater assets. She had placidly agreed to the marriage
which showed that she did not regard him with disfavour,
and he did not think her willingness had anything to do with
politics. There seemed no valid reason why Anne should
greatly wish for a friendship between Burgundy and England.
So it seemed likely that she did not find his person dis-
pleasing.

He was handsome, they said. But did they not often say
that of Princes? He had a finely arched nose and well defined
chin but he was inclined to put on flesh and his skin was too
highly coloured, perhaps the result of much exposure to
weather. However he bore a resemblance to his brother
Henry and he felt that was in his favour.

Anne was a good deal younger than he was, but that was
often the case in marriages such as theirs.

As they rode towards Paris he wanted to reassure her that
he would be a good and faithful husband to her.

He said to her: 'There is some surprise concerning our
marriage among the people.'

She answered: 'It is to be expected.'

'England and Burgundy ... at such a time.'

'My brother is no friend to Charles of France.'

'One would not expect him to show friendship towards his
father's murderer.'

Her face was sad. It was tactless of him to have referred
to the murder. After all, the victim had been Anne's father
also.

'I am sorry,' he said.

She looked at him with surprise.

'I reminded you of your father,' he explained. 'It was tactless of me. It was a great blow to you to lose him.'

'Murder is terrible. I wish there could be an end to bloodshed.'

'There will be,' he promised. 'It shall be my aim to make
France prosperous again and that can only be done through
peace.'

She turned to smile at him and he felt a glow of pleasure.
She was very beautiful and perhaps she could grow fond of
him.

It was a happy man who rode into Paris. This was a great

step forward. Married into the House of Burgundy to the sister of the Duke with a dowry of 150,000 golden crowns and the promise that if Philip should die without a male heir the county of Artois should be hers! And even if Philip should have an heir, Anne should have as compensation 1,000,000 golden crowns.

A good marriage. A magnificent dowry, a young and beautiful girl—and the greatest matter for rejoicing was the alliance with Burgundy.

*   *   *

The palace was magnificent and the festivities to celebrate the wedding must be equally so. There were banquets and balls but all the time John was aware of an uneasiness. It seemed difficult for everyone—including Anne—to forget that he was the alien conqueror.

In time, he told himself, it will be forgotten. Time? How long? And he was realist enough to know that even if he kept a firm hold on the government of the country there would always be factions to rise against him. Charles was no mean enemy. He might be weak, impetuous, and often listless but the French still regarded him as their true King and would go on doing so—him and his heirs for centuries to come. Occupation was never easy.

All through the celebrations he was aware of suspicions; he knew that he was watched furtively. He would be strong though. He would be as Henry would have been. Henry had married their Princess; he had done the next best thing: he had married into the House of Burgundy.

He wished he could be sure of them. He even wished he could be sure of Anne.

She was young, inexperienced, an idealist and he found great delight in her. She was docile, eager to please him, but he felt that he did not really know her. He wondered how much Burgundy had had to persuade her to the match. Would he have bothered? Oh yes, indeed, Burgundy saw the marriage as a way of flouting Charles VII and at the moment his bitterness against the murderer of his father was uppermost in his mind.

But John had other matters to occupy him as well as his marriage. A soldier could not give too much thought to his personal affairs except when they were closely connected with his duties. This marriage of course was a very important part of them. But now it was accomplished. He must always try to emulate Henry. Henry had been delighted with Katherine, but he would never have sought the marriage if she had not been the daughter of the King of France.

Messengers were constantly arriving at Les Tournelles. He was eager to know how his forces were faring at D'Orsay for that town had been in a state of siege for more than six weeks and the stubbornness of the townsfolk was an irritation to him for it meant expending so many men and so much ammunition to enforce the siege.

It was time D'Orsay collapsed; it must before long, he assured himself, and then he thought of the siege of Rouen which had caused his brother such anxieties. But it had been successful at last and had indeed been a decisive factor in Henry's victory. D'Orsay was hardly as important as that but at the same time he was anxiously waiting for news of that beleaguered town.

It was while he was thinking of this matter that news came of the surrender of D'Orsay.

Anne was with him. He smiled at her. 'At last,' he cried. 'Who would have thought such a place could hold out so long.'

She smiled at him sadly. He remembered that smile later. It was not always easy to remember that these people who were holding out against him were her countrymen.

He stood at the window watching the bareheaded prisoners being brought into Paris. These were the men who had made the siege of D'Orsay such a costly matter.

Anne was beside him.

'You look sad,' he said.

'I was thinking of those men. Where are they being taken?'

'To the Châtelet,' he told her.

'Prisoners,' she said.

'What would you expect them to be, dear lady? They have killed my soldiers; they have fought against me.'

'In defence of their town,' she replied.

He sighed. 'It was foolish of them. Had they surrendered six weeks before they would have saved us and themselves much suffering. They must pay for their folly.'

He turned abruptly and left her.

When he was asked to pass sentence on the prisoners he said it should be death. The citizens of France must learn that it did not pay to hold out against the Regent and severe penalties must await those who did; it was the only way to deter others.

There was gloom in the city of Paris. The people did not like these public executions. They hated to see their own countrymen led out to be slaughtered. For what reason? Because they had defied the usurpers!

On the morning of the day fixed for their execution, the streets were deserted. That was better, thought John, than having them crowded round the place of execution. It was a good sign. Sullen they might be but they were resigned.

He was sure that he was doing the right thing.

Anne came to him as he sat at his table in the antechamber. He rose and bowed. 'You wished to speak with me?' he asked.

'Yes. It is about the prisoners.'

'They are to be executed today.'

'John, please do not do it.'

He softened. 'It has to be,' he explained gently. 'They are an example, you must understand. I cannot endure many more of these pointless sieges. They drain our resources too much. They take too much time. I cannot have great bodies of men concentrated round one town because the people are so stubborn and will not give in.'

'Please understand that they are only defending their homes.'

'They would have defended them better by surrendering to my men. What good have they done. They have starved the citizens of their town; they will leave their wives without husbands and their children without fathers.'

She turned passionately towards him. 'My lord ... pardon them.'

'Pardon them! You do not mean that surely?'

'I do,' she said. 'I ask you. Pardon them.'

'My dear lady, do you understand what this means? To pardon them would be to advise others to do the same. They would say I was weak ...'

'They might say you were strong.'

He laughed. 'Never.'

She said: 'I should think it showed strength. To kill them shows that you fear that others will do likewise.'

She bent her head to hide the tears in her eyes and he was overcome by a sudden tenderness.

'You do not understand these matters,' he said gently. 'My dear lady wife, you must allow me to decide. You are too gentle, too good. You do not understand the perils of war.'

'I understand too well,' she replied. 'There has always been war ... War between my house and the Armagnacs ... War between France and England. Everyone in this poor war-torn land knows war, my lord.'

'Sweet lady, you must leave these cruel matters to men.'

'War has always been a man's game, has it not? A game ... yes that is it. It *is* a game. You play with living men as you would play with toy soldiers. You forget that they are not wooden soldiers ... they are living flesh and blood.'

He tried to take her hand but she withdrew it and sharply turning ran from the room.

He stared after her. He was upset by the encounter. She saw him as cruel, indifferent to suffering. She saw him as a monster crazy for power. It was not so. He had been brought up to fight. It was part of a boy's education. If he did not excel in the jousts he was considered to be a weakling and was despised by those about him. Anne did not understand.

An hour passed. He was still thinking of her. She had seemed more beautiful in tears than she had in her magnificent wedding gown.

What had she said? It showed weakness. It was nonsense. The men had to die. It would be folly to allow the people to think that they could flout his army and be forgiven like naughty schoolboys.

He must forget Anne's outburst. She was hysterical; she was illogical; she brought a woman's reason to that which was a matter for men.

He sat staring before him. He went to the window and looked out on the empty streets. Then he called to one of the guards.

*　　*　　*

Anne stood before him. Her eyes were shining and he saw that her cheeks were wet.

She was smiling at him. She said: 'You did it then. You stopped the order.'

'You spoke for them so earnestly.'

'But you said ...'

He went to her and took her hands in his. He kissed them.

She said. 'Thank you.'

Then he put his arms about her and held her close to him.

He was rejoicing in his marriage—not friendship with Burgundy, not the promise of Artois, nor all those golden crowns ... but simply because he loved her.

THE DUKE'S MISTRESS

Humphrey, Duke of Gloucester was in his element. He thrived on intrigue. His marriage to Jacqueline had focused attention on him and there was nothing he enjoyed more than being at the heart of a controversy.

'Ha,' he said to Jacqueline, 'this has made my brother realize that there are other members of the family besides his important self. It has pricked the pride of proud Burgundy. Imagine the consternation in the camps of these two worthy gentlemen, sweet wife.'

'I can well imagine it,' retorted Jacqueline, 'but what concerns me most is when we are going to get control of my territories.'

'All in good time our lands will be ours. Leave it to me.'

He looked at her slyly. He did not greatly care for her. Stripped of those delectable lands she would have no appeal for him at all. Her nature was not what he would call warm —quite the reverse. She indulged in what he called bed frolics with something less than enthusiasm. It was clear to him that if he had married her for her lands she had married him that he might get them for her.

Never mind. The project was a pleasing one and it still intrigued him.

He was constantly sending messages to Europe. He was trying to get the Pope, Martin V, to agree that Jacqueline's marriage to Brabant was not valid—Benedict did not carry enough weight—for although he was not entirely pleased with his marriage it was very important that it was recognized to exist.

There were disquieting messages from his brother John. It was a foolish thing he had done, insisted John. If he had been told that once he had been told twenty times. Burgundy was incensed, John added. Always Burgundy! John seemed to be obsessed by Burgundy. And he had married the mighty Duke's sister! Poor solemn old John forced into marriage because of brother Humphrey's feckless conduct!

'As a matter of fact,' he told Jacqueline, 'I am working very hard on our project. Do you know that e'er long I shall have amassed an army of five thousand? The time will soon be here when we are ready to cross the water, land at Calais and then march through to Hainault.'

'And you think Burgundy will allow that?'

'Burgundy will not be able to stop my gallant five thousand.'

'I trust you are right.'

She looked at him with narrowed eyes. How far did she trust him? She was no fool and she knew that any woman would have to be a fool to trust Gloucester far.

'So my love,' he went on, 'it is now for you to make your preparations. What say you to that? You will want to select your household, for I will not have you travel in any inferior style than that of a queen.'

'I have no intention of doing otherwise,' she told him.

He nodded pleasantly.

'Then, sweet wife, speed on your plans. Before October is out we should be on our way. We do not want to wait for the winter, do we?'

'As soon as that?' she said.

'Aye,' he answered, 'as soon ... or sooner. If you do not believe me, go and study the accounts my treasurer is compiling. He will be pleased to discuss them with you, for he is mighty pleased with his efforts.'

'I will,' she said.

He bowed as she went out and then made his way to the apartment which they shared together.

A woman was hanging up one of Jacqueline's cloaks in a cupboard. He had seen her before and noticed her. He had in fact come here in search of her.

'Why 'tis Lady Eleanor, I do declare,' he said.

She turned round. She had large dark brown eyes and thick dark hair; her cheeks were highly coloured and Humphrey thought of her as luscious. Her figure was voluptuous in the extreme, small waisted, large bosomed and ample hipped. The belt she wore at her waist accentuated this.

'Ah,' she said saucily, 'I too will make a declaration. It is Duke Humphrey.'

'And you are pleased to see him, mayhap?' he murmured.

'My lord, is there any reason why I should not be pleased?'

'Indeed no. There is every reason why you should be pleased. I will tell you this. I find you are a very pretty woman.'

'Ah.' She put her hands on her hips. 'Then you have not come to tell me that you are displeased with me and would dismiss me from the Lady Jacqueline's household.'

'Nay, nay, I have come to tell you that I would wish to take you into mine.'

'My lord jests,' she began but got no further because he had put his arms about her and his mouth was pressing on hers.

She was warm in her response as he had known she would be. He had had his eyes on her for days ... and he knew well enough that she had been aware of it and was cordially inviting him to proceed.

'You're a witch,' he said. 'You've bewitched me.'

'Mayhap. But it is not my occult powers that have done it.'

'Well, what shall we do about it, eh? What should you say?'

'I should say that you must remember your good wife, the Lady Jacqueline. But it might be that I will not say what I should.'

'Then what will you say?'

She drew away from him and put out her tongue provocatively. 'I shall say this, my lord. You are a man ... and men do what they will ... when they will, how they will. What does a poor woman do?'

'You mean ...' he said.

'I mean nothing, fair sir. Yet I could mean anything.'

He approached her again. He seized her. 'I want you,' he said. 'You know it.'

She opened her wide languorous eyes and said, 'When? Here?'

'Why not?' he said.

'You are a bold man.'

'You'll find me as bold as you wish me to be.'

She pushed him from her. 'Here? ... when my lady might come at any moment?'

'She is studying the accounts. I sent her to do so.'

'That you might come and see me?'

'You know I've had my eyes on you for days.'

'I saw the lust in them.'

' 'Tis not the first time you've seen such looks I'll warrant. Nor satisfied them either,' he added.

'My lord you are offensive.'

'You arouse a madness in me.'

'Never mind. Soon you will be overseas. Just curb yourself till then.'

'You will come with us. You must.'

An alert look came into her eyes.

'Shall I be there then?' she came to him and put her arms about his neck. 'I should not wish,' she went on, 'to find a man to my taste and then to lose him to the Dutch or the Zealanders or the folk of Hainault.'

'Is that what you want? To come with us?'

She put her head on one side. 'I'd have to try you first to see if I wanted that.'

She dragged him through a door. They were in a small closet. 'My sleeping apartment,' she explained. 'Small but it will suffice, I think, for at such a moment as this even the mighty Duke of Gloucester has other things to think of than his surroundings.'

'My God,' he said. And he laughed in triumph. He was in a fever of excitement such as he had rarely known before. His delight was increased when he realized that his eagerness was matched by hers.

He was convinced he had never before enjoyed such an encounter.

For a woman like this one he could forget not only Jacqueline but Hainault, Holland and Zealand.

*   *   *

Preparations for departure were proceeding rapidly and there were frantic messages arriving from Bedford.

'For God's sake,' wrote Bedford to his brother, 'do nothing rash. Burgundy is incensed. This could lose us his friendship.'

Humphrey laughed and bombastically declared to Eleanor that it amused him to see old John in such a panic. It might lose him Burgundy's friendship but it was going to bring vast advantages to Humphrey.

'Don't you think I should consider myself, sweetheart?'

Eleanor replied that indeed he should for it was something which he did to perfection being so practised in that art.

He could laugh at her; she amused him; she was ambitious for him too; she wanted him not only supreme in her bed but in the field. It amused her to have a powerful lover. She wanted him to be the most powerful man in England; and he would be when he regained Jacqueline's lands.

He had rarely been so pleased with himself. He was so proud of being Jacqueline's husband and Eleanor's lover.

Eleanor was with them when they left for Calais. He would not have sailed without her, so important had she become to him. She was the most erotically skilled woman he had ever known and he had known a few. The intrigue necessary to keep his liaison secret from Jacqueline excited him. He had rarely been so pleased with himself. He would lie with Eleanor usually in some secret place and when they were satiated with their lovemaking he would talk to her of his plans.

She applauded his schemes. She said when he had secured Jacqueline's territories he could turn his thoughts to England. It would be years before little Henry could rule and there was only John over in France. He would be likely to remain occupied there for some time.

'There is that old devil of Winchester,' Humphrey reminded her. 'A curse on these Beaufort relations ... the lot of them. Bastards all of them.'

She laughed and nibbled his ear.

Wonderful sessions they were. On the boat together arriving at Calais, the excitement of wondering what they would find; having to travel through country where they might meet Burgundy's forces. But there was no opposition. It was all so easy. Right to the borders of Hainault they came and there was no sign of an enemy. Instead the people came out to welcome Jacqueline. They had no love for the ex-Bishop of Liège.

Glorious days. The conquerors riding through Hainault, stopping at the houses of nobles who had nothing but a hearty welcome for them ... or in truth for Jacqueline; receiving the dignitaries with Jacqueline beside him and aware—oh very much aware—of Eleanor, hovering close. And then at odd times seeking a meeting. Anywhere, anyhow! How they laughed at the strange places in which they found themselves!

Two things had become clear to him. Conquest was easy and the more he knew of Eleanor the more he realized that he could not do without her.

Easy conquest, a wife who had achieved her ambition and was happy just then to make it her sole concern, and a mistress who delighted him more every time he saw her.

What more could a man ask?

*   *   *

It was too much to expect that life could go on like that. Rumours came through to the effect that Burgundy was preparing to come against him and that the mighty Duke had joined forces with Brabant.

Gloucester ceased so openly to sneer at Burgundy as the rumours grew more alarming every day.

One day one of Burgundy's messengers arrived, bringing with him the suggestion that Gloucester return at once to England and that Jacqueline go back to her husband the Duke of Brabant, and they both forgot this farce of a marriage to Gloucester.

There was a letter from Bedford too. He was urging Gloucester to take heed not only for his own sake but that of England, for Burgundy was on the point of concluding a truce with France. 'You can guess what a blow this is to us,' wrote Bedford. 'We are pressed as hard as we can be and if we lose Burgundy's support, which we shall undoubtedly do if you persist in angering him, we could be in a most unhappy position.'

Humphrey tossed his brother's letter aside. Did John think he was going to give up all these newly acquired possessions just because he was told to?

A further letter from Burgundy affected him more deeply. Burgundy was challenging Humphrey to a duel—the time-honoured method of settling a difference.

When Jacqueline heard she shrugged her shoulders: 'You have a fair chance of winning,' she said.

'Against Burgundy!' Humphrey quaked at the thought. Burgundy's reputation was such as to strike terror into the heart of any man. He sought an early opportunity of telling Eleanor.

'Duel?' she said. 'Nonsense. I don't want Burgundy to murder you ... or to return you to me in such a state that you are of no more use to me.'

They laughed but he was seriously disturbed.

'I'm tired of Hainault and Holland,' said Eleanor. 'I'm homesick. I want to go back to England. What are these places compared with home? I've always told you you are chasing the wrong things. Think what you can do at home ... a baby on the throne and you his uncle! Brother Thomas is no more. Brother John is engaged in France. That leaves Humphrey free of the field. I've always said it but I'll say it again. Get out ... before Burgundy comes in.'

'Jacqueline would never agree.'

'Then let her stay.'

'You mean leave her here?'

'I'll swear that is where she wants to be.'

'It would mean she would have to face Burgundy alone.'

'She doesn't have to if she doesn't want to. She could go back to Brabant.'

'I doubt it will come to that unless Burgundy insists. He seems to be the one everyone is afraid of.'

'He has great power.'

'Listen to me, my love. Let us go back to England. Would you agree to come?'

'You don't imagine I should let you go without me, do you?'

'Do you think anyone or anything could make me leave you?'

'No,' she said. 'You'd put up as big a fight for me as you would for Jacqueline's lands. But you're not going to put up a fight for either. Let the lands go ... Humphrey ... and keep close to me.'

'Let them go!'

'You are going to have to when Burgundy marches in. He's only waiting until he has made his peace with the French. You don't want to be humiliated in defeat do you, Humphrey? Of course you don't. We'll go to England before that can happen.'

'How can we?'

'It is easy. You will say you are going to raise fresh troops and to prepare yourself for your duel with Burgundy.'

'You are a clever girl, Eleanor.'

'I live to serve, my lord,' she retorted with a touch of irony in her voice.

It was amazing how easy it had been to deceive Jacqueline. She accepted all he said. Yes, they would need more troops. He must make preparations for his duel. He must go. She would hold the land until he returned. He could take only a few of his knights with him. It would be better to leave a large force with her.

To all this he agreed. He took a fond farewell of her and started out on the journey to Calais. He had a few anxious hours because naturally Eleanor could not ride openly with him. And of course it was expected that she would stay in Holland in attendance on Jacqueline.

They came to an inn where they would spend a night and still she had not joined the party.

He was beginning to fear that she had no intention of coming with him. Could it be that she had found a new lover and had worked to get rid of him? No, they had had such amazing times together; there could not be another person in the world who suited her as he did. She had interested herself so ardently in his affairs. She wanted to be beside him when he took power in England. She had been homesick for England from the moment she had set foot on foreign soil.

But there he was and where was Eleanor?

The horses were in the stables and he with his small band of men went into the inn. He was taken to a room. The innkeeper opened a door and he went in.

Eleanor was lying in the bed.

'How long you have been in coming,' she reproached him.

Then he fell upon her and his delight was greater than he had ever known.

THE DUKE AND THE BISHOP

HENRY BEAUFORT, Bishop of Winchester, was deeply disturbed when he heard that Humphrey of Gloucester was back in England.

He expressed his disquiet to Richard de Beauchamp, Earl of Warwick. Warwick was a man of good reputation, renowned for his honour and selfless devotion to the crown. Henry Beaufort prided himself on a similar loyalty. He was the second son of John of Gaunt and Catherine Swynford and he had never forgotten that he owed his advancement to his relationship with Henry the Fourth who was his half-brother. Their father had expected Henry always to care for the Beaufort branch of the family even though at one time they had been illegitimate—and this Henry had done.

Such a start was something never to be forgotten by a man like the Bishop, and he had sought to serve both his half-brother Henry the Fourth and his nephew Henry the Fifth with devotion. He was now ready to offer that allegiance to Henry the Sixth. He deeply deplored the fact that the new King was a baby and that others should have to be set up to govern during his minority. He had the highest regard for John, Duke of Bedford. It was a different matter with Humphrey.

Now Henry Beaufort was shaking his head and muttering that it was an ill day for England when Gloucester had come amongst them once more.

Warwick agreed. 'The mission abroad was doomed to failure before it began,' he said.

'And in addition is threatening to lose us Burgundy's support. My Lord Bedford is extremely anxious about the outcome.'

'And well he might be. Now Burgundy will doubtless walk in and take over Jacqueline's territories.'

'I would to God Bedford would return.'

Warwick understood such sentiments. Since Bedford and Gloucester had left the country Beaufort had taken on the responsibility of governing. He had been made Chancellor once more and was held responsible for all the unpopular measures which had had to be taken to support an army in France.

He and Gloucester had been enemies from the time of Henry the Fifth's death. Beaufort had never wanted Humphrey to have a place on the Council. He was, of course, the brother of the late King and uncle of the reigning one; but Beaufort believed him to be not only selfish and licentious but quite incapable of wise government. He had made this very clear to everyone including Gloucester which naturally did not endear him to the Duke.

At this time Beaufort unfortunately was undergoing a phase of unpopularity in London, and the citizens were expressing their preference for the absent Duke. Beaufort had brought in some unpopular laws and the Londoners were not slow in expressing their irritation with these. They declared he showed more favour to the Flemish traders than he did to the English merchants. Moreover he had approved orders made by the mayor and aldermen restricting the employment of certain labourers.

All the difficulties of city trading including the extorting of taxes were blamed on the Bishop.

'Bills have been posted on the gates of my palace,' he told Warwick. 'The labourers have been meeting and threatening what they will do to me if they lay their hands on me. I tell you, Warwick, there is no joy in this task ... even without the presence of the Duke of Gloucester. I have taken the precaution of putting a garrison in the Tower in case there should be trouble. I dread to think of what would happen now if Gloucester rode into London.'

He was soon to discover.

In a few days Gloucester was making it known that he was back and he was going to find out how deeply offended his friends the Londoners were with the Bishop.

In the first place he had sent messages to the Mayor, whom he knew to be on his side with the merchants who believed that the Bishop had treated them badly.

'My good friend,' he wrote, 'we must curb the prejudices of this upstart Bishop against our worthy citizens. I beg of you place a guard on the bridge so that when the Bishop would cross into the city he is prevented from doing so. It will let him know that I am back to uphold the rights of the Londoners.'

The Mayor obeyed Humphrey and when the Bishop was about to make his way into the city he was challenged by men-at-arms who told him that on the orders of the Mayor and the Duke of Gloucester he could not be allowed to enter.

As was inevitable, in spite of the Bishop's effort to curb it, fighting broke out between the Bishop's followers and those citizens who were determined to uphold the Mayor's decision.

Uneasily the Bishop retired. It was even worse than he had imagined. Not content with creating harm to English rule in France by angering the Duke of Burgundy, Gloucester was now set on making trouble at home.

The Bishop sought out Warwick once more. There was no need to explain to him what had happened at the bridge. It was common knowledge.

'The fighting was fierce while it lasted,' explained the Bishop. 'If I had not retired and called off my men there could have been a disastrous riot. Heaven knows how far it would have gone. I wonder, my lord, if you will agree with me that there is only one thing to be done. If you and the Council agree I propose to do it without delay.'

Warwick nodded gravely. 'I presume you mean that we must ask the Duke of Bedford to return.'

'That is exactly what I had in mind.'

'I fear it is necessary. It may be dangerous however for him to leave France at this time when the alliance with Burgundy has been so impaired.'

'Gloucester has made trouble in France; he could make greater trouble in England.'

'That is true. And when all is weighed and considered it is England which must be defended first ... if it is a matter of making a choice.'

'I see you are in agreement with me. I must send an urgent message to the Duke of Bedford. However much his presence is needed in France it is even more urgently needed here.'

That very day the Bishop dispatched an urgent message to the Duke of Bedford.

* * *

Little Henry was being dressed in a crimson velvet robe. It was a lovely April day and it was decided that he must appear before the people at St Paul's. The opinion seemed to be that the sight of their baby King might help to appease the angry discontent which was beginning to prevail among the Londoners since the return of Humphrey.

Katherine looked rather sadly at her little son. He would not be four years old until December. It seemed a pity to force him into these ceremonies. She wondered what he thought of all the pomp. He showed no sign of being disturbed by it.

She had tried to explain to him.

'It is because you are the King, my dearest. The people want to see you.'

'Are you a King too?' he asked.

'No, only boys can be Kings. I am a Queen.'

'Is Joan a Queen? Is Alice?'

Poor sweet child! What a lot he had to learn.

'You must smile at the people when they cheer you.'

'Why will they cheer me?'

'Because you are the King. Because they like you.'

He smiled then. Dame Alice was a little stern with him. After all, she had been given the right to chastise him. Not that she did very often because he was a good boy, scarcely ever in need of chastisement. And he never bore a grudge against Alice any more than he did against Joan. He loved them dearly. They were part of his life as his mother was. And Owen, of course.

When he sat on his pony Owen led him round the field. He enjoyed that. Owen talked to him in a soft Welsh voice which Henry liked. If Owen stopped talking he would say: 'Go on, Owen. Go on.' And Owen would talk about the Welsh mountains and when he was a little boy no bigger than Henry and although Henry did not understand all that was said he liked to hear Owen talk.

His mother liked to be there. She would put her arms about him and smile from him to Owen. He liked the three of them to be together like that.

Now he was going to ride through the streets of London and all the people would come to see him because they liked him, so he had to remember to smile at them and like them.

'Alice,' he said, 'suppose I don't like them?'

'You'll like them,' said Alice. 'You've got to. They're your people.'

His people! Like his horse. Like the beads on a stick which his mother had given him. His, like that, he wanted to know.

Well not quite, was the answer but one day he would understand. It was often One Day. There was so much he would know then but when would One Day come?

His mother showed him the little velvet cap turned up round the brim above which was a little crown.

They put it on his head.

'I don't like it,' he said. 'It's heavy. It hurts me.'

'Come, sweetheart,' said his mother. 'You have to wear it, you know.'

'I shan't,' said the King, snatching it off his head.

Stern Alice took it and replaced it. 'Kings,' she said very solemnly, 'have to wear their crowns whether they like them or not.'

That seemed to settle it. He was wondering about Kings and the people who were his and forgot about the crown on his hat.

How the people cheered him! They loved him. He looked so incongruous in his royal robes with the miniature crown on his head and his fat little hand clutching the miniature sceptre. He smiled. They liked him. They were his in some strange way which he would understand One Day.

They took him into St Paul's and there he was set upon his feet and two lords so magnificently clad that he wanted to stare at them and examine the jewels on their robes walked with him to the high altar.

There was a great deal of talking and it seemed to go on for a very long time but he was very interested in the proceedings and afterwards they led him out of the church and placed him on a beautiful little white horse and he was led through the streets of London. All the traders in the Chepe stood watching him with wonder and several women called out 'God bless him.' He was their darling little King. They threw kisses at him.

And he thought then that it was a very nice thing to be a King after all.

* * *

John discussed with Anne the letter he had received from the Bishop and the Council.

'It seems,' he said, 'that my brother Gloucester creates trouble wherever he is. I really think it is imperative that I return to England.'

The Earl of Warwick had come to France and he had disturbing stories to tell of the troubles which were working to a climax in England. 'Your brother,' he said, 'is determined to oust Henry Beaufort from the Chancellorship.'

John shook his head. 'My uncle is a good and honourable man. Would I could say the same for my brother.'

'The Duke of Gloucester is a very ambitious man, my lord. And when a country has a King who is a minor that can create a difficult situation.'

' 'Tis so, my lord Warwick. I would to God my brother Henry had not died and left us this burden.'

'A tragedy indeed. One so able ... so noble ... and to die in his prime when he was needed as few have been needed before.'

'It was a stroke of great misfortune for our country. But we must do what we can to avert disaster.'

'Which means, my lord, I think that your presence is needed to sort out this trouble.'

'I am not happy about the state of affairs here in France.'

'Nay, this affair of Burgundy ...'

'He was my friend, Warwick. His sister is my wife.'

'Let us be thankful for that, my lord.'

'Oh, I am fortunate in my marriage. Anne will do all she can to keep her brother at my side. But it is disquieting that Holland and Zealand are already in Burgundy's hand. When the ex-Bishop of Liège died—most conveniently—Burgundy declared himself the heir and marched in. There remains Hainault and I understand Burgundy is attacking that unhappy land at this time.'

'What chance has Jacqueline against him?'

'None.'

'And she is left alone to face him.'

'Deserted by my brother. But it would have made no difference if he had been there. Burgundy will conquer Hainault in no time. You see what my brother has done. He has alienated Burgundy from us and at the same time increased Burgundy's power.'

'He will be filled with remorse.'

'Will he? He will not regret the harm he has done me. He will just mourn the loss of the lands he tried to win.'

'And, my lord, can you leave this field now?'

'I must, Warwick. I cannot allow dissension in England. What I propose to do is to leave men whom I can trust here while I go to England. I hope my stay there will be brief. But go I must. Warwick, it pleases me to see you here and I am going to appoint you to remain here and with the help of Salisbury and Suffolk to look after matters in my absence.'

Warwick bowed and said that he would do all in his power to serve his country, and Bedford was pleased.

Then he returned to Anne.

'I wonder how you will like to journey to my country?' he said.

'I shall like better to go to your country with you than for you to go there alone,' she replied.

Their relationship had deepened since he freed the men of D'Orsay at her request. She was with him ... even when it meant going against her brother. It had not come openly to that yet. Bedford fervently hoped it never would. But he was grateful for her loyalty and it was a joy to him to be able to talk freely to her. She could sometimes give him good advice for she knew the minds of the French; and she could always offer comfort.

So they left Paris and began the journey to the coast. As he was riding towards the town of Amiens a band of hostile men were waiting for him. They sprang out and attacked his followers—of whom there were not many; he was afraid for Anne and kept her close to him. However, the crowd were only armed with bill hooks—nasty weapons perhaps but not much use against skilled guards—and they were quickly dispersed; but it was a warning always to be on the alert and it brought home the truth that in spite of the fact that he had brought a certain prosperity to France he was still regarded as the usurper.

When he reached England he was greeted by the news that

Philip of Burgundy had beaten Jacqueline's forces and she herself was his prisoner.

*   *   *

Humphrey was feeling decidedly displeased with the manner in which life was going.

He was fast losing interest in Jacqueline. He wished he had never involved himself with her. He did congratulate himself, though, that he had left her in good time. It would have been disastrous if he had been there when Burgundy had marched in. What if the mighty Duke had captured him as well as Jacqueline! He had been wise to listen to Eleanor's pleadings to return to England. It was the best step he could have taken in this sorry business. He had no time in his ambitious life for lost causes and he was beginning to believe that Jacqueline's was that.

She had sent him urgent calls for help. But what could he do? She was in Burgundy's hands now. It would need an army to go to her aid; and was the English Parliament going to grant him the means of raising that? Not likely.

What was occupying him now was his quarrel with his uncle Beaufort. Bastard uncle, he reminded Eleanor. Thinks himself as royal as I am. That was the trouble with these legitimized bastards. They could never forget that they were in truth bastards. It rankled. It made them want to assert themselves.

Beaufort should be ousted from the post of Chancellorship. Indeed he should be ousted from the country. 'For,' he told Eleanor, 'he is no friend of mine.'

It was not long, of course, before Bedford arranged a meeting with his brother.

He has aged somewhat, thought Humphrey. It is all that responsibility in France. He does not know how to live, this brother of mine. He has the power. There is no question of that. He's King in all but name, but how does he enjoy himself? That wife of his ... Burgundy's sister. What is she like? There is often little fun in these marriages of convenience.

Bedford was cool. He was indignant of course that he had been brought to England when the situation in France— partly due to Humphrey's feckless behaviour—was not very secure.

Was he ever going to be allowed to forget that he had

offended the all-mighty Burgundy? And now he was at odds
with Bastard Beaufort and John did not like that either.

'It seems,' said John with that aloof manner which made
many men respect him and few like him, 'that you leave a
trail of trouble wherever you go.'

'It is others who make the trouble.'

'It seems strange that you are always at the heart of it.
Burgundy...'

'Oh please, brother, let us give Burgundy a rest, eh? I am
tired of that sacred name. Believe me I have had the power
and importance of the gentleman served to me morning, noon
and night.'

'He happens to be of great importance to our success in
France.'

'I know, I know ... and you have married his little sister
to placate him. A wise move, brother, and one I should
expect of you. I hope the Lady Anne is not too burdensome a
duty.'

'I insist that you do not speak disrespectfully of the Duchess
of Bedford. Nor have I come to discuss the disasters your
actions have caused in France. That sad story is well known
to us all. This quarrel with the Bishop of Winchester must
stop.'

'So Uncle Henry has been whining to you, has he?'

'I have the report of the Council.'

'Are they too against me? Oh, sly Uncle Henry has primed
them, I don't doubt.'

'No sooner do you return to England than you are quarrelling with the Chancellor who, with the Council, has kept
order very well during our absence.'

'Has he? Have they asked the people of London?'

'The merchants of London are often disgruntled. They
resent the taxation which is necessary if we are to bring the
crown of France to England and keep it there. It is for you
to explain to them the need for taxation. They want us to be
victorious. These things have to be paid for. Moreover, do
you imagine that if the Bishop ceased to be Chancellor taxes
would be any less?'

'Brother, he tried to keep me out of London. He was in
a plot to kill me. Do you know he planned to seize the King.'

'That is nonsense. Why should he seize the King?'

'That he might rule. That he might have charge of the
boy. That he might set his own men about him.'

'Humphrey, you talk nonsense.'

'I'll tell you more,' went on Humphrey. 'Do you know that he plotted against our brother Henry? Do you know he counselled me to take the crown from our father?'

John looked at his brother in dismay. Was there no end to his folly?

John ignored the outburst and went on to talk of the need for unity in England. To bring such charges against the Chancellor, and a member of their family at that, could do nothing but harm.

'But if they are true, if we nourish a viper in our nest ... should we not bring this matter to light before he can do much damage?'

John said no more. It was useless trying to reason with Humphrey; his one desire was to patch up the quarrel so that he could restore some sort of harmony and get back to the important business of governing France.

He discussed the matter with members of the Council and explained the charges which Humphrey had brought against his uncle. No one believed them; but Humphrey was after all the King's uncle, and when Bedford was in France he was the Regent of England. The Bishop had only assumed the role because both brothers were out of the country.

It was decided that to satisfy the Duke of Gloucester there must be an enquiry and that the Bishop should be asked to prove that the charges brought against him were untrue.

That such charges could have been sufficiently believed that they had to be proved untrue was a great blow to the Bishop's pride. To have been accused of treachery towards his half-brother, Henry the Fourth, and his nephew, Henry the Fifth, and in fact also to the little Henry the Sixth was so unjust that he could only express his amazement.

Bedford tried to placate him. 'It is better to have the matter settled as amicably as possible. All you have to do, is show these accusations to be ridiculous and they will be dismissed.'

Beaufort could see that Bedford was right. Because his accuser was the son of Henry the Fourth, uncle to the little King and brother to Bedford, he had special privileges and one of these was to invent arrant lies about others.

Wounded and humiliated, the Bishop faced the Council, confounded his accuser, made it clear that he had never committed treason, and was exonerated.

'I will hand in the Seals,' he said, 'for I will not remain Chancellor after such accusations have been made against me. I have long intended to make a pilgrimage and this I will now prepare to do.'

Bedford was disturbed. 'I shall have to return to France in due course,' he told Anne. 'I dare not stay away too long. Gloucester will be my deputy here which alarms me.'

'Could you not persuade the Bishop to return to office and since your brother has shown himself incapable of keeping the peace take the government out of his hands?'

'You have learned a little about Gloucester. He regards the Regency as his right. While I am here it is mine, that is true; but if I am not, he is the next in succession. I fear if I attempted to appoint someone else there would be trouble. He has his supporters. He is popular with the Londoners. Men such as he is often are. I must stay a little longer.'

'I have heard rumours that he is interested in a woman of not very good reputation.'

'Yes, that is Eleanor Cobham. She is the daughter of Lord Cobham ... or said to be his daughter. Some will tell you she is of doubtful antecedents. It may be that she is a bastard of Cobham's whom he has brought up in his household.'

'Your brother seems to be deeply enamoured of her.'

'Humphrey is rarely enamoured of anyone or any project for very long. It seems likely that his obsession with the woman will pass. But, my dear, I am more concerned with the political strife he seems to delight in raising. His women are of no great concern of mine.'

'Then we must perforce resign ourselves to staying in England for a while.'

'At least you enjoy seeing my country.'

'That I enjoy, but I do not enjoy seeing you anxious.'

'Ah,' said Bedford smiling. 'That is the cross I have to bear as do all those who live close to the throne.'

'The cross sits lightly on your brother Humphrey's shoulders.'

He looked at her very seriously. 'Sometimes I wonder how it will all end for him.' And for a moment he let his thoughts dwell on how pleasant life could have been if he had been born a humble squire and Anne a lady of no great birth. They could have found much to interest themselves and occupy them in a country estate shut away from the perils and intrigues from which he knew they would never escape.

Sometimes such thoughts came even to the most ambitious men.

He was further disconcerted when the Pope offered Henry Beaufort a Cardinal's hat and nominated him cardinal priest of St Eusebius. Beaufort had been offered this during the reign of Henry the Fifth, who had sternly forbidden him to accept it. To become a Cardinal would direct Beaufort's efforts, and even loyalties, away from England and towards Rome. Henry had been very much against that.

Now Beaufort accepted.

'My brother's work once more,' muttered Bedford.

THE QUEEN PLIGHTS HER TROTH

CHRISTMAS had come and Katherine decided that it should be kept at Eltham. The King was now five years old and earlier in the year his uncle Bedford had made him a knight and several other boys had received their knighthoods at the hands of young Henry himself. That had been an interesting ceremony and Henry was now beginning to realize that he was different from other boys. People bowed to him, kissed his hand, cheered him, applauded him and made him feel very important in every way. He found it pleasant and was now beginning to expect to be treated in this special way by everyone as soon as he escaped from the nursery. There his mother, Joan and Dame Alice remained in command.

There were great festivities at Christmas. He very much enjoyed the giving and receiving of presents. Joan Astley helped him to choose a pair of gloves for his mother and hide them so that they would be a surprise for her. He had great difficulty in keeping the secret and on more than one occasion nearly let it out. His mother had caught Joan putting her fingers to her lips and had looked very bewildered. He had enjoyed it all very much. He loved the smell of pies baking and meat roasting and his mother had told him that there would be mummers and dancing and Jack Travail would be invading the castle with his merry companions.

Eltham, that palace which had been built by Edward the First, was some eight miles south of London on the road to Maidstone. Henry was used to living in palaces but it was exciting to come to this one at Christmas time and to pass over the ivy-covered bridge with its four groined arches. As they entered the great hall he held his mother's hand and the retainers came forward to kneel before him. He extended his hand for them to kiss with a natural grace. It was all part of being the King.

He could scarcely wait for Christmas morning when he would give the gloves to his mother and see what he was to be given.

Among his presents were some coral beads which delighted him more than anything else for they had once belonged to his great ancestor Edward the First. Joan Astley told him stories of the great Kings of England and the glorious lives they had led. Edward the Third interested him particularly because he had been a boy when he had come to the throne— a little older than Henry it was true. Quite old, Henry thought him. But everyone said he was just a boy.

There were a few other children who had been brought to the palace to share his games—the sons and daughters of noblemen—and they played bob apple and blind man's buff in which the elders joined. Then there were the players who performed a miracle play. Henry found this a little dull but when Jack Travail and his companions came into the hall and entertained them all with his games and plays Henry was enchanted. He clapped his hands with the rest and cried: 'More! More!' much to Jack Travail's delight. Henry wished it was always Christmas.

Dame Alice came all too soon and declared that it was well past bedtime. The other children were seized on too and Henry was taken, protesting a little, to his bed where he was soon fast asleep.

In the hall the Christmas merriments continued.

Katherine seated on a low stool surrounded by a few of her attendants watched the dancing. It was four years since she had been a widow. A long time. She should marry again, all said it. She was surprised that they did not try to persuade her to do so and perhaps persuade forcibly. She supposed her father's death and the preoccupation of her brother who was trying to regain his throne and the fact that she was a French princess who had her home in England, were all reasons why she was given some respite.

Besides, when a woman has married once for State reasons she should be allowed to make her own choice of a second marriage. That had always been a kind of unwritten law, not always adhered to, of course, especially when a woman was a specially good bargaining counter which she would have been but for the upheaval in France.

Because of that she was allowed to live her quiet life at Windsor whenever the fancy took her.

The ladies and the squires were dancing together. She declined to join in. She wanted to sit quietly and watch. Christmas had made her thoughtful. Lately the question of what her future would be had been constantly in her mind. She was twenty-five years of age. No longer a girl.

Her eyes went to Owen Tudor who was partnering one of the ladies in the dance. He was scarcely graceful. Dancing was not one of Owen's attributes. Dear Owen! He was often quiet and thoughtful nowadays. She wondered if the same thoughts occupied him as did her.

The dancers were pirouetting which some of them performed very gracefully. She clapped her hands. 'See who can turn the longest,' she cried. 'Come closer that I may see.'

So they approached and she called on one at a time to perform before her. The ladies applauded and some of the men were laying stakes on who should be able to do the most turns on tiptoe.

'Come, Owen Tudor,' she called. 'It is your turn. I wish to see you perform this pirouette.'

'My lady,' he said, flushing a little, 'I am no good at it.'

'Nevertheless you must try,' she said.

He lifted his shoulders in a gesture of despair which amused everyone, then he came close to her and began to turn on his toes. In a second or so he had toppled forward. The Queen put out her arms and he fell into them.

It was the first time they had made such close contact and both were aware of a tremendous excitement. It could only have been a few seconds that they remained so, looking at each other but the true nature of their feelings was revealed to them ... and perhaps a hint of them was given to others.

Owen recovered himself first. 'My lady ...' he stammered. 'A thousand pardons ...' He scrambled to his feet, his face now scarlet.

The Queen laughed on rather a high note. ' 'Twas no fault of yours, Owen,' she said. 'Methinks, alas, you are not going to be the champion.'

Everyone was laughing now. Owen Tudor was happier on a horse than pirouetting in the ballroom, they said.

'Happier still,' whispered one of the men, 'in the company of Queen Katherine ... alone.'

When the Queen retired for the night she was very thoughtful. She had known for some time, of course. When she went out riding and he was a member of the party the day brightened. If they could contrive to be alone then it was indeed a happy day.

She faced the truth. She was in love with Owen Tudor.

One of the women who was combing her hair said to her: 'My lady, have I your permission to speak openly to you?'

This was a faithful friend, one who believed because of the favour Queen Katherine had shown her she was especially privileged.

'What is it?' asked Katherine.

'It is being noticed, my lady, that you show much favour to Owen Tudor.'

'Owen Tudor. The Welsh squire? He is a very good squire. The King is greatly attached to him.'

'My lady, people talk.'

'Of course they talk. They have tongues have they not?'

'At times mischievous people talk slanderously.'

'Against me, you mean?'

'Yes, my lady. Against you and ... Owen Tudor.'

'What say they? Tell me that.'

'That he would be your lover ... and that he is low-born and you are a Queen of England and a daughter of a King of France. Also, he is Welsh.'

'Welsh? What of that?'

'They say the Welsh are barbarous savages.'

'Then they speak nonsense, do they not? Owen Tudor has shown he is as gallant and cultivated a gentleman as any we have at Court.'

Her vehemence frightened the woman who had thought only to offer a gentle word of warning. She did not believe for one moment that the Queen could possibly take a low-born Welsh squire for a lover.

'Ah,' said Katherine, 'I am not English either. Do they say that I also am a barbarous savage?'

'You are a French Princess, my lady. The Welsh are not as the French. The Welsh live in the mountain valleys like peasants.'

'Oh,' cried Katherine angrily, 'they are advancing a little as we talk. The savages have become peasants. I did not know that there was the difference in the races on this British island.'

'Forgive me, my lady. I did but tell you what I had heard because I thought you ought to know.'

Katherine stood up and laid a hand on the lady's arm.

'You are my very good friend,' she said. 'Do not fret. I shall do nothing to disgrace you.'

Then she leaned forward and kissed the woman's cheek.

The woman shook her head. The manners of the French were unaccountable, she thought.

Never mind. She had done her duty.

*   *   *

Katherine rode beside Owen Tudor. They had missed the rest of the party on purpose.

'I have to speak to you,' she said.

'I know,' he answered. 'They are talking about us. It was at the ball.'

'You fell into my arms,' she said.

'It was not my intention. I was no good at their dancing.'

She burst out laughing. 'You looked so ... funny, Owen, and I liked you for it. I liked it very much and then when you fell I held out my arms to catch you.'

'It was unpardonable of me to fall upon you.'

'Then the unpardonable is pardoned,' she said.

'You are so good to me,' he murmured.

'Owen,' she answered, 'is it not time that we faced the truth?'

He did not answer for a moment. Then he said staring ahead of him: 'You must send me away. I could go to France. Men are constantly being sent to France. The Duke of Bedford is raising a new force to take back with him when he returns.'

'I forbid it,' she said firmly. 'Are you not *my* squire?'

'Aye, and one whose mission is to do you good service. It is why I know I must go to France.'

'No,' she said. 'You shall do as I say ... that is if you want to. Dismount, Owen.'

'Dismount, my lady?'

'That is what I said.'

He obeyed. 'Now help me to dismount.' When he came to her she put her arms about his neck. She kissed his lips. He was hesitant but only for a moment.

She slid to the ground and they still stood together, their arms about each other.

'It has slowly come upon us,' she said, 'but now there is no denying it. Do you love your Queen, Owen?'

'With all my heart,' he said. 'I would die in her service.'

'And live in it?'

'I will do whatever she commands me now and forever.'

'That is a true lover's vow. I will make mine now. I love you, Owen Tudor, and here solemnly in this green sward I take you as my husband, my true husband that needs no mumbling of priests ... no grand fine vestments, no signing of contracts ... nothing but love.'

Owen said: 'How I have longed to hold you thus.'

'And I to be held. Shall we walk awhile and talk? Let us tether the horses.'

'What if we are discovered?'

She laughed. 'I am the Queen, Owen. I shall do as I please.'

'We will have to take care. If this were discovered ...'

She was silent suddenly. 'Yes,' she said, 'you are right. You could be in danger. Oh, Owen, that frightens me. I will be careful but, Owen, we are not going to be denied each other. That I insist on ... but only if you will take the risk. Will you?'

'I would risk my life for you.'

'My fear is for you. For myself I care not. But we cannot be denied, can we? We have faced the truth. Owen, we love each other. We are going to be together for I could not endure my life without you.'

'Nor I mine.'

'Then we shall meet ... we shall be as husband and wife together. I am so happy. For so long I have been lonely. I was fond of Henry but this, Owen ... this is wonderful. This makes everything worth while for me. Does it for you, Owen?'

'My love,' he whispered, 'we shall forget everything but each other.'

'Shall we plight our troth here ... in the greenwood?'

He closed his eyes and held her close to him.

'Let us find a spot,' she said, 'away from the world where no one can find us.'

*   *   *

Gloucester was as enamoured of Eleanor Cobham as he had ever been. Not only was she voluptuous and skilled in erotic arts so that she continued to surprise even his jaded palate, but she was ambitious too. She kept a close grip on affairs. She had been immensely amused by his conflict with the Bishop of Winchester and when he was inclined to be depressed by the dismal nature of his prospects she would point out his successes. It had been a complete victory over his old uncle, hadn't it? Beaufort had had to give up the Chancellorship and being a Cardinal got him out of the way.

That, said Eleanor, was subtle politics, for which, with her help, he had a decided talent.

He did occasionally have a twinge of conscience about Jacqueline. She had relied on him and had really believed he would get her estates back for them both to share. And it might have worked, of course, if they had been able to hold onto the estates and if Eleanor had not come along.

Now his great desire was to be with Eleanor and to spend their time exercising their considerable talents in bed—and that came first—and then in political intrigue.

It was true in some measure that he had won the battle with his uncle; but it had had the result of bringing brother Bedford to England, and that was not so good. He could very well do without the presence of his brother. John took command and everyone held him in such high respect that whatever John said they were inclined to agree was right.

John criticized Humphrey's rule generally. To be at the head of government was a task not to be taken lightly, he reiterated. One must dedicate oneself to the needs of one's country. One must subdue one's own personal desires, one's greed. That was the burden of John's song. Let him live up to it. It was not brother Humphrey's way. 'Let my brother govern as he will while he is in the land,' he said to Eleanor. 'For after his going over to France, I will govern as seems good to me.'

Eleanor agreed.

'You can be sure,' she said, 'that as soon as John feels he can safely leave, he will be off.'

Appeals were constantly coming from Jacqueline. It was no use, he told himself. She should give up. How could she stand out against Philip of Burgundy? If he could not send troops, she wrote frantically, could he send her money?

He approached certain members of the Council. If they would grant her a little money it would ease his conscience. He was not sure whether it was his conscience which bothered him or the desire to harry Burgundy.

John came to see him. Very soon now he would return to France. 'For which mercy let us be thankful,' Humphrey had said to Eleanor.

'You have asked the Council for money to send to Holland,' he said. 'This is madness.'

'Madness ... to consider a request from my wife?'

'Do you want to anger Burgundy still further?'

'Burgundy! Burgundy! Burgundy!' sang out Humphrey. 'He has become your patron saint, has he not, brother?'

'I do not have to explain again, do I, the importance of his friendship to us?'

'If you did it would have been for the ten thousandth time.'

'The need to hold that friendship is more important now than it was when you first heard it. Now, give me your promise. Your adventures in that direction are at an end. Be thankful that they were not even more disastrous.'

When brother John talked in that way it was wise to put up a semblance of agreement. John was the most powerful man in England as well as France.

Never mind, the field would be clear when he went back with his precious Burgundian wife.

'I shall not allow my brother to dictate to me,' he told Eleanor.

John left for France and as soon as he had gone Humphrey approached the Council again and asked for five thousand marks to send to Jacqueline.

It was refused. Humphrey shrugged his shoulders. He had done what he could, Jacqueline's was a hopeless case. This was confirmed when one day a message came to him from the Pope. His marriage to Jacqueline had been annulled.

'Burgundy's work,' he said to Eleanor.

She was pleased. There was a sly expression in her eyes. Why not? She would enjoy being the Duchess of Gloucester. For once she applauded Burgundy's action. She would not suggest it just yet. She would wait and shrewdly implant the suggestion into his mind, so that he thought it was his own idea. However, nothing must be done hastily. Divorces were tricky. She did not want to go through a form of marriage with Humphrey and then to have someone prove that it had been no marriage at all. And what if by that time he would have outgrown his desire for her company? One could never be sure. Men who had indulged as freely and consistently as Humphrey could become suddenly satiated. Eleanor was cunning, and one of the lessons she had learned was never to come to too hasty a conclusion to important matters.

*   *   *

The delegation was being discussed everywhere. In some it aroused amusement, in others concern.

'They say it was made up of very respectable women.'

'All very well dressed, I heard.'

'That was so, no rabble. They came in orderly fashion. Well, it *is* a scandal.'

'He used to be so popular with the Londoners, remember.'

'Yes, they showed clearly that they preferred his rule to that of the Bishop. But what they strongly object to is that woman, of course. She is so blatant and he takes her everywhere. He remains besotted by her. They say he has never been faithful to one woman long.'

So the gossip continued.

Humphrey was annoyed. Eleanor was more so, for really it concerned her most.

The fact was that a body of merchants' wives had presented themselves to the Council and announced that they were deeply shocked by the conduct of the Duke of Gloucester. He had abandoned his wife and was now flaunting his harlot Eleanor Cobham who was beside him wherever he went. Her manners were bold and she proclaimed with every gesture the nature of her relationship with the Duke. The wives of the merchants demanded more propriety in their rulers.

The women were graciously received by members of the Council. Nobody wanted to offend the merchants and they guessed that to offend their wives might be even more disastrous. It was pointed out to them that the Duke's morals were really no concern of the Council and that the Pope had actually annulled his marriage.

This the women had to accept; but it did show the growing unpopularity of the Duke and when he rode out into the streets of London boys who could quickly dodge out of sight before they could be caught, called after him.

The Council told him that his authority must be curbed. He could not expect the same power as that extended to his brother. He protested but that was little use. The housewives of London had had their effect. Before he had relied largely on his popularity with the Londoners. That that had waned considerably was obvious.

While he was grinding his teeth over his encounter with the Council the Earl of Warwick came to see him.

He had never liked Warwick. One of those honourable upright gentlemen, friend of John, loyal to the crown, not a man to diverge one little step from what he considered to be his duty. He had been a close friend of Henry the Fifth and very highly thought of by the late King.

Warwick characteristically came straight to the point. 'My lord, I come to tell you that I have been formally committed to the task of guardianship of the King.'

Gloucester narrowed his eyes.

It was his place to have the guardianship of the King. Was he not his uncle? Who should have charge of the child but his nearest relative—and it was understood that he could not indefinitely be left to the charge of his mother. John was the elder brother, it was true, but Humphrey was here on the spot.

But to appoint Warwick was an insult to him.

'And who has bestowed these powers on you?' demanded Gloucester. 'I have not been consulted.'

'The Council, my lord, but you will remember that the late King, your noble brother, named me as guardian of his son. He bequeathed the care of his education to me and now that the King is of an age for serious education I would fulfil the promise I made to his father.'

Gloucester ground his teeth in dismay. But what could he do? Those housewives of London had unnerved him more than anything else. He felt as though the ground was moving under his feet.

'The King is now seven years old,' went on Warwick. 'He should have his own household and a body of knights and squires whom we shall choose for him.'

'I see that the matter has been decided,' said Humphrey shortly.

'It is as you would expect, my lord Duke. I have sworn to teach him to love, worship and dread God. I shall develop his character along virtuous lines and let him know that God favours righteous Kings.'

'Does He?' asked Gloucester.

'My lord, I believe virtue to be the true way to happiness and that no joy can come to a ruler or his nation through avarice and ill doing.'

'I hope your wisdom matches your piety, my lord Warwick.'

'I have been commissioned to teach him, nurture him, to give him a good grounding in literature, language and all other arts and to chastise him when he does aught amiss.'

'Take care with the cane, Warwick. Kings have long memories.'

'I shall not allow such a consideration to cloud my actions. Also, my lord, I am to have the power to remove from him any persons who I consider shall be harmful to him.'

'Great powers are yours, my lord.'

'I shall do my best to use them wisely. The castles of Wallingford and Hertford have been chosen for him during the summers and Windsor and Berkhamstead for his winter residences.'

'I can see that it has all been well planned. And his mother?'

'He will see her frequently.'

'Perhaps then she will emerge from her widowhood. It has been a long one.'

'I am sure the Queen will never cease to mourn her husband.'

'Maybe. Maybe. I wish you well of your task. I think you are going to need all the good wishes you can get.'

'I am well aware, my lord Duke, of the gravity and importance of my task.'

Warwick left the Duke. It had been easier than he had hoped. Gloucester was angry that the care of young Henry had been passed to him; but he was still smarting too strongly from the signs of his unpopularity in the city of London to raise objections as he might otherwise have done.

'Warwick has the King,' Gloucester told Eleanor. 'I don't grudge him the task. Henry is not the meek boy some think him.'

Eleanor said: 'You should take care not to lose your influence with him.'

'Nay, I'll be favourite uncle. Moreover tutors who are

stern—and Warwick may well be—don't always keep their pupils' affection. The cane is a good way of beating out future favours. I imagine Warwick is too upright to consider this axiom. He'll not spare the rod and that may well spoil his future chances.'

They laughed together. The appointment of Warwick was nothing more than a minor irritation.

* * *

So Henry had passed out of his babyhood. He must no longer stay under his mother's influence. She should be grateful, she supposed, that they had allowed him to stay so long.

She thought: It will be easier now. There will be less attention focused on me. Perhaps I can live now like a humble country lady. That would suit her very well, for the most important part of her life was those hours she spent with Owen.

What an ecstatic relationship was theirs! Perhaps the more so because it was to be carried on with secrecy. Now that the King had left, important people had left with him. If she could go on living in obscurity in the country she must be thankful for this. She had contrived that Owen visit her bedchamber when the household was asleep, and he had climbed up and in at her window. But that could not go on for ever. It had been the happiest night of her life. Then she had been able to cast aside all pretence—for they had both pretended for many years; she that he was just a good squire; he that he was not in love with the Queen.

'I love you,' she told him twenty times during that first romantic night; and he had left her in no doubt that he shared her feelings.

She had come alive at last—alive as she had never been before. A fervent passion possessed her and she knew that it would be deep and abiding. She was not a girl any more to love romantically and this emotion had built up between them over the years. They had both tried to deny it, knowing that it would present difficulties, insurpassable difficulties they had seemed, but nothing was insurpassable before this torrent of love. It swept all aside. What cared she if he were a humble squire? What cared he if she were a Queen? They were lovers, meant for each other from the first moment they had been together. Now this love would not be denied. Her love for Henry had existed. But it was not to be compared with what she felt for Owen Tudor.

It was inevitable that those about her should notice the change in her. They saw the expression in her eyes when they alighted on the Tudor; they heard the inflection of her voice when she spoke of him.

Dame Alice and Joan Astley shook their heads together. They would not remain long, they knew, for their task was done. Their little one had been taken from their care and they were two sad women. When they were not talking of him and hoping that the Earl of Warwick would not be too harsh with him, they were wondering about the web the Queen was weaving about herself.

They were wistful. It had not been like a royal household. How pleasant it would have been to contemplate the arrival of more little ones who would be delivered to their care.

Dame Alice wondered whether she should warn the Queen that people were whispering about her and Owen Tudor.

*   *   *

Eleanor Cobham picked up the news. She prided herself on having what she called 'her ear to the ground'.

She was greatly amused and lost no time in telling her lover of the rumours she had heard.

'The Queen has a lover, eh?' said Gloucester. 'Well, are you surprised? Did you imagine the dear creature was living the life of a nun down there in the country? How did you think she spent her days?'

'She was devoted to her son. But now he has gone she is following her own inclination it seems.'

'I hope it is a worthy inclination.'

'I have heard it is some humble squire. A Welshman at that.'

'Is that so? Lucky squire! Katherine must be very loving to have chosen someone from the stables.'

'They say they are deeply in love. That the Queen has always lived most virtuously before.'

Humphrey was thoughtful.

'It is at such times that there is danger,' he said. 'She must not be allowed to forget that she is the Queen.'

It was a somewhat delicate subject. Eleanor had never suggested that Humphrey marry her, but he did wonder whether it was in her mind. He wondered how he would act if she started to bargain for marriage. Therefore he did not wish to discuss this passion of the Queen's too closely. It could open up that other subject.

But he did think that the Queen's future was a matter he should take up with the Council and he would do so without delay.

He must tread very carefully where his own affairs were concerned. As though to remind him of this there was more news of Jacqueline. Burgundy had defeated her completely and she had realized that she had no chance against him. She had signed a treaty at Delft in which she submitted to Philip's wishes. She recognized him as her heir and co-Regent of her territories. By this she did not lose everything. But she had to promise that she would never marry without his consent for the form of marriage she had gone through with Gloucester was declared null and void. She renounced him utterly and accepted the fact that she had never been married to him.

*   *   *

The realization had come to Katherine that she was to have a child. At first she was overwhelmed with joy. This seemed the perfect outcome of her love for Owen. Then she began to consider what this would mean.

She was a King's widow. Where could she go while her child was born? Some women might be in a position to hide themselves away for a few months. It was difficult with a queen.

Moreover she was unmarried. Would it be possible for her and Owen to go through a ceremony of marriage? Why not? Her priest could marry them. This must be so now that there was to be a child. She would marry Owen and then proclaim to the world what she had done. The Council couldn't stop her once the ceremony was over. Moreover what affair was it of any but herself and Owen? They had their work to do governing the country. What could the marriage of a late King's widow mean to them? They could now concern themselves with the young King. They had taken him from her.

No, she was of no importance. She had been once, of course; and they had made full use of her to help bring about the peace between England and France. That was over. Henry was dead and she had been free for six years.

She was longing to tell Owen. How delighted he would be ... and yet afraid. Only for her, of course. That was why he felt fear, as she did for him. For themselves each was ready to face whatever storm they had to, for the sake of what they had been to one another.

He came to her during the afternoon. Those who lived close to her could not help but know of the relationship between them, for it had been impossible to keep it secret from them. So Owen came and went frequently to her apartment and they were used to seeing him there.

She clung to him and then she told him. He was silent and she dared not look into his face.

When she did she saw that he was overjoyed and yet fearful, as she had known he would be, but the wonder of it was too great at the moment for him to give full vent to his fears.

'Our child,' he could only murmur. 'Oh Katherine ... my Queen ... to think that you and I are to have a child.'

Then he was all concern for her. She must take care of herself. She would have to have special attendants ... He stopped, remembering. Then he looked at her, fear uppermost now. 'Katherine ... how ... ?'

'I shall arrange it,' she said. 'I have faithful friends who will help me.'

He took her hand and kissed it. 'We should marry,' he said, 'for the sake of the child.'

She nodded.

'I could find a priest who would do it,' she said. 'And we will ... simply ... and speedily.'

'Before the child ...'

'Oh yes, before the child is born. Owen, I shall send for Dame Alice and for Joan. They have been unhappy since Henry was taken from us. They will help me.'

'A child,' he said in a bewildered voice. 'Our child. Oh Katherine ... how happy you have made me. Shall we have a girl, or perhaps a boy?'

'We will be content with what we are given,' she said. 'This is like a miracle. They took my son from me ... and now you have given me this.'

'It will not be easy.'

'Dearest Owen,' she said, 'I am no longer young and I am old enough to learn that the best things in life do not often come easily.'

ORLÉANS BESIEGED

JOHN, Duke of Bedford had returned to France to find the
position as indecisive as ever. He must bring this deadlock
to an end. It was true that Burgundy having settled his
quarrel with Gloucester and Jacqueline to great advantage to
himself was more inclined to be friendly. Anne, to whom he
was devoted, had a certain influence with him, and John was
more hopeful than he had been since the miserable affair of
Gloucester's marriage—or mock marriage—had given him
such anxieties.

His great desire was to put an end to the fighting and he
wanted to strike one decisive blow which would make it
perfectly clear to the French that it was useless to continue
with their resistance so that they would resign themselves to
English rule and settle down to bring prosperity back to the
country.

He knew that it was asking what was almost impossible of
a proud people. The Earls of Salisbury and Suffolk on whose
counsel he set great store were of the opinion that if they
could capture Orléans they could take a very large step towards victory.

Bedford was dubious. Not, he hastened to add, that he
questioned the importance of Orléans but he did feel that
the taking of it would be a lengthy operation. It would mean
keeping a large contingent of men to besiege it. The winter
was coming on; who knew how long such a siege would
last?

'The winter is even more cruel for the besieged than for

the besiegers,' Salisbury pointed out.

'True enough,' agreed Bedford, 'and we could bring in supplies for our men. But it would be a mighty task nevertheless.'

'I believe most fervently that until we take Orléans and get command of the Loire we cannot proceed very far. Orléans is as important on the Loire as Paris or Rouen on the Seine.'

'And as well defended as those cities.'

'It could be taken by siege, my lord,' said Salisbury, 'and it is essential to our cause.'

John knew that he would be unwise not to listen to the Earl of Salisbury who was one of the most experienced captains of the English army—it might not be too great an exaggeration to say the finest. He had waged successful battles in Champagne, Maine and Normandy and he had been in England recently for the sole purpose of gathering an army to, as he said, bring such a reckoning to the French that they would no longer have the stomach to fight. Enthusiastically he told Bedford of the ease with which he had recruited bowmen to his armies. It had been more difficult to get cavalry and men-at-arms, for they were too comfortable at home to want to go to a country which had for long been suffering the effects of war; but he had had a moderate success and had persuaded more than four hundred men of that kind to accompany him, while he had garnered more than two thousand archers.

He had his eyes on Orléans. The key to the problem, he called it. He was adamant. They must take Orléans ...

At length John was convinced and in the misty month of October the siege of Orléans began. Philip of Burgundy sent a small force to help the English and John was grateful for this show of friendship. But the Orléannese were stubborn; they were proud of their city—and justly so. They would make no easy surrender to the English. There was a strong conviction within those walls that this was no ordinary siege. It was not just their city which was at stake. It was the whole of France. A certain fatalism had come to them and this showed itself in a determination to accept any hardship rather than give in.

Orléans was a very fine city, lying on a bend of the River Loire—a city of stone and wood houses with high slate roofs, of towers and steeples, of long winding streets which had changed little since the days when it had been under Roman occupation. Its walls were six feet thick rising high above a moat, and these walls were flanked by towers, thirty-four of them, each of which had five gates and two posterns. All along the walls were parapets with machicolated battlements from which boiling oil or paving stones could be thrown most effectively down upon an invading enemy.

A stone bridge led from the town to the left bank of the Loire. Set on nineteen arches it was more than a bridge; it was the dwelling place of many of the Orléannese for houses lined the bridge on either side. On the eighteenth of the arches a small castle had been built and this was known as Les Tourelles.

The Orléannese were not surprised to find themselves in siege. They had in fact been expecting it to happen for some time. They knew that town after town was falling to the English and it must in time be their turn. For the last three or four years they had been collecting arms and storing them in their Tower of Saint-Samson; they had dug dykes and even built fortifications. They were as prepared as it was possible for them to be for the Earl of Salisbury when he came. So it was no shock when on that September day the Earl reached the town of Janville, which he took with ease, and from there sent a message to the townsfolk of Orléans that he was marching towards their city and that he demanded their surrender.

They formed into an orderly procession and, with priests and merchants, women and children, rich and poor, marched through the streets singing psalms as they went into the churches to ask God and their patron saints to come to their aid.

They would need it, for Salisbury had brought with him the flower of the English army. The result of the battle for Orléans could be decisive in settling the outcome of the war. Salisbury had convinced Bedford of this and he was now as certain of it himself as he was of anything. With him rode Thomas, Lord of Scales, William Neville, his nephew Lord Richard Grey, William Pole, Earl of Suffolk and William's brother John Pole and many other nobles. One of the best captains in the army was also there—William Glasdale, a squire of more humble birth than the noblemen, but one on whom Salisbury relied as he did on few others.

Salisbury saw at once that the little castle of Tourelles, which was really a fort, prevented their crossing the bridge and his first move, therefore, must be to take it.

The Orléannese put up a desperate fight for Les Tourelles, but after a few days were unable to hold out against the superior strength of the English and when they were forced to abandon Les Tourelles they had to face the fact that they had lost one of their most effective defences.

It was a Sunday afternoon when the strange event occurred. The flag of St George was flying from the fort. The French turned their eyes from it in rage and dismay while the Earl of Salisbury eyed it with the utmost pleasure because now he had a vantage point. From the topmost point of the tower he could see right over the walls and into the city.

He ascended the tower in the company of Captain William Glasdale and a few others and for some moments they stood overlooking the city. Then suddenly the window was shattered. A cannon ball had taken off a corner of the window; a paving stone came away and this struck the Earl carrying off half his face. He fell senseless to the ground.

While his companions picked him up Glasdale looked round and realized that the shot must have come from the nearby tower of Notre Dame which appeared to be deserted apart from one small child casually standing there.

It was a very mysterious event, and disastrous for the English and within a few hours of being taken to Meung-Sur-Loire Salisbury was dead, never having regained consciousness since the blow struck him.

They had lost their leader, the man who was certain of victory, and they were appalled. It was more than the loss of a great General, for this was the beginning of the strange stories which were to be circulated in Orléans and the surrounding countryside.

People who had been near Le Tour Notre Dame when the cannon had been fired swore that no one had been there, except a young boy who had been playing quietly.

Had he fired the cannon which killed Salisbury? He could not be found that he might be asked. He had appeared briefly and slipped away.

Could it be a sign from Heaven? asked the desperate Orléannese. It must be. They had to believe it. They needed help so badly and who better than Heaven could supply the kind of help they needed. Orléans was thirsting for miracles. So when something happened that might be one they glorified and magnified it.

It was a sign from Heaven, they said. They would yet be saved.

*   *   *

Winter was coming in. The people of Orléans still refused to surrender and the English living uncomfortably outside the walls of the city suffered as many hardships as those within the city. The Bastard of Orléans had been sent to the aid of the Orléannese. He was a warrior of great skill and charm and he brought new heart to them. The son of the Duke of Orléans and his mistress Madame de Cany-Dunois, he was a man of power in France. His bartardy had been of small inconvenience to him; he was after all a Prince's bastard. He was at this time advancing in his twenties and he had many successes behind him. He brought further hope to the city, for with him were warriors of great reputation such as Maréchal de Boussac and the Lord of Chaumont. Lord Scales, William Pole and Sir John Talbot had taken over command of the siege since the death of Salisbury and as Christmas was coming on they sent messages into the city to suggest to the Bastard of Orléans that they should call a halt to hostilities for Christ's birthday.

There was an air of expectation within the city. They believed that their prayers had been answered. The story of the death of Salisbury was discussed constantly. It had now become a miracle. The cannon, it was believed, had been fired from an empty tower. The only one who had been seen there was a small child. Could a child have fired a cannon? It was hardly likely. A mysterious hand had removed Salisbury from their path. Heaven was helping them.

One story in circulation was that an English cannon ball had fallen on a table where several people sat at dinner. The cannon ball bounced off the table and no one was hurt.

A better story was of the cannon ball which had fallen near La Porte Bannière for in that spot there had been several hundred people yet it had done no harm except knock off the shoe of one man. Laughingly he cried: 'The English go to a great deal of trouble to make me put on my shoe twice in one day.'

These stories multiplied and the wonder of them increased with the telling. The people of Orléans were looking for a miracle. It was very comforting indeed to believe that God or the saints were giving them these signs.

So on Christmas day they were all ready to call a halt for the sake of Jesus Christ who was born on that day.

The Bastard himself sent his best musicians over to Les Tourelles; and all through the day there came the sound of their music and the singing of English carols.

The Orléannese stood on the city walls listening, without fear, and the English forgot the hardships they were enduring.

The enemies were friends ... just for Christmas day.

*   *   *

There was a certain air of excitement among the Bastard and his friends for their spies reported that the English army was very short of food and that it had been arranged that a large quantity of victuals was to be brought to them from Paris.

'They are in dire need of these supplies,' said the Bastard. 'If we could intercept them and prevent their arriving, we should be turning the tables. They cannot go on without food. This could be the saving of Orléans.'

God was indeed on their side. They were sure of it now. It should not be difficult to waylay the convoy and capture it. It could be put to very good use in Orléans.

The Bastard left the city in a mood of hope and people crowded into the churches to pray. It was another sign, they said. They only had to be patient, believe in God and His miracles and not only Orléans would be saved but the whole of France.

In Paris the Bastard encountered the Count of Clermont, a young man of royal blood and exceptional good looks and charm of manner, who had received his spurs and was full of his own importance. The Bastard instructed him to take his men and watch along the road for the coming of Sir John Fastolf, a seasoned English warrior who was in charge of the convoy.

Clermont was determined to distinguish himself and he wanted the honour of capturing the stores to be his alone. He was not going to let the Bastard of Orléans take all the glory. The importance of this encounter was clear. To stop that convoy reaching the English would starve them out. They would have to give up the siege and the glory of saving Orléans would be his.

The Bastard parted company with him to go off in another direction and as Clermont was riding merrily along at the head of his troops so certain of victory, a messenger came galloping up to them. Some Gascon soldiers had sighted the convoy. They believed they could take it easily for the English were quite unaware of any danger. They could at this time catch them ill prepared for an attack.

'Make no attempt to before I arrive,' cried the jaunty young Count. This was going to be an easy victory, but it was his.

Meanwhile the English realized they had been sighted and that an attack was imminent. They had three hundred carts and wagons full of much needed provisions, and they were accompanied only by a few guards, archers and cavalry men with some merchants who had supplied the goods and a few peasants to help unload them.

Sir John Fastolf, with Sir Richard Gethyn, knew they were in a very dangerous situation from which a great deal of ingenuity would be needed to extricate them. They were in the worst possible country as they were completely unprotected and if a strong force came against them they would be quickly overcome.

But Sir John was a seasoned warrior. This was not the first difficult position he had been in and he was ready to try any expedient which might be of use.

They had seen the Gascons and wondered why they did not atttack. If they had done so the convoy could have been lost.

'God has given us time,' cried Sir John. 'It is what we needed, and with His help we may pull through.'

He then outlined his plan. The wagons should provide that defence which their position in the plain denied them. There were three hundred wagons—one hundred and fifty a side when they were lined up with a narrow passage between them. All around the wagons they placed stakes pointing towards the attackers; behind the stakes stood the archers so when Clermont arrived full of confidence, the English were prepared. He gave the order for his cavalry to advance, which they did. A shower of arrows met them; the horses stumbled on and broke their legs on the stakes. It was then not a difficult matter to rout Clermont's men after that, and when the Bastard arrived he was wounded in the foot and narrowly escaped being taken prisoner.

Clermont, seeing his glory vanishing, sulked and refused to go to the aid of the wounded Bastard. Three hundred Frenchmen lost their lives in the battle before the wagons— very little the worse for their part as fortifications—were trundled on to the walls of Orléans.

There was great rejoicing among the English when the outcome of the battle was known. They had their supplies— the loss of which could have meant the need to abandon the siege.

Sir John Fastolf was a hero and when the wagons were unloaded and their contents seen to consist largely of herrings, this encounter was known from henceforth as the Battle of the Herrings.

*   *   *

The Orléannese were dismayed. God had not been on their side this time. He had allowed that silly young Comte de Clermont to deprive them of victory.

The little miracles of the cannon balls were losing their power to comfort.

The Comte de Clermont might be the King's cousin but when he entered Orléans he was received with contempt. Even the Bastard recovering from his wounds was disconsolate and Maréchal de Boussac who had returned with him was hinting that his presence was needed elsewhere.

The Orléannese were losing that buoyant hope. They sadly needed a miracle.

The citizens talked together. They were being abandoned by those who had come to help them and that could mean only one thing. These men believed that the case was hopeless.

Some of the forces of the Duke of Burgundy were outside the walls with the English. Suppose they offered to surrender to Burgundy? That would prevent their town falling into the hands of the English.

It seemed to them that there was nothing else to be done. They could not go on starving and holding out against desperate odds. They would offer then to surrender themselves to Burgundy.

Philip of Burgundy was by no means displeased. He would

be happy to take Orléans, he declared, and the town should be surrendered to him.

But it was hardly to be expected that the Duke of Bedford would stand quietly by and see Burgundy walk into Orléans. Why should he agree to this when it was clear that the Orléannese were on the point of surrender. He and Burgundy were allies it was true, but uneasy ones. Burgundy was already too powerful. Why should he, Bedford, make him more so? When he thought of all the men, time and money he had wasted on this siege he was incensed.

'Indeed this shall not be,' he said. 'I do not care to beat the bushes so that another may get the birds.'

Burgundy, all prepared to march into Orléans, was furious. He immediately withdrew his troops and there was a rift between the allies.

'We will continue with the siege,' said Bedford grimly, and the Orléannese were as stubborn as ever. They would go on enduring hardship rather than give way to the English.

Then even he became aware of the rumours in the air. He paid little heed to them. He had learned from his ancestors that leaders only believed in superstitions when they worked in their favour.

This one was set about by the French. And a lot of nonsense it was. He laughed to think of it for it showed how desperate they were to fabricate and circulate such stories in the vain hope of bringing comfort to a people who had had their fill of suffering.

There was a young maid, said these rumours. She had heard voices telling her that God had chosen her to save France.

John laughed aloud. Let them indulge in their fantasies. Poor things, perhaps it could bring a little comfort to their hungry bodies; their good sense must tell them that defeat was in sight.

A peasant girl indeed. A virgin. They stressed that. She was going to ride into battle and drive the English out of France.

He was surprised that the French allowed themselves to indulge in such superstition.

The weary siege continued but as the weeks passed the name of Joan of Arc was heard more and more frequently and even John, Duke of Bedford could not ignore it.

*   *   *

Katherine was at Hadham in Hertfordshire. It was quiet there and she could rest in peace and make plans.

She had sent for Dame Alice Butler and Joan Astley. They knew why before she told them. Dame Alice said she could see it in her face.

'As you know,' said Katherine, 'I have taken a husband.'

They bowed their heads and waited.

'Our union must of course remain secret ... for the time. But now I find I am to have a child.'

'We shall look after you, my lady.'

'I knew you would,' replied Katherine. 'You loved my son so much. It is a pity these men see fit to take children from those who have nurtured and loved them.'

'They will make a King of him before he is a child,' said Dame Alice.

Joan nodded.

'We must perforce keep quiet about this matter,' went on the Queen, 'until I know what the Council will do about it. I would not wish ill to befall my husband.'

The women understood well. Owen could be taken from her. He could be imprisoned for what he had done and being of humble birth his actions might be construed as treason. He might be sentenced to the traitor's horrible death.

These women understood very well the delicacy of the situation; but their chief concern would be to bring the baby safely into the world.

Joan was handy with her needle and she was able to arrange Katherine's garments so that her pregnancy was not as obvious as it would otherwise have been.

Katherine sent for her priest. She told him that she was going to take Owen Tudor for her husband and that she wished him to perform the ceremony without delay.

He was astounded and reluctant. Katherine was a Queen, and he could place himself in danger if he performed this ceremony.

He shook his head. 'My lady, methinks you should inform the Duke of Gloucester of your intentions. If he is agreeable we can perform the ceremony without delay.'

'I am with child,' she said. 'The ceremony must take place at once.'

The priest was horrified. He wanted none of this matter.

'Are you a man of God?' demanded the Queen. 'Will you deny me marriage to the father of my child?'

The priest had no answer. She cajoled; she persuaded; she threatened; and when she pointed out that he was going against the laws of the Church by denying her marriage, at last he promised to perform the ceremony the next day.

Later that day one of her women came to her in a state of great agitation. It was a rumour she had heard.

It was said that the Duke of Gloucester had induced the Parliament to make a law prohibiting any person marrying the Queen Dowager or any lady of high degree without the consent of the King and his Council.

'This cannot be true,' she cried. 'Why ... after all this time? Why does he do it now?'

She did not need an answer to that question. It was because he knew.

But Gloucester could only have heard rumours of her liaison with Owen Tudor.

'What will become of us?' she cried in terror. But she was not one to give way to despair. Perhaps the horrors of her childhood had prepared her to fend for herself.

Gloucester or no Gloucester she was going to marry Owen Tudor. She was determined that her child would be born in wedlock.

Perhaps, she thought, it was better not to mention to the priest that there was this rumour about her marriage. If he married them in innocence he could not be held to blame. She would tell him that it should be a very secret affair. Only her immediate circle should know it had taken place. They would go on just as before. She would have her baby to care for and she would hope that Gloucester and his Council would lose interest in the mother of the little King.

The ceremony took place in an attic at Hadham and everyone present was sworn to secrecy. The priest asked permission to leave as soon as the marriage had been completed, which Katherine readily gave.

So she was married.

A few days later Gloucester's new law forbidding her to marry without consent was passed and she was officially informed of it. What could she do? It was too late now.

'Say nothing,' she said. 'These matters pass.'

She was now completely absorbed by her love for Owen and the imminent arrival of their child.

*   *   *

The Duke of Gloucester was a source of great irritation to the Council and it occurred to them that his power could be considerably diminished if the King were crowned. He would then no longer need a Protectorate. The King, though a boy, would rule in his own right. Thus the power of Gloucester could be curbed at one blow.

The Council were in unanimous agreement and on a clear and bright November day young Henry was brought to Westminster.

The Earl of Warwick led him to the high scaffold which had been set up in the Abbey and there he sat looking before him very solemnly, a little sad but conducting himself, as all agreed, with humility and devotion.

The crown was placed on his little head and he knew better now than to complain of its heaviness. He had already learned that although it was sometimes gratifying to be a King it had its drawbacks.

After he had been crowned he must go in procession to Westminster. There three Dukes walked before him carrying three swords which were symbolic of mercy, estate and empire, and Henry himself was led by two Bishops and six Earls with the Barons of the Cinque Ports carrying his pall and the Earl of Warwick his train. Judges, barons, knights and all the dignitaries of the city of London must attend.

The Bishop of Winchester—now a Cardinal—sat on his right hand at the feast and the new Chancellor, John Kemp, was on his other side. It was very formal and Henry was sorry for the Earls of Huntingdon and Stafford because they had to kneel beside him during the feast, one holding the sceptre and the other the sword of state—although he was uncomfortable enough himself in his heavy robes and crown.

And when he was seated and the hereditary champion rode in to challenge anyone who did not agree that Henry was the rightful King, the boy held his breath and looked about him anxiously wondering what would happen if anyone disputed that fact.

No one did and the feast began. Henry wished that he were back in Windsor talking to his mother while Dame Alice and Joan Astley served him with his simple food.

So he was crowned and he was most forcibly reminded that he was King of England.

His uncle Bedford sent messages from France.

He approved of the crowning of the King; he now wished

him to be crowned King of France. That was very important.

So no sooner had Henry come through one coronation than he was to prepare himself for another.

*   *   *

It was in an atmosphere of mystery that the little Tudor came into the world. It was impossible, of course, to keep his existence completely secret but only those in the household need know.

If visitors came they would not want to see the nurseries. The servants were loyal. They had to be if they would keep their positions and most of them were fond of the Queen.

Katherine had determined that it should all be achieved as comfortably as she could make it. And she did very well. Owen now continued with his duties as squire but he lived in the Queen's apartments.

They were two happy parents with a baby son.

They discussed what he should be called; Owen suggested Edmund and as Katherine wished all the time to please Owen she agreed to it.

So little Edmund flourished and it was not long before Katherine was once more pregnant.

By that time the strange stories of a peasant girl were reaching England.

She was said to be a virgin endowed with commands from Heaven.

Katherine talked of her a little. She was mildly interested because the girl was French and said to come from Domrémy, a part she knew slightly.

But there was too much to interest her in her own household for her to give much thought to a strange story about a certain girl they were calling Joan of Arc.

PART TWO

JOAN OF ARC

EARLY DAYS IN DOMRÉMY

SOME sixteen years before the siege of Orléans began Jacques d'Arc and his wife were waiting with mingled excitement and apprehension for the birth of their fourth child. It was not that the newcomer would not be welcome. Far from it. Jacques and his wife Isabelle—known affectionately as Zabillet—loved their children dearly. But times were hard—when had they been otherwise?—and the arrival of a new baby would mean that there was one more mouth to feed.

Jacques originally came from Arc-en-Barrois and having no legal name was called after his birthplace. He had in time found employment about the castle of Vaucouleurs and while there he had met Isabelle Romée. They had fallen in love and married. Isabelle—or Zabillet—though far from rich was not entirely penniless and on her marriage inherited the house in Domrémy where she settled with Jacques, and there the children were born. It was by no means a mansion but it served as a home for them and there was a small piece of land attached which enabled them to grow a few crops and with this and the permission which was given to all the villagers to graze their cattle in the nearby fields they managed to feed and clothe their young family.

Domrémy was situated on the River Meuse about twelve and a half miles from the town of Vaucouleurs and a little nearer to Neufchâteau. Adjoining it was the village of Greux and on the other side of the river was Maxey; a few miles away were Burey-le-Grand and Burey-le-Petit, and away on the heights lay the Château Bourlémont.

Until the wars had flared up again it had been a peaceful spot in which to live. News came slowly; the villagers were like one family, in and out of each other's houses, sitting at their doors in summer, gathering round the fires in winter, very often in one or other of their dwellings that one fire might serve several, fuel being not always easy to come by. The villagers lived carefully, making the most of everything they could wring from the land and now and then saving a little money to put by for emergencies. There was some excitement when travellers came, which they did now and then, for close by was the great road which had been there since it had been built by the Romans and along this came the messengers to and from the Court; merchants travelled along it too, so Domrémy was not as cut off from the world as some villages might be. Sometimes these travellers stayed at the village and begged a bed for the night and in exchange for that hospitality would give accounts of what was happening in the outside world. Moreover because the house of Jacques d'Arc was more commodious than others in the village he was usually the one to receive the guests.

It was a long low house with a heavy slate roof held up by great beams. In the front there were put two small windows so high that the interior was very dark indeed. The floor was of earth and the house was very sparsely furnished with only the barest necessities—a rough table on trestles, a few stools and spinning wheel and kneading trough; rough partitions divided the rooms. There were window seats in the fireplace and the walls were blackened by years of smoke. But on those walls in each room hung a crucifix, for Jacques and Zabillet were fervently religious and determined to bring up their children to be the same.

So close to the house was the church that its dismal graveyard was the first thing the family saw when they emerged into daylight. The days were punctuated by the sound of bells. They seemed to be ringing all the time, not only for mass and vespers, matins and complines but for all the ceremonies of the village, christenings, marriages and burials. The church dominated the village.

So it was at that time when the fourth member of the d'Arc family was about to make an appearance. Young Jacques—named after his father and given the name Jacquemin partly out of affection and the custom in the family of bestowing nicknames and partly to distinguish him from his father—

was already working in the field with his father. So was his younger brother Jean; and even little Catherine was helping in the house and learning to spin. Like all the children in the village they worked as soon as they were able. In time the new baby would join them—if it survived—and Zabillet was constantly telling Jacques that although the more children they had the more food had to be found, they all earned their daily bread. Jacques agreed and so in the little village of Domrémy they awaited the birth of their child.

There was no lack of helpers when Zabillet's pains started. The wives crowded into the dark interior where she lay on her pallet. The men were still working in the fields but Jacques knew that as soon as the baby arrived he would be called.

Birth was easy in Domrémy—but then so was death. Zabillet was serene enough. It was the fourth time she had been in this condition; and already she loved the baby.

And so the child was born. A little girl.

Well, they had two boys and girls were useful. They could spin and cook and look after the men; they could also do their stint in the fields.

She was a perfect child and it was decided to name her after one of her godmothers. Jeannette was a name well loved in France. It was the female of Jean and Jean had been Jesus Christ's best loved disciple. It was a good name.

Moreover it was a compliment to one of her godmothers—Jeannette de Vittel who had come to Domrémy from Neufchâteau for the ceremony and was very highly thought of because her husband Thiesselin de Vittel was a scholar and could read.

There were many godparents, as was the custom, and little Jeannette was baptized by the Curé Jean Minet in that church which was dedicated to Saint Rémy.

*　　*　　*

Jeannette was little more than three when she first noticed talk of war. It came into her parents' conversation a great deal and her brothers often talked of it. Now other riders galloped along the great road and sometimes stayed the night. She was well aware of the excitement when the neighbours crowded into the house, if it were winter to sit around the fire and listen to the news the traveller brought, or if it were summer gather outside the house on the green.

There was a new baby now—Pierre known as Pierrelot—
and it was Jeannette's task to mind him, which in spite of her
tender years she did tolerably well. She was a very serious
little girl and tried hard to understand what the grown-ups
were talking about and why news sometimes made them very
sad and at other times pleased them.

It was at this time she first heard the word Agincourt. She
did not know what it meant except that it was something
bad and shameful. People grew angry when they talked of
the Godons who, she guessed, were some sort of wicked devils.

As she grew a little older she began to learn more of these
matters. There was a wicked and cruel enemy of France.
These people were the Godons. They did not believe in God
and used wicked oaths. God Damn was the one which was
constantly on their lips—spoken in their barbaric tongue—
and from this came their name. They had won the battle of
Agincourt and so humbled France and made the King very
unhappy. Another name for the Godons was the English.

Because he had a bigger house than most of the villagers
but chiefly because he was a man of strong character Jacques
d'Arc had become a sort of headman of the village. People
came to the house to talk of their problems; if action was to
be taken they listened to his advice. Jeannette liked to sit
quietly in the shadows and listen and so when she was very
young she came to have a fairly clear understanding of what
was going on.

It was War. That was a hateful word and she wanted to
shut her ears to it. People forgot it for long spells at a time
and were happy, and then she would hear the word War again
and they would be miserable—more than that, afraid.

'Why do we have to have war?' she asked Jacquemin. 'What
good does it bring? Why don't they stop it? It only hurts
people.'

Jacquemin gave her a scornful look. She did not understand, he told her. She should get on with learning to spin.

She did that, she reminded him, but she could think at the
same time.

In time she learned that there was trouble between the
Armagnacs and the Burgundians and that had been going on
since the Duke of Burgundy had murdered the Duke of
Orléans and now it seemed the Armagnacs had murdered the
Duke of Burgundy in retaliation.

And what had this to do with the peasants of Domrémy? wondered Jeannette. Sometimes there was no talk of war for a long time. There were happy feast days. Jeannette loved the solemnity of them, the singing in the church, the ringing of the bells. She loved the statues in the churches and it was her delight to go and kneel before them, and she liked it best when she was alone in the church. Her mother had taught her the Paternoster, Ave Maria and the Credo. She learned these with avidity; it seemed wondrously beautiful to her to go into the church and sit on the floor in the nave below the pulpit and listen to the priest. All the women of the village went and Zabillet took her children there as soon as they could walk.

The church seemed to Jeannette something which was beautiful in a life which was full of hardship and dominated by the need to survive. The church gave a promise of paradise to some; it offered beauty and colour in drab lives. The peasants could sublimate their hard struggle in their religion. But although it was a religion of great promise of sublime happiness, it also had its dark side. It was a religion of contrasts—just like life itself—and as there was Heaven for the virtuous, there must be Hell for those who failed to achieve that perfection demanded at the pearly gates before a soul entered. It seemed one must spend one's life earning the right to enter and Jacques and Zabillet were determined that their children should not be denied entry.

Jeannette loved Rogation Sunday when the banners were brought out and the cross lifted from the wall and all the people walked in procession led by the Curé to the sacred tree on the river's edge known as L'Arbre des Dames. The little boys came first, then the women and the girls, and after them the men. As they went they chanted prayers and when they reached the sacred tree the Curé would read the gospels before they returned to the village chanting praises to God and the Virgin.

It was a solemn occasion but that which occurred on the fourth Sunday in Lent was less so. That was the children's day —the day they called Laetare. Then the earth was waking to Spring and the countryside would be looking beautiful and as they tripped along carrying their precious burdens of cakes, tiny loaves, apples which had been saved through the winter, nuts, cheese and perhaps a sweetmeat or two if they were lucky, they would go to the tree and there sing and dance.

Sometimes a piper came with them and played tunes for the dancing; and the children gathered wild flowers and made them into chains. These they hung on the trees or took home and cherished them in their homes until they faded, which was very soon.

The tree was a symbol. It must have been so since pre-Christian days but the villagers gave no thought to the fact that the worship of it was an inheritance from the past. There was a strong superstition in Domrémy that the fairies whom they called the Little People still inhabited certain parts of the woods. Some of the peasants laid out food for them—which they could ill afford—but the fact was that they were afraid of offending them, for fairies were not always good and some people held the theory that they were really people who were not good enough for Heaven and not bad enough for Hell and having been refused admittance to either must roam the earth.

There was a spring at the source of the river which was called La Fontaine-aux-Bonnes-Fées-Notre-Seigneur. It was but a mile or so from the village at the edge of the wood called Bois-Chesnu; and this spring was said to have magical powers. The sick came to drink its waters but as it was also a haunt of those fairies who could not be trusted, it was considered to be rather daring to visit it for instead of good health one might incur the wrath and curses of the Little People.

Jeanne—known as Jannet—Aubrit who had been one of Jeannette's godmothers, said she had seen the fairies dancing round L'Arbre des Dames and Jannet was the wife of a very important man who worked for the lords of Bourlémont; Jannet was too pious to have told a lie. So there were fairies but Jeannette was more interested in the saints.

Thus she was growing up in an atmosphere of extreme piety with a belief in miracles and a growing awareness of the horrors of war as it crept close to Domrémy. She heard the talk of the days before the Godons came. Then apparently all had been peace, though there had occasionally been skirmishes between the Armagnacs and the Burgundians. But the Godons were devils who came from over the seas and were determined to take France from its rightful King.

When she was alone in the church Jeannette knelt before the statue of the Virgin and prayed that the Godons might be driven back to their own lands and that France might be happy again.

Jeannette had some little friends in the village. When she worked in the fields or was spinning in the house she would be joined by Isabelle Despinal and Mengette Joyart who would bring their distaffs with them and they would all laugh and talk together. Isabelle and Mengette were a little older than she was but Jeannette was advanced for her years and this passed unnoticed. There was a young girl, Hauviette Sydna, who liked to join them. She adored Jeannette who never failed to make her welcome in spite of her youth; and the girls were very happy together.

They had very little spare time when they were not spinning or working in the fields or carrying water into the house but one day when they found there was no yarn left for spinning and they had done their work in the fields, Jeannette said she was going to walk to the Chapel of Notre Dame de Bermont.

'It's a long way,' said Isabelle.

Jeannette said she would go even though it was. She was used to walking and it was only for very long distances that she would be allowed to take the little mare.

Hauviette begged permission to join them, so they all made their way to the chapel.

'Once,' said Isabelle, 'the lord and lady of Bourlémont used to lead the processions.'

'Why don't they now?' asked Hauviette.

'Because they are dead, silly,' said Isabelle.

'How was Hauviette to know?' asked Jeannette.

Hauviette took her hand and pressed it. Jeannette was kind, though she could be sharp with those who displeased her, but she was always gentle to Hauviette, because she was younger than the others.

She turned to Hauviette now and said: 'Madame d'Ogivillier is now the owner of the Lord of Bourlémont's lands. There were no children to have them so they have gone to Madame d'Ogivillier who was his niece.'

'She lives in Nancy,' said Isabelle, to show her knowledge equalled that of Jeannette.

'And she married the chamberlain of the Duke of Lorraine,' added Mengette.

They were all silent with awe.

Isabelle then pointed out to them the small castle in the

distance. It was on a little islet in the middle of the river.

'That's the Château de l'Isle,' she said.

'We know that,' Jeannette reminded her.

'It belongs to Madame d'Ogivillier now,' added Mengette.

'How wonderful to have a castle of your own,' sighed Hauviette and they all laughed.

At length they came to the chapel.

'What shall we do?' asked Hauviette. 'Shall we pick flowers and lay them at her feet?'

'No,' said Jeannette. 'We'll just pray to her.'

The children went on their knees and prayed as they did in the church of Saint Rémy.

Isabelle rose after a few moments and Mengette did the same.

'I've prayed,' said Isabelle. 'Come on, let's go into the field. There is a little time before we leave.'

Jeannette said: 'You go. I wish to stay awhile.'

Hauviette hesitated and stayed with Jeannette, kneeling beside her, thinking how the hard floor hurt her knees and she was about to tell Jeannette when she noticed that her friend with her hands together as in prayer was staring up at the Virgin, and her face had become more beautiful.

Hauviette was overawed and words died on her lips. She waited.

And for some time Jeannette remained as though enrapt.

Then she arose and looked at Hauviette as though she were surprised to see her there and was wondering who she was.

She took Hauviette's hand. She said: 'It was as though the Virgin spoke to me.'

Then they ran out of the church and joined the others in the field. They gathered wild flowers and chased each other, but Hauviette noticed that Jeannette still looked enraptured as she had when she said the Virgin had spoken to her.

*   *   *

It was considered right that godparents should see their godchildren from time to time and therefore when Madame de Vittel declared that it was time for Jeannette to visit her in Neufchâteau Jacques and Zabillet agreed that the girl should go.

They could spare her for a week and she could make her-

self useful in the Vittel household. It was good for her to be
with such learned people.

Jeannette made the journey of some seven miles on the
little mare and it was a great pleasure to her to ride through
the countryside. The woods were beautiful with oaks, ilex
and chestnuts. In those woods bears lurked but they did not
come out by day. At night they were very bold and if they
were hungry they would venture into the village. People
never went about singly after dark because the bears could
be vicious and any night wanderers had to be prepared for
them.

During daylight it was safe. Daylight was like peace,
thought Jeannette, night, like war. Bears were like Godons,
wicked and cruel, trying to snatch what did not belong to
them.

Jacquemin was accompanying her and she rode behind him
on the little mare. He would stay one night in Neufchâteau
and go back to Domrémy the next day. He could not be
spared longer. It would have been so much more convenient
for Jeannette to have gone alone for it was hard to have to
spare two little workers together. However Jacquemin would
soon be back and Jeannette's visit would not be so long and
there was no doubt that godparents should see often those
whom they had sponsored. Perhaps Jeannette and Thiesselin
de Vittel would bring the child back.

Past the castle of Bourlémont they went, past the little
castle on the island—all familiar landmarks—and after a
while they came to the rocky valleys below the heights of Les
Faucilles and followed the winding river until the walls and
towers of Neufchâteau came into sight.

There was a warm welcome for the children at the house
of the Vittels. Jeannette de Vittel was delighted with her
little goddaughter and Thiesselin embraced her and told
her how pleased he was that she was staying with them for a
while.

'I would that Jacquemin might too,' he said.

Jacquemin looked wistful. 'We cannot both be spared,' he
said.

That was understandable and there was a wonderful meal
with meat such as the children rarely tasted at Domrémy. By
the d'Arc standards the Vittels were rich. It was because
Thiesselin was a scholar. He could read and write. There
were books in his house and Jeannette was allowed to hold

them and open them and study the strange shapes on the pages which Thiesselin could so miraculously decipher.

There was a school in Greux and some of the boys in Domrémy went to it. The Arcs could not be spared. Jeannette was not sure whether she would want to go. She had seen the horn book which belonged to one of the boys in the village and it had not held the same charm for her as the statues in the church and the beautiful sound of the bells.

Still, it must be wonderful, she admitted, to be a scholar like Thiesselin.

The next day Jacquemin departed. Jeannette did a little spinning for her godmother, some housework and weeding in the garden. In fact she worked as hard in Neufchâteau as she did in Domrémy. But there was more to eat, different and more delicious food; and when the day was over instead of going to bed as they did in Domrémy, Jeannette lighted two candles—a great extravagance for at home in Domrémy they never had more than one going at a time—and they talked and sometimes Uncle Thiesselin—as she called him—read to them from the wonderful books.

It was from Thiesselin that she first heard the stories of Saint Catherine and Saint Margaret.

All her life she would remember sitting on a stool in that darkening room with the two candles throwing their light on the book which lay open on the table before Thiesselin.

'Catherine was the daughter of the King and Queen of Alexandria,' read Thiesselin. 'The King was King Costus and the Queen Sabinella. Her body was beautiful but her soul was dark for it was blackened by idolatry. She worshipped idols. Many in her father's kingdom sought her hand in marriage because of her beauty. But she said no to them all. "I want a husband who is handsome and rich and the most noble in the land," she added. Then one night the Virgin came to her and in her arms she held the most beautiful child Catherine had ever seen. "Will you take him for your husband," asked the Virgin, "and will you, my son, take this beautiful girl as your bride?" And the Christ child said: "No, for she worships idols. But if she will be baptized I will put my nuptial ring on her finger." '

Jeannette listened wide-eyed to how Catherine was secretly baptized and there in a vision saw Christ who put the nuptial ring on her finger.

'Now Maxentius, the Emperor of the Romans, sent out a

command that all the people must offer sacrifices to the idols they worshipped. Catherine was now a Christian; she could not partake in the offering of such sacrifices, nor could she stand by silently and see this done, and when the Emperor and all his retinue came to Alexandria to witness the sacrifices and were gathered in the great square, Catherine went before him and called him a fool because he sacrificed to false idols. He was proud of the fine buildings he set up, she told him. He loved them to idolatry, but he should love the trees and the earth, the stars and the sky. That was God's work and superior to that of man.'

Listening avidly, Jeannette was there in the great square at Alexandria. She glowed with the ardour which was Catherine's. In those moments in the candlelit room she *was* Catherine.

Thiesselin went on to read of how Catherine was arrested and because her beauty had impressed Maxentius he said that his wise men should parley with her and confound her in argument and when they proved her folly to her she should be given the opportunity to recant.

'Now,' read Thiesselin, 'God spoke through Catherine so that she confounded those so-called wise men, and so impressed were they that they declared Catherine to be the one who spoke the truth.'

It was vivid; it was real.

Thiesselin paused and said: 'That is enough for this night. Tomorrow I will read more of the story of Catherine.'

Jeannette lay on her truckle bed as though in a trance. It had been a wonderful experience. She could scarcely get through the day and when that hour came when the candles were lighted and Thiesselin sat at the table and continued with the story of Catherine she was trembling with excitement.

She listened to how the infuriated Emperor caused the wise men to be burned to death, but although the fires raged round them they emerged unscathed.

'It was a miracle,' breathed Jeannette.

'It was God proclaiming the Truth,' said her godmother.

'And what did the Emperor do then?' Jeannette wanted to know.

It seemed that he had been struck by Catherine's beauty and offered her a place in his palace, second only to that of his Empress. There should be a statue to her set up in the town and she should be worshipped as a goddess. But first she must make a sacrifice to the idols the Emperor worshipped. Catherine's response was that she was the bride of Christ. Then the Emperor ordered that she be cast into a dungeon after being scourged by rods and there she should be left to starve. He then departed on his conquests. But an angel came to the Empress and she believed him when he told her that Catherine was a saint.

The Emperor returned and when he heard that Catherine was not dead but seemed unscathed by her ordeal he ordered that wheels with sharp spikes be made, the intention being that Catherine's body should be broken on these, but just as they were about to be set in motion they broke asunder and the pieces were scattered, killing several who had come to gloat on the sufferings of Catherine. The Empress, seeing what had happened, came to the Emperor to protest and to say that she had had a vision and as a result had become a Christian. In his rage the Emperor ordered her head to be cut off.

The Emperor then offered Catherine a choice. She could be his Empress or her head should be cut off.

'So her head was cut off and it was not blood that flowed from her body but milk. And from Heaven there was heard sounds of celestial music when Catherine ascended to join her bridegroom.'

Thiesselin shut the book and there was deep silence in the room.

Jeannette's godmother blew out one of the candles. 'Jeannette, are you asleep?' she asked.

Jeannette opened wide eyes to stare at her. 'Asleep! Dear godmother, I was there . . . I knew what was in her mind. And the milk which flowed from her body was purity. It is the pure who see God.'

The Vittels looked at her in amazement. She seemed transformed.

'Go to your bed,' said Jeannette de Vittel kindly.

Jeannette rose. 'Shall there be more reading tomorrow?' she asked.

Thiesselin laid his hand on her shoulder. 'My dear child,' he said, 'I will read more stories of the saints. Saint Catherine was not the only one to die for God and the faith.'

And that visit to her godmother was an important landmark in the life of little Jeannette. She waited through the days patiently doing the tasks set her and while she was at her spinning wheel she dreamed of what the saints had done for God and she thought that they were the truly great ones. Not great soldiers like the mighty Dukes of Burgundy and Orléans, not like the King himself ... But the holy saints who cared not what happened to them and lived only to die in the service of God.

She would always adore Saint Catherine, and when she heard the story of the blessed Margaret these two became as friends to her.

Eagerly she listened to how Margaret, daughter of Theodosius a priest of the Gentiles, was baptized in secret and how Olibrius the Governor of the city saw her and admired her beauty. He ordered that she be brought into his house and when she refused to become his concubine he had her hung from a wooden horse and beaten with iron rods while her flesh was torn with iron pincers. Her blood came from her body like the freshest water. She suffered other tortures at the hands of Olibrius but she endured them all and refused to give in. Finally she was beheaded and those watching said that as she died a pure white dove flew up to Heaven.

Jeannette thought a great deal about the saints and her godmother took her to the church and showed her the images of St Catherine and St Margaret, and she longed to be like them.

As she lay on her pallet at night she thought of them; she dreamed of them and it was as though they spoke to her in her dreams.

There was one significant factor about their lives, and that was their insistence on their virginity. Jeannette knew that many girls and boys were interested in each other; she had seen Mengette Joyart flirting with a young soldier who came from one of the nearby villages. She was constantly bringing the name of Collot Turlant into the conversation.

Jeannette shuddered. She wanted none of that. She wanted to live as Catherine and Margaret had. She vowed as she lay in her pallet that she would remain a virgin for then she might be chosen as Margaret and Catherine were.

There were more stories of the saints. The days and evenings passed too quickly, and in due course Jacquemin arrived to take her back to Domrémy.

Regretfully she rode slowly back. One day, she promised herself, I shall be among them.

The conviction had come to her. It was the first step in the direction she would go.

* * *

There was great excitement in Domrémy. Horsemen galloped to and fro on the roads but sometimes stopped to rest at the village.

Jeannette was ten years old, able to understand something of the terrible torment through which her country was passing.

She knew that the most wicked of all the Godons, the King of England, had made terms with the poor mad King of France and his wife the Bavarian Isabeau whom many people said was at the root of their troubles. Consequently the King's daughter Katherine had become the wife of the wicked King, and that King was calling himself the King of France.

There was consternation everywhere. The skirmishes between the Armagnacs and the Burgundians were as nothing compared with this. This was disaster. This would change the entire face of the countryside.

'How could the King do this?' demanded Jeannette of her brothers. 'How could the King take the Dauphin's inheritance and give it to this Godon?'

'Because he was forced to do it, of course,' said knowledgeable Jacquemin. 'You cannot think he would have done so otherwise.'

'But why ... why ... ?'

'Because the Godons have more men and money ... because we have a Queen who is a Jezebel and a King who is mad ... and Frenchmen who fight against each other.'

Her brother Jean looked ashamed. Domrémy was for Armagnac and Greux for Burgundy and Jean had had many a scuffle with the boys of Greux on account of that loyalty. He did not know what it was about—except that Armagnacs were for Orléans and Greux for Burgundy and when they confronted each other they fought.

'All Frenchmen should stand together,' said Jeannette. 'They would then have a better chance of driving the Godons away.'

'What does a girl know about it?' asked little Pierrelot.

'I know that the Godons will be driven away,' said Jeannette, 'and that France will belong to the French once more.'

Jean grimaced at Jacquemin. Jeannette was in one of her moods again, he implied.

The troubles did not decrease because of the treaty the King of France had made with the King of England. There were still French towns who would not submit to the conqueror and fighting went on which made the Godons angry. They had won; they had beaten the French to their knees; they wanted an end to the war and when the mad King died their King Henry was to be crowned the King of France. They showed small mercy on the rebels.

The Duke of Burgundy was a traitor—even the Burgundians of Greux were finding it hard to make excuses for him— and because he hated the Armagnacs whom the King favoured he had become the ally of the Godons.

It was all very disturbing. Everyone knew that the Godons were the enemy but otherwise they could not be sure who was fighting whom.

There were frightening stories of what happened when the soldiers passed through villages. They took all the food; sometimes they set fire to the houses; they took the women and raped them, regarding them as the spoils of war no less than the food they could lay their hands on.

The people of Domrémy gathered about the house of Jacques d'Arc. He was a man not only of deep piety but of far-sightedness. Just before the treaty which had given France to the Godons he had conceived an idea which some of them had thought a little foolhardy at the time and which they now saw was a stroke of brilliance.

When the Lord of Bourlémont had died without an heir he had left the small castle which stood on an island in the River Meuse to his niece Jeanne de Joinville. Mademoiselle de Joinville had married Henri d'Ogivillier who held a post in the King's service and she had gone to live in Nancy, so the castle was uninhabited and she had decided to let it on lease, for an annual rent, to the highest bidder.

It would never have occurred to the people of Domrémy that they could rent the castle until Jacques pointed this out to them. The castle was an ideal place for defence, being built on the end of the island and bounded on three sides by the river. The fields of the island were included in the deal and these could be put to very profitable use. Cattle could be kept there; in fact a colony of people living there could be entirely self-supporting.

Jacques had talked to the villagers very earnestly. They must between them acquire the castle if at all possible. There were sporadic outbreaks of war, and they would continue for a long time since it was hardly likely that the French would submit to the intolerable English yoke. They knew what happened when a rough soldiery of either side passed through villages. People lost their possessions; they were left with nothing and no prospect before them but to roam the countryside as beggars. And the women, what of the women?

'Will you not do everything within your power to protect your wives and daughters?' he demanded.

It was this which made them more determined and when the women added their voices to those of the men it was decided that they must do everything they could to secure the use of the castle as a means of defence for the people of Domrémy.

Jacques and a few of his neighbours did the bidding and rather to the surprise of everyone secured the use of the Château de l'Ile for nine years. The fact was that few had wanted it, for not many were as far-sighted as Jacques d'Arc. They must pay fourteen livres a year plus six bushels of wheat and if this payment was kept up the whole of the island was theirs except of course the Chapel of Our Lady which had stood there for centuries and which was open to any.

The renting of the castle had been a success. The land was fertile and they made the most of it. Jacquemin, who by this time had married a girl in the village, went over there to live and Jeannette often rowed over to look after the cattle or to weed and hoe the fields.

But it had not been acquired, Jacques pointed out, merely to provide extra grazing land and a home for some of those who married and being members of large families found their houses overcrowded. No, the object of renting the castle had been for defence. Jacques had set about turning the castle into a fortress; in front of the castle—the only part which was not bounded by the river—he had moats dug and these were kept filled by the river; four other young men with their small families joined Jacquemin and it was the duty of these five families to keep the island ready in case it should be needed. The villagers crossed frequently and Jeannette loved the peace of the place and sought opportunities to go there to work in the fields.

There came a day when a traveller on the road stopped in Domrémy for the night and seated round the fire in the house of Jacques d'Arc he told the family and as many of the villagers who could crowd into the house that the King was dead and that some months before the wicked Godon King had died also.

'Then,' said Zabillet, 'who is now the King of France?'

Jeannette said fiercely: 'It is the Dauphin. He should be crowned King.'

There was silence and all looked at Jeannette because it was not fitting for young people to talk as their elders might, and in the company of strangers it was behaving with a forwardness which was frowned on in all well conducted households.

Jacques was about to deliver a reproof when Zabillet laid a hand on his arm. Zabillet loved this daughter dearly; she had had a strong feeling from the day of her birth that she was different from the others.

'Jeannette is deeply moved,' she now whispered to her husband. 'Let her speak as she wishes.'

And for some reason he could not explain, the reproof died on Jacques' lips.

Then Jeannette went on: 'He will be crowned. He *shall* be crowned.'

The traveller said: 'Nay, little maid, 'twill not be our Dauphin who is crowned. It is a little baby who lives in England. He is now the King of England and calls himself the King of France.'

'Wicked men call him so,' said Zabillet. 'He is too young to be blamed for that.'

Jeannette's outburst had been passed over and the traveller went on to tell them that the little boy, the son of their own Princess would be brought to France to be crowned when he was a little older.

'By that time,' said Jacques, 'perhaps God will have come to our aid.'

'Yes,' said Jeannette, 'He will come. I know it in my heart.'

'Bring some wine for our guest, Jeannette,' said her mother. 'He will be thirsty.'

As Jeannette went away to do her mother's bidding there was certain exultation in her heart.

*   *   *

Times were growing worse. There were only brief periods of relief. A traveller coming one day told them that the Duke of Bedford, who had become Regent on the death of King Henry and whose ally the Duke of Burgundy had been, was now not on such good terms with Burgundy. It seemed that Bedford had a brother called the Duke of Gloucester who had deeply offended Burgundy.

'Let us pray that this will bring the Duke's loyalty back where it belongs,' said Jacques. 'But for this warring within our country we should not now be in this bitter position. If this quarrel brings Frenchmen together then it is God's work.'

But God's work, if it were, brought little relief. The next news was that the Duke of Bedford had married the sister of the Duke of Burgundy and this had strengthened the weakening alliance between them.

'How can a noble French lady marry a Godon?' asked Pierrelot. 'They are not as we are. They have tails like monkeys.'

'That is nonsense,' Jeannette told him. 'They have no tails. They are men and women as the French are. Their wickedness is in their souls which they have sold to the devil.'

'And have all the French sold their souls to God?' Pierrelot wanted to know.

'Let us pray they will do so,' said Jeannette.

Jeannette was growing more pious every day. They all noticed it. 'It will pass,' said Zabillet gravely. 'But only in a measure I trust. My Jeannette is a good girl. Sometimes I think she is different from the rest of us.'

The struggle between the Armagnacs and the Burgundians was as strong as ever. The Armagnacs had never forgiven the Burgundians for murdering Louis of Orléans and now the Burgundians were not going to forgive the Armagnacs for retaliating by murdering John the Fearless, Duke of Burgundy. Duke Philip was determined to avenge his father. In the meantime so did he hate the Armagnacs that he was supporting the English against the very crown of France.

There was even conflict between the villages. Domrémy was staunchly for Armagnac and that meant the crown; but the village of Maxey on the other side of the river was staunchly Burgundian. When the boys of these villages met it would not be long before they were fighting each other. Jeannette often saw her brother come home bruised and bleeding and when she asked how he had come to be so would be told: 'Oh, it was fighting against Burgundy.'

* * *

There followed a period of increased anxiety. The war was coming nearer to Domrémy. Sometimes they saw the smoke of burning villages in the distance and they knew that the soldiers were near. Whether it was English against French or Armagnac against Burgundy they did not know. Did it matter? Jeannette asked angrily. It was a stupid, senseless war.

Every night there were watchmen on the tower of the church and sometimes when a warning was given they would round up the flocks and herds and go across to the island fortress.

So far Domrémy had escaped.

But there was one terrible night when the battle came very near. From the castle Jeannette watched the flames rising to the sky and she knew that it was the village of Maxey which was being pillaged. Her first thoughts were for Mengette and her husband Collot Turlant whom she had married two years before. They should have joined them in the castle and yet, thought Jeannette, if any of these soldiers were of a mind to take the castle what would prevent them?

In the morning they went back to Domrémy. Everything was as they had left it, and although the relief of the return was almost unbearably great, everyone knew that they should not rejoice too gladly because from the safety of one day they could be plunged into the disaster of the next.

That turned out to be a sad day after all. Mengette came to Jeannette as she sat at her spinning wheel and one look into her face told Jeannette what she had feared.

She rose and took her friend in her arms.

'What is it, Mengette?' she said.

'Collot,' whispered the young wife. 'I saw it ... the cannon struck him ... and he fell. There was blood on the ground, Jeannette ... his blood.'

'Oh Mengette, my poor Mengette!'

'It was so short a time that we had together. It is only two years, Jeannette, and then ... these stupid wars. Why do the men make wars? Do I want wars? Do you? Did Collot? If they want wars, let them fight and die ... not us ... not us.

What does it matter to me ... Armagnac or Burgundy ...
France or England ... ?'

'Hush,' said Jeannette. 'You are overwrought. I will get
you some wine.'

Mengette shook her head.

'I hate them all. I hate them,' she said. 'They have taken
Collot. What harm did he do? It was La Hire ... the Gas-
con ... It was his men. He comes from the Dauphin to kill
Frenchmen ... good Frenchmen, like Collot.'

Jeannette had heard of the ferocious soldier of Gascony,
Etienne Vignolle, who was known as La Hire; his men would
have attacked Maxey ostensibly because that village was Burgundian in its sympathies, but these men revelled in war,
not for a cause but to satisfy their lust for blood. They killed
people like Collot Turlant and turned Mengette into a
widow.

What could she say to comfort her friend?

She stroked her hair. 'My dear little Mengette,' she whispered, 'you must try not to grieve. One day everything will
be good again in France. I heard a prophecy today. Do
you know what it was? It was Merlin long, long ago who
said that a wise virgin would arise from the people of France
and repair the damage which had been wrought by a wicked
woman.'

Mengette was not listening; she sat staring blankly before
her, thinking of all she had lost.

Jeannette went on: 'The wicked woman is the Queen of
France, Isabeau of Bavaria. She has cheated our King and our
country; she has been false to both and she has given our
crown and our Princess to the English. She is the wicked
woman of whom Merlin spoke, Mengette. But the wise virgin
will come.'

It was a few days later when a party of soldiers rode into
Domrémy. The villagers hurried into their houses and prepared for the worst. The soldiers dismounted and selecting
the house of Jacques d'Arc because it was the largest in the
village and in a prominent position close to the church,
rapped on the door.

Jacques opened the door and faced them.

'What would you have with me, sirs?' he asked.

'A word. Just a word,' was the reply.

They came in. Jeannette was at her spinning-wheel so she
heard everything.

'We are in the service of the great Robert of Saarbrück,' they announced.

Jacques became very uneasy. This man was well known throughout the villages of France. He was one of those who made a profession of war and sought to fill his own pockets through it.

'As you know, my lord of Saarbrück has declared for the Armagnac cause against the traitor Burgundy and this village I believe stands staunch for Armagnac.'

Jacques said: 'We are for the King of France, he who is now called Dauphin and is in truth our King.'

'So thought our master and he has sent us to offer you protection from the Burgundians and the Godons. As you know many of the villages hereabouts lie in ruins. We do not wish this to happen to Domrémy. We are going to protect you.'

'I thank you,' said Jacques. 'Methinks we may well be in need of such protection.'

The soldier went on: 'Such protection, which you so badly need, must be paid for. My master will need two hundred and twenty gold crowns to be delivered to him before St Martin's day this winter.'

'Two hundred and twenty gold crowns! But that is impossible. I have nothing like that.'

'My good man, it shall not come from you alone. There are many in this village. Let them all contribute. It is nothing so much when divided. Say two *gros* from each household, eh? That is what my master would have us say to you. If you value the safety of Domrémy, my good man, think about it. What is two *gros* when compared with the loss of your homes, your property ... ?'

Jeannette sat looking at her father as she listened to the sound of the soldiers galloping away. His face was ashen; there was anger and despair in his eyes.

After that there were many meetings in the house and on the green. Could they find the money? They must, said Jacques. He had sensed a threat from Robert of Saarbrück's men. It seemed they had enemies on every side.

War, thought Jeannette, accursed war; and she went into the church to kneel before the statue of the Virgin and pray.

*   *   *

Life was not all gloom. Catherine was very happy at this time. She was married to Colin, one of the field workers from Greux; they had been in love for a long time and Colin used to follow them when they went to dance at L'Arbre des Dames; he would tease them when they went into the chapel to pray and tell Catherine that she must not be as pious as her sister.

Catherine and he were always going off together and as they were now of an age to marry nothing was put in their way. Catherine went to live at Greux and as that was no distance from Domrémy the sisters saw a great deal of each other and were as happy together as they had always been.

Catherine was always urging Jeannette to think of marriage. She was personable enough. One or two of the boys in the village had cast their eyes on her. Whenever Catherine talked of marriage Jeannette became very serious and declared that she did not think she would ever marry.

Catherine laughed with the wise look of a knowledgeable married woman; and although Jeannette genuinely had no wish to marry herself she was delighted to see her sister's happiness.

It was a great hardship to find the money for Robert of Saarbrück but for a few months there was comparative peace. Hope was springing up because there were rumours of a rallying of the French armies and that the Dauphin was recruiting mercenaries from Italy and Spain. There were fierce Scots too, for the Scots had always hated the English, and were never averse to giving a hand against them.

This was to be the battle to end the tragic state of affairs. France would rise again, and a more hopeful spirit prevailed in Domrémy than had been known for a long time. Even the church bells rang out more gaily, it seemed to Jeannette.

They waited for news. The English were not as strong as they had been, they reminded themselves. The Duke of Bedford was no Henry the Fifth. He wanted to go home. His brother was causing trouble. Burgundy was not and never could be—a true friend.

There came the day when the road was busy with messengers riding to and fro. There were soldiers as well. Some stopped at Domrémy. Yes, there had been a battle, a bloody battle, that of Verneuil.

Victory for the French? Indeed not. The English had done it again. When would the French find a way of defeating those showers of arrows, those spikes turned towards the enemy which broke the legs of the French horses as they advanced?

So ... disaster at Verneuil and little hope of driving the Godons back across the sea. The sacking started again. There were sudden descents on the villages. No one was safe.

One night the tocsins rang out. Soldiers were coming in the direction of Domrémy. They were almost upon them and there was no time to save the cattle as well as the villagers.

They fled to the castle. They heard the sounds of shouting all through the night. Anxiously they watched for the flames.

In the morning they returned fearfully to the village. Their houses were untouched but all the cattle had been stolen.

Poverty stared them in the face. How could they live without cattle? Their flocks and herds were their livelihood.

Jacques declared that he would send a messenger at once to Jeanne d'Ogivillier, the owner of the Castle on the Island; she had influence in high places; she was a good and compassionate woman and she would know what the loss of their cattle would mean to the villagers. Moreover she was related to the Comte de Vaudémont. Could she appeal to him? The villagers had done no wrong, but they had had their means of livelihood snatched away from them in the night.

Perhaps none was more surprised than Jacques when the cattle, on the command of the Comte, were returned to the village. What joy there was! What bell ringing! The village congregated on the green to celebrate their good fortune and Jeannette went into the church to pray to the Virgin.

'Help them, Holy Virgin,' she prayed. 'Help me to do what I can.'

VOICES

IT was soon after that when she heard the first of the voices. She had rowed over to the island to tend the sheep. It was a warm day and everything around seemed peaceful. She was thinking about the past year and all the horrors they had gone through, the loss of the cattle, the difficulty in finding the tribute to pay Robert of Saarbrück, the death of Mengette's husband, and the constant fear in the night and the rising up from her pallet when the church bells rang out to warn them. Church bells should be beautiful, peaceful as they were when rung for church services. She loved the bells. She had always thought that one of the most wonderful moments of the day was when she was in the fields or tending the crops in her father's patch and she heard the bells of the angelus ringing out. Then she would kneel wherever she was and give thanks to God.

Alas, life was full of anxieties and would be until peace came back to the land. Even then life had its troubles, harvests failed, people died. She thought then of Catherine. She had not seemed well lately. Jeannette had noticed that she was becoming increasingly thin and she had a persistent cough. She herself would go to Greux more often. She would insist on helping with her work, for Catherine did seem to be easily tired.

She looked up at the sky. A dark cloud had sprung up suddenly. She held out her hand. It was raining quite hard now. On the island apart from the main chapel there was the ruin of an old one which could not have been used for fifty years. The walls had been battered by weather but what was left would offer a good shelter from a shower of rain.

The rain was now teeming down and she stepped under the protruding roof. It was clear that this had been an altar to the Virgin, and as always, when close to holy places, Jeannette experienced a lifting of her spirits. She knelt down to pray as she often did, and the burden of her prayer was, as usual, that Heaven might see fit to save her tortured country from the enemy.

And as she prayed a strange drowsiness came upon her. She could not understand quite what had happened when she thought of it afterwards. Whether she fell asleep she was not sure. It was a conviction rather than anything she saw, but it was clear and different from anything that had ever happened to her before. It was like a vision in which she heard the voice of God telling her that she had been chosen to go to the aid of the Dauphin.

She awoke ... if sleeping she had been. The rain had stopped and the sun had come out. It was shining on the wet grass and bushes, and she could smell the freshness in the air.

What a strange dream! Yet not a dream. Had she heard a voice? She was not sure. It was just a wild dream and yet she was filled with an exultation, as though she had been in communication with God.

She herded the flocks together and told herself she had fallen asleep and dreamed. The terrible state of the country was constantly in her mind. Wasn't it in everyone's mind? No one could escape from it. Perhaps that was why when she dozed for a few moments she should have such a dream. But no. It had been a preposterous idea. How could she, a simple peasant girl, go to the aid of the Dauphin!

It was a few days later—a hot summer's day. She was working on her father's patch when suddenly from the direction of the church she heard the voice again.

It said: 'Jeannette, I have been sent by God to help you live a good and holy life. Be good and God will help you.'

She stood up. A sudden fear came to her. She was in the presence of the supernatural.

'Have no fear,' went on the voice. 'Be good. If you are, you will have the protection of God.'

Jeannette's fear passed away and she fell to her knees. She believed it was Christ claiming her as his bride as He had St Catherine.

'I will be good,' she murmured. 'I will be the bride of Christ. I belong to Christ Jesus for as long as He will keep me in His almighty power.'

It was a strange experience. She rose from her knees. If any had seen her they would not have been very surprised. They knew how obsessed she had been for some time by her piety. Mengette and even Catherine had said that it was unnatural. Colin, Catherine's husband, openly laughed at her.

But there was some great meaning in life and she felt that she was on the verge of a revelation.

So she told no one of what she had heard and as a day or so passed she even began to wonder herself whether she had heard it.

She was not long left in doubt for a few days later she had another experience. She was in the fields once more when she heard the voice again. It was admonishing her to be good. And on this occasion she saw strange images ... figures bathed in light. In the midst of these was a majestic figure with wings whom she knew at once because she had seen many statues of him. He was the Archangel Michael.

'Jeannette,' he told her. 'You are the chosen one. Two saints of whom you have heard will be sent to guide you. Saint Catherine and Saint Margaret will come to you. They are appointed to guide and counsel you. Do as they say that that which God has ordained may come to pass.'

She was no longer in doubt. This was the reason for her excessive love of the church and the saints; it was the answer to those who wondered why she was apart, different from them, why she preferred to kneel and pray to the saints rather than dance in the fields and chat with the boys. She was the chosen one.

She was exalted.

'What has come over you, Jeannette?' asked her mother. 'You dream the hours away.'

She wanted to tell them; but she dared not. They would not believe her and just at first she could not endure their disbelief.

She waited every day for the voices to come, for the visions to appear. They always came and as the Archangel Michael had told her she saw the Saints Catherine and Margaret as well. They were beautiful beyond human understanding, bathed in celestial light and smelling of the sweetest perfume

more intoxicating than that of roses. They talked to her
gently, always soothing her fears. She fell on her knees before
them and swore that she would preserve her virginity even as
they had. She was one of them. She was the bride of Christ and
she would remain pure in His service.

'Have no fear, Jeannette,' they told her. 'Trust in Heaven.'

She could scarcely eat or sleep so great was her excitement.
Her mother watched her anxiously.

'I am anxious about Jeannette,' she told Jacques. 'The girl
is too pious. It is not natural. She should be with the young
folks. She will not now go to dance under the tree.'

'She will soon be of an age to marry,' said Jacques. 'She will
calm down then.'

Vaguely Jeannette heard them talking about the war.
There was a strong commander at Vaucouleurs called Robert
de Baudricourt. He was staunchly for the Dauphin and was
inspiring new hope in the neighbourhood.

Jacques shook his head. 'What can he do?' he asked. 'There
is so much ground to be recovered. We have lost so much.'

Jeannette said: 'It will not always be so. A time will
come...'

They looked at her oddly. Her eyes were shining. She spoke
like a prophet.

'What do you know of such matters, girl?' said Jacques
sharply. 'Look to your spinning.'

And she was silent—seeing that it would be impossible to
tell them.

She walked over to Greux to see Catherine. Her sister was
lying on her pallet looking very pale.

'Catherine, what ails you?' she asked. 'Do you feel pain?'

Catherine shook her head. 'It is my cough mostly, Jeannette, it weakens me. Do not tell Colin. It worries him. If I
rest like this I can be up and about when he comes in from
the fields.'

Jeannette cleaned the house and cooked a little and spun—
doing Catherine's share as well as her own.

'Thank you, sister,' said Catherine.

'I would I could do more for you, Catherine ... a strange
thing has happened to me. I have heard voices.'

'Voices?' she said. 'Whose voices?'

'Voices of angels and saints ... They speak to me,
Catherine.'

Catherine looked at her warily, a little frightened. Jeannette realized that their mother must have told her that Jeannette had been acting strangely lately.

Catherine would not understand and she did not want to frighten her. Poor Catherine had anxieties enough of her own —not that this was an anxiety, but Catherine might think it so.

'Have you been dreaming again?' asked Catherine. 'I used to when I was younger. I don't now. I'm glad. Dreams can be frightening when you are afraid the soldiers might come in the night ... and we seem always to have been afraid of that.'

No, she could not speak to Catherine.

Colin came in from the fields. He smiled to see her. He was glad she had come to give Catherine a helping hand.

'What,' he cried, 'have you taken time off from church to come and see us!'

He teased of course. No, she could tell no one in her sister's household.

Why should she want to tell? She did not know. Perhaps it was because she was going to be given some task and she would need help. I am so ignorant of life, she thought, just a simple peasant girl. Could they really have chosen me? Have I dreamed it?

There was one to whom she could whisper something. That was little Hauviette. Hauviette had always listened, always wanted to be with her since those days when a very small Hauviette had followed them about and tried to share in their games.

When Hauviette came to the cottage to spin with her, she chatted merrily all the time and did not notice Jeannette's silence. When it grew dark the young girl asked if she might stay the night as she used to. She had told her parents she would and even though she had not far to go to her home it was advisable for her not to be out after dark in case some marauding bear showed his face.

The two girls lay on Jeannette's narrow pallet and Jeannette tried to explain how angels and saints had come to her and told her she was chosen for a great task.

Hauviette listened rather drowsily, and after a while she began to murmur something unintelligible. Jeannette realized then that she was half asleep and that she had thought Jeannette was telling her a story about a saint who had the same name as herself. Hauviette did not really believe that

Jeannette, whom she had known all her life, could really be like Saint Margaret or Saint Catherine.

She would tell no one. No one would believe her in any case.

A few days later a visitor came to Domrémy. This was a member of the family for whom Jeannette had always had a special friendship. Durand Laxart was some sixteen years older than she was and had married her cousin Jeanne le Vauseul. Jeanne was the daughter of Zabillet's sister Aveline, and Durand had known Jeannette since she was a baby. He had been attracted by her because even then she had seemed apart from the other children. He used to carry her on his shoulders and walk through the fields with her, cut whistles for her out of wood and tell her the names of the birds and the trees.

Durand sat round the fire and talked of what was happening in Petit-Burey where he lived with his wife and her parents. They had suffered in the same way as Domrémy and like those of that village were haunted by the shadow of war. Durand was not so very frequent a visitor because Petit-Burey was five miles from Domrémy and although that was not so very far it did mean travelling ten miles if the visit was to be made in one day only.

He told them that Zabillet's sister Aveline was pregnant and that was a piece of news for them to discuss endlessly. When Zabillet was alone with Durand she told him that she was a little concerned about Jeannette.

'Her father is worried about her too,' said Zabillet. 'She is not like other girls of her age.'

'She never was,' said Durand.

'She spends so much time in the church in prayer. I believe she is there when she should be tending the flocks or tilling the ground. She neglects her work ... It is not that she is lazy ... and there is a strange look about her.'

Durand thought he would try to find out and when he saw Jeannette going into the church he followed her and there he found her kneeling before the statue of the Virgin. He stood waiting for her and when she came out he noticed the look of exultation on her face.

'Jeannette,' he said. 'What has happened to you?'

She looked at him and said simply: 'God has spoken to me through the Archangel Michael and His saints.'

'Tell me about it,' said Durand.

So she told him and he listened intently. He was the first who had taken her seriously.

'I am chosen,' she said. 'I have been told.'

He was thoughtful as they went back. Suddenly, as though on impulse, she said to him: 'Durand, you would help me, would you not?'

'If it were possible, with all my heart,' he assured her.

When they returned to the house it was to hear that there was a message from Colin. Catherine had become very ill and wished to see them all.

They left at once for Greux and there lying on her pallet so pale and small that she seemed almost to have wasted away, lay Catherine.

There was little they could do but mourn. Poor Colin had lost all his gaiety. He was just a bewildered boy. He stood staring at the figure on the bed as though trying to convince himself that this was the girl with whom he had danced round L'Arbre des Dames and whom he had married in the church of Saint Rémy not so long ago.

Jeannette was stricken. She forgot everything but that she had lost a beloved sister. She even forgot her voices.

She could not stay in the stricken house but wandered out into the patch of garden which was close by and as she did so the voices came to her.

The Archangel Michael appeared to her and the two saints were with him. They were looking at her with compassion and she knew that she must not grieve for earthly losses, for this day Catherine would be with her Father in heaven.

'Daughter of France,' said a voice, 'you must leave your village and make your way into France. Take your standard from the hands of the King of Heaven. Carry it with courage and God will help you.'

She was trembling. The voices were telling her she must act, and she did not know how to.

Then the Archangel Michael spoke to her.

'You shall lead the Dauphin into Rheims and there he shall be crowned,' he told her.

She covered her face with her hands for a few moments. Her heart was filled with sudden terror. This was something beyond her imaginings. She could preserve her virginity; she could die for her faith; but how could she, a country girl, go to the Dauphin?

'You must go to Captain Baudricourt in Vaucouleurs and

in time—though not at first—he will give you guides to take you to the Dauphin.'

The brightness had gone; the voices faded away and she was alone.

Had she heard aright? Go to the Dauphin? Go to Captain Baudricourt? She had heard his name and she knew that he was in charge of the garrison at Vaucouleurs. But how could she go to him?

* * *

It was a sad day when they buried Catherine. Jeannette walked with her brothers and her parents behind the coffin when they carried it into the church.

Durand Laxart was with them. He could not stop looking at Jeannette.

She looks so frail and ill, he thought. She will be the next.

When Catherine was buried Jeannette went into the fields and listened for the voices. They came again and repeated that she had been chosen by Heaven to stop the senseless war, to drive the English out of France and crown the true King at Rheims. Her first task was to go to Captain de Baudricourt and though he would not listen to her at first, she must persevere and she would succeed in the end.

How? How? Jeannette asked.

She must be good, was the answer, and it would come to pass.

When she returned to the house Durand was with her parents and her mother said to her: 'Durand thinks you should go and stay with him and Jeanne for a while. He thinks the change would do you good. Your Aunt Aveline will be feeling her condition. She is no longer young and child-bearing can be a strain at her age. It will be good to have an extra pair of hands to help in the house.'

Durand was looking at her intently. 'What say you, Jeannette?' he asked.

A great exultation came over her. She thought, Heaven has put this chance in my way.

So when Durand Laxart left Domrémy, Jeannette went with him, riding on the back of his mare, and while they journeyed across the five miles which separated Domrémy from Petit-Burey, Jeannette told him of her gratitude to him for his kindness in taking her away.

She would have to broach the subject of his taking her to Captain de Baudricourt very cautiously. Although he was sympathetic he would not perhaps go as far as that. She realized that to go to this worldly captain and tell him that she had heard voices commanding her to take the Dauphin to Rheims and there have him crowned would most certainly arouse his ridicule.

But she had taken the first faltering steps towards her goal, and she had been warned that it would be difficult. But she felt less frightened now. The steps must be slowly and cautiously taken—and Heaven would help her.

There was work to be done in the home of the Le Vauseuls where Durand and his wife Jeanne lived with Aunt Aveline and her husband. Aunt Aveline was delighted to see Jeannette, for not only was the girl a good worker but she had always been a favourite of hers.

Jeannette was prepared to help all she could and she found that there was much less to be done here than at home in Domrémy. There were also opportunities to talk to Durand, and make him aware of the enormity of this thing which had happened to her.

At first he was incredulous, but so eloquent was she and with such natural simplicity did she explain, that gradually she began to convince him and he felt the reflection of her ecstasy. She reminded him of Merlin's prophecy that the country would be ruined by a woman and delivered by one who would be a young virgin.

Could it possibly be that the one chosen for this mission was a member of their family—a humble peasant girl like Jeannette who had never even learned to read and write?

Jeannette had been right when she had believed that if anyone would help her that one would be Durand.

So Durand was at length persuaded to take her to Vaucouleurs. There had to be a reason, of course, and Jeannette and Durand put their heads together and tried to concoct one. Jeannette must see Captain de Baudricourt, implied Durand, in some connection with the protection money which was paid to Robert of Saarsbrück and as it was unseemly for a young girl to go so far alone Durand would take her there . . .

It was the month of May when Durand and Jeannette set out. Jeannette was exultant. The countryside was at its best. The fields were bright with daisies, buttercups, and little black and white lambs sported with their mothers while young girls like Jeannette herself watched over them.

On a gentle slope the little town of Vaucouleurs spread out before them. At the top of a hill was the castle, and it was to this fortress, the main defence of the town, that Durand and Jeannette made their way. The sentries were alert for there could never be any knowing when the enemy would be sighted but the countryman and the young girl with him aroused little attention. They were able to enter the castle and made their way to the Great Hall where Captain de Baudricourt was at that very time conducting the business of the garrison. Many people were passing through the great hall and not only soldiers; there were several citizens who had business to conduct and soldiers and messengers from the various parts of the country. Jeannette looked about her eagerly and she had no difficulty whatsoever in picking out Robert de Baudricourt. It seemed to her that the Voices were close and that they whispered to her: 'That is the man you are to see.'

Fearlessly Jeannette approached him.

'I am sent to you by Messire,' she said, 'that you may send to the Dauphin and tell him to hold himself ready, but not to give battle to his enemies at this time.'

She did not know why she said those words except that she was prompted to say them.

Robert de Baudricourt was staring at her. He could not believe he had heard correctly. He was very much a man of the world, a life of soldiering had made him so. He was a little sharper than most of his kind and like most he was for all the profit he could get. He was a rich man. He had married twice and on both occasions had had the good fortune or good sense to choose wealthy women, and he made sure that he profited from his battles even as his marriages; he had a quick wit and a lively humour which had carried him far. Moreover he was a good soldier and although he could only think that the chances of driving the English out of the country were poor, he was loyal to the Dauphin.

For a few moments he was speechless. He looked incredulously at the young peasant girl in her shabby red skirt and blouse, and wondered what she was talking about. She sounded mad. But she had a certain radiance about her which made him pause for a moment before shooing her away.

'Who are you?' he demanded.

'I have been chosen,' she told him. 'I am Jeannette d'Arc.'

'And what is it you say?'

'That I am a messenger from Messire who instructs that the Dauphin is to remain defensive and not yet go out to face the enemy. Assistance will come to him from Messire, and his anointing will follow.'

Baudricourt cried out: 'Messire! Messire! Who is this Messire?'

'It is the King of Heaven,' answered Jeannette simply.

Baudricourt was even more astounded. 'Who are you?' he demanded of Durand.

'I am her cousin, my lord. I have brought her to Vaucouleurs to see you.'

Baudricourt looked from one to the other and then his eyes rested on Jeannette. 'You want to go into battle, do you? You want to lead the Dauphin to Rheims?' He laughed at several of the men who were standing by watching with amazement. 'There is one useful service she could perform in the army, eh? Yes, yes, I think our men would like her well enough.'

Jeannette's face had grown pale and Baudricourt could not take his eyes from her. He softened suddenly. She was very young and very ardent, and she had conceived some mad notion. It was not to be surprised when it was considered what life was like for these country folk. They could never sleep soundly in their beds.

He turned to Durand. 'You waste my time. Take that girl home. Take her back to her father. Tell him to give her a good whipping. That's what she needs to knock some sense into her.' Some of the men were sniggering now. Baudricourt shouted: 'Don't bring her here again. If you do I'll find a place for her in the army ... one which will be better suited to her talents than leading the Dauphin to Rheims. She's a pleasant looking creature. So ... take care.'

Durand took Jeannette's hand and drew her away.

'Get her married off quickly,' shouted Baudricourt. 'That's what she needs.'

As they made their way back to Petit-Burey, Jeannette was not disconsolate. The voices had said that it would not be easy and had told her that Baudricourt would not listen the first time.

*   *   *

Jeannette now knew that there would be a waiting period, for the voices had told her that the time for action would be in the middle of Lent. But Lent had passed and her meeting with Baudricourt had come to nothing.

She was not disturbed. It had all been arranged, she told Durand. She would know when the time had come.

Aveline's child was born and she must go back to Domrémy. It was clear to her that some time had to elapse before she would be again called upon to act.

Back in Domrémy there was even greater anxiety than before. Soldiers were roaming the countryside, falling on undefended villages. From day to day no one knew if theirs would be the next.

There was great consternation throughout the village because the lease to Le Château de l'Ile had run out. Perhaps this was not after all such a calamity as none knew better than Jacques that a band of trained soldiers bent on looting, rape and murder would in a very short time storm the castle if they had a mind to.

He called together the people of the village and told them that he had a plan and if they agreed with it they had better put it into practice without delay.

He proposed to them that they get the flocks and herds together and leave Domrémy. They would take with them what they could carry and stay for a while in the town of Neufchâteau where they would be comparatively safe at least from the roving bands of soldiers who were more to be feared than the disciplined armies.

Those who agreed with him should follow him; those who did not could stay at home.

There was no man, woman nor child in Domrémy who did not want to go. Thus they set out like the Israelites of old fleeing from tyranny, and in due course arrived in the town of Neufchâteau.

As the party came into the town they were hailed by a big red-haired woman who was driving a small cart filled with flagons of wine.

'By all the saints,' she cried. 'Is it you then, Jacques d'Arc, why and Zabillet with you and Jeannette and Pierrelot! What do you in Neufchâteau? And come with the whole village and all ... Don't tell me. You're not the first. They're raiding again, are they? God curse them.'

She had descended from the cart and was embracing every member of the family.

Jacques told her it was true and that they wished to get out of Domrémy until things quietened down a bit.

'You'll find lodgings for all here,' she answered. 'We feel for you. How do any of us know when we shall need help ourselves. If it's not the wicked Godons it's the Armagnacs ...' She laughed and put her hand to her lips. Domrémy was Armagnac and Neufchâteau was part of Burgundy's inheritance. 'Oh never mind,' she went on, 'what are these things among friends? You and your family will stay at our inn until you find another place to go. Come ... You can help, all of you. There's work and enough in the inn, I can tell you.'

So Jacques and his family left the rest of the people of Domrémy who went on through the town looking for somewhere to stay and they themselves came to lodge with Jacques' old friend, Jean de Waldaires, and his loquacious wife, who was known throughout Neufchâteau as La Rousse on account of her red hair.

'How fortunate we are,' cried Jacques. 'Here we can stay awhile and we can all work in the inn. We'll be safe here and if the rioters visit Domrémy they may burn down our houses but at least we shall have saved our flocks and herds.'

It was indeed a satisfactory arrangement particularly as there was a small meadow attached to the inn where the livestock could graze. La Rousse was delighted to have them, particularly Jeannette who was such a good worker and so proficient at the spinning-wheel. She declared to Jean de Waldaires in the intimacy of their bed at night that they were a good bargain all of them—and especially Jeannette.

But it was a time of trial for the girl. Now that she had actually taken some action and confronted Robert de Baudricourt—even though it meant nothing but humiliation to her, she longed to continue. Her fear had left her. She had done what a year ago she would have believed impossible. She had faced the great Governor of Vaucouleurs and, although he had jeered at her, she had learned that she would never care if people scoffed at her; she cared only that she do well what Heaven asked of her.

She ate little; she had no desire for food. She liked to get out alone in the meadow and commune with her voices. They came to her though not as frequently as they had in the past. They had made her understand that she was destined for some mission and when the time was ripe they would tell her what to do.

She lived in a state of exultation and this so overwhelmed her that one day she mentioned to Michel le Buin, one of the labourers who worked on the land at the back of the inn, that a virgin, who was not far away from him at that moment, would lead the Dauphin into Rheims, and there see him crowned.

Michel le Buin stared at her and said: 'Are you telling me *you* are that girl?'

She did not answer. He thought she was mad and he whispered to others what she had said. They laughed together. 'Jeannette d'Arc has a touch of madness,' said some.

Others whispered: 'Is she a witch?'

No, they could not believe that of little Jeannette whom they had known for years and was religious and went to church so often. Such a churchgoer could not possibly be involved in witchcraft.

But it might be that the fairies had laid a spell on her, suggested someone; and that seemed to be the general opinion.

Jeannette d'Arc was undoubtedly strange if she fancied herself riding beside the Dauphin in a suit of armour and taking him to Rheims.

'Jeannette wants to ride with the army,' they said.

A rumour of this must have come to Jacques' ears for one night he awoke in a state of great agitation.

Zabillet rose from their pallet and asked what ailed him.

'It's a dream I have. By the holy saints, Zabillet, I could swear it was real. I saw her ... our daughter ... Jeannette ... riding away with the soldiers.'

'It was an evil dream.'

'It was so real I could believe it. I could see her so clearly. Riding with the soldiers, Zabillet ... that girl of ours ...'

'She would never go for that life, Jacques. You know full well. She is a good girl. You know we have said she spends too much time in church and neglects the flocks because of her love of the saints.'

'Zabillet,' he said sternly, 'if I thought my dream would come true I would ask you to tie a stone about her neck and throw her into the river.'

'I ... her mother to do such a thing? You are mad, Jacques.'

'If you would not do it,' he said sternly, 'I would. I would see her dead rather than disgraced and dishonoured.'

'Go to sleep and dream no more. It is a wild, impossible

dream. Our Jeannette is a good religious girl. Nothing would be farther from her mind than to go off with the soldiers to a life of sin.'

Still Jacques could not sleep and lay awake for a long time thinking of the disgrace of such a thing happening to a daughter of his.

'I wish some good young man would come along to ask us for her hand in marriage,' said Zabillet.

'Aye,' said Jacques. 'I confess I shall never feel easy until that girl is a wife.'

'I will take a candle to the church and pray for it,' Zabillet reassured him.

As though in answer to her prayer a few days later one of the young men of the village came to see Jacques to tell him that Jeannette had betrothed herself to him when they were in Domrémy and he thought it was time that they should be married.

Zabillet kissed this young man solemnly on both cheeks. He was a good worker, a pleasant boy; she knew his people well.

'We will arrange for the marriage without delay.'

When Jeannette came in from her work on the land, Zabillet went to her and put her arms about her. She looked from her mother to her father and to the young man with some amazement wondering why there was this unusual demonstration and atmosphere of solemnity.

'We are well pleased, daughter,' said Jacques. 'Our consent is given and we see no reason for delay even though we are away from home.'

'Of what do you speak, my father?' asked Jeannette, looking bewildered.

'Of your marriage, daughter. We have heard of your betrothal.'

'My betrothal!' she burst out. 'There has been no betrothal.'

'Jeannette, you know full well there has been. You promised ...'

Jeannette turned fiercely on the young man.

'You lie!' she cried.

'Silence,' cried Jacques. 'You use the language of these soldiers of whom you are so fond.'

Zabillet could see that he confused his dream with reality and she was afraid for her daughter.

The young man had turned to Jacques. 'I assure you, sir, that your daughter has promised me marriage and I shall insist on my rights.'

'And,' cried Jacques, 'I shall insist that you receive them.'

Jeannette ran out of the house. She went to the meadow and stood there with her hands folded together, staring up beseechingly at the sky.

'Have no fear, Daughter,' said the voices. 'They will try to force you, but they will not succeed.'

She felt calmer then and after a while she went back into the house.

There her father was waiting for her. He looked angry. He had always been stern but there had been a rough sort of kindness before. All that was gone now. He was looking at her as though she were ... unclean. Her mother was frightened too, she saw.

'It is time you were married,' he said firmly. 'What is wrong with this young man? He is a good worker. And he is determined to marry you in spite of the way you have behaved towards him. You *shall* marry him.'

'No, my father, I shall marry no one. I have vowed to remain a virgin for as long as Heaven shall command me to.'

'The girl's wits are addled,' said Jacques.

'Jeannette,' put in her mother, 'it is right that you should marry and this is a good offer. He will look after you. You will have children of your own ...'

Jeannette would have been very frightened, but she could feel the heavenly presence nearby assuring her that all would be well.

*   *   *

Jacques was triumphant. Her suitor, determined on marriage, swore that Jeannette had given her sacred promise to marry him, and after the custom of the day he cited her to appear before the tribunal in the town of Toul whither he had taken his case to the ecclesiastical court. This council decided all matters which concerned Domrémy and the neighbouring villages and the finding of the court would be final. If it decided that Jeannette was indeed betrothed she would have to marry, for betrothal was tantamount to taking a vow and such vows were considered sacred.

If she did not appear at the court it would be presumed

that she had given in and accepted her fate, so there was only one thing she could do, and that was go and plead her cause. She had made no promise and she would not be bludgeoned into marriage.

'Will you go to the court then?' asked Jacques.

'I will go,' she answered.

'Do you know that it is twenty-five miles from here?'

'I do know it.'

'And how will you get there?'

'I will find my way.'

'I'll not come with you ... nor shall anyone in this household.'

'I need no one. I shall go alone.'

So she prepared herself. Zabillet was very worried.

'We cannot let her go alone,' she said to Jacques. 'Think what might happen to her on the road.'

'She will not go,' retorted Jacques. 'Twenty-five miles! A girl alone! Stop fretting. She'll set out and be back in an hour or so ... and then she'll come to her senses.'

'She has a strong will.'

'She would never stand up to the court. Even if she made the journey, she would have to give way. They would be of the same opinion as we are. Marriage is the best thing for her.'

Jacques was wrong. Jeannette made the journey without mishap. She was certain she would because her voices had told her so. She faced the court; she was calm and so serenely vowed that she had made no promises, that the court regarded her objections very seriously indeed. She was sent away and told that her case should be considered.

Confidently she returned to Neufchâteau for her voices had told her that all would be well. She had not been back more than a day or so when two messengers arrived. One was to say that the young man who had lyingly declared that she had promised to marry him had been thrown from his mare and had died instantly. The other messenger came from Toul. The court had considered her case and accepted her story. It was not she who had been at fault and she was free to remain unmarried.

Jacques was subdued. Zabillet did not know what to think. And very soon after that Robert de Baudricourt had brought about a temporary truce and it was considered safe to go back to Domrémy.

THE MEETING AT CHINON

IT was a sad homecoming to Domrémy, for there was clear evidence that the soldiers had passed through. The villagers were grateful for Jacques' far-sightedness in leading the exodus to Neufchâteau. Once again he had been proved right. Even so the soldiers, no doubt enraged at finding no food to be taken, no girls to be raped, had wreaked a certain amount of damage on some of the houses. One or two of them had even been burned down.

'Let us thank God that no greater harm has been done,' said Jacques; and the entire village set to work to rebuild where necessary. Jacques' own house, by some stroke of good fortune, had been left unscathed.

Those were difficult months for Jeannette to live through; she was deeply aware of the suspicious, watchful looks which came her way. That they all thought she was strange there was no doubt; in the village they whispered about her, and Jacques continued to fear that she would go off with the soldiers and become a camp follower. Any profession less likely to suit Jeannette it would be hard to conceive but after his vivid dreams her father could not get the idea out of his mind.

Mengette, now recovering a little from the shock of her husband's death, remonstrated with her. 'Remember you are still young,' she said. 'You could marry and have children. Believe me, it is the best life.'

Pierrelot cried: 'What is the matter with you, Jeannette?

Why can't you be like other girls? People are saying you are strange.'

'Let them,' she answered. 'Let them say what they will. I have my destiny to fulfil and it is a matter for me, not for them.'

Only Hauviette felt the same towards her as she ever had. 'Whatever it is, Jeannette, that has happened to you, it is good,' she said, 'and you will do what you have to do and do it well.'

The young girl would sometimes come and sit beside her in the meadow while she watched the sheep, or bring her distaff so that they could sit and spin and only with Hauviette did Jeannette feel a certain peace.

With the coming of autumn there was a great deal of traffic on the main road and news came to Domrémy that the important town of Orléans was under siege. People talked on the green outside the church and they spoke gravely for there had been so many reverses for the French and if Orléans fell into the hands of the English it could be the beginning of the end of French resistance.

Jeannette chafed against her inadequacy. The voices had spoken to her of Orléans. She had been told before she knew there was one, that she was to raise the siege of that city and march triumphantly in to the rescue of the citizens.

Now the siege had begun and she was still in Domrémy where her father watched her with stern eyes and she knew that if she attempted to run away she would not be allowed to get very far.

What could she do? She was failing in some way. She felt foolish, helpless, unworthy of the task for which Heaven had chosen her.

It was October. How long could Orléans hold out? And what use was she, here in Domrémy?

She was sick with anxiety and she went to the fields and waited for the voices.

They came. 'Have no fear, Daughter,' she was told. 'Durand Laxart will help you again. His wife Jeanne is to have a child and when it is born he will ask that you go to look after her. Then you will go once more to Captain de Baudricourt. This time you will succeed in reaching the Dauphin.'

She was considerably comforted.

The news from Orléans was bad. The English were surrounding the town and the Duke of Burgundy was on the side of the English. That was shameful.

And here was Jeannette waiting for the call from Durand Laxart.

The English had captured the fort of Les Tourelles and the Earl of Salisbury, who was recognized to be one of the greatest soldiers in Europe, was in charge of operations.

And still there was no summons from Durand.

Then they heard that the Earl of Salisbury had been killed rather mysteriously, through a cannon ball as he looked from Les Tourelles on Orléans and it seemed that the tower from which it had come had been empty. Someone had seen a young child calmly walking away from the cannon ... but that was all and it was impossible for a child to have fired it.

It was the first of the mystic happenings.

Rumours came to Domrémy every day. English cannons had been fired into the city. One ball hit a table where a family was at a meal. It bounced off the table and none was hurt. Another fell in a square where a crowd was gathered and once again no one was hurt.

'The hand of God is in this,' said the people.

Jeannette was certain of this. She was in a fever of impatience. Then the summons came from Durand. His wife Jeanne was in labour. Jeannette must come to help them at once. So she left for Petit-Burey.

It was only five miles away and she could walk that easily, so she set out at once and her feelings as she passed through the village were a mingling of sadness and exultation.

She saw Mengette who ran out to embrace her.

'You'll soon be back,' said Mengette.

Jeannette did not answer. She knew that she would never come back.

'I'll call Hauviette,' said Mengette. 'You will want to say good-bye to her.'

'No, no,' cried Jeannette. 'Not Hauviette ...'

That she could not bear. The young girl was very dear to her; if she saw her she might weep; she might even cry out that this was their last farewell.

She must not see Hauviette.

She turned to take one last look at Domrémy before she went on to Petit-Burey.

*　　*　　*

In the garrison at Vaucouleurs there was great consternation about the possible fate of Orléans.

Robert de Baudricourt was seated at a table drinking wine with one of the commanders in the garrison and naturally the conversation was of Orléans.

'If the city falls that will be an end to French hopes,' said the commander Bertrand de Poulengy.

'Well, a big blow, I admit.'

'You know, Captain, that Orléans is the key to the Loire. It's what Paris and Rouen are to the Seine.'

'The English know that. It is why they are determined to take it.'

'And we should show an equal determination to hold it.'

Baudricourt looked at his companion and raised his shoulders.

'Our Dauphin is hardly the man to lead his country to victory.'

The two men fell silent as they went on sipping their wine.

'Strange things have been happening, Captain.'

'Oh you mean the death of Salisbury. A blessing for us. That man would have been inside Orléans in a week or two.'

'He died by that cannon ball. They say it took off half his face. He died in agony two hours later.'

'Well?'

'Is it not strange? He died from a cannon that seemed to have been fired from nowhere.'

'So they tell us.'

'And there were the English cannon balls that alighted on people and failed to harm them.'

'H'm,' murmured Baudricourt.

'You are sceptical, Captain.'

'In a way, yes. If you ask me, Do I believe that God or one of His saints fired the cannon that killed Salisbury, the answer is no. Even if you ask me if He put the idea to fire it into the head of a small child, it is still no. But if you ask me whether it is good for people to believe this was so, I will say Yes! Yes! Yes! I tell you this, Poulengy: the people of France are in desperate straits and if they can believe that a helping hand is coming from Heaven it is just possible that they will pull themselves out of the mire into which they have sunk through their own lethargy, their mad King, their scheming Queen and their internal feuds.'

'Captain, do you remember some months ago a girl came here?'

'You mean mad Jeannette. Oh, I remember her all right. A pleasant looking creature. Dark hair springing from a high forehead and the most earnest eyes I ever saw in my life. I thought she wanted to be a camp follower at first.'

'Don't speak of her in that tone, Captain, I beg of you.'

'Why? What's come over you, Poulengy?'

'I was there in the hall when she came. I heard what she said. I watched her. Do you know, I have often thought of her since.'

'Well, she's a tasty little piece, I grant you.'

'No, no. Do not speak thus. It could bring bad luck. I believed her, Captain. When she said that Messire had sent her and you asked who Messire was she answered that Messire was God. I believed her, Captain. I believe her still.'

'By all the saints, you amaze me, Poulengy.'

'There have been these strange happenings in Orléans. There is talk about the girl. They say she is going to crown the Dauphin King and drive the English out of France.'

'Was that not what she told us?'

'I believe it to be true.'

Captain de Baudricourt was silent. He poured more wine into his companion's glass and as he did so they were joined by another of the commanders. This was Jean de Novelempont, who came from Metz and was always known as Jean de Metz. Baudricourt poured him a goblet of wine.

'Thanks, that's good,' said Jean de Metz. 'You look solemn. Is the news bad?'

'As bad as it can be without complete disaster,' said Baudricourt. 'We were talking about God.'

Jean de Metz looked from one to the other in amazement and Bertrand de Poulengy said: 'We spoke of Jeannette of Arc. She came here once to see the Captain. He sent her back with orders that she should be returned to her father and soundly beaten for her temerity.'

'Poulengy believes she was indeed a messenger of God,' explained Baudricourt.

Jean de Metz looked at the Captain steadily. 'So do I,' he said.

Baudricourt leaned back as though to get a better look at them. He was silent for a moment. 'There was something about the girl,' he admitted thoughtfully.

Poulengy leaned forward. 'If she were to come again, Captain, would you listen to her? Would you treat her with respect?'

Baudricourt laughed. 'Do you know, with so many men in whose wisdom I have some confidence believing in her, perhaps I should. Yes, if she came again, I would see the wench. I would listen to her. I would do what I could to help her.'

There was silence at the table as they went on drinking their wine.

*   *   *

It was January when Jeannette with Durand set out once more for Vaucouleurs. Her cousin's baby had been safely delivered and because Durand took Jeannette very seriously, so did his wife.

As they set out from Petit-Burey Jeannette and Durand looked an insignificant pair and none would have guessed Jeannette's great mission. Her smock and thick red skirt were covered by a shepherd's cloak to shut out the bitter winds and these were the only clothes she possessed, but she was completely unconcerned about her appearance. She knew that this time she would succeed because the voices had told her she would.

Durand had arranged for them to stay for a while at the house of a wheelwright friend. Henri Royer and his wife Catherine immediately fell under Jeannette's spell. Indeed she had changed from the girl she had been on her first visit to Vaucouleurs. The radiance of her face and the shining purpose in her eyes inspired new confidence in those about her. They were beginning to believe that she had truly been endowed with special powers from Heaven.

The day after their arrival Jeannette with Durand beside her presented herself at the castle.

Baudricourt recognized her at once. 'So you have come to see me again,' he said. 'You did not take my advice and marry.'

'You must know, sir,' said Jeannette, 'that God has told me His will and that is that I must go to the gentle Dauphin who is the true and only King of France, that he may give me fighting men that I may go to Orléans and raise the siege. Then I shall take him to Rheims to be crowned.'

Baudricourt was amazed. Jeannette was so precise in her

demands, and they were quite preposterous. A girl go to the Dauphin, take men and lead them against the English outside Orléans!

How could a young girl live with rough soldiers? It was not difficult to guess what would become of her ... And if she failed they would laugh at him as a fool for believing in such nonsense. If she succeeded they would say she owed it to witchcraft. He did not think for one moment that the girl was a witch but a woman did not have to be a witch to be accused of being one.

The Court was at Chinon. What would they think of him if he sent a girl to them?

And yet on the other hand ... some people believed in miracles. He had been considerably impressed by the views of Poulengy and Jean de Metz. Those two—hardened soldiers both of them—were ready to believe that Jeannette had powers from Heaven!

And what if she had?

He listened to the girl; he talked to her; he tried to trap her, and found that it was impossible. She was simple and direct; she made no mistakes.

He had always found that in such a situation delaying tactics were the wise ones to take.

He would see Jeannette—certainly he would. She should talk to him every day. Meanwhile it might be well that Chinon would hear of her and send for her. What a happy solution that would be. No responsibility to be taken by him.

In the meantime her friendship with Catherine Royer was growing. They would sit spinning together and Catherine was greatly impressed by Jeannette's skill. She half wished that Jeannette would give up this project of hers and settle in Vaucouleurs. Catherine could foresee many a happy hour exchanging skills.

But Jeannette was getting more and more restive. It had at first seemed wonderful that Baudricourt had seen her and listened to her with respect. Now she was realizing that he was playing a game of prevarication.

One day as she went once more to talk to Baudricourt she came face to face with Jean de Metz and Bertrand de Poulengy.

'Good day to you,' said Bertrand, bowing with respect. 'So you are back with us.'

'What are you doing here in Vaucouleurs?' asked Jean de Metz.

'I have come to stop the King of France being driven from his throne and to save this country from the English. You may think my place is in my father's cottage but it is the will of my Lord that I should be here.'

'What Lord?' asked Jean de Metz.

'The Lord God,' answered Jeannette.

'I believe you,' said Bertrand de Poulengy.

'Thank you,' said Jeanette and passed on.

There was another fruitless interview with Baudricourt. She went back to the wheelwright's house in despair.

'Durand,' she said, 'I shall go by myself because I see I shall find little satisfaction from Baudricourt. Will you come with me?'

Durand hesitated. He had come so far. He had left his home and brought her to Vaucouleurs. She would never make the journey to Chinon on her own, he pointed out. She needed an escort. Did she think the Dauphin would ever receive her if she arrived footsore and weary ... a peasant girl? The project was doomed to failure. And he had been long from his family.

Then Jeannette had an idea. She remembered the two young men with whom she had spoken. She went to find them. They were together as though waiting for her.

'Will you take me to the Dauphin?' she asked.

'When do you wish to start?' asked Jean de Metz.

'Today if possible. If not, tomorrow.'

'We will take you,' said Poulengy, 'but we are under orders to Captain de Baudricourt and must first give him our resignations.'

'When will you do that?' asked Jeannette.

'Now,' said Jean de Metz. 'Go back to your lodging and prepare.'

Jeannette obeyed and the two men went at once to Baudricourt. They told him of the conversation which had taken place and of their intentions.

Baudricourt looked at them solemnly. 'You are rash, gentlemen,' he said.

'I swear this girl is a saint,' retorted Poulengy.

'I feel sure she is a good girl,' said Baudricourt. 'She has the outward guise of a good girl. But these guises could come from the devil. There is none who more than I would wish to see the siege of Orléans raised, the Dauphin crowned and the English driven back where they belong. But how do you know, gentlemen? How can you be sure?'

'I would stake my life on her honesty,' said Jean de Metz.

'You are over ready to stake your life, my good fellow. Make sure. Get the Curé to make a test before you commit yourself. Then take her. There will be no harm done and it may be that the Dauphin will consent to see her.'

In due course Baudricourt persuaded them that at least Jeannette should be put to the test and consequently the Curé visited the Royer household and in the room which Jeannette occupied confronted her in all the vestments of his office, holding the cross before him. He commanded her to come forward if she were indeed virtuous. This Jeannette did and convinced them that she had no traffic with the Devil as she was able to approach the priest and take the cross in her hands and kiss it.

While she was waiting to leave, a summons came from the Duke of Lorraine in Nancy. She was overjoyed. Her fame had travelled before her and now the Duke of Lorraine himself had sent an escort to bring her to him.

She set out at once and was full of hope when she reached the ducal castle in Nancy and was told that the Duke was all impatience to see her. She was taken immediately to his apartments. She had never been in such sumptuously decorated rooms. Indeed she had never imagined there could be such grandeur in the world. The Duke was a very important man and could take her immediately to the Dauphin.

She was led into an apartment hung with rich velvets and there seated on an ornate chair was the shrivelled figure of the Duke. He was wrapped in a cloak of purple velvet and seated on a stool; at his feet was a woman, the immodesty of whose attire shocked Jeannette so utterly that she was for a moment speechless.

'You are the maid who is known as Jeannette d'Arc?' said the Duke. His voice was the softest and most melodious Jeannette had ever heard but her spirits were drooping lower at every moment. This man—Duke though he might be—did not have the air of one who would lead a crusade.

'You have magical powers, I hear,' went on the Duke. 'News of you has travelled here to Nancy.'

Jeannette had found her voice. 'My Lord Duke,' she cried, 'I have no powers save those given me by Heaven. I am sent with a purpose and that is to take the Dauphin to Rheims and there have him crowned.'

The Duke did not seem to be listening.

'I am no longer young,' he said. 'Ah, how I miss my youth.'

'My lord,' said Jeannette, 'I see that you would be unable to lead me to Chinon. But you have a son-in-law, I know, René of Anjou, the great Duke of Bar.'

The Duke looked testy. 'What is the wench talking about?' he asked.

The woman on the stool was laughing, and Jeannette said: 'My Lady Duchess ...'

'The Duchess has gone,' she said. 'He could not endure her pious ways. I'm Duchess here now. He's getting old, you see. That's why he has sent for you. He wants to be able to frolic like he used to. You understand?'

Jeannette recoiled in horror. She thought of the weary journey to Nancy and she knew it had been in vain.

'My good girl, I reckon you've got the wrong idea of my lord's desire,' went on the woman. 'All he wants is to be young again. He was sure you could do it. He thought you were some sort of fortune teller ... someone with special powers.' She stood up, then bent over and put her lips to the Duke's ear.

'She can do nothing. She just wants to go to the Dauphin.'

'She's mad,' said the Duke. 'She's come here under false pretences.'

'The pretences were on your part,' said Jeannette. 'My time has been wasted. Now I need an escort back to Vaucouleurs without delay.'

'Get you gone and don't bother me,' said the Duke. 'You come here pretending you could make me young again ...'

'I did nothing of the sort,' said Jeannette. 'It is you who have wasted my time and God's.'

'Get out of my sight,' muttered the Duke.

The woman whispered something to him which sounded as though she were warning him.

Weary and bitterly disillusioned, blaming herself for her simplicity in being so easily duped, Jeannette emerged from the castle to find a groom waiting for her with a black horse. The Duke was giving it to her to ease her journey and there was a purse containing four francs to help defray the cost of it.

Jeannette was about to refuse when one of the escort

pointed out that the horse was a good one and she could ride that more comfortably than the one she had had before. Moreover the money might be useful to expedite their journey back to Vaucouleurs.

She rode back dismally wondering how many more trials she would have to overcome before she reached her goal.

As soon as she arrived in Vaucouleurs she went to see Robert de Baudricourt.

She was vehement in her denounciation of him.

'You see how you have wasted my time. Because of you we have suffered another setback inside the walls of Orléans.'

'What setback is this?' he demanded, and she could not tell him.

Back at the wheelwright's house Catherine Royer received her with great affection. She was greatly relieved to see her back safely.

'Jeannette,' she cried when she had assured herself that her friend was well, 'I have news for you. Your parents have been here. They were deeply distressed.'

Jeannette's eyes clouded with grief. 'They will not understand,' she said. 'This is the hardest part for me to bear.'

'They had heard that you had left Petit-Burey. They came here to find you. Your father was in a state of great despair. He seemed to think that you wanted to follow the army. I think your mother did understand in the end.'

'What happened? Where are they now?'

'They went back to Domrémy. I told them that I believed you were carrying out a mission from Heaven and that Durand believed it too. I said you were the purest girl I had ever known and your father the most mistaken of men.'

Jeannette laid her hands on Catherine's shoulders and looking at her earnestly said: 'They love me so dearly. That is what this means, Catherine. If they loved me less it would be easier for them.'

'Your mother believes now that you are the chosen of God. I am sure of it. She tried to soothe your father. I think she made him see that you were no longer able to resist this call and that was why they decided to return.'

'Oh, Catherine, how I wish I did not have to cause them pain. I must send word to them. But how? Oh, Catherine, why did I not learn to write and read? Perhaps if I had begged them to let me go to school they would have allowed it.

You see, I never wanted to. It was almost as though I wanted only to allow myself to remain ignorant. And now ... and now ...'

'There is the letter writer. He will write what you wish to say and it can be sent to your parents.'

'Oh, Catherine, that is what I must do. And now ... now ... I feel a sense of urgency. Terrible things are happening in Orléans. I should be there ... the Dauphin beside me, I know it, Catherine.'

'Let us go at once to the letter writer. When that is off your mind you can make your plans.'

So they went to the letter writer.

What could she say to them? How could she make them understand? Who would believe in those voices which were so real to her? How could she explain to her father—that most upright of men, but one who had never been guilty of flights of fancy? The nearest he had come to such a state was to believe in a dream of her following the soldiers to battle.

'God has entrusted me with a mission. He has chosen me, dear father and mother, perhaps because I am a simple maid. It is easier for those who are simple to believe without question. I have seen choirs of angels. I have seen the Archangel himself. I have seen the saints. They are guiding me and even though it has meant causing you pain I must go on. Great men are beginning to agree with me. Captain de Baudricourt believes me; he will give me an escort to Chinon where I shall see the Dauphin. Other men of importance are with me. My dear parents, I beg you pardon me for the grief I have caused you and give me your blessing for it is something I ardently desire.'

She felt happier when that was sent to Domrémy and then she presented herself once more to Baudricourt.

He was clearly shaken. He said at once: 'You told me that our army was facing another disaster. I have news of it. They are calling it the Battle of the Herrings. We had the greatest possible chance of diverting stores which the English badly needed. If we could have captured this convoy it would have been the end of the siege of Orléans. But once again a handful of Godons beat a far greater number of our best troops. There's a curse on us it would seem. They have the Devil with them, these Godons.'

'Never fear, my lord Captain. Soon we shall have God with

us. But for the sake of His name, delay no longer. Give me my escort and let me leave for Chinon.'

He caught her arm suddenly. He was genuinely disturbed. To his amazement he found he had grown fond of her.

'Jeannette,' he said, 'do you realize the dangers you will face travelling with rough soldiers?'

'I am not afraid.'

He said: 'You can trust Poulengy and Jean de Metz.'

'I know this,' she told him.

'But no one else,' he added.

She nodded.

They made their plans. It was better, said Poulengy, if they travel as merchants. They should not be in a large party of soldiers. There would be simply Poulengy and his servant, Jean de Metz and his; and with them would travel an archer named Richard and Colet de Vienne, who had come from Chinon at the request of Baudricourt, who wished to get some sort of permission from the Dauphin's court before he allowed Jeannette to go to him.

It was Jean de Metz who pointed out that Jeannette could not travel dressed as she was. Somehow they had to convert the young maid into a boy.

'The first thing,' said Jean, 'is her hair. That must immediately be sacrificed.'

Jeannette said willingly would she let it go, and in a short time her appearance was transformed. The thick dark hair lay at her feet and what was left looked like an upturned black basin on her head.

'If you go into battle,' said Jean, 'you will now be able to wear the *salade* helmet and the high gorget.'

He found some clothes which had belonged to one of his servants. It was not easy to fit her for she was by no means tall, being just under five feet with the sturdy figure of a peasant. She wore a shirt, short trunks and long dark hose which could be fixed to her doublet. Over this she wore a cloak reaching to her knee. She wore long leather boots and looked like a young man, comfortably off but not wealthy.

'She will need a sword,' said Poulengy.

It was Baudricourt who gave her one and she knew that his blessing went with it. He hoped she would succeed. She understood him well. He wanted to help her, provided he did not jeopardize his future by doing so. Thus, she thought, it is with ambitious men.

On his advice they set out at dawn and he had sent a message on to the Abbey of Saint Urbain to tell the Abbot to
expect them. Oh yes, undoubtedly they had the goodwill of
Baudricourt.

So, riding between Poulengy and Jean de Metz, Jeannette
rode out of Vaucouleurs on her way to see the Dauphin at
Chinon.

*   *   *

Colet de Vienne and the archer Richard rode at the back of
the little cavalcade.

They whispered together.

'Have you any doubt?' asket Colet de Vienne. 'She is a
witch. How else could a simple peasant girl have come so far?
It's as clear as fields in the sunshine.'

'It is clear,' agreed Richard.

'Shall we be laughed to scorn for taking a witch to Chinon?
And I tell you this: when she is known for a witch ... for how
would she stand the tests ... shall we be accused with her as
accomplices?'

'Nay, we should take care.'

'Poulengy and Jean de Metz guard her day and night.'

'They sleep.'

'With her between them.'

'Maybe they share her favours.'

'And why shouldn't we?'

'I have a plan. Let us try the witch first. She's young enough
to make it pleasant. And if she's a virgin so much the better.'

'She's no virgin. Witches must all consort with the Devil
before they become his own.'

'Well, then, why shouldn't we share in the fun? We'll take
her one dark night ... creep up when her guards are sleeping.
Smother her so that they don't hear her cries.'

'And afterwards?'

'We'll strangle her and throw her in a ditch.'

'Perhaps get her accused of witchcraft. They burn them
alive for that.'

'And there'll be glory for us for having discovered her true
nature.'

'A reward, do you think?'

'They say they are talking of her in Orléans. She is one of
their new miracles.'

'I say she comes from the Devil. Tonight, then. When they're sleeping.'

'Tonight,' agreed Richard.

*   *   *

There was just a crescent moon in the sky and a peppering of stars to go with it. There was danger in the air. Jeannette felt it.

'Have no fear,' said the voices. 'Trust in God. You are on your way.'

She lay there on the ground. On either side of her were the two she trusted, Poulengy and Jean de Metz. Not once had they attempted to touch her. If any man glanced her way their hands went to their swords.

God has chosen them as surely as He has chosen me, she thought.

For some reason, tired as she was, she found it difficult to sleep that night. She lay there thinking of Domrémy and her father and mother, of her brothers and dead Catherine and herself. She was only a simple country maid. Why had this task been laid on her? I must do it, she said. I will do it.

The crackle of undergrowth. The sound of a stone's being displaced, a light footfall.

'Have no fear,' said the voices.

Poulengy and Jean de Metz lay in deep sleep. It had been an exhausting day. She wondered why she did not sleep.

Someone was behind her, looking down at her. She looked up.

It was Richard the Archer.

He stood still staring at her. Then Colet de Vienne was beside him.

She just looked at them.

It was Colet de Vienne who spoke.

'I thought I heard you call for help,' he stammered.

She shook her head.

'Then all is well?'

She nodded.

They slunk away.

They looked at each other in the faint moonlight.

'What happened?' said Richard. 'It went not as we planned.'

'Did you ... know ... ?' asked Colet de Vienne. 'Did it come to you as it did to me?'

Richard nodded. 'She is pure,' he said. 'Indeed she comes from God.'

'I knew it too. We have been saved from eternal damnation.'

'From henceforth I believe in her,' said Richard. 'I shall guard her with my life.'

Jeannette felt a sudden peace steal over her. In a few moments, she was fast asleep.

*   *   *

They were in sight of Chinon. Jeannette's eyes were shining as she looked at the embattled walls, the ramparts, the barbicans and turrets of what was known to be the finest castle in France. And now it was of special importance because the true King of France was there—though Jeannette always thought of him as the Dauphin, and would do so until that glorious day when he was crowned at Rheims.

They rode into the town.

'You are to be lodged at an inn at the foot of the castle until the Dauphin gives you permission to come to him,' Colet de Vienne told her.

She was content. She could wait a few more hours. She had come farther than she would have deemed possible a year ago. Moreover she wanted to give thanks to the Holy Virgin and the saints for aiding her in her mission.

So between prayer and resting and preparing herself for her ordeal Jeannette passed the time while waiting for the summons to the castle.

Chafing against delay she lived through the waiting hours until men came from the Dauphin to question her.

'Have I not been questioned enough?' she demanded. 'Has not the Dauphin himself promised to see me?'

'Why do you come here?' they asked. 'What is your mission?'

'I have told you many times. I am sent from Heaven to raise the siege of Orléans and take the Dauphin to Rheims to be crowned King of France.'

They went away. She would hear soon, they told her.

And finally the command came. She was to present herself to the Dauphin.

With exultation she prepared herself. She had succeeded so far. It was as her voices had told her it would be. The impossible had been achieved and this was just the beginning.

She left the inn and rode to the castle. The guards eyed her with interest.

As she passed one shouted: 'Here comes the Maid! So this is the Virgin girl. Give me a night with her and she'd be no longer so.'

Jeannette turned to look at him. 'You are bold,' she said, 'to offend God ... you who are soon to die.'

She passed on and the man stood looking after her, trembling.

She heard later that a few hours afterwards he was so overcome by remorse that he had drowned himself.

People discussed the matter throughout the town. Every such incident helped to enhance her reputation. If she found it difficult to convince those in high places, it was not so with the ordinary people. The belief was fast growing that Jeannette d'Arc had been chosen by God to save France.

And so she made her way into the castle.

*　　　*　　　*

The Dauphin sat in the crowded hall surrounded by his courtiers and advisers. He had been so long undecided as to whether he would see this peasant girl. In fact his whole life had been one of indecision. Charles was unsure whether he would live through one day to the next; he was unsure of those about him; he lived in fear of what awful fate might overtake him; but what he was most unsure of was whether he was his father's son. He had been so ever since his mother —surely the most wicked Queen France had ever known— had told him that he was a bastard.

His life had been haunted by that fear. Had he no right to the throne of France? The King had been mad, passing clouded years of his life in the Hôtel de St Pol. The fertile Queen had taken a succession of lovers. How could any of her children be sure who their father was? Moreover, she seemed to hate her children—not all the time, for when she had seen a chance of marrying Katherine to the King of England she had seemed positively to love the girl. When the Dauphin's two elder brothers had died mysteriously it was thought that the Queen wanted the crown for her youngest son. But she turned against him, and had taunted him with the doubt which had haunted him ever since. Was he the true heir to the throne or was he the result of one of his mother's encounters with her numerous lovers?

Perhaps that had been at the very root of his lethargy.

He was now twenty-six years old and looked nearly fifty, for he had lived a life of excess; he had taken after his mother in that respect, but while she had kept her outstanding beauty he, who had never had any pretensions to good looks, had grown steadily more ill favoured.

He had begun life as an unattractive child. His face had been puffy from birth; his nose was long and wide—bulbous and purple, it seemed to hang over his flabby lips. His small eyes were almost hidden in folds of flesh. He had found great consolation in the arms of serving girls who while they did not find him personally attractive were bemused by his royalty. His legs were bowed which gave rise to a shuffling manner of walking. He was by no means a figure to inspire confidence.

And he lived in fear. There were times when he fervently wished he had been a nobleman with no responsibilities except those concerned with his estates. He loathed conflict of any kind; and he could not bear the sight of blood. He considered himself unfortunate to have been born at this time when France was engaged not only in this bitter struggle with the English but internal strife. He lived in terror not only of the Duke of Bedford but the Duke of Burgundy who was his own special enemy, for Burgundy held him guilty of the murder of his father.

Fear dominated the Dauphin's life. When he was staying at the castle of La Rochelle the ceiling had collapsed and only by a miracle was his life saved. From henceforth he had lived in fear of collapsing ceilings. He refused to live in large rooms. He wanted to feel that if a ceiling came down it would only be a small one.

He was subtle in a way; he was wily and shrewd, but he was overshadowed by his environment. Vaguely he longed to break away from the past; he longed to be declared the legitimate son of the King of France and in a way he dreaded it. His childhood had been flawed by a mad father and a wanton mother, and memories of a life of hardship endured with his brothers and sister in the Hôtel de St Pol lingered on. The fearful uncertainty of not knowing from one day to the next

what would happen to him had left him nervous and apprehensive. He was like a man in prison waiting to be released
that he might prove himself.

At this time his life was governed by doubt. Was he the
legitimate heir to France? Did he want to be? Did he want
to fight to free his country from the English yoke?

He was unsure.

And now they were bringing this girl to see him. Did he
want to see her? At one moment he cried, No. Then he remembered that the people were talking of her wherever she
went. They said she was indeed sent from God. They were
beginning to believe she would work miracles. Hardened
soldiers were moved by her.

He would see her. No, he wouldn't. Why should he waste
time with a peasant girl? It was preposterous. And yet ...

'People talk of Merlin's prophecy, my lord,' said Colet de
Vienne, that man who had gone forth as a cynic and returned
converted. 'They say that a maid would save France.'

It was true. He had heard the prophecy.

'My lord, she has travelled here from Vaucouleurs. The
country is overrun with rough soldiers. There are robbers
everywhere. It was a hard and perilous journey but she, a
simple girl, has come here.'

The Dauphin said he would see her.

'Let us hasten,' cried Colet de Vienne, 'before he changes
his mind.'

It was an impressive scene in the great hall which was
lighted by fifty flaring torches. Jeannette entered modestly
and yet clearly unafraid.

She looked about the hall and went straight to the Dauphin.
She had been told by Colet de Vienne what she must do, and
that was kneel before him and embrace his knees.

'God preserve you, sweet Prince,' she said.

The Dauphin tried to confuse her. He was a little shaken
that she had come straight to him. How had she picked him
out from this crowd assembled here? He thought wryly that
many of them looked more kingly than he did.

He pointed to one of his courtiers.

'There is the King,' he said. 'I am not he.'

She smiled and continued to look at him—impelled to do
so, she thought afterwards.

'Nay,' she said, 'it is you who are the Dauphin.'

He was nonplussed but still unconvinced. Could she have

seen him somewhere? It was hardly likely, but she might have heard a description of him. Heaven knew he was ugly enough to be picked out.

'Who are you who comes thus to my Court?' he asked.

'Gentle Dauphin,' she answered, 'I am a simple peasant girl and people call me Jeanne the Maid. God has sent me to bring you to your Kingdom. He sent a message and I am his messenger. You are to be anointed and crowned at Rheims and shall be His servant to rule France under Him.'

'You speak strange words,' said the Dauphin.

'I come from God,' she answered simply.

In spite of his disbelief he wanted to talk to her.

'Come,' he said, 'sit beside me. I will talk with you.'

Someone brought a stool and she sat close to him. He waved his courtiers to stand back.

She said quietly: 'My Lord bids me tell you that you are indeed the true heir of France and the son of a King. You should be troubled no more on this matter.'

He stared at her incredulously. How could this simple girl know of that matter which for so long had been uppermost in his mind?

He felt transformed. He believed her now. She came from God. She had been endowed with special powers; and he was indeed the son of a King.

She spoke to him then of the need to save Orléans. They must raise the seige. She must have men and arms. He must give them to her and with God's help she would lead the French to victory. In Orléans they already knew of her. They were waiting for her, expecting her to bring deliverance.

He listened entranced.

Earnestly she talked to him. He was astonished that a simple country girl should know so much.

Jeanne glowed with triumph. She was ready now to take the road to Orléans ... and Rheims.

VICTORY AT ORLÉANS

IT was some weeks later, at the end of April, when Jeannette seated on a white horse given her by the Dauphin, and clad in armour entered the city of Orléans after dark through the Burgundian Gate. On her right rode the Bastard of Orléans and before her was a standard-bearer carrying her banner on which were depicted two angels holding the fleur-de-lis. Behind her rode captains and men-at-arms, those whom the Dauphin had sent to accompany her.

The people were waiting for her. She was their saviour. Gone was their despondency. It was not so long since, after the Battle of the Herrings, they had believed themselves to be lost. They had even offered to surrender to the Duke of Burgundy. Now they rejoiced. It was God's will that they should hold out; and He had sent this messenger to save them.

Several had fought for the honour of lodging her and this had fallen to the lot of Jacques Boucher, the trusted treasurer to the Duke of Orléans. He was wealthy and had married a wife as rich as himself and had given a great deal in money and goods to preserve the city against the invaders so to him fell the honour of being host to the Maid.

It was the custom in such houses for the guest to sleep with the host, so Jeanne shared a room with Madame Boucher and her little daughter Charlotte, actually sleeping with the child in her bed.

The little girl was overcome with wonder at the prospect of sleeping beside one who was a kind of angel. Jeannette did not look in the least like an angel. In fact the child had never seen anyone like her before. She might have been a boy and yet she was not, and she had come from Heaven. That meant that Charlotte had to be extra good and remember all that she had been told. She must not lie in the middle of the bed but keep to the edge; she must lie still and not fidget and above all she must keep her mouth shut and not snore.

Jeannette was reassuring. She whispered to Charlotte that all was well for she was so tired and would not notice if she fidgeted just a little.

After a night's sleep Jeannette was ready for action.

First she would call upon the English to make peace. She wanted to write to them and once again she reproached herself for never having made any attempt to learn to read and write. There was no alternative but to get someone to write for her and the written words would be those dictated by her voices.

'King of England,' she dictated, 'and Duke of Bedford who call yourself Regent of France, Earl of Suffolk, My Lords Scales and Talbot who call yourselves lieutenants to the said Duke of Bedford, I call on you to yield. Give up to the Maid the keys of those towns which you have taken by force. The Maid comes from God to make peace if you will render proper account. If you do not, I shall be a great war chief and I shall make your people leave France. If they will obey the wishes of God, mercy will be shown them. I who have come from Heaven to thrust you out of France, promise you that if you do not leave there will be such tumult in France as has not been seen in a thousand years.

'Duke of Bedford, self-called Regent of France, the Maid sent by God does beg you not to bring destruction on yourself and your army. But if you turn from justice, she will defend the French, and the finest deed that was ever done in Christendom shall be done.

'Writ on Tuesday in the Great Week.

'Listen to the news from God and the Maid.'

The letter was delivered to the English camp. As was expected there was no reply.

'Now,' cried Jeannette, 'we must prepare to do battle.'

There was an immediate consultation and differing opinions as to when the attack should start and what form it should take. Dunois, the Bastard of Orléans, was in command of Orléans. A great soldier—one of the finest in France—he was completely loyal to the crown. He was good-looking, wise, brave—in fact a model of a man; and of course was royal being the illegitimate son of Louis of Orléans, he who had been the lover of the wicked Isabeau and murdered by the Duke of Burgundy when coming from her apartment. His mother had been one of Orléans' most favourite mistresses, Marriette d'Enghien, Madame de Cany-Dunois. On the murder of the Duke, the Duchess of Orléans had been so impressed by the Bastard, who was only eight at the time, when he had offered to avenge his father, that she had insisted he be brought up with her children and accorded those privileges which would have been his if his parents had been married. Always he had been known as the Bastard of Orléans but his royalty was never in doubt.

This was the commander with whom Jeannette was brought face to face; she must consult with the Gascon soldier Etienne Vignolle known as La Hire whose reputation for fierce ruthless warfare Jeannette had heard of when she was a girl. There was also the handsome young Gilles de Rais, a good soldier but one who loved finery and ostentation to such an extent that he travelled in much state with trunks of glorious garments. Among other captains and commanders was the Sire de Gamaches, an impulsive young man whom she sensed from the first was none too pleased to find an uneducated girl sharing their conferences.

Jeannette was impatient. So much time had been wasted. Her mission could so easily have failed. The people of Orléans had not so long ago been ready to surrender to the Duke of Burgundy. What if they had? Everything would have failed. The Duke of Burgundy was no less the enemy of France than the English. It was divine intervention which had caused the Duke of Bedford—usually so astute—to refuse to allow that surrender. He had said he would not beat the bushes to let someone else get the birds. That matter of the birds was one which would be regretted by the English for a very long time.

But there must be no more wasted time. They must go into action.

La Hire agreed with her. He was rash and he had scored most of his successes through taking quick action.

'The people are in a mood of exultation,' he said. 'They believe in the Maid. They will fight as never before.'

The Sire de Gamaches pointed out that it would be folly to attempt to attack without the backing of the force which had been promised from the troops at Blois.

'We should not wait,' said Jeannette. 'We have waited long enough.'

Dunois considered both sides. There was much to be said for either.

De Gamaches seeing his hesitation lost his temper. 'I see,' he said, 'that more attention is given to a wench of low degree than to a warrior knight. I will bandy no more words. I will give up my banner and fight as a poor esquire. I will not lead men in an action which I feel to be folly.'

He handed his banner to Dunois who wisely refused to take it.

'Listen,' he said with patience, 'this is not the time for quarrelling amongst ourselves. It is true that the people are in a mood of euphoria. They think that the Maid will work miracles. We have to fight for victory and we must make no more mistakes. It is true that much time has been wasted. It is also true that we need the help of the troops from Blois. Take back your banner, my lord. I myself will leave at once for Blois. I will return with the troops. Then we shall start our action.'

It was agreed that this was the wisest plan and chafing with impatience Jeannette consoled herself that in the Bastard of Orléans they had an inspired leader.

It was proved how right he was for when he reached Blois it was to find that those who deplored Jeannette's spectacular rise to importance were determined to destroy her—even if it meant the loss of the city of Orléans to the English.

Her chief enemy was Regnault de Chartres, Bishop of Rheims, who had resented the effect she had had on the Dauphin and wanted to prove himself right. A most ill-favoured man—with rough hair and beard and a mouthful of bad teeth—he hated her fresh youth. And when Dunois arrived at Blois he was just in time to change the decision to ignore the call for troops to come to Orléans.

There was consternation among the English outside Orléans. They talked constantly about Joan the Maid. They had anglicized her name and although some tried to mock her they did so with apprehension. There had been a change in the attitude of the French since her arrival. She was bold and it was clearly a strange thing that a young girl should arise in such a manner and force herself into the presence of the Dauphin, as she apparently had done.

It was all very well to call her a strumpet. She was scarcely

that. It was said that she insisted on all recognizing her virginity, and that though she had passed her nights in the
company of rough soldiers, none dared attack her. She said she
was sent by God.

It smacked of witchcraft, said the English.

But the fact remained whether God or the Devil it was
beyond the understanding of natural men and either of those
two would be an extremely uncomfortable adversary.

The English watched the arrival of the troops from Blois
and wondered what the future held. They would be glad to
see an end to this siege. It had gone on too long and they had
endured too many hardships. They were waiting for the day
when they should enter the city and enjoy those rewards of
conquest which were the very reason why so many were engaged in the profession of war.

*   *   *

So they were ready. Jeannette was exultant. She had no
doubt of the issue. Her voices were urging her on. Now she
was going to carry out the first part of her mission and free
Orléans.

Many were going to die. She was sorry for them. And many
would go unshriven as was the case in war. If she could only
convince the English that they must give up Orléans, that it
was the Divine Will that it should be given up, much bloodshed could be avoided.

She mounted the bastion which directly faced that of Les
Tourelles, the chief stronghold in the hands of the English.

She called for Sir William Glasdale whom she knew to be
the captain in charge.

'I call you to give up,' she cried. 'I have the command of
God and His saints, and I tell you that your place is not here.
Go away that your lives may be saved.'

Sir William Glasdale laughed at her. 'Go back to your
fields, cow girl,' he shouted. 'It is where you belong. Meddle
not in matters beyond your understanding.'

'You speak bold words,' retorted Jeannette. 'But consider
well. You shall soon depart. You should repent with haste.
Many of your people will be slain but you will not be there
to see it.'

Glasdale descended from the tower.

He was a little shaken. There was something about the girl,

he decided. She unnerved him. What was it? An innocence? Should he, a hardened soldier, be afraid of innocence?

She is a witch, he told himself.

But in his heart he did not really believe that. There was a radiance about her, a brightness. It was as though a prophet spoke through her.

He was very uneasy. It was no way for a commander to go into battle.

*   *   *

The battle had raged for several days. The Orléannese were certain of victory because God was on their side; Jeannette had said so and they believed Jeannette. It was no easy fight. The English had become accustomed to victory since Agincourt and they really believed that one English man was worth half a dozen French. But the French had found a new inspiration. They had the Maid, and the Maid came from God.

She was in the thick of the battle—a small figure but easily distinguishable because of her size, the litheness of her movements and the words of encouragement she constantly offered.

When she was wounded in the foot, there was consternation. How was it that God and His saints could forget their own? She felt a tremor of uneasiness—not for herself but for the effect this would have on those about her.

It was nothing, she told them. She felt it not at all.

Les Tourelles must be stormed and taken, she knew that. If that could fall into French hands not only would the English have lost their most important bastion but the effect on both sides would be tremendous.

But the English would not give in easily. They had heard that Joan of Arc had been wounded. That was good news. She was just a milkmaid, a cow girl after all. For some reason she had wormed her way to the fore and the French were using her as a symbol. God's messenger indeed! If God wanted to help the French why didn't He strike all the English dead? Not very difficult for God, surely. Why go to all the trouble of bringing forward a peasant girl?

The battle was now beginning to sway in favour of the English.

'We must take Les Tourelles,' cried Jeannette desperately.

There were some French who wanted to call off the battle.

'No, no,' cried Jeannette. 'You have done that too often. This time we are going on until we win. We are going to take Les Tourelles.'

She took a scaling ladder and had started to climb when an arrow struck her between the neck and shoulder and she fell.

There was a shout from the English.

'The Maid is down. The Maid is dead. So much for God's messenger!'

Someone was bending over Jeannette. It was the Sire de Gamaches who had so resented her at the counsel of war.

'Take my horse,' he said. 'Get into safety. I have wronged you. Forgive me. I admire you. Bear me no malice.'

'Thank you,' said Jeannette. 'I bear you no malice. I never saw a more accomplished knight.'

The Sire de Gamaches called one of his men. 'Take her to safety,' he ordered.

She was put on a horse and taken within the city walls. She was half fainting as they removed her armour. They shook their heads when they saw the ugly wound, with the arrow still protruding.

One of the men knelt by her. 'Save yourself,' he said. 'You have powers. You can cure it with words.'

'I know no such words,' she answered. 'If I am to die then die I must.'

'The English are saying you are dead. Our men are losing hope.'

'Then,' she replied, 'I must show them.' She seized the arrow in both hands and with a mighty effort pulled it out. For a moment she lost consciousness but only for a moment.

Dunois had heard what had happened. He came hurrying to her.

'Jeannette,' he said. 'Oh little Maid, is this the end then?'
She opened her eyes.

'How goes the fight?' she asked.

'They saw you fall,' he said. 'They jeer. "So much for God's help" they say. I think we cannot hold out much longer. We must retreat behind the walls.'

'No ... no ...' she cried.

He was looking at the ugly wound in her shoulder. Someone was applying oil and lard, the known remedy in such cases.

As the wound was padded the faintness was passing.

'Help me into my armour,' she said. 'I am going out there.

We are going to be inside Les Tourelles before nightfall.'

So they brought her armour and she rode out once more.

When the French saw her they sent up a cry of joy. This was a miracle. She had fallen seemingly fatally wounded and now here she was as though nothing had happened.

The English saw her too. They could not believe it. She must have risen from the dead. Truly she had Divine powers. God was against them ... God or the Devil ... and in either case what chance had they?

It was the turning point of the battle. Sir William Glasdale saw at once that they would have to abandon Les Tourelles. He called for the retreat. While he was passing over the drawbridge a shot from the walls of the city broke down the bridge. Wounded Glasdale fell into the water and drowned with several of his men.

The French stormed into Les Tourelles where they discovered food and ammunition. The English had fled clear of the city and the French took possession of the rest of the bastilles which were equally well provided with the provisions they so sorely needed.

The English were in retreat, and the siege of Orléans was over.

TRIUMPH AT RHEIMS

SHE had accomplished the first part of her mission. Orléans was free. Now she must bring about the second: the crowning of the Dauphin who should be Charles the Seventh of France.

Messengers had been sent with all speed to Chinon and Jeannette was preparing to leave Orléans immediately with most of the army. There was no time to spend rejoicing in Orléans. The Orléannese would do that. She must meet the Dauphin at Blois and they would go on from there to Rheims.

She had expected him to have arrived already, all jubilation, all eagerness to take his rightful place in his country. It was disappointing to wait two days at Blois and still find he had not come.

In due course a message came that he was about to set out for Tours and Jeannette immediately left Blois for that city.

She met the Dauphin just outside Tours. Their horses drew up almost touching and Jeannette removed her bonnet and bowed low. The Dauphin took her hand and kissed it. It was a deeply moving moment.

She thought he looked transfigured and she did not see him as the debauched young-old man. To her he was the King and all kings had an aura of sanctity to folks in Domrémy; and this one was the chosen of the Lord. She had been singularly blessed, selected for her simplicity and given this task by Almighty God.

The Dauphin was moved. She had saved the city of Orléans —this young peasant maid. She had magical powers, it was certain. She had assured him of his legitimacy; then gone on to save the all important city for the French. Why should a girl do this? He should have ridden at the head of his troops instead of skulking in Chinon. If he had been a great warrior like some of his ancestors this domination by the English would never have taken place.

What could he say to the saviour of Orléans? He could welcome her; he could kiss her hand; he could treat her with respect—but he could not repress the twinge of resentment for he was envious because she had done it, when that duty was his.

Together they rode into Tours. What rejoicing was there in the streets, but even while Jeannette revelled in success it was as though an icy hand clutched at her heart. This was how it must have been on that Sunday long ago when the people waved their palm leaves and welcomed one other, crying Hosanna.

They rested at Tours. Jeannette was all impatience to be gone but the Dauphin was uncertain. This was pleasant ... here in Tours. The people were for him. They liked to see him riding with the Maid. It reminded them that God was on their side and God, they said, was invincible.

But how Jeannette chafed against delay and how the Dauphin revelled in it! It was so pleasant at the moment, he thought. Why not linger in such a happy state?

But they must ride on, said Jeannette.

It might mean riding on through hostile country to Rheims, she was reminded.

'So be it,' she replied. 'We have come so far. The Lord God will not desert us now. It is His Will that the Dauphin should be crowned at Rheims and it is for this purpose that I am here.'

The Dauphin was surrounded by his advisers, the chief of whom was Georges de la Trémoïlle—a coward of a man but sly and shrewd. He looked like a great barrel so fat was he. He was vicious, and a man to be watched for those who offended him had a way of disappearing from the scene. He was always at the Dauphin's side and his word carried weight.

It was disconcerting to men such as he was to see so much adulation given to an ignorant country girl.

It suited La Trémoïlle to see the Dauphin weak, depending on him; he had always advised a policy of shilly-shally.

So when Jeannette urged them to make the journey to Rheims La Trémoïlle, with the Chancellor Regnault de

Chartres, strongly opposed her.

'There are not enough troops nor money for such a journey,' they insisted; and the Dauphin following his long habit listened to them. Delay was part of his nature, no less than theirs. He dreaded change. It was wonderful to have achieved this victory but now he was realizing that it was rousing him out of his lethargy. Did he want that?

Jeannette was not easily brushed aside. She sought the Dauphin in his private apartments and none dare stop her. If Trémoïlle and Regnault despised her, others in the King's entourage did not. They had for her an awesome respect.

She fell onto her knees before him, and told him that it was imperative that they leave at once. Her voices were urging her. Her voices must be obeyed. He must come to Rheims.

'There are too many obstacles,' he told her. 'There are towns still in the hands of the English. Do you not see that they will be doubly fortified ... after Orléans.'

'I see only that we must go to Rheims. My voices demand it, sire, and they must be obeyed.'

At length hers was the voice that convinced him and the Dauphin with his Court and an army of twelve thousand set out for Rheims.

There were difficulties along the road. Jeannette had known there would be. At the town of Troyes it was particularly disheartening for there was a garrison there consisting of six hundred English and Burgundians. They would not lightly surrender.

Of course Trémoïlle and Regnault pointed out that they had no provisions to mount a siege. There was only one thing to do and that was to turn back.

'No, no!' insisted Jeannette. 'Oh, my gentle Dauphin, listen to God who speaks through me. Wait here before your town of Troyes and by love or force within the space of a few days I will make it yours.'

Jeannette prepared for battle. She was camped outside the walls and the following day she donned her armour, mounted her horse and carrying her banner rode forth crying that she came in the name of the Lord God.

There was no fighting. Within the city there was a call of 'We surrender' and the townspeople came out declaring that they would not resist the Maid.

She rode into the town side by side with the Dauphin. She

was triumphant while Trémoïlle and his friends murmured that it could have gone the other way.

Dunois came to her with great emotion shining in his eyes. 'You are indeed God's messenger,' he said.

'You know it now, my lord,' she said. 'Make good use of me while I am here for I shall not be here much longer.'

Dunois seized her arm and said earnestly: 'Why do you talk thus? What do you fear?'

'Treachery,' she said. 'I feel it in the air. It is that which will destroy me.'

'Jeannette, you know you are going to die. When?'

'I do not know when, but that it will come I know full well. I am at the will of God and I shall accomplish what I have been commanded to do. I raised the siege of Orléans; I must now see the Dauphin crowned at Rheims. When that is done ... it may be my work will be also.'

'Pray God, Jeannette, that He will preserve you.'

She smiled at him. 'I would like it well if He sent me back to my mother and father. I would like to tend the sheep again and know that my work is done.'

Dunois turned away. He was surprised at his emotion. He was fond of her, not as a mystic—he was not even sure that he believed whole-heartedly in that—but because she was simple and humble and ... he sought for a word to describe her. He thought, It is Good. Jeannette is good with a goodness rare in men and women.

The army was camped some ten miles from Rheims. Trémoïlle declared the town would stand out against them.

'Not so, my lord,' replied Jeannette. 'You will see that the leading citizens will come out of the city bringing the keys to the Dauphin.'

And this was what happened for no sooner was the cavalcade in sight of Rheims when the leading citizens came out as Jeannette had said they would and they had the keys of the city in their hands. Eagerly they were awaiting the arrival of the Maid with the Dauphin and within a few days he should be crowned King of France.

*   *   *

It was the custom in France for its Kings to be crowned on a Sunday and the people of Rheims were determined that this should be observed. All through the Saturday of the 16th of

July they were making their preparations. They knew that their Dauphin had taken up his residence at the Castle of Sept-Saulx some ten miles outside the town.

At nine o'clock in the morning Charles came into the church and beside him was Jeannette. It was what the people expected. It was because of her that he was here and if there were some who deplored it, still it must be.

His magnificent robes were open at the neck and shoulders in preparation for the ceremonial anointing which would signify that he was being endowed with renown, glory and wisdom. He stood before the high Altar and with him were the Duke of Alençon and the Counts of Clermont and Vendôme.

The anointing oil, contained in the Holy Ampulla, a crystal flask which had been brought out from the tomb of the Apostle, was said to have been used by the Blessed Rémi at the anointing of King Clovis.

Jeannette watched the proceedings with jubilation. This was the climax. This was where her Voices had led her. It was the moment of fulfilment and the happiest in her life.

The Archbishop had taken the crown from the altar—not alas, the crown of Charlemagne with its rubies, sapphires and emeralds decorated with fleur-de-lis, for the royal ornaments were all in the hands of the English and were said to be at St Denis.

That mattered not. It was the act of crowning which was important and the Dauphin was now in truth King Charles the Seventh.

The trumpets were sounding, and the people shouting: 'Noel! Noel!'

Jeannette came forward and knelt at his feet. Tears were streaming from her eyes.

'Sweet King,' she cried, 'now is God's pleasure done. It was His will that I should raise the siege of Orléans and bring you to this city of Rheims to receive your holy anointing, making it known that you are indeed the true King and telling the world to whom this fair realm of France belongs.'

The King lightly touched her head with his fingers and the people cried out in their joy.

'*Vive le roi. Noel! Noel!*'

The King then moved on to his banquet which would be held in traditional fashion in the old hall of Tau. The table had been extended into the street so that there might be feasting for all. There would be free food and free drink and hundreds of sheep, chickens and oxen had been slaughtered. There was Beaune and Burgundy for everyone.

Dunois was watching Jeannette with affection. She had achieved a miracle. She should be content now. She should go back to the country and live peacefully for the rest of her days. Let her go back to the simple life, perhaps take a husband, look after a household, have children. She was as skilled in the crafts of the home as she had become in those of war.

This was no life for a young girl. She had been called on to perform a miracle and that was what she had done.

'Jeannette,' he said, 'you know the inn called Ane Rayé. You should go there. I think you will find something to interest you.'

She looked at him in surprise. She knew he understood that she had no feeling for the revelries which must follow the coronation.

'What shall I find there?' she asked.

'I will take you,' he said, 'and you shall see for yourself.'

People made a path for her and the Bastard of Orléans. Eyes followed the Maid and she was treated to an awed silence; but today was the King's day. The miracle was over; now they would enjoy the fruits of it. Rich red meat. Flowing wine. The Maid had done well; they loved the Maid. But this was the day to eat, drink and carouse and sing *Vive le Roi*.

She could not believe her eyes when she walked into the inn. In a matter of seconds she was in her mother's arms. Her father was standing by; and there were her brothers Jean, Pierrelot and her cousin's husband, Durand Laxart.

Releasing herself from her mother's arms she faced them all.

Her father took her hands and kissed them. 'I have come to ask pardon,' he said.

She shook her head, her emotions threatening to choke her. 'My father, you understand now. I had to do what I did. I had to hurt you. It was a command from Heaven.'

'You saved Orléans. You are a friend of the King ...' That was Pierrelot. 'I can't believe it even though I have seen it with my own eyes.'

'We are so proud of you,' Jean told her.

Jeannette turned to Durand Laxart who was standing a little apart.

'So much I owe to you,' she said. 'I shall never forget that.

You helped me when I needed help. God will reward you.'

'I believed in you ... from the first,' Durand told her.

'And we were the ones who rejected you,' cried Jacques. 'May God forgive us.'

'He will. He has already done so,' said Jeannette. 'What you did, you did for love of me. It was what any father would have done.'

'How were we to know that our sister Jeannette was to be the saviour of Orléans?' cried Jean.

'And now we are here, let us be happy together,' said Jeannette. 'There is so much I want to know. How are matters in Domrémy?'

'We are all so proud ... so proud ...' murmured her mother.

'And Mengette ... and Hauviette?'

'They await news of you. Poor little Hauviette, she was heart-broken when you went ...'

'I knew she would be. It was the reason why I could not say good-bye. My dear little Hauviette. Take my love to her. Tell her to be happy. Tell her I think of her ... often.'

'She will be so pleased that you remembered her,' said Zabillet.

'Remember her! Hauviette! As if I should ever forget her!'

'You have so many matters to occupy you.'

'There would always be a place for Hauviette.'

'Come let us sit down,' said Jean. 'I have ordered a little food and wine.'

So while the people of Rheims were feasting in the streets and the King in the banqueting hall, Jeannette sat down to a simple supper with her family. They were amazed at how little she ate. She wanted nothing but small pieces of bread soaked in wine. She had grown accustomed to such fare, she told them; and she needed little else.

Pierrelot tried to coax her to eat.

'Hush you,' said Zabillet. 'You should know it is no use trying to persuade Jeannette when she has made up her mind.'

Later her father took her on one side and whispered to her that there was a matter of some concern to Domrémy and he wished to speak to her about it.

She listened attentively while he went on: 'We are as poor as ever, and you know what that means. We are finding it hard to meet the new demands from the treasury. The villagers have begged me to have a word with you to ask if you could persuade the King to give us exemption from the new tax. You are his friend they say. You have given him his crown. Will he give your native village this concession if you ask for it?'

'I know he will,' said Jeannette. 'Rest assured I shall ask him.'

Jacques looked greatly relieved. He had made this journey chiefly to make this request. He wanted to see Jeannette in her glory, of course, but he was still a little suspicious of it. Her strangeness had worried him a great deal and that she, his humble daughter, should have been selected for such a task still seemed like some sort of necromancy. He had heard it whispered in some quarters that she was a witch. That would be the final degradation. But to see her, so radiant, so self-effacing, so beloved of the people and respected by great men such as the Bastard of Orléans and the King himself, lulled his fear though not entirely.

He was greatly relieved when the King decreed that Dom-rémy and Greux should be exempt from all tallies, aids, sub-sidies and subventions. He said also that the family's expenses should be paid and that they should be provided with horses to take them back to Domrémy.

When they said good-bye, Zabillet clung to her daughter.

'Jeannette,' she murmured, 'why do you not come back with us? You have done your work. This is what you set out to do, was it not? You saved Orléans for the French and had the King crowned at Rheims. What else is there for you, Jeannette?'

'I shall not be happy, dear mother, until there is not a single Godon left in France.'

'Jeannette, God has guarded you so far. Come home now.'

Jeannette shook her head.

'God rest you, dear mother. Go and live in peace. I shall know what I must do when the time comes.'

Zabillet sighed. As she said earlier to Pierrelot, it was no use trying to persuade Jeannette.

DISASTER AT COMPIÈGNE

LATER, in her darkest moments she believed that she should have gone. That was the moment ... the time of glory. She had accomplished her mission. She had obeyed the commands of Heaven. She had been the instrument through which God had imposed His Will.

Why did she stay? Was she a little intoxicated by glory? Had she come to believe herself not merely that instrument but the possessor of divine powers? She had seen a miracle come from her work; she had heard the acclamation of the crowds. In Rheims at the time of the coronation the poor had come to kneel at her feet. They asked only to touch her hands, to touch the hem of her garment. Great men had bowed to her, listened to her, followed her wishes, showed their respect for her. The Bastard of Orléans, the Duc d'Alençon, the Sire de Gamanche, the King himself—had all treated her with something like reverence. Had the sin of pride come very close to her? She had stressed her humility, her origins, her lack of education ... But even in that was there a touch of pride?

How could she tell? It was easy to look back afterwards and say: I should have done this. I should not have done that. If ... If ...

She believed now that she had a further mission. She would not rest until every Englishman had been driven from the shores of France. Perhaps having accomplished one seemingly impossible mission she must have another.

'Come back with us to Domrémy,' her mother had said. 'You have done what God commanded.'

Should she have listened? It was easy to say 'Yes' ... looking back.

There were many who loved her; but there were others who hated her. Rich, powerful people there were who wanted to destroy her. The King was her friend ... but what was the friendship of kings ever worth, and Charles the Seventh had never shown himself as a steadfast character. There was the wily Duke of Burgundy, who was the ally of the English while not averse to a little flirtation with the French and ready to jump whichever way was best for Burgundy. He hated the King because he had instigated the murder of John the Fearless, the last Duke, and that was something which the present Duke Philip could never forget.

And did she think the great Duke of Bedford would stand quietly by and see his armies defeated by a peasant girl from Domrémy?

There were enemies closer to her. There was Georges de la Trémoïlle—as treacherous a man as ever lived. His father had been attached to the Duke of Burgundy and Georges had been brought up at that Court with Duke Philip. It was not unlikely that Georges would still retain a certain liaison with his boyhood companion; and the Duke would deem it beneficial to have a man who must feel some friendship for him living so close to his enemy the King.

Georges de la Trémoïlle was unscrupulous in the extreme —a man who would not hesitate to murder. His treatment of his first wife had created a scandal at one time. He had married her, taken all she possessed and then driven her from his house. She had died as the result of the condition into which he had forced her. His reason for getting rid of her was that he had his eyes on another woman who was both comely and extremely wealthy and he thought it would be not only pleasant to marry her but profitable also.

It had not been a difficult matter for Trémoïlle, favourite as he was with the King, to arrange for the murder of the lady's husband and marry her himself.

Such a man would have no scruples and little difficulty in removing Jeannette, once her great popularity had died down. It would be dangerous, of course, to do it at the time when she was regarded almost as a saint throughout the country and had many friends in high places.

But Trémoïlle had always been a man who knew how to wait.

Regnault de Chartres, the Chancellor, could easily be handled by him. Regnault, Bishop of Rheims, was a man of ambition and he sought to satisfy that, as so many had before him, through the Church. He hated Jeannette. If God had wanted to guide the King to Rheims, why should He have chosen a simple country girl to do it when the Bishop of Rheims was standing by?

He wanted to get rid of Jeannette but like Trémoïlle he realized that they must wait until the tumult was over.

He and Trémoïlle were aware that the two most important men in the country were Burgundy and Bedford; Bedford was going to find some means of staining Jeannette's image. He had to. It was the belief in her supernatural gifts which had defeated his army. It was not force of arms which had raised the siege of Orléans. It was fear of the powers of light or of darkness—it mattered not which, they were both equally effective for striking fear into men.

Moreover Burgundy was not going to stand by and see Charles victorious. As soon as he was free of his present commitments he would spring into action.

As for King Charles, they had little respect for him. They would know how to handle him when the time came.

Jeannette was now planning to march on Paris. She knew that until the capital was in French hands there could be no true victory. The girl had learned her military tactics well, they had to admit. She wanted to march on Paris and take it for the King while both Trémoïlle and Regnault saw that if she succeeded in this it would be impossible to destroy Jeannette. What they wanted was to gain Paris through negotiations—*their* negotiations and they believed this should be done through an alliance with Burgundy.

Charles hated bloodshed and it should not be difficult to make him listen.

Jeannette knew very well that the Duke of Burgundy was the enemy of the King of France. He would always regard him as his father's murderer and if anyone reminded him that Louis of Orléans had been murdered at the instigation of a Duke of Burgundy that made no difference.

Thus Jeannette had powerful people working against her. Moreover her voices rarely came to her now. When she was involved in a skirmish, sometimes she was successful, at other times not. She was filled with a burning desire to drive the Godons from France, but secretly she was beginning to wonder whether God no longer desired her services.

With the people she was still Jeannette, the wonder girl from Domrémy who had achieved miracles. It would take a little time for such a reputation to be destroyed, but many had short memories. Already it seemed the King did not listen to her with the same respect. His advisers Trémoïlle and Regnault had his ear; and she did not like what was going on. Sometimes she was very depressed; she longed to hear her voices and they did not come. She followed the King from Château-Thierry to Senlis, from Blois to Compiègne. She was obsessed by her devotion to him and to France. But she missed the divine inspiration. She had become a good commander; but so were Dunois, Alençon and a score of others; and they had not been able to save Orléans.

The Duke of Bedford had brought five hundred of his dreaded archers to Paris. One division of his army there carried a standard on which was embossed a distaff and a spindle. 'Now, fair one, come!' was its inscription. Jeannette was eager to attack Paris and she still had influential supporters. One was the Duc d'Alençon who had complete faith in her. However the attack failed.

Then the English left Paris in the hands of the Duke of Burgundy—a signal to the French that he was their trusted ally—and Jeannette was forced to retreat to Compiègne where she made the acquaintance of the garrison captain there, Guillaume de Flavy. It was only later that she discovered he was Regnault's half-brother and had been brought up by him.

She was uneasy. She knew that Trémoïlle and Regnault were in secret communication with Burgundy. She mistrusted Burgundy and she begged them to do the same. 'There can be no peace with him except at the point of a lance,' she insisted.

It was May of the year 1430. Almost a year had passed since the crowning of the King and they were no nearer driving the English from France than they had been at that time. Jeannette had gone on an expedition to Crépy and while she was there news was brought to her that Burgundy was laying siege to Compiègne.

'We must return at once,' she said. 'We must fight our way into the town.'

She was reminded that they were only three hundred or so strong—a small company to fight its way through Burgundy's

forces; and when at daybreak she came in sight of Compiègne
and the besiegers did not attempt to stop her entering the
town, she thought she had recovered her old inspiration.

She went at once to the church of St Jacques, convinced by
her easy entry into the town that she was back in grace and
was receiving help from Heaven.

People thronged about her and followed her into the
church where she heard Mass. And as the children gathered
round her touching her armour and seeking the honour of
having spoken to the Maid, she heard herself saying—and it
was as though a voice spoke within her: 'Children and dear
friends, soon I shall be betrayed and delivered over to death.
Pray for me.'

A great depression settled on her then. She knew that it
was her voices who had been with her so little of late who
had spoken in the church.

Nevertheless that evening she wanted to make a sortie out
of the town and in spite of the feeling of despair which had
come to her she was eager to go on with her plans.

She commanded Guillaume de Flavy to have boats ready
on the river Oise to help the troops return and to see that all
the gates of the town were securely locked and only the bridge
gate left open.

Very quickly it was realized that the venture was a failure.
'We must retreat,' shouted the men.

But Jeannette would not retreat. 'Never!' she cried. 'Let
us stand and fight.'

'We are lost if we do,' was the rejoinder. The men had
suddenly realized that it was only a peasant girl who was
asking them to risk their lives. It had been all very well when
God was with her but clearly He was not involved in this. It
was folly to stay, they believed, and they were not going to do
so. They scrambled into the waiting boats.

Jeannette held off the enemy who would prevent the troops
escaping, until the boats had taken them to the drawbridge
and they all passed into safety. She was left outside with one
or two faithful supporters.

Guillaume de Flavy made a decision. He knew she was
outside. So were the Burgundians and they were ready to
storm the town. He ordered that the drawbridge be pulled
up and the portcullis let down.

Jeannette, left outside, was soon surrounded.

There was a shout of: 'The Maid. We have the Maid.'

Someone pulled at her surcoat. She was down. They surrounded her.

'Yield,' cried one of them.

She was beaten. It had come to pass as she had known it would. This was her destiny, and she must face it with courage.

One of the men who was different from the rough soldiery bade her rise. She must go with him and he would take her to his master, Count John of Luxembourg.

The cry went up: 'We have the Maid. She is in our hands.'

This was the end of the miracles, for how could God let His chosen one fall among her enemies?

She was praying silently as they led her away.

*   *   *

The news spread rapidly through the country. It was received with exultation and with sorrow. There was lamentation in the village of Domrémy.

'I knew this would come,' said Jacques. 'It was never right. She should never have left us.'

'It was her purpose in life,' Zabillet answered. 'Pray God that He will treat her well.'

The King took the news calmly. He did not know whether he should mourn or rejoice. It had been clear lately that God had deserted her for there had been no more spectacular successes. She had done as any other commander would do ... no more.

The Duke of Burgundy was excited. Exultantly he sent messengers to all those to whom the news would be of the utmost interest. The Maid captured and in the hands of the Count of Luxembourg—a vassal of his. What should be done with her? As a prisoner taken in battle she should be treated with some respect. She should be ransomed as such people were. Ransomed! Some would pay a big ransom for her. The King of France? He owed it to her to pay her ransom and set her free. God knew she had done enough for him. Bedford would be itching to get his hands on her for while she lived and went into battle his men would always be afraid of her. The citizens of Orléans should ransom her if they could afford the price. She had done much for them.

How had she been captured? wondered Burgundy. Guillaume de Flavy had drawn up the bridge and let down the

portcullis knowing she was on the wrong side of it, exposed
to her enemies. And Guillaume de Flavy—the half-brother of
Regnault—had been brought up by him. Had Flavy been
doing his half-brother a favour?

Well, however it happened it was done; and Burgundy
must turn it to good account.

The citizens of Orléans were stunned. The people gathered
in the streets chanting the Miserere; in Tours and Blois many
walked barefoot to the shrines of the saints. They could not
understand why God should have deserted His messenger. It
was a further sign, they assured each other. She would miraculously escape, and that would be yet another display of
Divine protection.

Georges de la Trémoïlle was in a state of great delight. This
was indeed good fortune for him. He suspected Regnault
since it was his half-brother who had shut her out and left her
to her enemies. Good work, he thought. He went to the King
at once and they discussed the news. He pretended to be
grave.

'She is in the hands of Burgundy, not the English,' Trémoïlle pointed out.

'The English will endeavour to get her into their hands.'

'It was a risk she took and if she was really sent by God He
will protect her. She was always rash. Never listening to advice
—always going her own way.'

Charles was uneasy. He had so much for which to thank
her. When she had come to him and read the suspicion of his
illegitimacy in his mind and had reassured him, he had
known she had Divine powers. She had saved Orléans; she
had had him crowned at Rheims. It worried his conscience
that she had fallen into the hands of her enemies.

Trémoïlle knew his royal master well. Charles was worried.
He might try to act—or at least he was thinking about it. He
would be expected to act. The people would demand it of
him. He would find all sorts of reasons why this or that could
not be done, of course, but it was a dangerous situation.

Fate played into Trémoïlle's hands. Perhaps it was natural
that after the impact Jeannette had made on the people of
France imitators should spring up here and there.

Before Jeannette's capture a matron named Catherine de
la Rochelle had declared that she too had had visions. She too
had been selected by Divine Powers to partake in the salvation of France. She wanted to tour France and explain that a

vision had come to her at night—a lady dressed in cloth of gold who had told her that she must exhort the population to bring their treasures from their secret store and give them to the King of France to prosecute the war. She had met Jeannette, and Jeannette had dismissed her as a fraud. So, reasoned Trémoïlle, Catherine de la Rochelle might be useful now.

A shepherd boy was brought to him. This Guillaume of Gévaudan had had the signs of the stigmata on his hands. He said that it had been revealed to him that God had suffered Jeannette to fall into the hands of her enemies because she had become hardened by pride. She had grown to love fine armour and beautiful horses so well that she had lost sight of the fact that she was working for God.

As for Catherine de la Rochelle, she was ready to swear that Jeannette was a witch. She had seen her in visions having intercourse with the Devil.

These facts Trémoïlle could lay before the King, and Charles' conscience was only too ready to be eased.

The Duke of Bedford could scarcely contain his excitement. Earnestly he discussed the matter of the Maid's capture with the Earls of Warwick and Suffolk.

'It's the best piece of news I've heard for a long time,' declared Suffolk.

'It would have been better if she had fallen into our hands instead of Luxembourg's,' commented Bedford wryly.

'Which,' added Warwick, 'is tantamount to falling into Burgundy's hands.'

'What will Luxembourg do, think you?' asked Warwick.

'You know that grasping one-eyed Count. He'll ransom her.'

'You think the French ... ?'

'My lord,' said Bedford firmly, 'we must see that the French do not pay that ransom, and the only way we can do it is by paying a higher one ourselves.'

'I agree,' said Warwick. 'We must get the Maid into our hands.'

'And prove her to be a witch,' added Bedford firmly.

'Our troubles will continue until she is removed,' agreed Warwick. 'I've no doubt of that. It is not her skill in war—though that is remarkable for a simple country girl. But the French believe her to be God's messenger. And for that reason they fight as never before.'

'And our men ... what do they believe?' asked Bedford. 'That she comes from the Devil? She does. She's a witch. There's no doubt. But whether it is the powers of light or darkness, they are working against us and will continue to do so until she is destroyed.'

'What action then, my lord?'

'I have already sent to England. Nothing must be spared. There will have to be new taxes if necessary. And there is no time for delay. Money must be sent in readiness. When Joan the Maid is put to ransom, we are going to be the ones to pay it. Make no mistake of that.'

'It's the only way. Joan will soon be in our hands.'

'We have to go warily. Watch Burgundy. He'll try to make the utmost out of this. If he forbids Luxembourg to take a ransom Luxembourg will have to obey. But we must be ready.'

'We want Joan of Arc.'

*　　　*　　　*

A terrible desolation had come to her. Something had gone wrong. She had disobeyed her voices in some way. She had always known that when the Dauphin was crowned her mission was accomplished. Her family had been at Rheims. That was the sign. She should have returned with them. Why had she stayed? Because after her experiences nothing could be the same again. She had said she wanted to return to the quiet life of the country, but did she? She had lived with great happenings. Ever since her voices had come to her— and she had been only thirteen then—she had dreamed of great events. How could she go back to being a simple peasant woman?

Nothing could be the same again. She wanted it to go on. She had wanted to lead men into battle. Before the coronation she had known inspiration, something strangely divine. After the coronation, it was withdrawn and she had been only a human being with a great purpose, dedicated though it was. But she had failed and she had fallen into the hands of her enemies.

She was taken to Beaulieu Castle which belonged to her captor, the Count of Luxembourg. He would ransom her as was the custom with all those people of rank and importance who were captured in war. She was of no rank but no one in France was more important.

'Jesus,' she prayed, 'do not let me fall into the hands of the English.'

She was half way there, she knew, for Luxembourg was the vassal of Burgundy and Burgundy was the ally of the English. But her dear King Charles would never let that happen. As the days passed and there was no news from him she was tormented by doubts. She tried to call on her voices. She heard them but distantly. 'She must not despair. God would look after her.'

She wanted to be free. What was happening at Compiègne? She should be there. Surely Charles would send someone to capture the castle, to restore her to freedom?

There was much coming and going. The Duke of Burgundy was in the castle. She heard the great man's name whispered. He came to see her. The interview was brief.

She reproached him for taking sides against the King of France, to which he replied he was avenging the death of his father.

She pointed out to him that his father had paid the price of his vengeance.

Burgundy was cold. 'You should not speak of matters which do not concern you,' he said. 'By God's Truth, girl, you have enough matters of your own with which to occupy yourself.'

There was nothing to be gained by that interview.

She did not trust the Count of Luxembourg. He was most ill favoured, having only one eye; but it was not that so much as his mean expression which repelled her. He was clearly greatly amused to find himself in this position and on the rare occasions when Jeannette saw him, he enjoyed hinting that he would probably be forced to hand her to the English.

This was why she planned her escape. It would be difficult, but it was possible and with the help of God she could do it.

If she could get out of her room and run along a passage there was a spot where it would be possible for her to slip through a narrow space in the wall. She was small and as she had scarcely eaten since her capture and even before then existed on pieces of bread soaked in wine, she was very thin. She knew that with a little effort she could slip through that gap. Then she would have to pass the guardroom. But if she could lock the door from the outside, they would remain captive while she slipped out of the castle.

For several days she thought of this. She imagined the joy of the people when she showed them once more that God was with her and had effected her escape. She prayed all through the day and at dusk was able to slip through the gap as she had thought; she was able to turn the key which imprisoned the guards.

'Oh God help me,' she murmured, 'I have done it.'

She ran round the spiral staircase. A porter was standing at the bottom and he caught her as she attempted to run past him.

'Where are you going to?' he asked. 'You are my lord's prisoner. Did you think to escape as easily as that?'

She was taken back to her prison but the Count of Luxembourg was alarmed.

She might have escaped. And what would have happened to him, if she had? He would have been blamed. Obviously Beaulieu was not a strong enough prison.

Jeannette was transferred to the castle of Beaurevoir close to Cambrai where she could be much more closely confined.

*   *   *

She was desperately unhappy. She had been so certain that God would help her escape. Piteously she called on her voices. They came to her sometimes, but faintly and as though far away. Sometimes when she lay on her straw after a day of fasting she saw the Saints Margaret and Catherine.

'Have patience,' they said. 'You are not forgotten.'

But there were times when she thought she was and a terrible fear came to her. She was obsessed by the English. She must not fall into their hands. She hated them fiercely. They were wicked ... all of them ... they had dared overrun her country and had called the boy king Henry the King of France. She had changed that. She had brought about the crowning of the real King. But what would they do to her if she fell into their hands?

And she would. This cruel Count of Luxembourg would not be able to resist the ransom they offered. Besides, he was a vassal of Burgundy and Burgundy had become a traitor to France when he became the friend of the English.

She could not bear it. She looked down from the narrow slit of her window to the stony courtyard below. If only she were down there. If only she were free.

And one day the impulse came to her. She was at the top of

a seventy foot tower, but the saints would carry her down. They would not let her fall. If she had the courage to step out they would carry her down to safety.

She stood on the ledge. The cool air fanned her face. She stepped out into nothing.

They found her lying unconscious on the stone floor and carried her in. She was badly hurt and unable to move. The Count was deeply disturbed. She might have killed herself. The English would have been pleased, but what of his ransom?

Jeannette wakened to find two women at her bedside. As she opened her eyes she thought they were Saints from Heaven because of the sweetness of their faces.

One of the women was very old, the other much younger, but she sensed the kindliness in both of them.

'Ah, you are awake,' said the older of the two. 'You have had a bad fall but you are going to recover. You must rest though. There is nothing to fear. We have been looking after you.'

'Where am I?' asked Jeannette.

'In the castle of Beaurevoir.'

'Still here.'

'Yes, you fell from the window.'

'Who are you?'

'I am the Countess Jeanne of Luxembourg—the Count's aunt, and this is his wife, Jeanne of Bethune.'

Jeannette closed her eyes. She knew now that her attempt had failed; she was not in Heaven; she was still a captive in the hands of her enemies.

But the two women could scarcely be called that. As Jeannette recovered she realized how much she owed to their kindness. She began to understand that the elderly lady was of some importance for she held the Luxembourg estates and, if she decided to, could leave them to someone other than the Count. He was therefore most respectful to her which amused Jeannette. The young Countess of Luxembourg was a gentle girl and deeply religious; both of these women were sorry for Jeannette and nursing her when she was close to death had made them aware of her piety. They could well believe that she had been following a divine purpose and although they were on the other side through Luxembourg's allegiance to Burgundy, they did not hold that against her.

They said she should have some women's clothes to wear.

'Something attractive,' suggested the young Countess.

'We will send for materials,' said the elder one.

Jeannette shook her head. She wanted no women's clothes. Her voices had said she must dress as a man until they told her otherwise. She would keep to what she already had.

For the first time since her capture she began to feel a little happier. Her position was desperate, she knew, and still the threat of being passed to the English hung over her, but there was comfort in the society of other women.

*   *   *

The Count of Luxembourg was in desperate need of money and the capture of Jeannette d'Arc seemed to him like a gift from Heaven. He was avaricious by nature and was unsure of his inheritance. He had to be very careful not to offend his aunt; he had just built the castle of Beaurevoir and as usual such projects turned out far more costly than had at first been calculated. He needed money badly.

He was desperately anxious to get that ransom. The Duke of Burgundy, he guessed, was toying with the idea of paying it himself. He was one of the few who would be able to afford it. In fact so rich was Burgundy that it might well be that even the English would not be able to outbid him. He could see Burgundy's motive. He would hold Jeannette as a threat to the English. That was an uneasy partnership. Even though Bedford had married Burgundy's sister there was a great deal of suspicion between them.

But it was the English who would get her in the end. The Count was certain of that and he was waiting for the day.

While he was thinking of this and imagining the gold trickling through his fingers his aunt came in to see him.

'She will recover,' she said. 'Poor girl. She's little more than a child.'

'A child, my lady, who wrought a great deal of havoc in a very short time.'

'She sees it as good.'

The Count shrugged his shoulders.

'I believe in her,' said the Countess. 'So does your wife. That girl is good. Be careful how you treat her.'

'She will be no concern of mine once she has passed out of my hands.'

'What will her fate be at the hands of the English?'

'They will make her out to be a witch.'

'She is no witch. She is a good saintly girl.'

'Dear lady, it is not for me to say.'

'But it *is* for you to say. You must not let her pass into the hands of the English. Charles should pay the ransom. How can he not? Consider what she has done for him!'

'Charles could not afford to pay the ransom for which he would be asked.'

'By you?'

'I am the fortunate man who holds the prize.'

'Jean, you must not sell this girl to her enemies.'

'My dear lady, you do not know what difficulties I find myself in. The building of this castle has cost so much. And if my Lord Burgundy should decide the girl should be given over, then so must it be. He is my master.'

'He understands the laws of chivalry enough to let the matter rest with you.'

'You do not know the Duke of Burgundy.'

'I know myself, nephew. And I should be most displeased if you sold Jeannette d'Arc to her enemies.'

She swept out of the room. She had always been a forceful lady, fond of getting her own way. She was warning him that if he accepted a ransom for Jeannette d'Arc she might decide to cut him off from the Luxembourg estates.

*   *   *

The Duke of Bedford was with the Duke of Burgundy, and the matter they were discussing was Jeannette's fate.

They had both heard of the attempts at escape.

'The angels had deserted their posts while she jumped,' commented Bedford wryly.

'Indeed so,' replied the Duke, 'and what they were doing to allow that porter to be on guard when she might have slipped out of Beaulieu I cannot imagine. Seriously, the girl is a fraud.'

'How did she manage to inspire the Orléannese?'

'Fear. You know that well enough. You should have allowed the town to surrender to me.'

'After I had spent time and men and money making the siege?'

'You were not going to beat the bushes for someone else to get the birds. Remember? That was one of your rare blunders.

The Blunder of the Birds. But for that Orléans would not
have been lost to Charles.'

Bedford was silent. He was a man who had made very few
mistakes, which was why he deplored them when they did
occur. The affair of the birds was only half a mistake. He
would not have been very happy to see Orléans in Burgundy's
hands—better than Charles' though, he had to admit, and
that his men had been beaten by this strange girl was indeed
a disaster.

'Luxembourg wants the ransom,' said Burgundy, 'but his
aunt has forbidden him to take it.'

Bedford raised his eyebrows.

'A very pious lady, most virtuous. She has been nursing the
Maid and will not allow Luxembourg to take the ransom.'

'And he dare not?'

'He stands to lose a great deal if he displeases the lady.'

Bedford was mildly relieved. He was by no means an impulsive man. He was content for matters to remain as they were
for the time. Joan of Arc could do no harm in prison, and he
was not quite ready to pay the heavy ransom which would be
demanded.

'The old lady won't last long,' said Burgundy. 'She is very
old and not in the best of health. As soon as she has gone, then
you will see.' He leaned towards Bedford. 'I have thought of
making a bid myself.'

Bedford was horrified. Burgundy was the one bidder he
feared. The richest man in France, he could offer almost anything and Luxembourg by reason of his position would have
to accept Burgundy's offer even if it were less.

Burgundy was smiling slyly. There was little he enjoyed
more than watching his ally's discomfiture.

'You would be very unpopular, my friend, if you harmed
the Maid,' suggested Bedford.

'Not with her enemies.'

'What would you do with her?'

'She's a witch,' said Burgundy. 'I have little doubt of that.
I might keep her in prison for the rest of her life. I might
burn her as a witch.'

If he burned her at the stake ... all well and good, thought
Bedford. But he wouldn't, he was too wily. He would hold
her and keep her to threaten his English allies whenever he
felt the need to do so. The Maid must not fall into Burgundy's
hands.

Bedford said: 'Trade with the Flemings flourishes in England.'

The Flemings were in Burgundy's vast domains. They lived by their weaving. There would be a revolt if their trade were interfered with.

Burgundy was thoughtful. Bedford could stop their woven goods being exported to England at the stroke of a pen.

Burgundy was thoughtful. He did not really want to be burdened with Joan of Arc.

When the time came he would let the English have her.

Soon after that the time did come. The old Countess of Luxembourg was found dead in her bed one morning. No one was very surprised; she had been ailing for some time. Her estates naturally passed to her nephew who was delighted to have the threat of her displeasure removed for ever.

Then the English came along with a very good offer and Burgundy, thinking of the Flemish weavers, allowed his vassal to accept it.

So Jeannette passed into the hands of her enemies the English and was taken to the capital of Normandy, Rouen, there to await the judgment they would pass on her.

FINALE AT ROUEN

It was in cold December, two days before Christmas, when Jeannette arrived in Rouen. She was deeply depressed. That which she had greatly feared had come to pass. She felt deserted by the King and worse still by her voices.

Her prison was a cell in the tower of the castle. It was not small but very dark. There was nothing but a straw pallet on the floor and only one window too high for her to see what was outside.

Twice she had tried to escape and her captors were determined that she should not do so again. They put fetters on her legs and an iron belt was fixed about her waist—and all these were chained to the wall.

There had been a great deal of talk about her purity. If she was to be condemned as a witch she could scarcely be a virgin, and it was very necessary that she should be condemned as a witch. Therefore her gaolers were chosen from that most brutal section of the army notorious for its barbarous behaviour. When these men raided towns and villages they brought terror to the inhabitants who had given them the name of *houspilleurs* which meant tormentors. Among those selected to watch over Jeannette there were two men whose reputations was slightly worse than those of the others. They were William Talbot and John Grey. When she saw them such fear as she had never known in the heat of battle seized Jeannette. One look at the brutalized faces of these men was enough to tell her what their intentions would be. She prayed then with an even greater fervour than ever before.

How could this have happened to her? It had all been so gloriously successful. She had believed she would go on until she had driven the English out of France. How foolish she had been! She had loved the glory and had sought it after her mission was done; and now she must pay for it. It seemed that God and her voices had deserted her. When she had recovered in Beaurevoir castle after throwing herself from the window, she knew. Right up to then she had believed they would save her. Perhaps she had thrown herself down being tempted as Christ was in the wilderness.

'If they are going to kill me,' she prayed, 'oh God let them do it quickly.'

All her chains would allow her to take were three paces forward and back.

There was no heating in the cell and the weather was bitterly cold. The one window which gave little light and no view for her, provided the draughts. She was to be tried and proved to be a witch and she was in the hands of the Inquisition who had their special methods for proving a prisoner guilty.

Her gaolers sought to insult her at every turn. They teased her, they liked to frighten her. Their words did not frighten her; it was their acts she feared.

They had set up a table and stools and played with dice. While she watched them, inwardly she prayed for the strength she would need when the time came, as she knew it would.

They would sit in a corner of the room with their dice— cursing and swearing. They muttered about her. 'But for this naughty Maid we should not be here in this cold room passing the hours away. We should be out ... in the taverns ... having a good time with the wine and the wenches.'

'What think you of her?'

'Not very comely.'

'Nay ... nay ... but she says she's a maiden still. I always had a fancy for maidens.'

'What even when they're dressed to look like a man!'

'There are parts which are like a woman.'

They hiccupped and roared with laughter.

She thanked God for the clothes she was wearing—the sort of clothes soldiers wore under their armour, padded doublet of linen laced up in the front; short breeches of deerskin and long woollen hose fastened to the doublet by eyelets and laces.

Her shoes were of padded leather. She looked like any soldier divested of his armour.

There was a certain protection in such clothes; that was why she knew she must cling to them and resist all temptation to assume feminine attire.

Now she must lie here, or take her few paces and wait for her trial while she endured the coarse conversation of her gaolers and hoped—in vain she guessed—that they would not try to put their coarse words into action.

Yes, indeed it seemed that God had deserted her.

It was not long before the onslaught came, as she knew it must.

She was exhausted and lying down; they were throwing their dice. She could hear their slurred voices, and although her body craved sleep she knew that she must stay alert.

One of them came over to her.

He touched her with his foot. She rose as well as the chains would permit.

'Get ready,' he said. 'They're going to smear you in sulphur and take you to the stake tonight.'

It was a lie, she knew.

'Go back to your dice,' she cried.

'Are you not frightened, little Maid? Think of the hot flames licking that virgin body of yours. It's a shame to die young, you know. You don't want to feel the flames of hell before you've had a few pleasures on earth, do you?'

'You lie,' she said. 'There has been no such order.'

'How do you know that?'

'God has told me,' she said. And the radiance was there on her face as when she rode into Orléans.

It seemed to the men then that there was a strange light in the cell.

William Talbot was a little afraid but he was not going to let John Grey know that. John Grey felt the same in respect to William Talbot.

Talbot caught her and pulled at the laces of the doublet.

With all her strength she hit out at him and sent him flying across the cell. He fell knocking his head against the wall.

John Grey burst into laughter at the sight of his friend.

'You like me better, eh, little Maid?' he said.

She brought up her knee and caught him. He reeled back. The other men at the door looked in. They saw the two notorious *houspilleurs* lying on the floor groaning.

They stared in amazement.

Jeannette stood there, the radiance still on her face.

She lay down on her pallet. She could sleep now in peace. She knew that she was not completely deserted.

*   *   *

There were visitors to her cell. Five important gentlemen had come to see her. She recognized Jean, Count of Luxembourg immediately. Three of the others she did not know. Luxembourg told her who they were. The great Earl of Warwick who was tutor to the young King of England; the Earl of Stafford who held a high place on the English Council; the Count's brother, Bishop of Thérouanne; and the fifth was Aimond de Macy, a man who had come to see her at Beaurevoir.

She did not hope for help from any of these men. The English she knew were out to destroy her; she distrusted Luxembourg and any friend of his; as for Aimond de Macy he had offended her deeply when he had come, out of curiosity, to see her and had declared that properly dressed and groomed she would be a pretty girl. He had commented that she had very pretty breasts and had tried to handle them. He had laughed afterwards at the fierceness with which he had been repulsed.

For what then could she hope from such visitors?

Luxembourg who felt an irresistible desire to tease her knowing how frightened she must be to have fallen into the hands of the English—into which he had sold her—said: 'Good day to you, Joan.' They used the English version of her name now because it was what the English called her.

'Why do you come here?' she asked.

'I have come to buy you back on condition that you promise never to take up arms against us again.'

Why did he say such a thing? She knew it was only to tease her, to raise her hopes that they might be dashed again and she would then feel even greater depression than she did now.

'I know full well that you are mocking me,' she told him. 'You have no desire to do what you say ... nor have you the power.'

'I swear to you ...' began Luxembourg.

'Have a care on whose name you swear your falsehoods,' she retorted. 'I know the English will kill me. They believe that when I am dead they can regain the realm of France. Is that not so?'

She looked defiantly at the Earls of Warwick and Suffolk who were watching her closely.

She laughed mockingly. 'I will tell you this; that if there were a hundred thousand more English in France than there are at this moment, they shall never reconquer the realm. That belongs to our King Charles the Seventh ... the anointed of God and so shall it remain.'

The Earl of Stafford had grown white with anger. He was known to be an impulsive man. He drew his dagger and moved towards Jeannette.

Warwick drew Stafford back. 'Have a care,' he whispered. 'Would you strike a girl?'

It was an end to the visit; Warwick's desire now was to get away.

Jeannette sank onto her pallet. For a moment she had thought the enraged earl was going to plunge the dagger into her breast. She had almost longed for him to do so. Then there would have been an end to her misery.

She thought about Warwick. Was that a hint of pity she had seen in his eyes? It might have been. But he was a calm, shrewd man. He knew that Joan of Arc killed by the dagger of an angry English earl would have remained a martyr whose spirit would have marched on with the French armies after she was gone.

No. These English were going to prove her a witch. They had to. So perhaps it was for that reason that Warwick had restrained the Earl of Suffolk.

*　　*　　*

Pierre Cauchon, Bishop of Beauvais, was in charge of the case against Jeannette because she had been taken in Compiègne which was in his diocese.

He knew that it was expected of him to prove her to be a witch. His masters desired it of him. It was the only possible verdict. Joan of Arc must be shown to be a creature in league with the Devil and evil spirits.

Pierre Cauchon was an ambitious man; although he had risen high in the Church he sought, in addition, to try his talents outside it.

He had ingratiated himself both with Henry the Fifth and

the Duke of Bedford. He had supported John of Burgundy when he had been putting forward his case for murdering the Duke of Orléans and for that reason he had won the gratitude of Philip of Burgundy.

When he was fifty he had become Bishop of Beauvais; he was at this time sixty and one of the richest priests in France. A tall, broad man with rugged features, he had a powerful presence. His confidence in himself was complete. He was avaricious and not too scrupulous. He was the man Bedford needed to give the verdict which was so necessary to him.

So while Jeannette waited in her prison he was preparing the case against her.

One day Jeannette was told by her gaolers that as a great concession a fellow prisoner was being allowed to visit her. He came from Lorraine, her own province, and he was a cobbler named Nicholas Loiseleur.

Jeannette was delighted and wondered why her gaolers, who had so far shown so little concern for her comfort, should send her a companion.

Nicholas Loiseleur was a gentle creature; he was some forty years of age and his voice was soft. He spoke with an accent which had a hint of Lorraine in it but sometimes he lapsed into a more educated tongue.

He was very sympathetic and asked Jeannette a great many questions about her home in Domrémy. He was very interested in her childhood and he asked about the fairies and the dancing round the tree.

Had she ever seen fairies? he wanted to know.

She told him that she had only heard of them and had never seen them herself. She believed her godmother had seen them or so she had heard.

Then he wanted to know about her voices.

She began to notice that on his visits he talked little about himself, and suddenly it occurred to her that he had not the hands of a cobbler.

She tried to turn the questions and ask about him; and when his answers were not very satisfactory her suspicions were aroused. She noticed that he always spoke in a loud voice and that he turned his face towards the door.

What was this? Another enemy when she thought she had a friend!

It was a well known trick of the Holy Office to trap people, to lead them to betray themselves and to have some eavesdropper taking notes. So this was the function of her cobbler friend.

Was there no end to the humiliations to which she must be submitted? It seemed not. One day a great lady came to her cell—no less than the Duchess of Bedford who was also the sister of the Duke of Burgundy.

She had come in the company of two others to test Jeannette's virginity.

The Duchess spoke with a gentleness and understanding of this violation of Jeannette's privacy.

'I am sorry,' she said, 'that this must be inflicted on you, but I am convinced that you are a pure maiden and if we can testify to this it will be very helpful to you in your coming trial.'

'And if I refuse?' asked Jeannette.

'Alas, they will take no refusal.'

There was something very kind about the Duchess. There was no prurience in her manner such as that to which Jeannette had so often been subjected.

'I promise you,' said the Duchess, 'that I and my helpers will conduct this examination with as much speed and privacy as we can. Please submit. I assure you it is better that you help us rather than resist.'

Jeannette, knowing what the result would be and taking a liking to the Duchess who seemed so different from her tormentors and reminded her of the kindness of the ladies of Luxembourg, submitted to the examination.

When it was completed the Duchess said: 'You are indeed a maid and shame on those who have called you harlot. Rest assured all shall know the result of this examination and I want to send you a tailor who will make clothes for you.'

She went to the gaolers whom she had dismissed during the operation and said to them: 'Joan of Arc is a good girl. Pray treat her with the respect you would like others to show to your daughters.'

Jeannette lay on her pallet after the Duchess had gone and her spirits were lifted a little. It was comforting to know that there were some in the world who could be kind to her.

The Duchess was true to her word and a few days later her tailor, Johannot Simon, called to measure Jeannette for some clothes.

Unfortunately the man thought he could make free with

the prisoner. He was rewarded with a blow on the ear which sent him reeling across the cell.

The guards were amused. Two of them had suffered themselves.

The tailor had learned his lesson too. Joan of Arc was no ordinary prisoner.

*   *   *

In the chapel royal of the castle of Rouen the trial of Joan of Arc was about to begin.

The most important figure in the court was Pierre Cauchon, Bishop of Beauvais. Seated on the dais he looked magnificent in his robes of scarlet edged with gold filigree. On either side of him seated in the carved seats were the forty assessors clad in their black robes—a startling contrast to the red splash of colour provided by Cauchon.

Jeannette was a sorry figure—emaciated, pale, still in chains and wearing the clothes into which she had gone to battle she was a sight to arouse pity. But those assembled in the court had not come to feel pity but to do the bidding of their masters.

There was a great uproar from without. Voices could be heard shouting against her. They were the English who had feared when she came against them. They called her the Devil's milkmaid, Satan's cowgirl, the whore of Domrémy. It mattered not that she was proclaimed a virgin; they would not give up their belief that she was from the Devil, because the only other alternative was that she came from God and that was something they dared not believe.

The scribes seated below the dais stared about them in consternation; they had never before known such a tumult in a court of this nature and were uncertain how to act. The prisoner appeared to be calmer than anyone. She sat pale and aloof as though she did not care that her life was at stake.

Finally Cauchon succeeded in establishing order. He told Jeannette that she must swear to answer the whole truth.

She considered this carefully. 'But I do not know what questions you will ask,' she pointed out. 'It may be that you will ask about something I cannot tell you.'

Cauchon said: 'Will you swear to do as you are told?'

'No,' she answered. 'I can tell you of my home, of my parents and what I have done since I took the road to France.

But what God has revealed to me I will not tell except to
Charles the King.'

They were wasting time, said Cauchon. She must take the
oath otherwise her evidence would be worthless. But he had
to agree that she should answer questions about her actions
and her faith but might not find she could do so about her
visions.

If she would not take the oath and answer all the questions
put to her Cauchon could have condemned her right away,
but that would not have suited the Duke of Bedford. He
wanted to expose her, and the King of France with her, as
dabblers in witchcraft. That was what Cauchon's masters expected of him and it was to his advantage to please them.

The first session had come to an end. It seemed to have
been completely taken up by formalities. As Jeannette was
about to leave the Court Cauchon said to her: 'I must warn
you. Should you attempt to escape it will go ill with you.'

'If the opportunity to escape came, I should take it,' she
retorted. 'It is every prisoner's right and I have never promised
anyone not to do so.'

'Are you aware that you are the prisoner of Holy Church,
and that it is a terrible crime to wish to be free of that
Church?'

'I have promised to no one that I should not escape,' she
answered stubbornly.

'Do you believe you have God's permission to leave prison?'

'Yes. If the opportunity was given me I should take it.'

When the Court was cleared Cauchon discussed the proceedings with the assessors. How could they know what the
girl would say next? Young and ignorant as she was, she was
a powerful adversary. They would have to tread very carefully.

Later he talked to Jean Beaupère, a former rector of the
University of Paris who had been assigned to assist him in the
cross-examination. Cauchon had great respect for Beaupère.
He was a shrewd man, learned in the ways of the law as well
as in those of the Church. He was a man of calm, clear judg-
ment and he had argued that under clever cross-examination
a simple peasant girl would destroy herself; and when
Cauchon said she could be condemned after her first appearance in Court it was Beaupère who pointed out it would be
better for her to entangle herself. There would be repercus-
sions, they could be sure. They wanted a clear case of heresy

and witchcraft. They wanted the Inquisition to find her guilty and hand her over to the secular arm for sentence which would be—as it was for witchcraft—burning at the stake.

'The next session should be held in a smaller chamber,' said Beaupère. 'We do not want a repetition of today's scene. The girl has courage. Let the Court be conducted among ourselves. We do not want all that turmoil outside. It is against her now. It could turn to her.'

Cauchon agreed that this was wise and the next day the Court was set up in a small room and guards were placed outside the door to keep out the mob.

The Inquisitor Jean Le Maître was present, as he had insisted, not to question, but to observe, and among the assessors was the sly Loiseleur who had posed as a cobbler and sought to trap Jeannette.

She saw all these people and was less afraid than she had been when she had had to face the ruffians in her cell. She had heard her voices in the early morning and Saint Catherine and Saint Margaret had told her to be of good cheer. God was watching over her and above all she must be bold. She must speak out and say what was in her mind. Refuse to answer if they asked her something which she felt was too sacred to be spoken of. And on other matters, tell the truth.

Beaupère spoke gently. Had she been as simple as some thought her, she would almost have thought he was on her side. He asked a great many questions about her childhood. She had no objections to talking about that. But it was inevitable, of course, that they should arrive at that time when she had heard the voices.

'What form did the angel take?' Beaupère asked.

He wanted her to describe some humanized form because it seemed a good way to trap her. She was aware of this. It was as though her voices were warning her.

'I refuse to answer that question,' she said.

One of the assessors cried out: 'What does the prisoner mean—she will not answer! She is here to answer any question that is put to her.'

Beaupère looked at Cauchon. They understood each other. The girl could refuse to talk altogether. What then? They could torture her. There were many things they could do to her. But would that be wise? They wanted her to talk. They wanted her to betray herself through the answers to subtle questions.

Cauchon shouted to the assessor to be silent. 'Let the Court proceed,' he added.

Beaupère ignored her refusal and did not press for a description of the angel. Instead he wanted to know how she had picked out the Dauphin when she had been presented to him. He had tried to press someone else on her, had he not? But she had known him at once.

She was guided to him, she said.

'By what sign?'

'That I will not speak of.'

The assessors murmured amongst themselves. What sort of a trial was this where the prisoner continually refused to answer certain questions?

They turned to Beaupère, but he was biding his time. He believed he could force her into a position where she would entrap herself. That was what he wanted.

'So these voices came to you, a humble peasant girl. You were to do this strange thing ... leave your cows and sheep and lead the Dauphin to victory.'

'That was what I was told to do.'

'And what was to be your reward for all this?'

'The salvation of my soul.'

Beaupère was exasperated. He had not expected such quick thinking of a peasant girl.

Cauchon was getting exasperated. The girl was making such a good impression. Of course they would find her guilty but it must be done in such a way as to leave no doubt. They did not want her to be a martyr after her death.

At the next assembly he told her that he would have no more nonsense about her refusing to take the recognized oath. But she again refused to take it.

'I could condemn you for that,' he said.

'Take care,' she warned. 'I am sent by God. You put yourself in danger by your treatment of me.'

Beaupère smiled at her pleasantly. He pursued his questions concerning the voices—each one cleverly couched to catch her. He came at length to the rites that had been observed during her childhood. They were pagan ceremonies, he hinted, and she had taken part in them. There was a suggestion that during them she had become imbued with the witches' craft.

At the end of the session she was taken back to her dreary prison there to stretch out on her straw pallet and pray for guidance until she fell asleep exhausted.

A great fear had come to her. She would not be allowed to go on refusing to take the oath. She knew that behind the smiling face of Beaupère there was a wolf waiting to devour her.

During the next days her weariness was apparent. Beaupère was the first to notice. He was cutting the ground around her, teasing her with seemingly innocent questions, standing by waiting for her to fall into his traps.

At last he had finished. He had done her great harm she knew, but she was not sure in what ways. He had been so quiet, had seemed so calm—even compassionate.

Cauchon took up the questions. Weary and without much hope for she knew that everything was going against her, she cried out: 'I went to war on God's business. I do not belong here. Send me back to my home.'

'Are you sure you are in God's grace?' asked Cauchon slyly.

'If I be not,' she answered firmly, 'please God to bring me to it. And if I be, please God to keep me in it.'

Cauchon despaired of bringing the trial to a satisfactory end. He consulted with his friends as to whether they should threaten her with torture.

She must stop her appeals direct to God; she must show greater respect for the Church. And yet how could they condemn her for praying to God?

She was surprised when she was allowed to stay in her prison for a day or so. She did wonder what fresh trials were being prepared for her. Then she discovered.

They came to her and releasing her from her chains led her out of prison. She gasped with horror when she saw the instruments in that dark apartment to which they had brought her. This was the torture chamber.

'Let me bear it, oh God,' she cried.

Cauchon regarded her steadily. 'It is our desire to bring you back into the ways of truth,' he said. 'You have made wicked inventions and placed your soul in peril. Only confession can save your soul and if you will not save it without, torture may induce you to.'

In the midst of her terror a great calm suddenly descended on Jeannette and then words which came to her lips seemed to have been put there by the saints whom she so dearly loved.

'If you will you must tear me limb from limb and I can do

naught but submit. And if in the extremity of the torture
your cruelty imposes on me I admit what you wish me to say,
I should afterwards tell the world that it was lies forced from
me by your instruments of torture.'

Beaupère laid an arm on that of Cauchon.

He withdrew him to a corner.

'The girl is too clever,' he said. 'What she says is right. None
would believe the confessions which are extracted under torture. It will not do in her case. Our task is to prove her guilty.
We will not do it with torture. It is the sure way to setting
her up as a martyr.'

They took her back to her prison and the idea of torture
was abandoned.

But the end of the trial was in sight.

Back in Court she was told that she was disobedient to
Christ if she did not obey his prelates of the Church.

How could Holy Church survive if all its members might
make private treaties with Heaven? This was her sin. She
demeaned Holy Church. If any man or woman would have
contact with Heaven it could only be through the Church. In
setting herself up as a confidante of God and His saints she
was placing herself above Heaven's representatives on Earth
—the prelates of the Church. She had been guilty of pride
and witchcraft for they would not believe her voices came
from Heaven. She was guilty of bloodshed. But her great sin
was in denying the supremacy of the Church and any who
did that was guilty of heresy.

She lay on her pallet. Her body burned with fever. She
believed she was back in the fields of Domrémy ... dancing
under L'Arbre des Dames. She was young, only a child, and
she had not then heard the voices.

She tossed on her bed.

She was exhausted mentally and bodily. She had scarcely
eaten for days—nothing but a little bread soaked in wine.
She had tried to answer their eternal questions, being careful
to avoid those which she believed might give offence to
Heaven.

Sometimes she felt they were sustaining her, those voices.
At others she felt they had deserted her. When they spoke
ill of the King she defended him fiercely, but in her heart
she knew that he had deserted her too.

They came to take her to the Court. She looked at them
with unseeing eyes.

'God help us, she is sick,' said Cauchon. 'She is sick unto death.'

*   *   *

They sent doctors to her. She must not die. That would never do. They must have her condemned; that must show her to have been the tool of the Devil.

Cauchon sent the best doctors to her. She was exhausted, was all they could say. She needed rest, food, peace of mind.

The two first she could have. It was hardly likely that the third would be available to her.

After a few days when Cauchon came to see her he was relieved to hear that she was a little better.

'I rejoice to see you are recovering,' he said.

'For what purpose should I recover?' she asked.

'I sent doctors to you to comfort and ease you in your illness. Your answers at the trial were very wayward,' he told her, 'but I bear in mind that you are an unlettered girl. I can send good men to you to instruct and bring you back into the ways of truth. I must warn you that if you persist in your ways you will place yourself in great peril. We who are your mentors in Holy Church, wish to lead you away from this danger.'

Jeannette smiled feebly. 'Thank you,' she said. 'But I shall continue to rely on God. If I die, I trust it will please you to bury me in holy ground.'

'If you disobey the Church's laws,' replied Cauchon, 'you cannot be granted the Church's privileges.'

'Then,' she said, 'I must trust in God.'

*   *   *

She was well enough to leave her bed. She felt frail as though much of her strength had been sapped from her. She reflected that it was exactly a year since she had been captured. Oh God, she prayed, have I endured this torture for twelve long months?

She must go once more before her judges.

This was the end. If she admitted that her voices and visions were false, she might be saved.

It was Pierre Maurice, one of her assessors and a canon of Rouen, who urged her to deny her voices.

He was young; and he spoke sympathetically. There were occasions when Jeannette imagined that some of her judges were sorry for her and would help her if they could. Maurice was one of them.

'Jeannette, my friend,' he said, 'do not reject the Lord Jesus Christ. Do not take the path to eternal damnation with the powers of darkness who seek to distract men and women by taking on the shapes of angels and saints and saying they come from Heaven. Repel them. Turn your back on them. Listen to the words of those who would help you and who are the true servants of God.'

She looked into the earnest face of this young man and perhaps because she was so weak, having just risen from a sick bed, a flicker of doubt entered her mind.

Pierre Maurice was aware of this. He leaned towards her.

'Can you imagine the agony of death at the stake? It is not quick, my friend. You suffer the torments of hell ... a fore-taste of what will go on eternally if you die with all your sins upon you. Think. You are denied the rights of the Church! Oh think of it, Jeannette.'

She was silent, thinking of it. Where were her voices now? Where was her good friend the King of France? If only there could be some sign.

'Take her to her cell,' said Pierre Maurice. He gave her a gentle smile. 'Think of it, Jeannette,' he added softly.

She lay on her straw. She was amazed that she could sleep. But her sleep brought her no comfort. She dreamed that the flames had already begun to lick her body.

She awoke crying out in terror.

Only a dream but one which would soon be reality.

It was early next morning when they came for her ...

Beaupère with Pierre Maurice came into her cell.

'We are leaving at once,' she was told. Maurice laid a hand on her arm. 'Jeannette,' he said, 'listen to me. Recant while there is time. If you do not the Church will hand you over to the secular law.'

'And I shall be tried again ... and not by the Church.'

'You will be condemned. None would go against the judg-ment of Holy Church.'

She said bitterly: 'Holy Church must not shed blood. So it passes those it wishes to destroy over to the secular arm and it would go ill with any judge there who went against the wishes of the Church.'

She was surprised at herself. She had been brought up to revere the Church. She put her hand to her brow. She felt weak and ill.

She climbed into the cart they had brought to take her the short distance to the cemetery of the Abbey of St Ouen. There platforms had been set up and on one of these were seated several cardinals and officials of the Church. Among the Cardinals was the Bishop of Winchester, watching the proceedings with the utmost interest for they were of great importance to his nephew the Duke of Bedford, and indeed to the whole English cause in France.

A sermon was preached by William Erard Canon of Rouen who afterwards admitted that he had no heart for it.

Jeannette listened and it was as though her dream was still with her and already she could feel the heat of fire scorching her limbs.

She was afraid.

'The French had never been a truly Christian nation,' the preacher was saying. Oh, he was determined to please his English masters. And Charles who claimed to rule over that nation must be a heretic himself to trust to this woman who now stood before ...

Jeannette could not bear to hear the King spoken of in such a way. She rose and cried in loud ringing tones: 'You outrage our King who is the noblest of Christians ... None bears greater love to the Church than he ...'

The preacher went on to list the crimes the Maid had committed.

'Make your submission,' he thundered. 'Repent while you have time.'

Jeannette was still intent on defending the King.

'If there has been any fault it is mine alone,' she cried.

Pierre Maurice listening thought: She is weakening. She says 'if there has been any fault.' She would not have said that a week ago. Poor girl. Poor brave child.

They would excommunicate her, brand her as a heretic and hand her over to the secular law to carry out the sentence of death by burning.

Erard had turned to her. For the last time he was asking her to sign the submission, to confess to that of which she was accused.

She is wavering, thought Maurice. Poor girl, they have deserted her, all of them. She is worn out with suffering.

She said very quietly that she wished her case to be put before the Pope.

'The Pope is far away,' said Erard, 'and your judges are delegated by him. The time has come. I shall now read the sentence of excommunication.'

Jeannette lifted her hand in protest.

Cauchon watching closely signed to Erard and a paper was set before Jeannette.

She was going to put her cross on it.

Under great pressure, after a year of intense suffering, sick in body, ignored by the King whom she had helped, deserted by her voices for whom she had lived and worked for the last six years, she could endure no more.

She nodded her head.

'I would rather sign than be burned,' she said.

* * *

What had she done? She had denied her voices. She had betrayed Saint Catherine, Saint Margaret and the Archangel Michael. Worst of all she had denied God.

'They left me alone to my enemies,' she murmured.

She tossed on her pallet. In the dimness she thought she saw a light. She thought she heard the voices.

They admonished her gently, but they understood. She had suffered as few had been called on to suffer. They were with her. She would have nothing to fear. Eternal joy was very close now.

Suddenly it was all clear to her. Her voices had promised nothing but salvation. There was no way out for her but through death.

She felt happier now.

* * *

The streets were filling fast. It was the day so many people had been waiting for. The people were to have their spectacle after all.

She wore a long grey robe and on her head was a paper mitre on which were written the words Heretic, Relapse, Apostate, Idolatress. It was the end.

Pierre Maurice came to see her in the cell. She was touched by the sadness in his eyes.

'Where shall I be this night?' she asked.

'Have you no hope in Our Lord?' he answered.

'Yes,' she said and there was ecstasy in her voice. 'God willing I shall be with the saints in Paradise.'

They took her out to the tumbril which was waiting for her. There were one hundred and twenty soldiers to guard her on her short journey to the market place. All the little streets which converged on it were choked with people all eager to get a glimpse of the Maid's last moments.

Cauchon delivered his final announcement.

'In the name of God we reject you, abandon you, praying only that the secular power may moderate its sentence.'

It was ironical. There were some in the crowd who marvelled at the hypocrisy of a Church which could bring one of its members to this square with the sole purpose of submitting her to the flames and at the same time piously cast off the responsibility, knowing full well that no member of the secular arm would dare go against its wishes.

Now they were waiting. There was the pedestal, the ladder which she was to mount; there were the faggots which would be lighted.

They took her to the scaffold and forced her to mount the ladder. A chain was fastened about her waist to hold her firmly to the stake and almost immediately the smoke began to rise.

'So I die,' she thought. 'No cross to hold, no comfort to help me on my way.'

'Will you not give me a cross?' she cried in anguish and one of the English archers who had come to witness the spectacle was moved to sudden pity which he found inexplicable. He leaped forward and snatched a branch from the wood at her feet. He formed it into a cross and gave it to her.

She seized it gratefully and held it before her eyes.

One of the monks came up with a cross he had taken from the altar of a nearby church. He held it before her eyes.

The flames were thick now. The crowd was shouting so loudly that they could not hear the moaning mingled with the prayers of the victim.

Then suddenly there was a cry of 'Jesus'.

For a few moments there was a deep silence in the square.

Then an English soldier spoke and his words were clearly heard by those around.

'God help us,' he said, 'we have burned a saint.'

PART THREE

ELEANOR OF GLOUCESTER

THE WITCH OF EYE

THE young King was excited. For the first time in his life he was going to leave England.

The Cardinal had come to him with much solemnity and had explained to him that he was going to his land of France and would there be crowned as King.

But I have already been crowned once, thought Henry. He remembered well the weary ceremony and the weight of the crown they made him wear and all those people coming up one after another and kneeling to him. There were times when he heartily wished they had made someone else King.

But to go to France! That might be exciting.

He looked at the Cardinal, an old, old man he seemed and very serious. He had heard his uncle Gloucester refer to him as 'that old rogue'. That puzzled him. It was hard to think of the Cardinal as anything but one of those good men for whom the gates of Heaven would open wide when he made his journey there, which, thought Henry, judging by his age must be imminent.

In the meantime he was on Earth and appeared now and then to make sure that the King did his duty.

Henry missed his mother and Alice and Joan. Life had been very different when he was with them. But apparently people like himself who were born with the burden of kingship already on them, could not be brought up by women. They had to have people like the Earl of Warwick and the Cardinal of Winchester around them—and occasionally his uncles, stern Bedford and jolly Gloucester, both of whom, in spite of their different natures, alarmed him more than a little.

'There will be a service at St Paul's Cathedral,' the Cardinal was saying, 'and you must remember that God will be watching you—and so will the people.'

It was rather frightening to be so spied on; but if God loved him as much as the people obviously did, he thought he might be as welcome in Heaven as the Cardinal would be.

'You will understand,' went on the Cardinal, 'that a great deal of preparation has gone into this visit so it remains with you, my lord, to make sure that no one is disappointed in you.'

Henry replied brightly: 'The people shout a lot and cheer me and say "Long live the little King".'

'That is because you are a boy. But at the same time they expect a great deal from you. The higher the position the better you must be. You must never forget that you are King of this realm.'

'People are always telling me,' commented Henry, 'so I could not easily forget.'

'That is well,' said the Cardinal. 'After the service we shall go to Kennington and we shall be in Canterbury on Palm Sunday, where we shall celebrate Easter which will be fitting. Then we shall make our way to Dover.'

'Will my mother come with us?' asked Henry.

'No, no, indeed no,' said the Cardinal quickly. He did not wish to be reminded of the Queen Mother. There were some unpleasant rumours about her, some connection with a Welsh squire. There were anxieties enough without her adding to them. Things were not going well in France and the Duke of Bedford was deeply concerned about the abandoning of the siege of Orléans.

So the journey began as they had arranged it should. From Kennington to Canterbury where the people came out to cheer the little King. They remained there over Easter and all thought it was a good omen that Henry should set sail for France on St George's Day.

It was exciting to land in a new country. It seemed he was its King as he was in England. His father had won it. Henry was always a little disturbed when people talked to him of his father because the admonition usually followed that he must learn to be like him; and Henry was beginning to think that it was not going to be very easy to do that.

They rode across the country which was rather flat and not unlike England in many ways except that the people did not seem to love him so much. They came out of their houses to look at him but they did not cheer as they did in England and some of them looked as though they would rather he had stayed away.

He heard a good deal of talk about Joan the Maid. The servants were always whispering about her. 'Who is Joan the Maid?' he asked. 'She is a witch,' he was told.

A witch! His eyes were round with horror. Where was she now?

She was where she should have been long ago. In prison. They had caught her. Now she would have to pay for her wickedness.

He thought about her a great deal. That was because she seemed to be in everybody's mind.

She had used her witchcraft against the English, it seemed, and consequently they had lost some battles. They had taken that very badly. Battles, Henry had always thought, were won by the English. He was constantly being taught about Crécy and Poitiers and Harfleur and Agincourt. Nobody could withstand the bowmen of England—unless it was by witchcraft.

They were going to Rouen and soon he saw the towers of the capital city of Normandy which had been for so long the dominion of the English. William the Conqueror had made it so when he came to England; Henry had learned that years ago.

His uncle Bedford was at Rouen. Henry was greatly in awe of him. He was always so stern and never failed to remind him of his wonderful father. The Duchess was different. She was kind and friendly and seemed to remember quite often that although Henry was a King he was also only a boy.

Henry realized that they were all very concerned about Joan of Arc. They seemed to talk of nothing else. There was a sort of trial going on and his uncle Bedford was in close conference with the Bishops of Winchester and Beauvais and other men; they were all very grave.

They told him little. All he knew was that there was a wicked woman who was a witch and she had come to some arrangement with the Devil to crown the Dauphin of France who thought the crown of France was his although it really belonged to the English through the conquest of Henry's great father and something called the Salic law which the French followed and was no true law at all apparently.

Well, he had to prepare himself for his coronation and there was a great fuss about that too. The Kings of France were crowned at Rheims and owing to the witchcraft of Joan of Arc Rheims was now in the hands of the French and as the Dauphin had been crowned there it was hardly possible for Henry to be crowned there as well.

His uncle fumed about it. He had heard him cry out: 'The woman must be proved to be a witch.'

So then Henry knew that it had something to do with Joan of Arc.

He asked one of his squires about the witch. It was exciting —and frightening too—to contemplate that she was actually a prisoner in this very castle. Sometimes he would wake up in the night and wonder whether witches had special powers and that they might break out of their prisons. Surely that was a small thing to do. Suppose she came to him? She would be particularly angry with him because, as he had learned, it was due to her that the Dauphin had been crowned. She wouldn't like the true King very much.

One day his squire said to him: 'There is an aperture in her prison. People watch her through it. Would you like to take a peep?'

He hesitated. He was afraid of what he would see. He imagined an ugly old woman with warts all over her where the Devil had kissed her.

But he wanted to see. He wanted to be frightened and horrified.

He accompanied the squire into the tower and up a flight of stairs.

The squire lifted him and he put his eye to the aperture. He was looking into a dark room, bare as far as he could see of all furniture except a straw pallet. Seated on this, her eyes on the window high in the wall, which was the only place where any light came through, was a woman. She was not old. She was pale and her eyes looked large and luminous. He could not help staring at her. There was a quality about her which even he in his youth must recognize.

He could not have described her. The only thought that came into his mind was: She is not like a witch. She looks good.

Then he saw that there was another table in this room,

which he had not seen at first. Seated at it were three men whose appearance was so rough and cruel that they made an outstanding contrast to the girl seated on the bed.

As he looked there he felt suddenly a wretchedness which he could not understand. He signed to the squire to lift him down.

He wanted to burst into tears.

He said nothing as he was taken back to his own apartments, but he could not forget the sight of her. She haunted his dreams as she had before, but differently. Previously he had thought of an evil witch breaking into his apartments and putting some fearful spell on him. Now he thought of her quiet and sad ... staring up at the light as though she were talking to God.

There must be good witches as well as bad ones, he thought and he was convinced that she was a good one.

There came a day when the excitement in the town of Rouen had reached fever point. It was impossible to shut it out of the royal apartments. They were whispering together —from the highest to the lowest. Everybody wanted to be out in the streets on that day.

'It is the day when they will burn Joan of Arc at the stake,' he was told. 'You are not to go out to see it.'

He did not want to. He clenched his hands together. He did not want to see her burn.

But the tension had permeated the castle. One might not be there to see ... but one could feel.

The English were burning her. His uncle Bedford had said that was what must be done because she was a witch. She brought great harm to the English and had changed the course of the war. There would be no hope for England if she were allowed to live and lead French armies.

He could smell the acrid odour of burning wood and the oil they poured on it to make it burn the faster. And she was in the centre of it. The girl he had seen through the aperture in the wall.

He wondered if he would ever be able to forget her.

Uncle Bedford was brisk and obviously relieved. So was the Bishop of Winchester. Now they could go ahead with the coronation.

But it seemed that was not easy. It was all due to the fact that traditionally Kings of France should be crowned at Rheims and because of Joan of Arc the French were now in possession of that town and they believed that the true King was the French one who had already been crowned, once more due to Joan of Arc.

His uncle Bedford came to him one day and told him that shortly he would be leaving for Paris. He was going to be crowned there. It was a great pity that it had to be Paris but they could not wait until they had recaptured Rheims so he was to be crowned there and return to England for the people there would not want him to stay away too long.

He was glad that his aunt Bedford was there too. He liked her; she reminded him of his mother. She was kind and seemed the only one to understand what an ordeal a coronation could be to a boy of nine. That was it; she thought of him as a boy while these important men thought of him as the King. He was able to tell her that he had looked through the aperture at Joan of Arc.

'They should never have taken you to see her,' said the Duchess.

'But I was glad they did. I wasn't frightened after that. I used to dream that she came into my room at night and she was old and ugly and cast wicked spells on me. Then I saw her and I didn't dream after that … except to be very sad because they were going to burn her.'

'Hush,' said the Duchess. 'You should not speak of her to your uncle or to any.'

'People do speak of her,' he said. 'I heard someone say she was a saint.'

'No … no … no. That is treason.'

'Treason,' said Henry solemnly, 'is to speak and act against the King and the country. I am the King, so I can't speak treason against myself, can I?'

'Oh,' laughed the Duchess, patting his hand, 'you are going to be a clever one, I can see. Listen. It would be better now if you did not disturb yourself with these matters.'

But try as he might he could not forget Joan of Arc, even when they rode to Paris, that wonderful city of towers and turrets which enchanted him. He wished that he was going there to stay with his mother as they used to at Windsor and there were just the two of them with Alice and Joan and of course Owen Tudor. Then there had not been the anxieties of what he would have to do and whether he would perform it to the satisfaction of these solemn old men.

The people had hung out flags and banners for him, and

they cheered him as he entered by the Porte Saint Dennis, but they were the English conquerors of course. The French remained silent and sullen. He felt that he wanted to say to them: It is not my fault that I am here. I am the King but I still have to do what I am told.

He was to be lodged at Vincennes until the coronation, which, said his uncle Bedford, should not be delayed. The situation had been uneasy since the coming of Joan of Arc and now she was dead her influence remained. She was a martyr now and Henry had heard it said that martyrs were as much to be feared as the greatest generals.

Two days before the coronation he was taken to the Hôtel de St Pol to visit his grandmother.

It was an alarming experience. Isabeau, ravaged by the violent life she had led, was still beautiful but her grandson was repelled by her. She put down a hand which he thought was like a claw and drew him to her. He stared at her with solemn eyes. Her face was painted and she looked like some powerful goddess who would have the power to turn him into stone if he displeased her.

'So, grandson,' she said to him, 'you are to be crowned King of France. That is well ... that is well.'

'I am not sure that the people of France think so,' he answered.

She laughed. 'You are a clever boy, I see that. Stay clever, little one. There are two things which will bring you what you want ... beauty and cleverness. Once I had them both.'

He did not know what to reply so he looked at her steadily thinking she was magnificent although somewhat grotesque.

'Tell me of your mother.'

'She is well,' answered Henry.

'They have taken you from her care.'

Henry agreed that this was so.

'Tell me, grandson, did you know the Tudor squire?'

'Owen?'

'Was that his name?'

'Yes, he was Owen Tudor, grandson of Sir Tudor Vychan ap Gronw, and his father, Meredydd, was an outlaw accused of murder.'

'You concern yourself greatly with the affairs of a squire.'

'Well, this was Owen ...'

'A rather special squire I believe. Did your mother think he was a rather special squire?'

'Oh yes. She said there was none like Owen.'

His grandmother began to laugh.

'Your mother was my youngest child,' she told him. 'She became the Queen of England and the mother of its King! That is good ... considering the condition we were in. Beaten to our knees by your father, grandson.'

'Yes, I know about Harfleur and Agincourt.'

'I'll swear you do. The English boast of their successes. As all do. Now tell me more of your mother. Tell me of life at Windsor ... when you were with her. Tell me about Owen Tudor ...'

She made him talk a great deal and although she smiled kindly at him he was very glad when the visit to the Hôtel de St Pol was over.

Two days later he was crowned at Notre Dame by Cardinal Beaufort. It was not a happy ceremony. There was a brooding atmosphere of discontent throughout the proceedings and the people of Paris complained that there were too many English present. Surely, thought Henry logically, this should have been expected since the King was English, but the French did not like it. Moreover Kings of France should be crowned at Rheims and there *was* a King of France in any case. There was further complaint because many of the customs that accompanied a coronation were ignored. Certain prisoners usually received an amnesty and money was distributed to the needy. All this was forgotten by the English, so it was an odd kind of coronation from every point of view and one calculated to bring little comfort to the French.

The Duke of Bedford was aware of the discontent. He was a very worried man these days. He had been shaken by the exploits of Joan of Arc; and his alliance with the Duke of Burgundy was far from sound. The Duke blamed him for the loss of Orléans. If he had allowed the people to surrender to Burgundy the town would not now be in the hands of the French. It had been a great disappointment to Bedford that Henry could not be crowned at Rheims. In fact the position in France had not been so uneasy from an English point of view since before Agincourt. And to think it was all due to a peasant girl who had heard voices, infuriated the Duke. He would not have been nearly so infuriated if it had been due to superior fighting strength and strategy, but this was incomprehensible and even now that the Maid had been burned at the stake he was still bemused and uneasy.

He said to the Bishop of Winchester: 'The King should leave for England immediately. I cannot rest in peace while he remains in France.'

The Bishop agreed. 'But you will see that everything will change now. The witch is no more. Her influence has gone. It will be as it was before she came to disturb us all. Charles is a weakling—no Maid of Orléans can alter that. He is lazy, indecisive, not meant for war.'

The Duke nodded. 'I think of Burgundy ...'

'Your Duchess will make sure that the peace is kept between you and her brother.'

'Oh yes. Thank God for Anne. But her health gives me some anxiety, Bishop.'

'She is young. She is devoted to you.'

'I thank God for that. I pray for a child—so does Anne. She longs for it.'

'He will grant your wish in time,' said the Bishop.

The Duke found it difficult to shake off his gloom, and the Bishop thought: This affair of the Maid has unnerved him ... as it has us all.

On the Duke's orders the young King left Paris for Rouen, but it was the end of January before he landed at Dover where he rested for a while and by slow stages made the journey to London, where a great welcome awaited him and although it was cold February the people came out in their thousands to greet him. He looked very handsome in his robes of State with the crown on his head. 'The dear little King,' they called him. Banners fluttered from every possible place and the procession was halted again and again as it made its way through the streets of London. Young girls recited poems on the virtues of their King and they did not fail to stress the fact that he was King of France as well as of England.

It was all very pleasant and one of those rare occasions when he was glad he was the King.

Humphrey of Gloucester was there to welcome him back. He was never sure of Uncle Humphrey. He knew that Uncle Bedford, stern as he was, was a man of great honour and virtue. He was not certain what Uncle Humphrey was.

Humphrey had been Regent during his absence and he saw at once that there was a change in his uncle's attitude towards him. He was a little more deferential.

Ah, thought Henry wisely, it is because I am growing up.

When Humphrey had told him how pleased he was that he

had returned safely and how delighted that the people of London had welcomed him so warmly—both sentiments of which Henry with growing shrewdness was a little suspicious —he then began to tell him about the iniquities of Cardinal Beaufort.

Something would have to be done about that old rogue, said Uncle Humphrey.

To hear the dignified Cardinal referred to in such terms was bewildering. But then life often was to a King who was taking such a long time to grow up.

*　　*　　*

The Duchess of Gloucester was very pleased with life. From comparatively humble origins she had risen high, for who would dispute the fact that while the Duke of Bedford was absent from England engaged on the French wars, the Duke of Gloucester was the most important man in England —King in all but name; and as she held a powerful influence over him, this meant that the Duchess was a lady of great consequence.

It had been a great triumph to get Humphrey to marry her. As plain Eleanor Cobham she had enchanted and enslaved him and there were few, apart from Eleanor herself, who believed that she could continue to do so and with what effect. But Eleanor had complete confidence in herself. Humphrey had never met a woman like her. As deeply sensual as he was himself she could continue to excite him in that field which had always been important to him; but there was more than sexual accomplishment to Eleanor. She was as wily as any statesman; and she knew how to play a waiting game. There was nothing impulsive about her. She had her eyes well on the future.

There was a little King—a minor for some years to come— malleable as clay in the clever hands of those who knew how to mould him. He had two uncles and one was engaged in the French wars. That left the field clear for the other—Gloucester . . . or would have if those who tried to impede him were swept away.

She was waiting for her husband when he returned from greeting the King.

Humphrey came bursting into their apartments. She went to him and removed his cloak, then putting her arms about his neck gave him a deeply passionate kiss on the lips. He responded as he could never resist doing and said: 'Oh, Eleanor, Beaufort's back with the King.'

'That snake,' she said. 'It's time someone finished him.'

'We must.'

'Come,' she said. 'Will you eat? Will you rest? What do you wish, my love?'

'To be with you ... to talk and talk ... This thing's on my mind. He's got Bedford's confidence.'

'We'll eat first,' she said, 'and then go to bed ... and you can talk as you will.'

Later they lay side by side in the bed they delighted to share and they talked about the Cardinal ... and Bedford.

'My brother has aged. This woman has upset him.'

'One would not expect him to be upset by a woman.'

'No ordinary woman, I assure you, but one who heard voices ... a virgin no less.'

'And Brother Bedford would respect that!'

'He proved her a witch and burned her at the stake but she haunts him. I can see that. He's not sure. She was so convincing at her trial ... she confounded Beauvais and the lot of them. And how could a peasant girl do that? That's what they ask themselves. I can tell you that girl is responsible for more than the loss of Orléans and the crowning of the Dauphin.'

'But now she's dead.'

'She lives on in a way. The French thank Heaven she was on their side and that idea can't be shifted.'

'To let the girl burn at the stake! Heaven's help wasn't much use there.'

'It's made a sort of legend of it. After all they are saying Christ was crucified. If the girl had gone back to her flocks she would have been forgotten in a few months. Now they will never forget.'

'So Bedford suffers, does he?' The Duchess was smiling.

'He looks older.'

'And he is happy with his Duchess? You brothers are lucky in your marriages. Henry enjoyed Katherine. By the way, there is still scandal about her frolicking with the Welsh squire.'

'Let her,' said Gloucester. 'She's no threat to us.'

'No, and we waste time to consider her. Humphrey, if Bedford were to die ...'

'He is a young man yet.'

'In battle perhaps. After all your brother Henry died at thirty-five.'

'Yes, if he were to die what then?'

'What then indeed, my Humphrey. Do you realize that you would be next in line to the throne?'

'Young Henry is a healthy enough boy.'

'H'm ...' she murmured and there was speculation in her beautiful eyes. 'We must hope the way remains clear. Bedford may live for years yet. His Anne may have a son ... which God forbid.'

She was deeply thoughtful; ideas had come to her which she would not share even with Humphrey.

She had become a Duchess and no one would have believed she ever could. Was it possible for her to be a Queen?

There was one man who would ruin their plans if he had a chance and that was Humphrey's uncle, Cardinal Beaufort.

He must go. Humphrey had tried hard enough to get rid of him and had failed so far. It was a pity that the old Cardinal held such power. It was a pity that he was of a royal strain. It was all very well for Humphrey to call him Bastard. So might he have been born but old John of Gaunt's paternal instincts had been strong and he had cared so much for Beaufort's mother that he had insisted on her children being legitimized. And Henry Beaufort, Bishop of Winchester and now Cardinal, had shown his loyalty to the crown all through his life. It was hard to unseat such a man.

'I think we have him this time,' said Gloucester. 'We'll get him on praemunire. I have it on good authority that he has bought an exemption from the jurisdiction of Canterbury. He has given bribes. And look how rich he is. How did he come by such possessions?'

'To get him removed would be a great triumph,' said Eleanor.

'Never fear, my love, I shall do it.'

'I never doubted that you would. Tell me more of Bedford.'

'He is as ever ... determined to carry out my brother's death-bed wishes. A little upset about Burgundy though. He made a mistake over Orléans and should have let the town surrender to Burgundy. Wasn't going to beat the bushes to let someone else get the birds, ha, ha. He thought he was clever. And Bedford doesn't like to make mistakes.'

'You would say matters do not go well in France.'

'I would indeed say that.'

She put her arms about him and drew him towards her. 'We have matters here in England with which to concern ourselves,' she said.

*   *   *

It was May when Henry opened Parliament and a very unpleasant session it was because of the quarrel between Uncle Humphrey and Cardinal Beaufort.

During it the Cardinal rose and confronting him and his Uncle Humphrey demanded to know what accusations were being brought against him.

There was a great deal of recrimination and talk which Henry could not understand but he was well aware of the hatred between his Uncle Humphrey and his great uncle the Cardinal

He gathered that the Cardinal had made treaties with the Pope and that by so doing he had acquired special privilege; he had amassed great wealth; and above all his Uncle Humphrey would not rest until he had confiscated the Cardinal's vast wealth and exiled him from the country.

It was all very distressing for Henry who was afraid of both of them. He was glad they did not expect him to take any decisions as yet. That was all for the Parliament to do.

He was relieved when the Parliament told him to declare his faith in the Cardinal; but it was all very bewildering and it seemed that the Cardinal was not very happy about the proceedings. Henry had heard his Uncle Humphrey say that the Bishops would be rather excited at the prospect of the See of Winchester being vacant and that would be helpful. Henry could not understand that at all. It seemed to have nothing to do with the Cardinal's guilt.

After that they discussed seizing his jewels, which was also difficult for Henry to understand. Later he heard that the Cardinal had lent the crown a great deal of money so that seemed to settle the matter.

But Henry young as he was knew that his uncle would continue to hate the Cardinal and try to harm him; and the Cardinal would always be Humphrey's enemy.

*   *   *

As the Court was at Westminster for the session of the Parliament, it was easy for Eleanor to go on a little errand which had long been in her mind. Divesting herself of her jewels and her fine velvet robe, she put on the clothes of a merchant's wife and with one of her attendants likewise clad she slipped out into the streets and the pair mingled with the crowd.

They made their way in silence to an inn in one of the narrow streets. The innkeeper came out, his eyes lighting up at the sight of Eleanor, and he was about to bow obsequiously when a look from her restrained him.

'The horses?' she said.

'Ready and waiting ...' he answered promptly.

She nodded and with her attendant went out with the innkeeper to the innyard where two horses were already saddled. The innkeeper helped Eleanor to mount and did the same for her attendant. Then the two women rode together out of the yard.

It was not very far to the Manor of Eye-next-Westminster and having reached the little hamlet they went to an inn to leave their horses. They were received there with the same respect.

Although these precautions irritated Eleanor at the same time she was elated by them. An intriguer by nature she enjoyed the thrill of mystery. She wanted no one to know of her visits to Margery—not even Humphrey. Eleanor had great faith in Margery, and she had suffered a certain shock not so long ago when Margery had been sent to Windsor, suspected of sorcery.

Trust Margery to extricate herself from that, but even she could hardly hope to do so again if another charge was brought against her and it would not be advisable for the Duchess of Gloucester to be connected with her.

They came to the house; it was small, in a row of such houses, but there was something exciting about it because it was the home of Margery Jourdemayne, the Witch of Eye.

Eleanor rapped imperiously on the door. It was opened cautiously and there was Margery herself, her eyes bright with welcome.

'Come in, my lady. It warms the cockles of my heart to see you again.'

'Ah Margery, let me look at you. The same as ever. You don't seem to have suffered much from your ordeal.'

'That's nigh on three years back, my lady. And right glad I am to see you ... and to learn by hearsay that our little tricks worked. My lady Duchess now ... no less. A very great lady ... one of the finest in the land, they tell me. But what do we here? Come in, my lady ... and you too, my lady. There's always a welcome for you at old Margery's fireside.'

They were in a small room very sparsely furnished with a table, two chairs and a few stools. This was where Margery received her clients and it was scarcely different from other rooms in houses of its kind.

'Pray be seated,' she said and offered a chair to the Duchess. Margery herself sat on the other. The Duchess's attendant was given a stool.

'And what did you wish from me, my lady?'

'I believe you have a good complexion milk, Margery. You supplied it to me in the past. I miss it.'

'I know the one, my lady, my own special brew. 'Tis made from ... Ah, but I must not give away my secrets. 'Tis more than the herbs that goes into it. It's the wisdom and blessings of wise women culled over the years and passed down to their own.'

'It softened my skin and made it like velvet,' said the Duchess. 'Margery, take me to your workroom a while. I would select my own pot.'

'Assuredly, my lady.'

A covert understanding had passed between Margery and Eleanor. It meant they were to be alone.

The attendant rose and Margery said: 'Nay, my dear. You will stay here.'

It was an order. Eleanor turned to her attendant and shrugged her shoulders as though to say: We must humour the old woman, and then she followed Margery through a door which was firmly shut behind them.

'You know the way, my lady,' she said with a little laugh.

Eleanor nodded and Margery led the way down a flight of steps. With a key which hung about her waist Margery opened a door. They were in a kind of cellar with a barred window high in the wall through which a faint light came. From the beams hung herbs of many kinds all in the process of drying. There was a fire burning and on this stood a cauldron from which steam rose and the air was filled with the pungent smell of whatever was simmering. Eleanor recognized the appliances on a long bench which could be used for cutting, slicing, pounding and such like operations for she had seen it on previous visits.

'My lady's complexion milk. I have but to decant it,' said Margery. 'I made this for you before I went to Windsor. That's three years ago but it is of such fine stuff that it will last forever.'

They both knew that it was not for this that Eleanor had come. But naturally the Duchess did not want even her intimate friends and attendants to know the real reason. They were enough in her confidence to know that she visited the Witch of Eye, for Eleanor could not very easily have come alone. However that was as far as they should be in the secret.

Eleanor said: 'Margery, what happened at Windsor?'

'I was arrested you know with Friar Ashewell and the clerk John Virley and we were all charged with sorcery.'

'And you were released.'

Margery smiled slyly. ' 'Twas a surprise to all in Eye I can tell you when I came back. They were all set for Smithfield to see me in smoke.'

'Don't talk so, Margery.'

'Oh my lady, 'twas truth. But I had good friends ... and to my amaze as well as others, I was set free.'

'And came straight back and continued to sell your love potions.'

'There's no harm in them. They be good ... as you yourself have reason to know. It was like being tickled with ten thousand feathers when I heard you'd married the Duke. I said, "Ah, reckon she owes something of that to old Margery." Though mind you you're one of them ladies as a man finds hard to escape from once she makes up her mind she wants him. 'Tis good to see you so riz in the world.'

Old Margery had a respectful manner of speaking which nevertheless contained a reminder of Eleanor's spectacular ascent in the world. The old woman was telling her she remembered young Eleanor Cobham coming to her for a love potion or some aid to beauty, when she was no more than a woman of small consequence and thought herself so lucky to get the task of lady-in-waiting to Jacqueline who was then the Duchess of Gloucester.

Margery remembered well the elation of the lady when she became the Duke's mistress and how they had put their heads together and tried to work out a way of making her his wife.

Fate had favoured them with the wars in Holland and foreign parts but when the moment came, with Margery's help, Eleanor was ready—and Margery hoped the proud Duchess would not forget it.

'And the Duke is as loving as he ever was?' asked Margery wondering why Eleanor had now come back to her. After all it needed a little courage—not that Eleanor had ever been short of that—for Margery had been accused of sorcery once and had escaped by the skin of her teeth. There was no saying that she would not be taken again—in fact it was very likely. It would not look well for a high and mighty lady like the Duchess of Gloucester to have had traffic with her. So the inference was that Eleanor must want something rather badly to have come in person to the Witch of Eye.

'Yes,' answered Eleanor, 'as loving as ever and I know how to keep him so.'

Margery nodded slowly. 'Then ...' she began.

Eleanor burst in: 'We have no child. It seems strange, Margery ... that all this time ...'

Margery nodded. 'It is sometimes so ... Nature be a very odd critter.'

'I want you to make me fertile. I want a child.'

Margery nodded sagely. 'It is not easy,' she said.

'Not easy! I thought you could do these things.'

'I can be of help. But lady, there's others in it. There's nature and there's the man.'

'What do you mean, the man?'

'The Duke's first Duchess had no children.'

'He was hardly ever with her. She didn't appeal to him. I can assure you it is different with us. Besides there have been children of his—outside marriage.'

'I can use my art ... and if it be possible you will get your child ... But you must remember ... there be other elements in this ... elements such as my kind can have no hold on.'

'You said you could help me to marriage.'

'Aye ... and so I did. I gave you special unguents and lotions as few men can resist. But you was no night crow. You was a beautiful little singing bird. 'Twas part you, part me. There was only the two of us in it.'

'There was Humphrey.'

'And he could have stood out against it. But he was already half way there, now wasn't he?'

'Well, are you telling me I need not have come?'

'Indeed no, my lady, we can do all we can ... and it'll be a help.'

She took a piece of wax from a cupboard and putting it in a pan held it over the fire. When it was melted she took it off and left it to cool for a few minutes. Then skilfully she formed it into the shape of a child.

'There,' she said. 'There is our baby. We will cherish him. We will tell him not to be so shy.' She held up the figure and breathed on it. 'I breathe life into you, little child. Awake. You are wanted in this world. There, Duchess.' She held the figure out to Eleanor. 'Hold him tenderly. Kiss him. I will keep him here for nine months and whisper to him every day. At the end of that time if you have not conceived I will give him to you and you shall keep him and cherish him and assure him that he will be very welcome if he would but come.'

'Thank you, Margery,' said Eleanor, and she put a purse on the table.

Margery's eyes glinted as she looked at it. Wise witches managed to snare the noble in their nets. It was from them that the money came and help often in difficulties. A woman could just about live on the charms and love philtres she sold to humble folk but for the real prizes go to the gentry; and glory be, they were just as ready to consult the witch as the humbler folk.

'I'll give you the skin lotion, my lady, and a little something to slip in the Duke's wine ... just to keep him merry and loving.'

Eleanor nodded, took the bottles, slipped them into the pocket of her gown and went to rejoin her attendant in the room above.

THE DEATH OF BEDFORD

QUEEN KATHERINE awoke every morning to a sense of excitement. She would stretch out her hand to make sure that Owen was still beside her. He laughed at the habit. His hand would curl about hers and they would both remember to be grateful for what life had given them.

'Still here, little Queen?' he would say.

'I shall never be so accustomed to being happy that I forget it could pass.'

'Why should it?' asked Owen.

'Because ... Oh, but you do not need me to say. You know that we live here ... in secret ...'

'Secret ... when at any moment your servants will come in and see us here together?'

'Our servants ... Owen.'

'No,' he said, 'you are the Queen. I am your squire.'

'You are my husband.'

Owen was silent. Would they recognize him as such? Would they say that a marriage conducted in a garret was no true marriage for a Queen?

No. They would not care. They did not want to think of Katherine. Men like Bedford and Gloucester were so concerned with their own ambitions that they would not think the Queen a danger to them and therefore what would it matter to them that she had taken a Welsh squire for a husband. Let her beget children ... they would call them bastards if they wished.

Bastards! Little Edmund, baby Jasper. Oh no, they were

born in as holy a wedlock as the King himself.

He turned to Katherine and kissed her gently.

'Let us be happy,' he said. 'We have had much to be thankful for and shall continue to enjoy it.'

'Yes,' she said. 'Let us do that. It is what I want.'

Then she talked of the cleverness of Edmund. He was already babbling away ... nonsense mostly but there were words here and there. And baby Jasper was going to be as bright.

She loved her babies and all she wanted was to be allowed to live in obscurity with her family. Surely that was not asking too much?

So they talked of domestic matters and a servant came in to bring them wine with salted fish and bread which they would eat before rising.

Katherine was merry. It was a beautiful day. The sun was shining. Owen was beside her. When they had eaten and dressed they would go to the nursery and see the children. It was a lovely way of starting the morning.

But the next day she would awaken with the uneasiness upon her.

It was due to her strange childhood, Owen told her. Then she had not known from one day to the next what would happen to her. Awakening at Hadham was quite different from awakening in the Hôtel de St Pol. There she was governed by the madness of her poor father and the harsh rule of her rapacious mother. Here in Hadham she was the Queen, though living in obscurity; and she had her children to care for and a devoted husband to protect her.

'You are right, dear husband,' she said. 'Each day I thank God for you. Do you remember our first meeting ...'

Then she was happy again, recalling how they had tentatively approached each other, knowing in their hearts what joy they had brought one to the other, until that day when dancing he fell into her lap ...

'Let us thank God for what He has given us,' she said.

'And show our trust in Him by accepting that it will last all our lives,' added Owen.

'Amen,' she murmured.

It was only to be expected that Henry should visit his mother, even though he had been taken out of her care. Messages arrived at Hadham to announce the fact that the King was on his way.

This threw the household into a panic, not because of the King himself but all who would come with him. It was hardly to be expected that Henry would travel without a considerable entourage. After all he was not the boy Katherine had handed over to Warwick. He was growing up. He had been crowned King not only of England but of France.

As a mother Katherine longed to see her son, but as the wife of Owen Tudor she was afraid of what his visit might mean.

She talked long with Owen about it and they decided that Edmund and Jasper should stay in their nursery. After all, who would think to look for them and they were too young to understand that they were being put out of sight. Owen would return to his squire's quarters and they could rely on the discretion of their servants.

Katherine was tormented by her doubts and longings.

She was at the topmost turret to watch Henry's arrival. She saw him coming in the distance, pennants waving and his standard-bearers riding ahead of him. She was filled with emotions, remembering her pride when he was born and that faint twinge of apprehension which she felt then because she had disobeyed her husband's wishes and had borne their son at Windsor.

And there he was riding at the head of the cavalcade—her son, her little King. Oh yes, he had changed. She saw that at once. He had assumed a new dignity. Poor little boy. Did he realize the weight of the responsibilities which would be laid on his shoulders?

She went down to greet him, and when Henry saw her he forgot everything but that here was his mother whom he had loved so dearly in those days before he understood the difficulties of being King.

'Dear lady!' he cried and ran into her arms.

The Queen smiled at stern Warwick who of course did not approve of such conduct.

'Ah, you have not forgotten me then, my son.'

'Oh Mother,' he said, 'I am so happy to see you. Is Joan here still? Is Alice?'

'Oh yes ...' Katherine hesitated for a second or so and this was not lost on Warwick. She could not say that they had stayed with her to care for her other children. 'They will be delighted to see you ...'

'So they stayed after I went,' said the King.

'They had grown accustomed to our household.'

They walked side by side into the house.

'Do you like being shut away here, dear lady?' asked Henry.

'It serves me well,' she said.

'And how is Owen? Is he still here?'

'Yes ... he is still a member of the household.'

'I want to see him.'

'I doubt not you will.'

They were listening, all of them. She was aware of it. How much did they know? How much would they discover? Was this not so much a visit of the King to his mother as an investigation to discover the true state of affairs at Hadham?

She was delighted to see Henry again, although he did not seem her child now in the same way that Edmund and Jasper did. He had when he was their age, of course. I hope, she thought, that I shall be able to keep my Tudor babies with me forever.

She and Owen had been right when they had agreed they could rely on the loyalty of their servants. Joan and Alice were delighted to see their charge. They marvelled at his growth and his grasp of affairs. They questioned him and there was no doubt that Henry was happy to be treated as a child again.

He went to see Owen and they talked of horses and Henry kept recalling those days when Owen had helped him master a horse.

There was an occasion when Katherine had a chance to speak to her son alone. She wanted to know whether he enjoyed his life now as he did long ago.

'It is so different,' said Henry a little sadly. 'I am so rarely alone. Do you know, dear Mother, when I lived with you everybody did all they could to make me forget I was King; now they do everything to remind me of it.'

'Is the Earl good to you?'

'He is good *for* me, they tell me.'

He was developing a sharp wit, this Henry. Her father had been like that in his lucid times. A sharp fear shot through her. No ... no ... there was no resemblance between this solemn little boy and her deranged father.

'It is not quite the same thing,' she said quickly.

Henry agreed with that. 'He is a good and honourable

man. Sometimes I wish he were not quite so good and honourable. He is reckoned to be so chivalrous. He has done so much that is worthy.'

'It is why your father commanded that he should be your guardian. I hope he is not too hard a taskmaster.'

'No. Perhaps not. I had been used to you and Joan and Alice ...'

'They did not always spare the cane ...'

'But it never really hurt, dear Mother.' He was thoughtful for a moment. 'I went to France, Mother. I saw my grandmother.'

The Queen felt her heart beginning to beat uneasily as it always did at the mention of her mother. Her name brought back so many memories. She remembered the beautiful face distorted with rage, the cold aloofness when she ordered her children to be sent to the Hôtel de St Pol; she remembered one occasion when Michelle had clung to her skirts in an effort to plead for them all to be allowed to stay at the Louvre and not to be dispatched to that cold palace where they could hear the sounds of their father's madness. She could see, in her mind's eye, her mother angrily slapping Michelle's clinging fingers while her sister cried out in pain and let go of her mother's skirts.

'What thought you of your grandmother?'

'She was very kind to me. She is very beautiful.'

'She must have changed though since I knew her. Her life is very different from what it was.'

'She asked for you. She hoped you were well.'

Katherine was silent.

'And I saw the Maid, Mother. I saw Joan of Arc.'

Katherine caught her breath. 'When? You did not ...'

'No, I did not see them burn her. I looked through a hole into her cell. I saw her there with her guards. They looked ... brutish ... and she, my lady, she looked like a saint.'

'You have been listening to rumours and gossip. It's never wise to do that, my son. They tell me she was a peasant girl who had learned the witch's craft.'

'She was no witch, Mother. And then I was crowned in Paris because we could not get to Rheims. I think of her a great deal. She did not want me to be crowned King. That was why she came from her village to fight. Do you believe that saints can ... can harm those who go against their wishes?'

'Saints would not harm, my son. They do nothing but good. That is why they are saints.'

'Then she will not harm me for I know her to be good.'

Yes, indeed he had grown up. He had not only been crowned King of England and France but he had seen Joan of Arc, and her fame had travelled far and wide. People even talked of her in England. She was a witch, they said, who had fought with the French and won a few successes.

If King Harry had been alive she would never have succeeded; he would have captured her as soon as she appeared on the scene, tied her up in a sack and thrown her into the Seine.

But she had impressed Henry. She had made him thoughtful. But perhaps that was just the burden of kingship.

The stay would not be long and Katherine's feelings were mixed. She was not sure whether she wanted the King to go or stay.

Warwick talked to her after dinner while they listened to the minstrels. He asked her if she was satisfied with the quiet life she led. She told him that it filled her needs. They had agreed that it was not suitable for the King to be brought up by his mother and as her son's upbringing and education were in his capable hands she was sure that she need not concern herself on that account.

He said: 'You are well served, my lady? You are served as is fitting for the King's mother to be?'

'I am indeed well served. I have no complaints,' she answered.

'You have good menservants, bodyguards and the rest?'

'The best,' she answered.

'I see Owen Tudor remains in your service.'

'I see no reason to rid myself of a good squire,' she said. 'No reason at all.'

'Tudor has been long in your service.'

'Oh yes. The late King noticed him at Agincourt.'

'Ah, his place in the household was no doubt a reward for good service. Mayhap the late King would be pleased could he look down from Heaven to see that you treat well one who served with him at Agincourt.'

'He would be pleased to see Owen Tudor rewarded I doubt not.'

She was in no doubt that there were rumours about her and Owen. Warwick had come down to probe, and although she was sorry to lose her son she could not help being relieved to see the party ride away.

Then she could return to that cosy domesticity which meant so much to her.

*　　*　　*

John, Duke of Bedford was not a happy man. He could not understand why since the meteoric rise of Joan of Arc everything had seemed to go wrong. Ever since his brother's death he had been wishing that he had lived, but never more so than at this time.

What had happened? Since Agincourt the star of the English had risen high and there seemed no reason why it should not continue to dominate the sky over France. A vacillating King, son of an imbecile father and the Jezebel of the age, a country ravaged by war, powerful allies against it ... what chance had it? And then suddenly that peasant witch had changed everything.

It had been a terrible day when they had burned her at the stake. He had not gone near the square in Rouen. That would have been unwise. He had remained—some would say skulked—behind closed doors and heavily curtained windows. He did not want to hear how she had gone bravely to her death, how someone said he saw a white dove rise from the burning pyre at that moment when she called the name of Jesus in one last shuddering cry before the silence. He did not want to hear that people—even the English soldiery—were saying that they had burned a saint.

He did not want to hear the name of Joan of Arc again. But what was the use? The witch had appeared and that was the beginning of the end of English power in France.

But how could he help hearing her name? She was still spoken of and if he forbade her name to be mentioned what good would that do? It still went on repeating itself in his mind.

A curse on Joan of Arc! A curse on misfortune! What had happened to the victories, the successes?

They had just lost Chartres. Why should they lose Chartres? He had been so incensed that he had determined to make a great attempt to reverse this tide of misfortune. God help us, he said, we shall lose all that Henry gained if we go on in this way.

There was another matter which gave him cause for great uneasiness. Anne was looking ill these days. Sometimes he thought the witch of Arc had laid a spell on her.

She tried to soothe his anxieties by assuring him that she felt well, a little tired perhaps, but that was due to the heat, the cold or that she had perhaps ridden too far. Excuses which he did not believe.

Sometimes he thought she was more ill than she let him know.

Those were happy times he spent with her.

Once he had said to her: 'It is a marvel to me that we who married for State reasons should have been so singularly blessed.'

'I always determined that I would make a happy marriage,' she told him.

'And to be determined on something is the best way to succeed at it. Oh, Anne, I wish we could end this fighting. I wish we could be more together. I wish I could be more sure of your brother.'

She had been thoughtful. She knew her brother well. Proud, haughty, royal, he had always deplored the fact that the French throne had not descended to him and thought often how different life would have been for the French if it had.

Burgundy was not a man easily to forgive his enemies. When Charles as the Dauphin had been with those who murdered the old Duke of Burgundy he had made that Duke's son his enemy for ever. A feud was in progress which had almost cost Charles his throne ... and would have done but for this peasant girl about whom everyone was still talking.

But Philip of Burgundy loved his sister. He would listen to her, she knew, and whatever his own feelings towards the Duke of Bedford were, he was pleased that Anne had found happiness with him.

Anne had said: 'I shall do everything I can to keep that friendship between you and my brother warm, dear husband.'

And she had, comforting him as she always did. No, he had reason to rejoice in his marriage. He had a wife whom he loved dearly and the marriage had served its purpose which had primarily been to strengthen the alliance between Bedford and Burgundy.

And now her health gave him anxiety. But he had a great many causes for anxiety. He was afraid of the subtle change which was creeping over France. Surely the powers of witch-craft were not as great as they seemed? And yet it had all begun with the Maid.

It was always the same. It came back to the Maid. It seemed as though in spite of the fire the witch lived on.

As he brooded messengers came to him.

Eagerly he awaited what they had to tell. Good news, he hoped, from Lagni-sur-Marne to which he had sent out a strong force to take the place.

But alas it was not good news. Everywhere the French were showing a stubborn resistance. The Maid seemed to have imbued them with a new spirit. They were holding out and the English troops were getting short of provisions. If help did not come soon they would have to retreat.

He was in a quandary. The place was of no great strategic value but the English could not afford another defeat.

He made up his mind with a speed which was characteristic of him. He would have to go to Lagni-sur-Marne in person.

By God's Holy Writ, he thought, I will attack these French so fiercely that they will think twice before they put up such a resistance against us in future.

In a few days he was at Lagni. He went through the camp. There was something wrong, he knew. The English had lost the certainty that no one could beat them. The siege of Orléans had been demoralizing and so had the French victories which had led to the crowning of Charles at Rheims. If only Henry had lived; he would have known how to deal with this strange influence which had affected both sides. He, Bedford, knew that he was a good soldier, he was a great general; he served his country with devoted loyalty, always had and always would; but there were times when a special genius was needed, and such genius did not appear in every generation. If only Henry had lived! Everything would have been satisfactorily settled. He would have known from the beginning how to deal with Joan of Arc. Bedford had made few mistakes in his military career but there were two vital ones, he saw now. He should have let the Orléannese surrender to Burgundy. Burgundy would never forgive him for refusing to do so. Thus he had given the Maid her chance to save that important town for the French. That was the first mistake. An even greater one had been to burn Joan. That act had made her live forever. And for the rest of his life he would be haunted by it.

It seemed as though she had laid a curse on all the English, for fiercely as they fought they could not break the siege of Lagni. And then ... the shame of it ... French reinforcements —cannon and cavalry—came to relieve the town.

Where were the bowmen of England? They had lost heart. They believed that Joan of Arc was possessed of some Divine power and that in burning her they had burned God's elect. Heaven was against them. Many of the soldiers had been present in the square at Rouen on that day. They would never forget.

They retreated before the French and Bedford had the mortification of seeing his troops defeated.

He was even more discomfited when he learned that the victorious French were on their way to Paris.

He rode there with all speed and as he came through the Porte Saint Antoine the people were sullen. He was their master at this time they knew, but in their hearts they did not believe he would be so for long.

There was one consolation. Anne was in Paris. He went straight to her and even there horror awaited him. She could not disguise from him now the fact that she was very ill indeed.

'Anne,' he cried, 'Anne, my love. What is it? Why was I not told?'

She smiled at him wanly. 'You did not want to hear of my petty ailments,' she answered. 'It is nothing. I have had a bad day.'

He was desolate. God has indeed turned against me, he thought.

He spent a great deal of time with her. He tried to forget the dismal state of affairs. We are going from bad to worse, he thought, but he could really give his attention to nothing but Anne.

When he heard that some of the nuns of St Antoine, including the Abbess, had been in communication with Charles and were working to bring him to Paris, he was angry and ordered them to be imprisoned. He knew that the Parisians would turn against him to a man when and if the time was ripe to do so.

He could not speak to Anne of these matters. She lay still in her bed, her eyes closed, her fingers twined about his. He had married her for expediency but that did not mean that his love was any the less.

It did occur to him that if she died—and he greatly feared she would—his alliance with Burgundy would have suffered a great blow. Only he and she knew how very much she had worked to keep that friendship alive. It was an unnatural friendship—a Duke of Burgundy, member of the Royal House of France to be an ally of the English conquerors! But for Burgundy's intense hatred for the murderer of his father it could never have come about.

But it must be kept green, that friendship. It was the pivot on which success revolved. Henry had known it. He had mentioned it on his death bed. 'Do anything ... almost anything ... to keep Burgundy on our side.'

He had tried, as he had endeavoured to carry out every wish of the late King. He had always known that his dead brother was the great architect of success in France, and he greatly feared that without his skill in keeping it the firmly built victory would collapse into defeat.

November was a dreary month. He would hate Novembers forever more, for on the thirteenth of that month, Anne died.

She looked at him sorrowingly as though begging his pardon for dying. She knew how important her brother's friendship was to her husband and she knew that ruthless, brilliant and shrewd as Philip of Burgundy was, he would be ready to break that friendship at the first opportunity if it suited him to do so; it was her influence which had kept it alive.

'John,' she said, 'be happy. Tell my brother that it was my dearest wish for you to remain friends. I am sorry I must leave you.'

He could not speak. He was too overcome with emotion.

She was buried as she had wished to be in the Church of the Celestins. The people turned out in their hundreds to mourn her. She had been noted for her goodness and her beauty and being but twenty-eight years of age, she was young to die.

They even warmed to the Regent Bedford when they witnessed his grief.

He seemed much older, bowed down with sorrow and anxiety. He had no wish to stay in Paris. He left at once for Rouen.

*   *   *

How he missed her! Although it had been impossible for

them to be together a great deal, he realized that she had always been in his thoughts. During his dilemmas which had been frequent of late he had often said to himself: 'I will ask Anne that', or 'I will tell her that' or 'I wonder what Anne would think of that?'

So there was a great gap in his life. People thought him cold and aloof, but he was human after all; he was more than soldier, more than Regent. He had been, though briefly, a devoted husband.

Now of all times he needed her. Everything was going badly and he longed to talk to her, ask her advice, to get her to speak to her brother. He knew he could never forget her.

He was not popular even in Rouen where heavy taxes were demanded of the people in order to pay for the occupation. The people were sullen. They had hoped for better times when England took France, and what had they found? They were poorer than ever.

It was necessary to inflict heavy penalties on those who defaulted and what was even more disconcerting was the fact that some of the soldiers were talking of mutiny. They wanted to go back to England. They were tired of being away from their homes.

John knew that there was only one way of dealing with such people for they could undermine a whole army, and he dealt with them in that way. The severe penalties he inflicted increased his unpopularity.

Oh, for the comfort of Anne during those dark days. One day the Bishop of Thérouanne came to Rouen and in his company was his young niece, a girl of seventeen. Bedford welcomed them warmly for the Bishop was Louis of Luxembourg, and the Luxembourg reigning family was very rich and powerful. For some time Bedford had sought to make an alliance with them for the coolness in Burgundy's attitude since the death of Anne was becoming more and more apparent.

Moreover it was pleasant to be in the company of young Jacquetta. She was not only extremely pretty but very vivacious; she could sing charmingly and although she was young she had a certain grasp of affairs which seemed to Bedford admirable in a girl of her age.

He found that he was seeking her company a good deal and she seemed not averse to this. She took a great interest in the war and discussed the influence of the Maid, who, she was sure, was a witch.

'People remember now,' she said, 'but they forget quickly, do they not?'

That seemed to him a wise comment. Moreover it was something he wished to believe himself. He thought: We are always impressed by those who speak our own thoughts.

But she was an enchantress. She soothed the aching need for Anne.

He supposed it was inevitable and he was not surprised when the Bishop approached him.

'I have always wanted an alliance between our two countries,' said the Bishop.

Bedford admitted that he would not be averse to such an alliance either. He needed all the friends he could get.

'Jacquetta is a charming girl,' said the Bishop, and Bedford could not deny that either.

'I know that an alliance between the English Royal House and that of Luxembourg would give us great pleasure.'

And watching Jacquetta and seeking to assauge the terrible void made by the loss of Anne, he decided that to marry Jacquetta would be a good move whichever way it was looked at.

There was great rejoicing in Rouen. All citizens, even those who had grown sullen on account of too much taxation, loved a royal wedding. John sent to England for five fine bells to be made for the Cathedral. They were his gift to the town and they were meant as a thanksgiving for his newly found happiness.

So only five months after the death of Anne of Burgundy Louis, Bishop of Thérouanne, married the Duke of Bedford to Jacquetta of Luxembourg.

*   *   *

The Duke of Burgundy was incensed. Bedford had married within five months of Anne's death. That was a slight on Anne and therefore on the House of Burgundy. And he had married Jacquetta of Luxembourg which meant he had formed an alliance with a rich and important ally. There was an even greater cause for anger: Jacquetta was the daughter of Pierre, Comte de St Pol and Regent of Luxembourg, who was a vassal of the Duke of Burgundy and the Duke's permission for the marriage had not been asked.

'By God's eyes,' cried the Duke of Burgundy, 'indeed I was not asked! They knew full well that if I had been I should have refused permission for the match.'

He would make his displeasure felt by withdrawing all communication with the Duke of Bedford. If the Duke wished to convey his regrets to him he must be the first to move.

To hell with Burgundy! thought Bedford. He would marry where he would. It was no disrespect to Anne that he had married so soon after her death. It was because he had missed her so sorely that he had done so. Anne, my dearest, he thought, you gave me a taste for marriage. It was because I could not bear your loss that I sought so soon to try to fill the gap you left in my life.

Yes, Anne would understand. He could not expect Burgundy to. Burgundy could only see marriage as a political move and he naturally did not like the alliance with Luxembourg.

Perhaps he would come round, though. There had been disagreements between them before.

Cardinal Beaufort came to him and expressed his regret at the disunity between them and their important ally.

'I know, I know,' said Bedford. 'But I cannot consult the Duke of Burgundy on every detail of my private life.'

'I believe he feels this marriage to be some concern of his since the Duchess's father is his vassal ... and Burgundy's sister was your first wife.'

Bedford put a weary hand to his head and did not speak. Watching him closely, Beaufort was alarmed. What had happened to his nephew? Bedford had always been so alert. He had done well in France. The late King would have been pleased with him. But of late he had changed. It was since the coming of Joan of Arc. No, it must be something more than that. A peasant girl could not affect great men so strangely. Perhaps Bedford was past his first youth, and he had lost a wife to whom he had been devoted. Bedford must not tire now. There was so much to be done and so much gained could be easily lost.

'There should be a reconciliation with Burgundy,' he said gently.

'I have no intention of crawling humbly to him,' retorted Bedford.

'I did not mean for one moment that you should. There must be a rapprochement on both sides. I believe it would be a good idea for me to attempt to bring this about.'

Bedford wanted to shrug his shoulders and cry that he was tired of the whole affair. If Burgundy liked to sulk, let him. But of course Burgundy was not sulking. He was incensed as he always was when he believed there had been some attack on his dignity. He was a man obsessed by his own importance and his power; but it had to be admitted that that importance and power were very great.

The wise thing of course was for Beaufort to try to bring about a reconciliation.

'Perhaps you should make that attempt,' agreed Bedford.

Beaufort was relieved. Like everyone else he was disturbed by the way everything was going in France. He knew that his old enemy Gloucester would take advantage of his brother's discomfiture. How he hated Gloucester! A self-seeker; a man whose immediate ambitions came before everything else. He was even worse since he had made that mésalliance with his first wife's attendant. Bedford must regain his hold on affairs in France; and there must soon come a time when he could leave those affairs to a deputy for his presence was greatly to be desired in England where Gloucester had far too much power when his brother was out of the country.

The first step was to patch up the quarrel with Burgundy.

'I will make immediate arrangements for a meeting,' he told Bedford.

Bedford nodded wearily. At least he could trust his uncle.

The Duke of Burgundy with a certain condescension agreed to meet the Cardinal at St Omer.

From the first moment of the meeting the Cardinal knew that he was facing difficulties and that the breach was going to be very difficult to heal.

Burgundy said that the English appeared to be losing their skill in battle. 'It became noticeable after the siege of Orléans,' he said. 'If the Duke had not prevented the town surrendering to me, he would not be in such dire straits as to need an alliance with Luxembourg as a temporary measure to bolster up his strength.'

'My lord, the Duke of Bedford deeply regrets the matter of Orléans. If it had not been for the witch ...'

Burgundy shrugged his shoulders. 'Everything is blamed onto the witch but you, my dear Cardinal, a man of experience, do not believe for one moment that a simple peasant girl could have changed the course of events.'

'It was the effect she had on the people, not what she was, my lord, but what the French and the English believed her to be. Her influence is waning and if you two mighty lords forget these little minor irritations and are seen to be united, all that is lost will soon be regained.'

The Duke was silent. He is wavering, thought the Cardinal. God help us. It is true then ... this rumour that he is thinking of breaking his alliance with us and joining with France. That would indeed be disastrous.

'It would seem to be a most unfriendly act to marry into Luxembourg,' said the Duke stolidly. 'And if the Duke of Bedford regretted his act why does he not come to me in person? Why send an emissary ... even one so important as yourself, Cardinal.'

'I was not exactly sent by him, my lord.'

'You mean he is unaware that you have approached me?' The Duke was looking more haughty than ever. That would not do.

'Not so, not so,' said the Cardinal quickly. 'He was deeply grieved by your displeasure and when I suggested I should convey that sorrow to you he did not forbid it.'

'I see,' said the Duke. 'He was too proud to come himself. Let me tell you this, my lord Cardinal, if the Duke came to me in person it might be possible for us to dissolve our differences ... who shall say ... In the meantime ...'

The Duke paused mischievously. He knew that the rumours about the feelers the French were sending out towards him would have reached the English and he could well understand their anxiety. Let them be anxious. He had never forgiven Bedford for Orléans and it had been borne home to him then more strongly that it was unnatural for Burgundians and French to be fighting on opposite sides in a war of such vital consequences. It was all very well to conduct strife between factions in the country. The feud between the Burgundians and the Armagnacs was natural enough; but to fight a war against a foreign enemy and not to stand together ... Yes, it was indeed a bizarre situation.

Charles was being very meek; he was dissociating himself from the murderers of the old Duke of Burgundy. He might not have intended to murder. That could be well believed. He was a mild man, not given to violence by any means.

Perhaps that should be considered.

'It is a pity that there should be this discord,' said the Cardinal. 'It puts heart into our enemy even though Charles knows that you have sworn not to make a separate peace with France.'

So he had been correct in divining the Cardinal's thoughts. They were worried, were they. It was true he had sworn not to make a separate peace with France, but he was getting very tired of Bedford's going against him and the marriage into Luxembourg had really damaged their relationship. Anne was dead and he now no longer had to consider her. She was not there to plead with him and explain her husband's motives. Bedford owed a lot to Anne—yet as soon as she was dead he was off with this young girl from Luxembourg.

Burgundy had no desire to mend the quarrel. It suited him well at this time to keep it going.

He knew Bedford's pride so he made the gesture which he knew would not be accepted by Bedford.

He said: 'If the Duke of Bedford wishes to say he regrets his actions let him come himself to tell me so.'

The interview was at an end, and the Cardinal knew that he had failed.

Would Bedford go cap in hand to Burgundy and say he was sorry? How could Burgundy ask him so to humble himself? Why should the Regent of France do such a thing even for the sake of an important ally? Burgundy knew he would not come. That was why he had asked him to.

*   *   *

Humphrey of Gloucester was in a rage. His brother was coming home. Eleanor was sympathetic. She knew exactly how to handle him. He had not swerved in his devotion to her, and she undoubtedly had the power to hold him. She sometimes wondered how much she had to thank Margery Jourdemayne for that, but the fact remained that with Margery's aids and her own overwhelming sexuality she could appeal to the Duke—and what was more important, preserve his need for her—as no other woman had ever been able to do.

So far, though, she remained infertile. She could not understand it. She had paid several visits to Margery and had seen the waxen image. It looked very beautiful to her. Margery kept it in a tiny cradle lined with velvet. A beautiful article although so small. Margery said that she spoke to the image every day and she felt she was on the verge of getting a response.

'Any day now,' she said. But she had been saying that for months and still there was no sign of a child.

Eleanor knew that she could afford to wait a while. There were important matters always on hand and life with the Duke was never dull.

And now Bedford was coming home. She was sure he would strongly disapprove of her.

'There's nothing to fear from him,' she said blithely. 'He hardly comes home as a conqueror, does he?'

'It is disgraceful the way he is mismanaging things in France.'

'They should have let you handle them.'

He smiled fondly at her. She was always amazed by how childishly he responded to flattery. His military career had been without renown but he always saw himself as a great commander. She should not complain of that trait in his character. It made him more easy to manage.

'He will probe into the way things are at home.'

'Oh yes, no doubt, and find fault with everything.'

'You can be sure of that.'

'Well, let us begin by finding fault with him. That should not be difficult. You could tell the Council that you are not at all happy about the way he is conducting the war. Since he was so ignobly beaten at Orléans things have been getting worse and worse over there. A word in the ear of certain members of the Council . . .'

'You are right,' said Gloucester.

'Most carefully dropped as you know so well how to do . . . dropped on fertile ground. There are many who are not over fond of your noble brother, Humphrey.'

So they talked. Gloucester said that perhaps he should offer to go to France to set matters right.

Go to France! It was the last thing she wanted. What a terrible thought! Trailing from town to town, living in camps! No, she preferred the castles and palaces of England. But there was no harm in agreeing with him. She could be sure no one would take such a suggestion seriously.

When she saw Bedford she was struck by the fact that he

had aged considerably since she had last seen him. The sight of him sent little quivers of excitement running through her lively imagination. That affair of Joan of Arc had upset him more than seemed possible. And he had this merry little wife of half his age. He was still a man of distinction. He was very like his brother the late King, so it was said. He did command respect as Humphrey, bless him, never could. John was a fine figure of a man; not her taste really; no one would be able to tell him how to behave. He would never be the slave of his senses. He had been a virtuous married man with Anne of Burgundy, and now he had married this pretty little creature. But that was, of course, for Luxembourg.

No, she need have no fear that he would let Humphrey go to France; and the ageing looks of the great Duke and a certain unhealthy tinge in the colour of his skin did set her mind working.

Bedford faced the Parliament, well aware of the criticism of events in France. When things went wrong the leader was always blamed, he accepted that. He said that if any complaints against him had to be made this must be done before the King and the Parliament.

John Stafford, the Bishop of Bath and Wells, rose immediately to reassure him, saying that he and the Council had heard no such charges and that he had had word with the King who wished to add his personal thanks to those of the Parliament for the manner in which the Duke had conducted the war.

At the next meeting of the Parliament when the finances were discussed Bedford offered to give up a large part of the money paid to him for his services that it might be example to the people showing them how it was necessary to make great sacrifices in order to win great victories.

There were certain members of the Council who hinted that Bedford's presence was needed in England. This was an indication of Gloucester's unpopularity and Bedford was well aware of this. He had no confidence in his brother; he knew that he was rapacious and ambitious and even more so since his marriage. All the same it was quite impossible for him to stay in England, he pointed out. In view of the way in which the war was going his presence was needed over there.

Gloucester then offered to go to France in his place and he made boastful remarks to the effect that he would soon set matters to rights so that the English would be successful again.

Bedford was naturally furious at what this implied. He said that Gloucester must write down what he had said that Bedford might present it to the King.

Gloucester had no wish to indulge in an open quarrel with his brother so he withdrew his remarks, and his offer to go to France was not even referred to again.

But there was a meeting of the Parliament to which the young King—now thirteen years old and solemn for his years —had to attend.

Henry was more accustomed to these occasions now and he invariably pleased the Earl of Warwick by his demeanour during such sessions. He did not tell them that his attention often strayed and he had to concentrate hard to remember what they were all talking about. But on the whole he did not find them too taxing, though of course they would become more arduous as he grew older.

Often he thought of the easy days with his mother and Owen. He wished he could see more of them. There was a certain amount of whispering about his mother and Owen. Apparently their being so much together was not considered seemly. Henry thought it must be very pleasant to be them— living quietly in the country, being together and not having to attend long dreary sessions which were intruding more and more into his life.

He listened to his Uncle Bedford droning on about the setbacks in France which had begun with the unlucky siege of Orléans. 'Taken in hand,' he said, 'by God knows what advice.' Everybody knew then that he was talking about Joan of Arc and Henry's mind went back to that day when he had looked through the aperture and seen her. He found it hard to forget her completely and now and then the memory of her would flash into his mind.

Uncle Bedford was a very noble man—different from Uncle Humphrey he knew. Now he was saying that he would return to France and prosecute the war and that he would give up to it the whole proceeds of his estates in Normandy.

It was clear to Henry that those who had listened to the sly hints of the Duke of Gloucester were ashamed and now whole-heartedly applauded the Duke of Bedford.

A few days later he came to see Henry to say good-bye before he left for France.

'It rejoices me to see you growing fast, my lord,' he said. 'Why within a few years you will be able to take your rightful place and govern this land.'

Henry was glad Uncle Bedford was pleased with him but he was not really looking forward to when the crown should become a reality instead of a terrible burden to be worn on his head on State occasions.

*   *   *

There was no doubt that all parties were growing tired of the war and it was agreed that there should be a conference over which the legates of Pope Eugenius should preside. This was to be in Arras and it should not be a matter for the French and English only, but several of the European states should join in. The war between England and France for the right to govern France had been going on for nearly a hundred years. There had been times when it had seemed to be near conclusion with victory for one side or the other; then there would be more victories, more reverses and the tables would be turned. A short while ago it had seemed that the war was over with victory for the English, but then a peasant girl had appeared and there was change again.

It was a splendid occasion that took place at Arras in the July of that year 1435. The Papal legates arrived with great pomp and there were also ambassadors from Castile, Aragon, Portugal, Sicily, Denmark, Brittany and other states. But the principal parties were those from the King of France, the Duke of Bedford and the Duke of Burgundy.

The Duke of Burgundy arrived on the thirtieth of the month looking very splendid and escorted by three hundred archers all wearing the Burgundian livery. He caused some concern by riding out of the town to meet his brothers-in-law, the Duke of Bourbon and the Comte de Richemont, because naturally these men were fighting on the side of the French. Burgundy seemed to be drawing attention to the incongruous situation in which he, a member of the French royal family, should be in conflict with his own people. This seemed significant to those who were aware of the strain which existed between Burgundy and Bedford and which had never been healed since the latter's marriage because neither Duke would suppress his pride sufficiently to approach the other.

It was to be expected that an agreement would be difficult

to come by. The English did not want to make peace, which would have surely meant giving up all that had seemed to be in their hands before the coming of the Maid. They suggested a truce and perhaps a marriage between their King Henry and a daughter of Charles VII.

No, said the French, there must be peace; there must be an end to the war and English claims on France.

'We have no right,' said the English ambassador, 'to despoil our King of a crown to which he has a right.' He pointed out to the Papal legates that unless they agreed it was not possible for Burgundy to make peace with France for he had sworn not to do so without the consent of his allies.

As far as the English were concerned this seemed to settle the matter. They would agree to a truce only. Their claim to the crown of France could not be waved aside, and since the French would not agree to a truce merely the conference might never have been called for all the good that had come from it.

All thoughts were now turned to the Duke of Burgundy. His brother-in-law, the Comte de Richemont, talked to him very earnestly.

'You are French in blood,' he said. 'You are so in heart and wishes. You belong to the Royal House. You have seen this kingdom all but destroyed; you have seen the suffering poor. You do not love the English. You have often said how arrogant they are. Even at this time you are not on friendly terms with Bedford. He has insulted you and our sister. You went into this alliance because of the murder of your father. Brother, my lord, you do not fit into it.'

Burgundy listened with attention.

'You speak truth,' he said. 'But you know I have made promises. I have entered into treaties with the English. I do not wish to forfeit my honour.'

Richemont was persistent. He went to the Pope's legates. 'While the Duke allies himself to the English the war will go on,' he said. 'If we could break that alliance it would mean the English would have no alternative but to return to their own country. Burgundy wants to break it. It is unnatural. I beg you to help.'

As a result the legates spent hours talking with Burgundy.

'For the love of Jesus Christ,' they said to him, 'put an end to this strife. Put your country out of its misery. We are ordered by the Holy Father to beg you to forget your ven-

geance against the King of France. You must no longer seek
vengeance for the death of your father. Nothing would add
more to your fame and standing in the world than if you
forgave and forgot the injury you have suffered. The King of
France is close to your blood. He is your kinsman ... yet for
the sake of revenge you have joined his enemies and the
enemies of France.'

The Duke, who had always prided himself on his honour,
was deeply disturbed. He greatly desired to put an end to his
alliance with England, yet he did not see how he could extricate himself from the dilemma in which he found himself.

'I must have time to ponder this,' he said. 'It is a matter
which deeply concerns my conscience.'

The Comte de Richemont said that he should have
several days to consider.

'He is a wise man,' he said to the Papal legates. 'He will
see what is best.'

*   *   *

The Duke of Bedford rode back to Rouen. He felt old and
tired. The conference now in progress at Arras was an indication of how much had been lost since the ill-fated siege of
Orléans. Ever since then his health had declined with his
spirits. It was as though a curse had been put upon him.

God knew that he had tried to keep his word to his brother,
and he had always acted in a manner which he believed
would please him. That noble image had been before him
always and at first it had seemed that he could not falter.

And then ... the tide had changed, so swiftly, so unaccount-
ably that one could almost believe in supernatural influences,
and in spite of all his skill and dedication he had been fighting a losing battle ever since.

He would never understand it, but he would never forget
that fearful day in Rouen when he had stayed behind stone
walls but in spirit was out there in that square.

By the time the towers of Rouen came into sight he was
exhausted. What had happened to him? Only a year or so
ago he could spend hours in the saddle and hardly knew the
meaning of fatigue. Affliction had come to him swiftly. He
thought often of Henry, who had died so young. He had been
but thirty-five years of age. And he, Bedford, well he was
forty-six—not exactly young, ageing perhaps but not yet old

surely. Young enough to lead his armies for a few more years.

The Cardinal was watching him anxiously. There was something wrong. Bedford was the last man to betray any weakness and now he was too tired to attempt to disguise it. The Cardinal, too, was remembering how suddenly Henry the Fifth had died.

'It has been an exhausting matter,' he said. 'There is so much anxiety about Burgundy.'

'He is a man of honour,' said Bedford. 'He will not find it easy to break his word to me.'

'Nay,' said the Cardinal, 'but methinks it is only this one point of honour that keeps him with us.'

'If he breaks with us,' replied Bedford, 'we must perforce count him among our enemies.'

'He has always been an uneasy friend,' answered the Cardinal.

There was small comfort in the contemplation of a break with Burgundy. The last King had said his friendship was essential to them and that was as true today as it had been when he said it.

It was a period of great anxiety and Bedford felt too exhausted to consider it in all its menacing possibilities.

As soon as he reached the castle he went straight to his apartments and remained there. The next day he felt too weak to rise.

His young wife came to him in consternation. He had always seemed very mature to her but now he looked like an old man.

'My lord,' she said, 'you are ill.'

'Tired,' he said, 'just tired and disappointed.'

She knelt by the bed.

'Oh, my lord, what can I do?'

'There is little anyone can do,' he answered.

She said: 'I can send for the physicians.'

He lifted a hand to protest but dropped it again. He was too listless to care whether they came or not.

The next day he was asking for news from Arras. There was none.

The Cardinal came to see him. God help us, he thought. He has the stamp of death on him.

He went back to his apartments in a state of gloom. He prayed fervently for the health of Bedford. He dared not contemplate what the future would hold if Bedford were not there to apply his sane and steady judgments.

A few days later Bedford was in a fever. His thoughts were muddled. He was not sure where he was. He kept thinking that Anne was near him and that he could not quite reach her.

His eyes wandered round the apartment. It was in this very chamber where he had waited, while the crowds gathered in the square. He thought it was happening now. He could picture Joan with those calm clear eyes raised towards the skies as though she saw something there which was denied to the rest of those who were with her. What was it in those clear, limpid eyes? Innocence, he thought. Yes. Innocence of guilt, innocence of the world, innocence of evil. It was a beautiful quality.

'We should never have burned her as a witch,' he muttered.

And I ... am I to blame? I could have stopped it. They gave her to the English and we burned her as a witch.

Dear God, I had to do it. She was a menace to my armies. With what power had You endowed this girl that she could affect us so. We burned her; but it was her own people who betrayed her. And the King of France for whom she had done so much deserted her and allowed her to die ... miserably ... horribly. And yet they had said that when she cried out in her final agony they saw her soul in the form of a white dove ascend to Heaven.

I did it ... I did ... but what else could I have done? Forget her. She is dead. What of the future? Burgundy ... Burgundy ... will you break with us? Anne ... Anne won't let it happen. But Anne was gone and he was trying now to reach her.

'We should send for the priests,' said Jacquetta.

The end was very near, they all knew it.

The Cardinal felt a sudden despair. What would happen now ... not only to him but to England? It seemed that the future of both was very bleak.

Gloucester would now be next to the throne. If only Henry were older; if only he had a wife and an heir. But he was but a boy yet. It would be necessary to keep an eye on Gloucester.

The death of the Duke was received with a shocked silence throughout Rouen. People began to talk about the Maid. Was it not strange that the Duke had died here in the very town close to the very square where Joan the Maid had been burned at the stake?

Was it a curse on Bedford? Was it a curse on the English?

They buried the great Duke in the Cathedral at Notre Dame and they wondered gloomily what would happen now that he was dead.

*   *   *

'Dead!' mused Burgundy. His old friend and enemy!

Who would have believed it possible? Bedford with those ruddy healthy looks had seemed far from death.

And now he was gone and that, of course, made all the difference to Burgundy. His alliance had been with Henry the Fifth, a man whom he had admired as much as any other he had ever known; Bedford had followed his brother and he had admired him also. It had seemed good to ally himself with such men. But now they were dead and surely that could be an end to an alliance which had always seemed an incongruous one.

He understood Bedford well. An astute man, a far-seeing man. He would have realized at once that if he, Burgundy, signed the treaty of Arras and his old friend became his enemy that would be the end of English dominance in France.

The French were wooing him with sweet promises. Charles disowned the murder of the old Duke of Burgundy. It had been no wish of his, he declared. He would deliver up the murderers to the Duke; he would pay fifty thousand crowns of gold for the property which had been taken from Burgundy at the time of the assassination; he would place certain towns in the Duke's hands. This would compensate him for what he had lost in the war.

Yes, thought Burgundy, I will sign the treaty of Arras. The English have left the conference and now the only one to whom I owed allegiance is dead. Why should I not join my own kinsman?

This unholy alliance should be brought to an end.

*   *   *

There were scenes of joy throughout France. In the streets of every town Armagnacs were embracing Burgandians. The King of France called together the States General at Tours and there, kneeling before the Archbishop of Crete, after

Mass had been celebrated, he swore on the Bible to keep the peace with Burgundy.

All the nobles in the land from both sides of the dispute swore with him.

'For long,' said the King, 'I have prayed for this happy day. Let us thank God for it.'

The streets were ringing with the cries: 'Long live the King. Long live the Duke of Burgundy.'

The Cardinal returned sadly to England.

There could not be a greater blow for England, he thought.

There could also not be a greater blow for the Cardinal himself.

Thus the power of his old enemy Gloucester was increased.

God help England, thought the Cardinal. And God help me.

THE END OF AN IDYL

ELEANOR, Duchess of Gloucester, was on her way to Eye-next-Westminster to visit Margery Jourdemayne.

Margery's efforts to make her pregnant had come to nothing, but she had not lost her faith in the witch for all that. There were other elements to be considered, Margery had always pointed out, and Eleanor accepted that.

She had been in close contact with Margery for some time now and she had been in extremely good spirits ever since she had heard of the death of Bedford. She could feel almost dizzy with delight when she contemplated the future. Her husband was next in the line of succession to the young King and until Henry married and acquired an heir he would remain so.

The worst fate which could befall Humphrey and, through him, her, would be if the young King produced an heir.

She had a feeling that Margery was going to be very useful to her in the future.

It was very gratifying. Who would have thought that sober old Bedford would take to his bed and so obligingly die! Margery could not have arranged it better although no witches had had a hand in that happy demise . . . unless it was that one they were always talking about . . . the peasant witch of Arc.

Never mind how. She must just accept the good fortune. Bedford dead and Humphrey one jump from the throne.

Margery had guessed why she had come. Margery would know of Bedford's death. There was very little Margery missed. And she would already be considering possibilities, for Eleanor had always been a valued client even when she was nothing more than a higher servant in the employ of the first Duchess of Gloucester. But how quickly she had climbed out of that! And when she became the Duchess it was Margery's triumph as well as Eleanor's. Margery always hoped she would not forget that. She liked her clients to be grateful —and not only materially so, although of course that was of the utmost importance.

She could not complain. Eleanor was generous and Margery was becoming quite rich because of the connection.

Eleanor was taken down to the quiet of Margery's kitchen where the cauldron boiled and the black cat with the malevolent green eyes opened one of them to study Eleanor for a moment and then closed it again.

A seat for Eleanor and one for Margery—hers a sort of throne with cabalistic signs on it to remind high-born clients that Margery was the Queen of her own domain.

'My lady,' said Margery tentatively, 'I trust you are in good health.'

'Could be better,' said Eleanor shortly which was a reference to her inability to announce her pregnancy.

No more of that, thought Margery. The child is stubborn. He won't get himself born.

'You must be happy with the way things are, my lady,' she went on. 'Your lord has risen in the world since I saw you last, eh?'

'Bedford is dead ...' said Eleanor. 'That makes my husband one step from the throne.'

'Close,' agreed Margery. 'But one step is as far as a mile if it's never taken.'

Eleanor sighed. Then she looked full at Margery. 'He must take it, Margery,' she said firmly.

Margery looked stubborn. She shut her mouth tightly and nodded her head.

'It could never be done, my lady ...'

The best way to send the price up was to declare first the impossibility, reasoned Margery. And, by my spells and potions, I should need to be well paid to meddle in the ways of royalty.

'It could be done,' said Eleanor. 'There are surely ways.'

'My lady, you could bring us all to ruin. The stake for me

and what for you, my lady? Not that perhaps ... but a terrible fate I wouldn't be surprised.'

'Oh stop talking such nonsense, Margery. If Humphrey were King I should be Queen. I would see that you were protected, and who would dare touch a Queen?'

Margery was silent. Madame's ambitions surprised even her sometimes. She had become the Duchess of Gloucester. Wasn't that enough for her? No, it seemed my lady had her eyes on the crown.

'Everything will be different now,' went on Eleanor eagerly. 'Already it has changed. Can you feel it, Margery? It's in the air.'

'Oh yes, I feel it,' said Margery. 'I can also feel the flames creeping round my legs. They say they put oil on it to make it burn the faster.'

'What ideas you get. There shall be no question of trouble, I promise you that.'

'With all respect, my lady, I can't see how you could help it. You know ... as well as I do ... what would happen if you were found, say, with aught that might mean you were working against the King. The King, my lady. Our very own King.'

'He is a foolish child ... nothing more.'

'He's a boy who will grow up. We were all children once.'

'Yes and some of us knew what we wanted right from the start.'

'Mayhap he does, my lady, just as you do.'

'What matters that? I know what I want now. And I want Humphrey ...'

'You want your lord to be the King of this country.'

'Don't look so shocked, Margery. He is next in line. He is the son of Henry the Fourth.'

Margery was silent, looking down at her large-boned hands which were lying in her lap.

Then she sighed and went to the wax. She placed it near the fire and began to mould it.

Eleanor watched her avidly.

When Margery had finished the figure bore a fair likeness to the King.

*   *   *

She would tell no one—not even Humphrey—of her visit to
Margery. He did not know of her connection with the witch
so there was no need to tell him now. Humphrey was un-
predictable. Who knew what he would say if he discovered
that he had married Eleanor partly because a witch had
helped him fall into the trap laid for him.

He was delighted now, of course. He would no longer be
overshadowed by an elder brother whom everyone thought
was such a virtuous and noble fellow. He was free. He would
not have to answer to Bedford for anything again.

People were more subservient to him even than before.
He had taken a step up the ladder. It was not an impossibility
that he might one day be the King of this country. People
had to step warily. They might be talking to the future
King.

His vindictive nature set him looking round to see if he
had any slights to avenge. The greatest of his enemies was
his Uncle Cardinal Beaufort. He wondered how Beaufort
was feeling about the death of Bedford. A little uneasy, he
was sure. Let him remain so. The Duke of Gloucester was a
very powerful man now.

The Cardinal had come back weeping and wailing because
of the breaking of the alliance with Burgundy. Gloucester
raged against the Duke, calling him traitor. But never mind,
they would show him that the desertion of the Duke of Burgundy meant nothing to the English.

'We shall go in and win back all we have lost,' he declared.

His Council was uncertain. Beaufort, on whose judgment
many of them relied, was of the opinion that they should
seek peace. 'Think of our position there,' said Beaufort. 'We
have lost a great deal since the siege of Orléans,' he said. 'The
tide has turned against us and this has ended in the major
calamity of the loss of Burgundy's friendship.'

'It was not worth much,' said Gloucester.

'Your late brothers were of the opinion that it was worth
a great deal,' answered Beaufort.

'Well, it has proved worthless. Burgundy has deceived us.'

'He never deceived us. He made the treaty with your
brothers, not with England. They are both dead—God help
us—and therefore Burgundy can honourably release himself
—which he has done. Because of this it is time to think of
making peace in France.'

The Cardinal was a traitor, Gloucester declared to the

Council. He was working with France. Perhaps he was taking bribes from the French since he was so eager to bring about a peace.

The councillors shrugged their shoulders. There would never be an end to this feud between the Cardinal and his nephew until one of them died.

Gloucester himself wanted to go to France. He would take an army with him, and he promised them that in a short time he would win back all they had lost.

Did any of them believe him? Perhaps not. But it was decided that he should go.

Eleanor was secretly angry. To go out of England was scarcely the way to secure a throne. Moreover she was sure he would not shine as a military hero. He always *thought* he would, she knew, but there was a world of difference between dreams and reality.

He was delighted to be going to France. Well, let him. He had once again to learn the lesson.

Why did he want to go to France? she mused. Quick recognition? Military glory? Did he really think they were easily acquired? His brothers had been exceptional men—great soldiers, great statesmen. None knew more than Eleanor that her Humphrey was neither. She had to plan for them both. But let him have his game. He would never be satisfied until he had.

He had to snap his fingers at Beaufort. Beaufort thought there should be peace. Therefore Humphrey thought there should be war.

Bedford had won acclaim—in the days before the siege of Orléans, therefore Humphrey must win fame.

But it would not last.

At least Warwick and Stafford were with him so it might not be a complete débâcle. Perhaps they would save him from that. It might even be a glorious victory. In that case the services of Warwick and Stafford would be forgotten—only to be remembered if there was defeat.

Eleanor was right. There was a quick skirmish in Flanders from which Gloucester emerged without much triumph; then he decided that he could not conduct the war in that fashion. He must go home to consult with the Council.

It was clear that he had had enough of war. He would never excel at it. He wanted to return home to the possibility of becoming King of England and the warm bed of his still

attractive wife. So a few months after his departure he was
back in England.

*   *   *

It was a very pleasant existence at the manor of Hadham.
The passionate love between Queen Katherine and Owen
Tudor had developed into a steady devotion. They were completely contented with each other and their happy little
family which Katherine had said understandably grew with
the years. There were now six-year-old Edmund followed
by Jasper a year or so younger, and Owen and Jacina. They
lived quietly and simply and it seemed that visitors came less
frequently as time passed.

'Which is how I like it best,' said Katherine. 'I must confess, Owen, that I am just a little frightened when people
come to Hadham.'

'They have forgotten us now,' replied Owen. 'As long as
we do not interfere with the plans of ambitious men, no one
thinks of us.'

He did not know how true were his words.

The manor was pleasant, well off the beaten track. Katherine had become the lady of the manor house—she never
thought of being royal now. Royal days had not brought her
the happiness of this quiet existence. She took great pride
in supervising her household. It seemed of the utmost importance whether they should have leyched beef or roast
mutton for dinner; and whether it should be fresh or salted
fish for Fridays. She always rose at seven and went to the
chapel to hear matins in the company of Owen. As soon as
Edmund was old enough he should accompany them, she told
Owen. He laughed. Their eldest was little more than a baby
yet, he reminded her. 'He will soon be a young man,' she
told him; confident that this quiet life would go on for ever.
She had learned to weave and to make up the results of her
work into gowns for herself and her family. She could spin
like any matron, she said; and she could embroider like any
noble lady. She could use the kembyng-stok machine for holding the wool to be combed as efficiently as any of her servants;
she could be happily occupied in the still room and exult over
her triumphs there and mourn over her failures, of which
she proudly stated there were very few. She tended her children as few noble ladies did and rejoiced in the fact she could

spend so much time with them. Often she thought of her own bitter childhood, and compared her children's lot with her own.

'Lucky lucky little Tudors,' she thought. Ah, she could have told them of the terrors of listening to the cries of a mad father, of the horrors children could be subjected to through the cruel negligence of a wicked mother.

But I trust they will never know aught of that kind, she often said to herself.

And Owen, he declared he was the happiest man on earth. He was the squire and he was her husband and they had come to terms with their positions so that it did not matter in the least that she had been born a Princess of France.

There were times when she thought of her first-born. Poor little Henry. He was fifteen years old now and they were already thinking of marrying him. She hoped it would not be just yet and that his wife would make him happy when she came. He had been a good and docile boy, and she was quite certain that the Earl of Warwick had made sure he remained so.

So the happy days passed with little news from the outside world. Nor did they want it. All they asked was to go on living in their own little world, enjoying each day as it came to them; content in their love for each other and their growing family.

It was springtime and the blossom was beginning to show on the fruit trees in the orchard and there were black-faced lambs playing in the fields. Katherine and Owen rode out together in the woods and remembered the early days when they had begun to know each other.

Under the trees the bluebells bent their heads to the light winds and the fragrance of damp earth was in the air.

This was happiness, thought Katherine. Everything that had gone before was worth while to have come to this.

She had drawn up her horse and Owen had brought his to wait beside her.

She turned to him and smiled. He understood. It was often thus and there were occasions when they did not feel the need of words.

They would ride back to the house where the smells of roasting meat would tempt their appetites and they would go to the nursery and play awhile with the children and listen to the accounts of nursery drama and comedy. How young Edmund had astonished his tutor with his grasp of reading; how Jasper had written his own name; how young Owen had thrown his fish and eggs onto the floor; how baby Jacina had walked three steps unaided.

All these matters seemed of such moment. Katherine loved the significance of little things. The household affairs seemed to her to be far more important than all those struggles she remembered from her childhood: feuds between noble houses and the ascendancies of the Burgundians over the Armagnacs, her father's incapabilities and her mother's lovers.

'I shall never, never forget,' she told Owen. 'And I shall never cease to compare Now with Then.'

He understood as he always did.

'My love,' he said, 'I shall do all in my power to make that so until the end of our days.'

'Let us go together, Owen,' she said in sudden fear. 'That's what I ask of the saints. Let us stay like this until the time comes and then go together.'

That was what she said that day in the bluebell wood.

She had something important to tell him.

'Yes,' she said. 'Again. Another little one. Not for some time. I only knew for certain yesterday.'

'The child will be as welcome as the others were,' he said.

'I sometimes think our children are the luckiest in the world,' she answered.

A cloud crossed his face then. 'Katherine .... love,' he whispered. 'Don't tempt the fates.'

She laughed aloud. Oh she was happy then. So sure of happiness.

When they returned to the Manor a messenger had arrived.

The King was on his way.

*　　　*　　　*

They embraced warmly. This was an informal visit, as far as anything Henry did could be informal at this time. He was now fifteen years old; he was leaving boyhood behind him; and the days when he had lived in that sheltered nursery presided over by Joan, Alice and his mother seemed very far away, although he still remembered them with a loving nostalgia.

Katherine was delighted to see him—although he had

grown away from her and now seemed remote compared with
the importance in her life of the little Tudors.

'I would come to see you more often,' Henry told her, 'but
they are always wanting me to be in different places and I am
often in Westminster because I have to attend the Parliament and the meetings of the Council.'

'You must be becoming very learned in matters of State.'

Henry lifted his shoulders. 'I am still scolded when my
attention strays ... as it does often. They talk so much, dear
lady. Sometimes they all but send me to sleep.'

Katherine laughed and with every minute in her company
Henry seemed to become a boy again.

His stay could be only for one day, he told her. He would
leave on the next.

'You are welcome, my son,' said Katherine. 'But you must
forgive us if we do not accommodate you as you are accustomed. We are not used to entertaining royalty here at Hadham.'

'I come as your son, dear Mother, not as the King.'

'Oh, then,' said Katherine gaily, 'mayhap we can manage.'

In the kitchens they were preparing a special banquet.
'I doubt not,' said the cook, 'we shall have the King here
often now that he is growing up and can please himself
more.'

It was a good sign, was the general opinion. The King
visited them and that surely meant that he accepted his
mother's union. The members of the household were understandably a little disturbed because of all the secrecy that had
to be practised and although as time passed that had been
considerably relaxed, the marriage of the Queen and Owen
Tudor had not been officially acknowledged.

Henry, however, until this time had not been aware of
the nature of his mother's relationship with Owen. His visits
were so rare and so brief and when he came he was invariably
in the company of some powerful and notable men.

This time he was with a very small band of friends and
Katherine soon learned the reason for this. Henry himself
told her.

'Warwick is going to France. He has been appointed
Regent following the death of my Uncle Bedford.'

'Ah, that was a tragic matter. I liked your Uncle Bedford ...'

She was going to say better than his brother Gloucester, but

Owen had warned her to be careful what she said in the presence of the King. It was not that Henry would mean to harm her; he was a devoted son; but he was only a boy and if she said something indiscreet, it might slip from him. 'You cannot be too careful,' Owen had added.

'He was a great man,' said Henry. 'But he never was the same since they burned Joan of Arc.'

'That is long ago.'

'No ... no ... dear Mother. It is only five years ... but it is something not easy to forget.' He wrinkled his brow suddenly. 'I saw her ... briefly. They showed her to me in her cell. She did not see me for I looked through an aperture. Just for a short time ... yet I remember.'

'It was a very strange affair,' said the Queen. 'You were telling me that the Earl of Warwick is going to France. You will miss him.'

Henry nodded. 'He was very stern. So different from you and Alice and Joan, but I grew fond of him. He is a very great man I believe and he had to try to make me worthy of my crown.'

Katherine drew him to her and kissed him suddenly. He seemed in that moment her little boy.

She laughed—that rather childish laughter which had echoed through his childhood and which he did not realize until now that he had missed so much.

Katherine drew herself away from him though still holding him by the shoulders. 'I am forgetting,' she said. 'This is our King ... not my own little son any more.'

His royalty dropped from him; he put his arms about her. 'Dear Mother,' he said, 'I like it well when I am just your little son.'

She was wiping the tears from her eyes. 'You must forgive me, my dear little lord,' she said, 'it is my nature. Owen says I am too easily moved to tears and to laughter ...'

'Owen?' he said. 'Ah, Owen. He is here still?'

'You liked him, didn't you. I am glad, Henry. I am so glad because ...'

'Yes, dear Mother?'

'Later,' she said. 'Later.'

But she could not keep it to herself. She was so happy. Why should they not—here in this safe refuge—all be together like one happy family?

'Henry,' she said, 'did you ever wonder why I was so

contented living here alone?'

He shook his head. He did not say that he had been so busily occupied in learning to be a King that he had had no time to wonder about her.

'I have been so happy, Henry. I *am* so happy. And why do you think? Why?'

'Tell me.'

'You always liked Owen Tudor, did you not?'

'Owen. Oh yes indeed. I loved Owen.'

'That delights me. So did I, Henry. So do I.'

He looked at her in disbelief, and she went on: 'Owen is my husband. It is because of that I have been so content all these years.'

Henry broke into a wide smile.

'Oh ... my dear lady mother ... what an intriguant you are.'

She caught his arm. 'Henry, you are not displeased?'

'Displeased! You and Owen! I love you both. Where is Owen?'

'You will see him soon. He does not forget that you are the King. He holds himself aloof from royalty until he is summoned to the presence.'

'He is my stepfather now.'

'I can see the thought does not displease you.'

'I must congratulate you ... and him.'

'Oh, Henry, how happy I am that you have come. How I have missed you, and how I wish that we could all be together!'

'You must be very happy here.' Henry's eyes were wistful. He thought of the Court which surrounded him. The important men who bowed so obsequiously and yet were always telling him what he must do. It must be a wonderfully free life here in the country.

'We are. And Henry. There is something else. Come with me.'

She led him to the nursery. The children were all there. Young Edmund immediately came to his mother and stared up at Henry. Jasper toddled after him.

Katherine laid her hands on Edmund's head and picked up Jasper. 'The little Tudors,' she said. 'Your half-brothers, my lord.'

Henry was bewildered for a moment or two until the truth dawned on him. Then he was smiling; he was kneeling down to talk to Edmund. He was clearly delighted with his brothers.

'And you must not neglect Owen and even baby Jacina. They will be most put out.'

'Dear Mother, and all this time you have been here in the country raising a family!'

He admired the children. He was clearly amused and delighted.

'Now we have no secrets,' said Katherine. 'I always hated to have secrets from you.'

'Dear lady,' he said, 'why is it that this marriage is kept a secret?'

'But surely you know. They would say it is a mésalliance ... I Princess of France, Queen of England, mother of the King, to marry a squire!'

'But Owen Tudor ...' began Henry.

'They always told me that I had a very clever son. Yes ... Owen Tudor. That is the answer. The best man that ever lived, that is my Owen. Come, Henry, you know he is your stepfather now. I will ask him to join us.'

Owen was disturbed, as she had known he would be, to discover that she had divulged their secret.

'It is time my son knew he had a family,' said the Queen. Henry had always liked Owen; and he was very ready to accept him as his stepfather. He talked freely and much restraint dropped from him in the company of his mother and stepfather.

He told them about his life under the guardianship of the Earl of Warwick. How the Earl had insisted on his excelling at equestrian sports and how when he went overseas he had had a harness garnished with gold made for him. He told them a great deal about his stay in France and how he hated being crowned in Paris. 'It is depressing to feel the people don't really want you. I didn't want to be King of France. They already had a King in any case. He was crowned at Rheims which is the proper place for Kings of France to be crowned. Joan of Arc arranged that.' His expression darkened, and his mother knew that he continued to be disturbed by Joan of Arc. They should never have allowed him to see her. The woman was a witch and had clearly laid a spell on him.

But his melancholy did not last long. He was so delighted to find himself in the centre of a family.

It was a sad King who took farewell of his mother and step-father.

* * *

Humphrey of Gloucester was delighted that Warwick had been sent to France as Regent. He might have gone himself. No, that wouldn't have been wise. Eleanor had said that he should remain in England now and as usual she was right.

The King was only fifteen—a minor still; and as the next in succession he was closer to him than any.

They had one great interest in common. Many people had been amazed at Humphrey's love of literature. When he was surrounded by literary men his character seemed to change. He loved discourse and he seemed to throw off his arrogance and his obsessive ambitions in their company. He had amassed a collection of rare books and now and then would shut himself away to read. The scholar seemed quite apart from the sensual man of the world. It was as though two people lurked behind that countenance once so handsome and now considerably debauched.

Humphrey had undertaken the education of his nephew and had imbued him with a love of literature. It was the one ground on which they could meet, and Humphrey was delighted to discover in the King a willing pupil. Henry enjoyed the study of books rather than outdoor sports and on these grounds he and Humphrey were in tune.

'When you have the power,' Humphrey had said, 'you must do all you can to promote learning. You must keep the universities rich and able to perform their function. You must encourage men of letters.'

Henry fervently assured his uncle that he would.

They had visited the universities together. They went to Oxford, Cambridge and Winchester; Henry was very interested in the new university at Caen which his uncle Bedford had founded.

So he and Humphrey could be happy together with their books, for Henry loved to handle books, loved the thrill of opening them and discovering their contents.

But he too was already aware of the other side of Humphrey, and he seemed less interested in his books since his marriage to his new Duchess.

Henry did not like Eleanor. Sometimes he felt really uneasy when she was near. He would look up suddenly and see her eyes fixed on him and there would be an expression in them which he did not understand.

It was during one of those friendly sessions with Uncle Humphrey when he spoke of his visit to Hadham.

They were in Humphrey's library and Humphrey had talked for some time about a book which he wished Henry to read.

'When you have read it I think you will agree with me that the author should be encouraged. Perhaps a small pension ...'

Henry agreed with enthusiasm.

'He lives in Hertfordshire,' went on Humphrey. 'I have sent for him to come and see me. There are one or two points I want to talk over with him.'

'I was in Hertfordshire recently,' said Henry. 'I wish I had known. I might have sent for him. I was visiting my mother.'

He did not notice that Humphrey had become more alert.

'And how was the Queen?'

'Very, very happy ...'

'Indeed.'

'I don't know why there should be this secret. Owen is a good man ... He is worthy in every way.'

'I heard some talk of the Queen and Owen Tudor.'

'He is my stepfather.'

'Ah, there was a rumour. I knew that he was the Queen's devoted friend ... but marriage. There is a law, you know, about the marriages of people like the Queen.'

'The knot is tied now. They are so content. They have children, too. Four of them. Young Edmund is a very bright boy and I think Jasper will be too.'

The Duke of Gloucester seemed to have forgotten the author in whom he was so interested.

'So ... you have accepted your ... er ... stepfather.'

'Accepted him? Oh it was not a matter of accepting him. He exists. And he is a most interesting man. I was telling them about my coronation in France and how the people were ... and he said that they love me here and that is important.'

'It is indeed. But equally important that your French subjects should love you too.'

'Owen said they never will do that. They see themselves as French and French they will remain. He says it is the same in a way with the Welsh. He is Welsh, you know.'

'Your uncle Bedford never trusted the Welsh.'

'Uncle Bedford never trusted anybody.'

'It is often wise not to be too trustful.'

'Owen says ...' Gloucester was not interested in what Owen said, but he was disturbed at how often the Welsh squire was creeping into the conversation.

Henry was clearly impressed by his stepfather.

'I shall visit them again soon,' he said. 'I enjoyed being with them. My mother is so ... young still. She has such a joyous laugh and Owen is interesting to talk to ... and the children, they are amusing.'

The Duke of Gloucester was growing more and more thoughtful. 'I should be wary of visiting them,' he said.

Henry looked haughty. 'I am the King,' he said. 'I shall do as I wish.'

*   *   *

Eleanor wanted to know what was on his mind.

'Young Henry has been to Hadham and met his stepfather and his mother's new family,' he said.

'Did the foolish woman really marry the Welsh squire?'

'Whether she did or she didn't she lives with him and has produced four children.'

Eleanor felt a sudden anger surge up in her. Four children! And she could not get even one!

'That upsets you,' she said tensely.

'She can have fifty brats if she likes. What disturbs me is this pleasure the King takes in them. He says he is going to see them often and when I reminded him that that might be unwise he reminded me that he is the King.'

'High and mighty, eh?' said Eleanor. 'The stripling is becoming a man. The King indeed! Well, he has it so frequently drummed into him that it is not surprising that he knows it now.'

'He is obviously taken with the Welsh squire. It is Owen says this and Owen does that. By God's ears, you would think Owen was the Pope himself.'

'Obviously it must be shown that Owen is not the Pope. He is not even a Duke. He is just a Welsh squire who has managed by excessive good looks—I presume they are good looks—to creep into the Queen's bed.'

'They are a very happy couple, according to Henry,' said Gloucester.

'I am sure Owen is happy. Who would not be?' She was serious suddenly. 'What are you going to do about it?'

'Do? What can I do?'

'Well you are not going to allow Owen to become chief adviser to the King, are you? You are not going to bring his mother came back into his life.'

'They just want their life in the country.'

'Nobody wants just their life in the country.' Eleanor, with her overweening ambition, could not understand the lack of it in others; she was sure it existed and they pretended it did not in order to achieve it the more quickly.

'I fancy they do.'

She ruffled his hair and kissed him on the lips. 'You are a very romantic gentleman sometimes, dear husband.'

'You see,' he said, 'the Queen is really simple at heart.'

'Indeed. The Princess of France who married the King of England and dutifully produced the heir to the throne! She hated giving him up, did she not?'

'He is her son.'

'He is the King. No, I tell you Katherine is not so simple. She knows how to get what she wants. She fancies a country squire so she enters into an intrigue with him although she knows that the Council would never have allowed it. There is nothing simple about Katherine. And now when our dear little King goes to her he is shown the delights of domesticity. Dear Owen is so good to him. His mother loves him dearly. Why, Humphrey, what are you thinking of? They want to get the King in their grasp.'

He looked at her steadily. 'And if so . . . what can I do about it?'

'What can you do about it? You can act, Humphrey. That's what you can do. Now there is a law that noble ladies like the Queen cannot marry without the consent of the Council. You brought in that law. Have you forgotten?'

'It may be that they were married . . . before . . .'

'Before or after, what matters it? It may be that they are not married at all. This is an illicit union and one in which the Queen cannot be allowed to indulge.'

'What good would it do to break it up?'

'Great good, Humphrey. Henry is growing up. Do you

want him turning to anyone but you? His mother will have a great influence on him. She has already begun to. And our Welsh squire, his dear stepfather, will be advising him before long, when our Henry is a little more sure of himself—and he is fast becoming that. Were you not reminded, with a certain asperity I gather, that he was the King? Of course if you want to be ousted from your place as chief councillor by the Queen and her lover let well alone. Let Henry visit Hadham. Let them weave their spells around him. What does it matter if Humphrey of Gloucester be set aside for a frivolous Queen and a low-born squire.'

Eleanor certainly knew how to rouse her husband to action.

He said: 'I could arrest the Tudor for breaking the law.'

She went to him and slipping her arm through his nestled against him.

'There you speak more like the great Duke.'

She was smiling to herself. Their influence must be removed. Margery Jourdemayne seemed to be losing her touch. Although pins were inserted into the wax image of the King nothing had happened. He was still in good health.

'It takes a long time with a King,' Margery had explained.

Perhaps it did. But when one had great plans one did not want the loving eyes of a mother to see too much.

It should be an easier matter to remove the Tudor household from the sphere of influence than it was to bring a child into the world and drive a boy out of it.

*   *   *

The summer was passing but there were still pleasant days when one could sit in the garden. Katherine was nearing the end of her pregnancy. There was already a midwife in the house and she was expecting the child would be born any day now. Owen was beside her, taking great care of her. Edmund watched her wonderingly. He had been told that he might expect a new brother or sister. Jasper who was unusually advanced said that he wanted another sister and he would not accept another brother. He had two brothers already and he liked his sister Jacina best.

'You will love the baby whether it be boy or girl,' he was told.

'Will I?' he said wonderingly.

And there they were on that fateful day when one of the

servants came into the garden to tell them that visitors had arrived.

'I wonder who it is,' said Katherine beginning to rise. 'Perhaps it is someone come to tell us Henry is on the way.'

Owen said: 'Stay where you are. I will go and see.'

Katherine turned. Men were coming onto the lawn. Two of them came forward and stood one on either side of Owen.

'You are Owen Tudor, Welsh Squire to Queen Katherine?' she heard them say.

'I am.'

'We must do our duty and arrest you.'

Katherine felt her heart leap in terror. She started forward.

'On what grounds?' cried Owen.

'In the name of the King,' said the Captain of the guard.

Katherine started to run. 'Owen ... Owen ... stay here ... Don't go.'

He was looking back at her. She saw the anguish in his eyes and she knew that as long as she lived she would never forget his face as it was then.

'Katherine ... my ... Queen.' The words seemed to escape from his lips. He was holding out his arms. She stumbled towards him. She reached him and fell into them.

'Owen ... Owen ... what does it mean ...?'

'I don't know. It can't be much. I have done nothing wrong. It will soon be explained.'

'It won't ... it won't,' she exclaimed. 'They are taking you away from me ... It is what I always feared.'

The Captain said, almost gently: 'We must go now.'

'I want an explanation,' cried Owen.

'You will get that.'

'I won't let him go. I won't,' cried Katherine. 'Do you know that I am the Queen?'

'Yes, my lady, but this is the order of the King.'

'The King. My son. Take me to him.'

'We have orders to take the squire, my lady. Come, Squire. We must be gone.'

They were moving him away.

The sun seemed suddenly pitiless. She could hear Edmund and Jasper shouting to each other ... it seemed from a long way off.

'Owen, Owen ... my love ...' she called. He was looking back taking a last look at her as she stood there on the grass holding out her arms to him.

Something was happening. Owen had gone. Darkness descended on her and she was sinking to the cold friendless earth.

* * *

She was lying in her bed. She had been aware of intense pain ... and some fearful shadow hanging over her but she was not sure what it was.

She was in a strange world she felt; she was not on earth; she did not want to come back. She was afraid to because of the hideous shadow which would reveal itself to her if she did. Somewhere in her mind she knew that Death was very close to her and that because of that shadow she wanted it to take her.

'She will recover.' Those were the first words she heard, and she knew that she was coming back.

She opened her eyes.

'You have a little girl, my lady.'

'And ... my lord ... Where is my lord?'

The fearful shadow was revealing itself and the revelation was wrapping itself round her like a cloak of misery.

'My lord went away, my lady.'

'When ... when ... how long ago?'

'It is three days. You have been long in labour.'

'My children ...'

'They are well and here, my lady.'

She closed her eyes. Then it came back to her. That wonderful happiness which had been shattered in minutes. They had taken him away. Where? And why?

She must get well. She must go to him. She must bring him back. She could. She would. What harm were they doing anybody? Owen must come back to them. He was so necessary to them all.

They brought the baby to her ... a frail creature, not like the others. They had been lusty from the start. This one's entry into the world had been marked by sorrow.

'She is very frail,' she said.

'We thought, my lady, that she should be baptized without delay.'

Ominous words.

She tried to rouse herself and think. Where was Owen? She must get up. She must understand what this meant. She would send to the King. She would ask him to come and see her. He had so enjoyed being with them all. He would listen. He would tell her what this was about and he would send Owen back to her.

The child was christened Margaret. A few days later she died.

The Queen felt a sickening sense of loss; but it was Owen she wanted. The break up of her happiness was all she could think of. The loss of the child to whose coming she and Owen had looked forward was just another blow. But when one was stunned by disaster another did not hurt as it might have done if it had been delivered singly. She and Owen would have mourned the loss of this little one ... But then, had she not been subjected to that terrible shock, baby Margaret would have been as strong and lusty as the rest.

'What can I do?' she mourned. 'What must I do?'

The children came to her.

'Where is our father?' they demanded.

'He has gone away for a little while.'

'He did not tell me,' said Jasper.

'He didn't tell me and I am the eldest,' announced Edmund.

'There was not time to tell you. He went in such a hurry.'

'And where is the baby?' Jasper wanted to know.

'The baby has gone away, too.'

'With our father? He should have taken me,' said Jasper.

'No ... me ... I am the eldest ...'

'He will be back,' said Katherine and then because she was weak and some voice within her said, He never will, she could not hold back her tears.

The children watched her in amazement. They did not know grown-up people cried.

Then they were all crying with her. They knew some major catastrophe had struck their home.

*   *   *

They came to Hadham. There was a party of them including nuns.

The Abbess sought out Katherine and told her that it was the King's wish that she be taken to the Abbey of Bermondsey where she would be well looked after.

'I will stay here,' said Katherine. 'It may be that my husband will come back.'

'My lady,' said the Abbess, 'it is well that you should know. Owen Tudor is a prisoner in Newgate.'

'Why so? Why so?' she cried. 'What has he done that they should put him there?'

'He has married against the law. Or if he has not married he has lived with you as your husband.'

'He *is* my husband.'

'That is his offence. He has broken the law which forbids men of his rank to marry noble ladies.'

'I married of my own free will.'

'It is the law, my lady, and we have been ordered to take you to our Abbey in Bermondsey. There you will be nursed back to health. You have nothing to fear from us. We will care for you.'

'This is my home. I shall wait here for my husband and I have children ... young children ...'

'They are being taken to the Abbey of Barking. There they will be cared for and educated in a manner fitting.'

'They have broken up my home ...'

'Dear lady, the law forbids such a home.'

'Oh God!' she cried. 'I vow vengeance on those who have done this.'

'Do not invoke God's anger, lady. You have already sinned deeply in this marriage.'

'There never was such a good and pure marriage as mine with Owen Tudor.'

'Come, lady, we will nurse you back to health.'

'My children ...'

'They have already left for Barking. We thought it better to avoid the anguish of parting.'

'Oh my God, you have taken everything from me ... everything I cared for ...'

'My lady, you will recover. You will find peace in God.'

'I will find peace only with my husband and children. I beg you send for the King. He is but a boy but he loves me. He will not let them do this to me.'

'It is on the King's orders, my lady ...'

'I will never believe that!' she cried. 'He is but a boy in the hands of ambitious men.'

'You will feel better when you are in the peace of our Abbey. We shall nurse you and bring you back to health.

Then you will make your plans ... or you will stay with us. It is in your hands, my lady. But now these are orders. We are to take you to Bermondsey.'

She knew she was powerless. She must obey. She must bide her time and try not to grieve too sorely for her children or to yearn too unbearably for a sight of Owen.

*　　　*　　　*

She remained ill. The loss of her child, the sudden disappearance of her happy life—it was too much for her. There were times when she raged against fate and those who had done this to her and there were others when she lay listless on her bed.

Time was passing, she knew. She was always asking, 'Have you heard aught of my husband?'

There was never any news of him. Nor of the children.

What were they doing, those little ones, torn from their home and their parents? How could people be so cruel to little children?

She thought fleetingly of her own misery in the Hôtel de St Pol. But what was that compared with this? This was such tragedy that she could not think clearly. It had stunned her into a melancholy of inadequacy, a state of not caring, of longing for death.

Yes, that was it. If she could not have Owen and the children she wanted to die.

She prayed for death. 'Oh, God, take me out of my misery. I cannot live like this. I want Owen. I want Owen more than anything. I want my babies. Oh, God, how can You be so cruel?'

Some days her spirits would revive a little. She would fancy something could be done. She would ask for writing materials and write to the King. She would appeal to him, tell of her misery. He could not fail her.

But in her heart she knew that whatever she wrote to the King would not be allowed to reach him.

The Abbess and her nuns were growing anxious. There were times when the Queen seemed almost demented. At others she would be quiet as though she were already on the way to death.

'She has an unequable temperament,' said the Abbess. 'Remember who her father was.'

The Duke of Gloucester, who was the most powerful man in the country, enquired about her.

'Keep her well looked after,' were his orders. 'It must not be said that she did not have every attention. Of course she is a little wild. It may well be that she has inherited something of her father's affliction.'

The Abbess and her nuns would do their best.

But her health grew worse. She became devout. She told the Abbess that she thought she was paying for her sins.

That pleased the Abbess. It was a good conclusion for her to come to.

'You see,' said the Queen, 'I went to Windsor for the birth of the King's son. "Do not go to Windsor," he said. "I do not want my son to go to Windsor." And yet I went to Windsor. I don't know what possessed me. There was some prophecy. I was wicked. I think I have passed some evil spell onto my son.'

They tried to soothe her. God would forgive her, said the Abbess. If she repented, if she devoted herself to prayer and asked forgiveness sincerely enough she would be forgiven.

'I never shall, I fear. I fear for my son Henry. I have dreams, Abbess, terrible dreams ... that he is as my father was. You cannot understand, lady Abbess, what it was like to be shut up in St Pol and to know that a madman was there and that he was my own father.'

'It is now in the past, lady. You have the future to think of.'

'I have nothing on this earth,' she said. 'They took from me everything I loved.'

'You must rouse yourself. Take an interest in life. Perhaps you could become one of us.'

'There is only one thing that would make me want to live and that is if they give me back my husband and my children. I do not wish to live without them. I cannot live without them. Oh ... if I could have some news of Owen. What do you think they are going to do to him? If you could come and tell me that he is free ... that he is coming to me ... I would be young again tomorrow. My health would come back to me. But I need him so much. I want him, Abbess. I care for nothing. If I cannot have him and my happy life I just want to die.'

'This is sinful talk.'

'I care not, Abbess. I want my husband who is so cruelly

taken from me. I have had a sad life ... and then it was happy suddenly. I came to England and I loved the King who was good to me ... but that was nothing ... nothing to compare with my life with Owen. Perhaps there never has been ... for any ...'

'Then you should thank God that you were allowed to enjoy it even for a while.'

'Yes,' she said, 'I thank God for Owen ... for my children ... but to take them from me ... what sort of God is it that can do that?'

'You blaspheme, my lady.'

She began to laugh wildly. 'I care not. Let Him take me. Let Him do what He will. He could not do worse than He has already.'

'You should occupy yourself with prayer. Would that not be better than this wildness? You should pray for Owen Tudor. Perhaps then God would see fit to answer your prayers.'

Then she was silent.

She would pray. She would beg.

Oh God, give him back to me.

And so it went on.

＊　　　＊　　　＊

Her health was failing. She could not sleep. She scarcely ate at all.

The nuns said: 'She is dying.'

'Should we send to the King?' wondered one of the sisters.

The Abbess shook her head. The Duke of Gloucester had said there must be no communication with the King.

If she could only have news of Owen Tudor it would help her, but she knew nothing except that he was in Newgate.

She asked endless questions about Newgate. What happened there? How were prisoners treated?

And her children? It was easier to give her news of them. They were settling happily in Barking.

'Children adapt themselves,' said the Abbess. 'They quickly forget.'

'Not Edmund,' she said. 'Not Jasper. The little ones perhaps but not those two.'

But it was for Owen she mourned. Owen in Newgate ... a prisoner who had broken the law by marrying her.

The Abbess was growing more and more anxious.

'She is willing herself to die,' she said.

Days passed. Listlessly, she was aware of time. The sun rose; the sun set. Another day gone and no news of Owen.

She took to her bed. She was too weak to rise.

'Death, come and take me,' she prayed.

Often her thoughts drifted to the past; then she thought she was in the Hôtel de St Pol, clinging to Michelle ... poor Michelle, she was dead now ... as I soon shall be, she thought. Oh yes, that is the best for me. In the past she had fought to survive, all through that hazardous childhood. Then Henry's death which had seemed so terrible at the time. But it had all led to those ecstatic years with Owen and then ... to this.

If I had not been so happy I should not be so wretched now, she thought. God raised me to the heights only to dash me to the depths. Cruel. Cruel! Why could we not have been left alone?

And Owen? What was he suffering? She was selfish to think of herself. He would be longing for her and the children even as she longed for him; and in some dark cold damp cell. At least she had a bed in which to be miserable, good food brought to her which she would not eat.

One morning she awoke and was not sure where she was. For one brief moment she had thought she was at Hadham and that she had only to stretch out a hand to touch Owen. But no ... she was not there. Then where ... where ...

From a long way off she heard the nuns talking.

'She is in a high fever It was inevitable ... Such neglect of her health ...'

'If there was only news of Owen Tudor she would recover.'

The fever grew worse; she would not take the nourishing foods they brought to her. She turned her head away when they prayed by her bedside. She had no interest in anything.

And then one day there was a visitor at the Abbey.

He asked if he might have a word with the Abbess, and as it was clear that he had news of importance the Abbess agreed to see him.

'I come from Owen Tudor,' he said.

The Abbess stared at him in disbelief.

'He is in Newgate ... a prisoner ...'

'No more,' said the man. 'He has escaped ... with the help of friends.'

'Where is he?'

'That, lady, I cannot tell you. He wishes his wife to know that he is free and will find a means of coming for her.'

'I cannot allow this. She has been put into my charge.'

'You must tell her that her husband is free.'

The Abbess was thoughtful. She had orders from the mighty Duke of Gloucester. She was to keep the Queen here, virtually a prisoner though treated with the utmost honour. If Owen Tudor came here and took her away what could she answer to the all powerful Duke? He would be furiously angry; he would blame her, perhaps have her removed from her post.

Yet ... what that news would do to the Queen! She knew what effect it would have. If Katherine heard that her husband was free, that there was hope that they would be together again, she would regain her will to live.

The Abbess was a deeply religious woman. She had witnessed the suffering of the Queen and although she had obeyed orders to keep Katherine a prisoner in the Abbey, she had often deplored the part she had been forced to play in the drama.

Katherine was a weak woman; there was no doubt in the Abbess's mind of that—but she loved deeply; and surely love could not be evil—even carnal love between two people who were not married.

The Abbess knew that the Duke of Gloucester would not wish Katherine to be told of her husband's escape, but she made her way to the cell which was occupied by the Queen. She opened the door and went in.

Katherine was lying with her face turned to the wall on which hung the great crucifix.

'I have news, my lady,' cried the Abbess. 'Owen Tudor is free. He has escaped from Newgate. He has sent someone to tell you that he will come for you.'

Katherine did not stir.

The Abbess went closer to the bed. She laid a hand on Katherine's cold cheek.

'Holy Mother of God,' she murmured, 'it is too late.' Then she made the sign of the cross. 'God rest her soul, poor tragic lady,' she said.

*   *   *

When the King heard of his mother's death he was overcome with grief.

'When I was with her,' he said, 'she seemed so young ... she was so happy. Oh, how cruel it was to take her away from Owen and the children.'

His Uncle Humphrey explained to him. 'Owen had broken the law. Such acts cannot go unpunished.'

'I can see no harm in what they did.'

'My lord, it is always necessary to maintain the law.'

Stop treating me like a child, Henry wanted to cry out, but he said nothing. The Earl of Warwick had taught him to control his temper—not that he had inherited the Plantagenet one which was notorious. He was mild by nature but at times he could be angry and it was usually over something he considered unjust as he did this treatment of Owen and his mother.

He promised himself that he would do what he could to help Owen and his brothers and little sister.

First there was the funeral of his mother and that must be worthy of her. The King gave orders that she was to be brought to St Katherine's Chapel by the Tower of London and there lie in state and from there be taken to St Paul's for a memorial service and then be buried in the Lady Chapel at Westminster Abbey.

Henry then sent out an order that Owen Tudor should come to him as he wished to talk with him. He need have no fear. He promised him safe conduct.

When Owen heard, he was undecided. He trusted the King but the King was but a boy, he was a figurehead merely and had no real say in affairs. The King would never have agreed to imprison him and break up his mother's happy home. No, Owen could not risk coming to the King. Yet on the other hand he wanted to hear about his children. If he could see Henry alone ... But what was the use? It was a trap.

He came to London however but the nearer he approached the capital the more uneasy he became. And when he reached Westminster so certain was he of treachery, so eager to avoid a further incarceration in Newgate that he took fright and with it sanctuary in Westminster Abbey.

Eleanor and Humphrey were furious when they heard he had come so far and still eluded them.

'The King is too interested in Tudor,' said Humphrey. 'Let them get together and the boy will be showering honours on him and before we know where we are we shall have a favourite on our hands, telling him what to do and how the rest of us are concerned with our own ambitions.'

'It must never get to that,' agreed Eleanor. 'He must be lured out of sanctuary.'

'And how?' asked Humphrey.

'He is an old soldier and I have discovered that he used to frequent that tavern by Westminster Gate. If he could be lured there he could be taken and sent back to prison. After all he is guilty of escaping.'

'We will try it,' said Humphrey.

It was not difficult of course to find an old soldier who had served at Agincourt with Owen. Agincourt was a magic word to those old warriors. They could never resist talking of it and how they had taken part in and won one of the greatest battles in military history.

The old soldier would be delighted to work for the Duke of Gloucester. He would go into the Abbey, get into conversation with his fellow soldier and tell him of the stories which were told in the old tavern of Westminster Gate.

Owen was pleased to see a man whom he could not remember having seen before but who had undoubtedly served with King Harry's army. They talked a while of old times, but when the suggestion came to visit the tavern Owen was wary. There was too much at stake to risk it for the sake of a convivial evening. He was grieving deeply for the loss of Katherine and still could not believe that she was dead. She had seemed so full of life, like a young girl, and that she could have wasted away, died of melancholy still seemed an evil dream to him.

So the trick failed, much to the chagrin of Eleanor and Humphrey.

'I'll get him yet,' vowed Humphrey.

In the meantime Owen sought an opportunity of seeing the King. He knew that if he saw the boy alone then he could make him understand that he had committed no crime. He had escaped when he had been wrongfully imprisoned. There was nothing criminal about that.

He had the utmost faith in the King.

Greatly daring he decided to make his way by night to Kennington where the King was sitting with his Privy Council. The Duke of Gloucester was not present and it seemed a good time to state his case.

The King and the members of the Council were startled when Owen burst in upon them. Henry stared at him and he cried out: 'Owen, it is you then?'

And then a terrible desolation swept over the young King for he was reminded afresh of the death of his mother.

'My lord King, my lords of the Council,' said Owen. 'I come to beg you hear me. Have I your leave to tell you why I am here and to explain that I have been wrongfully imprisoned?'

The King astonished everyone by saying in a loud clear voice: 'You have our leave Owen Tudor to state your case.'

Owen addressed himself to the boy—Katherine's son, who looked a little like her; the same clear eyes, the same innocence. His spirits rose. His enemies were not present, he could hope that the King would help him, and he stated the facts clearly. He had loved the Queen dearly and she had loved him. She was no longer of importance to the country. Any children they had would be Tudors remote from the throne. They had loved and married before the law was brought in forbidding marriages such as theirs. The Queen was now dead. She had died of melancholy because she had been unable to bear the separation from her husband and children. He had been imprisoned. True he had escaped, but he saw no wrong in that because he should never have been imprisoned in the first place.

Then Henry spoke with an authority and wisdom which he employed at times and which never failed to astonish those who witnessed it. He finished by saying: 'My friends, Owen Tudor has stated his case with clarity. He has committed no fault against us and I say that from henceforth he is a free man.'

Owen fell on his knees before the King and kissed his hands. Henry, deeply moved, turned away. He could not forget that that happy home at Hadham had been broken up and he would never again experience the peace and happiness he had found there.

*   *   *

He sent for Owen. He had no longer need to play the King. He was just a young boy who had lost his mother.

'I did not see her much after they took me away,' he said,

'but I always thought of her. It is strange, Owen, but when I had to do something which I hated and which I was a little afraid of, like being crowned in Paris and going to the Parliaments in the beginning, I always thought of my mother.'

Poor Owen. He could not speak of her because his emotion choked him.

'And Owen, I remember you too ... You used to ride with me.'

'You were a bold little boy, my lord.'

'I was quaking with fear within and you always gave me courage. Owen ... it is so sad that she is gone ... and the house at Hadham ...'

'I don't want to go there again.'

'No ... nor I. What of the children?'

'They are at Barking still.'

'I will see that they are well cared for, Owen.'

'I am going to see them.'

Henry nodded. 'It is well that they are so young. They will forget perhaps.'

'The little ones yes ... not Edmund and Jasper ...'

'They will in time. Are you going straight to them now?'

'Yes, my lord. I shall refresh myself in the tavern at Westminster Gate and then ride to Barking.'

'God speed, Owen. Remember I am your friend.'

Owen took his leave and went to the tavern as he had said he would and he was accompanied by his priest and his servant and while he was there a man came in and sat beside him.

The man wore a heavy cloak but as he sat down beside Owen he allowed it to fall open and so disclosed the royal livery.

'I come from the King,' he said. 'He commands me to tell you that you should not go to Barking. Your enemies are waiting for you there as the first place to which you would go. On the King's commands you are to get away with all speed.'

Owen understood. Gloucester was not going to let him go free.

Owen hastily left the tavern with his two retainers, mounted his horse and turned his face to Wales.

They had not gone far when they realized that they were being followed and soon a company of armed men had caught up with them and surrounded them. Gloucester had sent

men to Barking but others had been lying in wait at Westminster.

What were three against so many? And when Owen saw
who his captors were he feared the worst.

*   *   *

So he was once more a prisoner. Gloucester had no wish
to appear in the matter and gave the prisoner into the hands
of the Earl of Suffolk. A dangerous man, said Gloucester, as
all men were who escaped from prison. 'We must see,' he
added, 'that there is no escape this time.'

It was more comfortable in Wallingford Castle than it had
been in Newgate but Owen chafed against his lack of freedom.

There was no reason to suppose that he would be allowed
to remain there. Gloucester wanted him back in Newgate.
The proper place, he said, for men who had the temerity to
marry queens in the hope of furthering their ambitions.

So it was back to Newgate. Owen realized then the futility
of appealing to the King. Henry wished him well; he was
honourable and a son of whom Katherine could have been
proud, but he was ineffectual in the hands of powerful men.

Gloucester wanted him out of the way. He would have
to be careful. He must plan. He must not give in. He must
find some way of getting out of Newgate for the sake of his
children.

There was one consolation. He had his servant and the
priest with him. They could talk together; they could plan.

The opportunity came. 'It must not fail,' said Owen. 'If it
does they will separate us; they will put us in closer confinement. We have to succeed and this time never give them the
chance to take us again.'

It was the time-worn method. Guards were always ready
to take a little wine, and if that wine had something a little
stronger in it, well, the plan might work.

It did. The drunken guards, the scaling of the walls, and
out to freedom.

They found horses which were supplied by a friend at a
nearby tavern and before the dawn broke they were miles
away from Newgate on their way to freedom and Owen's
native Wales.

THE RECKONING

THE Duchess of Gloucester was restless and disgruntled. Her plans came to nothing. The years were passing and the King was leaving his childhood behind. He was almost twenty. Some kings of twenty might be considered to have reached their maturity; not so Henry. He had always been a mild creature ready to be guided; sometimes it seemed that he was somehow lacking.

Eleanor liked to think of him as an imbecile.

Gloucester mildly reproved her. His nephew was by no means half-witted. In fact intellectually he was very bright. It was merely that he was not forceful enough to govern. He really was not endowed to be a King.

'This is the crux of the matter,' said Eleanor. 'He is not endowed with kingly qualities.'

And they were talking of marrying him which of course they would soon. It was strange that he had been allowed to reach the age of twenty without having had a wife found for him. It would not be long delayed and then there would be a child ... an heir to the throne.

No, thought Eleanor, not that!

Humphrey was deep in his feud with Cardinal Beaufort. It was amazing how they always took opposing views. Beaufort was all for making peace with France because he said that England could not afford to go on supporting a war. Humphrey had always dreamed that he would outshine his late brother Bedford and win back all that had been lost since the coming of Joan of Arc. Humphrey saw himself as another

Henry the Fifth. Beaufort wanted to release the Duc d'Orléans who had been a prisoner in English hands since Agincourt. He was an excellent bargaining counter. Beaufort was ready to do anything for peace. No, cried Humphrey, there should be no peace.

Eleanor supported him in this. Peace with France would inevitably mean a marriage for Henry with a daughter of Charles the Seventh.

There must be no marriage. Eleanor was frantic at the thought.

Something must be done before then.

She was disappointed in Margery Jourdemayne. In spite of the beautiful waxen image nurtured in its cradle she was still not pregnant. She had swallowed pills and potions which Margery assured her were destined to produce fruitfulness and Margery had been living very comfortably on the proceeds of the Duchess's patronage for years.

And yet nothing the Duchess desired came to pass.

The baby did not arrive and the King still lived.

Margery was getting desperate. She said that a certain familiar had come to her in a dream and said that the fault lay with the Duke.

'I do not believe that. Before our connection he had an illegitimate son and a daughter.'

'Bastards,' cried Margery. 'How can they be sure who their fathers are?'

'Arthur and Antigone both have a look of the Duke.'

'The Plantagenet looks are not uncommon in this land,' was Margery's excuse. 'It comes down through generations.'

But Eleanor was getting impatient and Margery was getting alarmed seeing the disappearance of her best source of income—and the one which had enabled her to not only live in comfort but stow something away for less lucrative days.

'My lady might like to consult a man I know of—a cleric— a man of the Church no less. He will tell your future. That is what your ladyship would like. I hear that he can foretell the stars. He is expensive ... Well, not to a lady like you. And he is worth every groat.'

'Bring him here,' said the Duchess.

So that was how she made the acquaintance of Roger Bolingbroke.

He appealed to Eleanor from the beginning. He was more sophisticated than Margery. He was not a witch; he was a soothsayer. He wore a long black cloak and his breeches and surcoat were also black. His appearance was impressive. The blackness of his garb was relieved only by a heavy gold chain which he wore about his neck.

He had penetrating eyes in a thin white face; there was an aura of another world about him. Eleanor was sure that he could help her.

He said he would consult the signs. Consultations were costly because they demanded so much of him and if he were to continue his work he must be aloof from financial worries.

Eleanor waved all that aside. She was ready to pay what he asked. She took a sapphire ring from her finger and gave it to him as a start.

Roger was delighted. He saw the beginning of a rewarding association.

The first meeting sent the Duchess's spirits soaring.

Roger stared at her over the strange objects he was handling on the table. He muttered to himself while Eleanor listened intently. Then he came to her and knelt.

'I hardly dare say what I see,' he murmured.

'Tell me! Tell me!' she cried.

He took her hand and kissed it.

'My lady, I see the Queen of England.'

'Who is she ... a bride for Henry ... ?'

'My lady ... *you* are to be the Queen.'

She was beside herself with delight. 'Tell me more. Tell me more ...'

'I can see no more now ... my lady. This one fact overshadows all else.'

He went back to his stool. He stared and muttered. Then he buried his face in his hands.

'The powers have left me,' he said. 'They have given me this blinding fact and they say that is enough ... for now ...'

'Then when ...'

'I will commune with the powers ... if that is what you wish. I need special implements. They are costly ... I have never dealt with such as this. I shall need time ...'

'Time ... time ... what for?'

'To acquire what I need.'

'There must be no delay.'

'Delay ... my lady ...' He lifted his shoulders.

She took a chain from her neck. 'Take that. I will pay for what you need.'

'My lady, I will give up everything to work on this.'

He was working on it. But he could go no further. She was going to be Queen, he said. The powers, however cajoled, would tell no more than that.

He would consult with a man he knew—that was if Eleanor was agreeable to bring another into the case. She must be warned that his services would be costly.

Impatiently she shrugged her shoulders.

'Spare nothing,' she said. 'I want to know how this can come about.'

Thus she met Thomas Southwell who brought a further respectability into the proceedings because he was a canon of St Stephen's, Westminster.

He confirmed Roger Bolingbroke's prophecy that Eleanor would be the Queen of England. But he said it would not come about easily.

What did they mean by that?

'There is someone in the way, my lady,' said Thomas Southwell.

'But if it is ordained that I am to be Queen he will be removed, surely?'

The two men looked at each other. It was not quite as easy as that. It was true that Roger had seen her in her regalia being crowned at the Abbey, but now that his vision had cleared it was made known to these seers that the brilliant destiny could only be reached if the lady had the courage to surmount a certain obstruction. Someone stood in the way. The King.

'I did not need to spend a fortune to discover that,' retorted Eleanor coldly.

The men were alert. She was getting impatient.

'The King has to be removed before he marries,' said Thomas Southwell. 'It can be done. Margery has special skills in this art. She should be called back.'

'Margery has been working on it for years and nothing has happened.'

'Margery has never worked with us.'

So the two wise men and the wise woman came together and Margery made an image of the King which she said would take her a few weeks because it was not merely constructing it in wax which had to be done but life had to be breathed into it. She had to repeat incantations over it every night. It must be done in accordance with the laws of witchcraft otherwise it would be useless.

'And when it is done?' asked Eleanor.

'It shall then be placed in a warm spot near a fire but not too near, and there it shall be left until the wax melts ... But that must be gradual. Then as it melts, so shall the King's life ebb away.'

'We have tried it already.'

'Not with us,' said Roger Bolingbroke.

She believed them. She knew that Roger had a good practice near St Paul's, that people of the Court visited him in secret and the fact that a canon of the Church was with them ensured success.

Eleanor waited.

*   *   *

Humphrey rode through the city towards Westminster. The people cheered him and that was a comfort. Strangely enough he had retained his popularity in spite of his failures. The people seemed to like some people and forgive them a good deal. They had never liked the Cardinal. They still thought of him as 'Bastard'. It amazed Humphrey often how the most humble people attached such importance to birth and despised those who, although far above themselves, were not of the highest.

He was growing a little tired of all the conflict, but his feud with his uncle Cardinal could still arouse fighting excitement in him; he could see though that the Council was swaying towards Beaufort. Perhaps in time the people would.

He had squandered men and money in Jacqueline's cause; he had married beneath him—not that he regretted that. Eleanor had been worth it. She could still please him, which was amazing considering how jaded he was. And she was loyal to him—or was that to herself? As he rose she had risen with him.

Oh, he was tired. He would go to the palace and there shut himself in with a new book which had just been sent to him. He was interested in the author and if he thought the book worthy he would arrange a pension for him.

He could hear shouting in the streets. Outside a house a crowd had assembled and guards were arresting a man.

Some malefactor, he thought. I wonder what his offence is?

The man was dressed in black—a strange-looking creature. 'Who is he?' he asked one of his attendants.

'My lord, it is the soothsayer, Roger Bolingbroke. It has been said for a long time that he deals in black magic.'

'Another of them. There are too many witches and such like in the country.'

He rode on to Westminster.

Eleanor was delighted to see him. They embraced warmly. Later she asked about the health of the King.

'Never very robust,' said the Duke. 'It often amazes me that my brother should beget such a son.'

'Not so well as normal, then?' she asked.

'Oh ... he always looks sickly to me.'

She was exultant. It is working, she thought. Very slowly the wax was melting. When it had disappeared completely the King would be dead.

'You had a good journey, my love?'

'Oh fair enough. The people of London cheered me.'

'Bless them. They have always been loyal to you. I set my trust in the people of London.'

'I saw a fellow being arrested near St Paul's.'

'Oh?' She was not interested. She was thinking of the slowly melting wax figure.

'Some sort of witch. It's time we looked into their activities a little more. Perhaps this is a sign.'

A sudden fear touched the Duchess.

'A sort of witch ... a man, did you say?'

'They're as bad as the women. This one looked the part. He was all in black ... looked like the Devil himself.'

'Oh ... near St Paul's you say?'

'Yes, I think I've heard his name mentioned before. Seems to be quite a fashionable sort of rogue. It was Bolingbroke— Roger Bolingbroke.'

The Duchess felt a little faint. She steadied herself by taking his arm.

'Are you all right, my love?'

'I'm all right, Humphrey.'

'Are you ...'

No, she thought angrily, not pregnant. And Roger arrested. What does this mean?

* * *

She was soon to find out. The whole Court was talking of it. The arrest and questioning of Roger Bolingbroke had led to his accomplice Thomas Southwell being brought in, and they had had some connection with Margery Jourdemayne the Witch of Eye who had faced charges at Windsor some years before and owing to the dark powers she possessed had somehow escaped conviction.

The interest was growing. The houses of the prisoners had been searched and there was an upsurge of interest when a half-melted figure of the King was discovered.

'You can be sure,' was the comment, 'that people in high places are concerned with this.'

It seemed possible, for why should men in the position of these two, and a poor old woman of Eye, risk their lives to replace one King with another?

Passions were rising. This was not merely the discovery of another witch. This was witchcraft with treason.

The Duke of Gloucester was very uneasy. As the next in line for the throne he felt eyes were turned to him. He was afraid to raise the subject with Eleanor for a terrible suspicion had come to him.

As for Eleanor she was in a state of great anxiety. They must not mention her. She must not be involved in this. But if they decided to put the men and Margery to the torture what would they divulge?

They were not brave men, either of them. They were clerks, minor prelates ... growing rich on practising the black arts.

And Margery, she had been in trouble before. How would she stand up to questioning? She had been ready to serve her Duchess assiduously ... but that was when she was being paid.

Anxious days followed and when the two men and the Witch of Eye were found guilty of practising witchcraft and of treason no one was surprised.

It was a Sunday in July, hot and sultry. Bolingbroke was to be present at St Paul's Cross where a stage had been set up. There he was to confess to the vast crowd which had gathered that he had practised the black arts. He now fully repented of his sins and was ready to pay whatever penalty was demanded of him.

Eleanor would have liked to be there but she dared not. She knew that Humphrey felt the same. He was not with her. He avoided her and she knew why.

But she had sent one of her women to mingle with the crowd and to report back to her everything that had been said.

She shut herself into her bedchamber. She must be alone. And at the same time she must give no indication that she felt an especial anxiety.

Already she knew that suspicious eyes were turned on her. People were asking themselves who would make a wax image of the King.

There was a knock at her door. It was the woman she had sent to St Paul's. The woman's eyes were wide and frantic.

'My lady,' she cried, 'you must fly. Roger Bolingbroke has admitted he practised black magic and treason and he says he did so on your command.'

She stood up and was at once afraid her legs would not support her. This was what she had feared. She looked about her frantically.

Where was Humphrey? But could Humphrey help her now?

Then she knew what she must do.

'Bring me my riding habit,' she said.

'My lady, where are you going?'

'Away from here ... before they come for me.'

She was helped into her riding habit. Her hands were trembling.

'My lady, you will not get far ...'

'I know ... but as far as I need, please God. I am going into sanctuary at Westminster.'

*   *   *

It was but a temporary refuge. She had needed it while she thought of what she must do.

Humphrey did not come to her. He dared not. This was entirely her affair. If he showed his sympathy with her he would immediately stand with her, accused.

No, she had used Humphrey. She had arranged this alone; now she must pay the penalty.

For a few days she was comfortless in Westminster. Some of her attendants came to her and brought her news of what was going on. Bolingbroke, Southwell and the Witch of

Eye were all in the Tower. It would go ill with them. Old Margery would not escape this time.

It was no comfort to know that a tribunal was being set up in St Stephen's Chapel, that it was headed by the Cardinal Beaufort and Archbishop Ayscough to enquire into charges of necromancy, witchcraft, heresy and treason. A formidable list of accusations.

Eleanor lay in discomfort in the sanctuary. To think she had come to this after her spectacular rise to fortune! The serving-woman of no account to become Duchess of Gloucester! Oh, if only she had remained content. But when were the ambitious ever content? First she had sought to displace the Duke's wife and having done that, to displace the King.

It would have worked, she thought angrily, but for those fools Bolingbroke and Southwell. How could they be so foolish as to get arrested ... and then to mention her! It was unforgivable.

She was called upon to attend St Stephen's to answer the charges brought against her. She would stand up to them. She had always been able to defend herself.

She was brought before them. Defiantly she faced them.

Yes, she had visited the Witch of Eye. She had bought lotions from her. She might have bought a spell.

She had used this, had she, to lure the Duke of Gloucester from his wife?

Oh no. It was only after he had parted from his wife, when she, Eleanor, had become his mistress. She had wanted to make their love respectable.

'Did the Duke know of these spells used against him?'

'The spells, my lords, would have been useless had they been known. And they were not used against him ... only to procure his greater happiness.'

'And the waxen image?'

She would confess to the lords that she longed for a child. She had been foolish. She had thought these people could help her. That was why she had asked them to make a waxen image.

'And to burn it slowly ...'

'My lords, I knew nothing of that.'

She might be wily but she did not deceive them. All the accused were indicted of treason. The three necromancers were sent back to the Tower, and Eleanor was placed under constraint in Leeds Castle until such time as there should be a further inquiry.

* * *

Leeds Castle in the lovely county of Kent was very beautiful, standing on two islands as it did, connected by a double drawbridge, but the beauty of her surroundings meant nothing to Eleanor. She was now awaiting a summons to appear before her judges and she was afraid.

Humphrey had not been near her. In a way she understood. He dared not. By coming to her he risked his life. He was the first suspect in this plot to murder the King; and he must show that he was entirely ignorant of it.

She was alone. She must defend herself. She wondered what they would do to her. They did not believe her when she said that the image was of a baby she longed to have.

October had come; the leaves were being torn from the trees; there was a warning of winter in the chill which came off the water that lapped the castle walls. She looked from her window across that water to the profusion of trees and the bronze carpet of leaves beneath them. She wanted to go out there and ride in the woods. She wanted to be free to go and come as she pleased.

Why had she not been content with what she had, when she had been given so much?

The summons came. Once again she was to attend St Stephen's Chapel where a special commission, on which sat the Earls of Suffolk, Stafford and Huntingdon, had been set up.

They eyed her disdainfully—a woman of no breeding, they had never been able to understand why the Duke had married her. A lusty mistress no doubt ... but a Duchess, and the Duchess of Gloucester, the highest in the land ... next the King!

Next the King! Ah, there was the reason.

She defended herself ably enough. She clung to the story that the image had been of the child for which she longed. She could not convince them though, for she could not explain why when it was found it had been half-melted away.

She was found guilty with the rest. The Witch of Eye was to be burned at the stake, and Bolingbroke and Southwell were to suffer the traitor's fearsome death of hanging, drawing and quartering.

She saw them turn pale when they were sentenced ... all except Margery who had come to terms with her terrible fate. After all she had come close to it before.

And now it was Eleanor's turn. She was guilty of conspiring against the life of the King. Only her nobility acquired through marriage and her connection with royalty saved her from the terrible fate of her fellow conspirators.

She was to be imprisoned for life but before she was taken to her prison would be required to walk barefoot through the streets of London carrying a taper which she would offer at various churches as yet to be named. For three days she should do this before she was taken off to her lifelong prison.

*   *   *

It was a holiday in London when the executions were due to take place. People crowded into the streets not to be done out of one little bit of excitement. Some went to Smithfield to watch the witch burn. Poor Margery Jourdemayne who had confounded her accusers some ten years before at Windsor and could not repeat her success in this more serious charge. She was philosophical until the flames began to touch her feet. It was one of the hazards of a witch's life.

And then the agony started. 'Save me God,' she prayed; and then protesting, 'Oh Lord, why did you send the lady Duchess to me!'

She was old and oil had been poured on the wood to make it burn quicker, so the agony was not prolonged.

So died poor Margery Jourdemayne, the Witch of Eye-next-Westminster.

The fortunate member of the party was Thomas Southwell. He had lived in an agony of fear since he had been arrested and when his terrible sentence was pronounced against him he was in such a state of shock that he scarcely knew what was happening to him, and when his guards went to arouse him on the morning fixed for his execution they found him dead. He had died of fright.

Not so Roger Bolingbroke; he suffered the entire grisly performance and his severed head was in due course set up on London Bridge and his limbs sent to Oxford, Cambridge, Hereford and York for as far afield as these cities the people had heard of the plot which the Duchess of Gloucester had contrived with these felons to kill the King and set up her husband in his place.

* * *

She walked barefoot through the city streets carrying a candle which weighed two pounds in weight. People came out to stare at her, to call names at her. Murderess, they said.

She looked neither to the right nor to the left. From Temple Gate to St Paul's she walked and there she set the candle on the altar. People crowded round her, plucking at her robes, reviling her.

This was the worst of all. She had been able to endure confinement in Leeds Castle but to be thus humiliated for one of her pride was punishment indeed.

She had still two more penances to perform and with only one day in between to bathe her aching feet blistered from walking barefoot over the dirty cobbled streets, she must start again. This was a Saturday and she must parade from the Swan in Thames Street to Christchurch and on the next day, Sunday, from St Paul's to St Peter's in Cornhill.

How they scorned her! How they loved to see the once mighty fallen low! Not so long ago when she rode through these streets, these people would have called out 'Long live the noble Duchess' and hope that she would throw a coin at them.

Now they were against her. They called her Murderess. They believed she had tried to kill their beloved King.

And after this, what was there but imprisonment for the rest of her life?

And Humphrey? Would he come to her?

She had arrived at St Peter's in Cornhill. The penance was over. Now they were ready to pass her into the hands of her gaoler. Sir Thomas Stanley had been chosen for this role and he was waiting to take her to Chester Castle while they decided where she should finally be incarcerated.

So had the mighty fallen. Here was an end to her ambitious hopes. The King would be married soon. He would produce a son. There would be no crown for Eleanor.

* * *

Humphrey was old and tired. Everything had gone wrong. Eleanor's ambitious folly had ruined their life together. He

saw little of her. She had been sent to Kenilworth Castle and
remained a prisoner there; and now there was talk of sending
her to the Isle of Man.

He missed her; and he had tried soon after the sentence
to bring about her freedom. Noble ladies, he declared, should
be tried by their peers in the spirit of Magna Carta. It would
have been possible to buy her freedom, surely. But he
was out of favour. The King was growing up. Henry was
horrified that there should have been this plot against him;
moreover he refused to believe that his Uncle Humphrey was
not involved with his wife.

'I shall never trust my uncle again,' he was reported to
have said; and Humphrey knew his nephew well enough to
realize that once such an idea came into Henry's mind it
would stay there.

Instead of furthering their ambitions Eleanor had blighted
them forever. Everywhere he was baulked. The King was to
marry and not the princess of Humphrey's choice. Once
Humphrey's great enemy had been the Cardinal. He was
still an enemy but he had been superseded in that respect by
William de la Pole, the Earl of Suffolk. As Humphrey fell in
the King's favour so Suffolk rose.

Suffolk had become very friendly with the Duke of Orléans
who had been imprisoned in England since Agincourt; it
was Suffolk who had arranged his release; and now listening
to his advice was supporting the idea of a marriage between
the King and Margaret of Anjou.

Humphrey wished for a marriage with the daughter of
the Count of Armagnac but ever since Eleanor's trial young
Henry remained suspicious of everything his uncle said and
did.

Henry was emerging as a King who found it difficult to
make up his own mind about anything. He was going to
be weak, that much was evident. Such a King set the minds
of ambitious men afire for power. Suffolk was just such a
man. He was in close amity with the Cardinal, but that was
safe for the Cardinal was an old man and had been ailing
for some time. Suffolk's great enemy was Gloucester; and,
since Gloucester's position had been considerably weakened
through suspicion of being concerned with his wife in a plot
to get rid of the King, he presented no great threat.

Gloucester was very much aware of this. He no longer had
Eleanor to bolster up his confidence and give him that solace

which it seemed she alone could give him. It was not that he was an old man but the life he had led had taken such a toll of his health, and there were times when a listlessness came over him and he did not greatly care about Suffolk's successes.

It was Suffolk who was sent to France to bring home the King's bride; it was Suffolk who was promoted to a marquisate; it was Suffolk who was in high favour with the new Queen. He was ready to take his place as chief adviser to the King as soon as the Cardinal died—which could not be long. And there was one whom he was determined to destroy—and that was Gloucester. Moreover fate seemed to be on his side.

Oh Eleanor, he thought, you wanted too much for us. We should have been content with what we had. Now you have lost that ... and it seems I am likely to do the same.

Henry had made it clear that he had no wish to see him. He did not trust his uncle and felt very uneasy in his presence. He had strengthened his bodyguards.

'I have my enemies,' he said, and everyone knew he was thinking of Gloucester.

However Humphrey still remained protector of the country; and this was a situation which could not be allowed to continue.

Parliament was meeting at Bury St Edmunds, and Humphrey had decided he would appear there and ask for the release of his wife. If he could take her away he would go and live with her in retirement.

Attended by about eight horsemen, most of whom were Welsh, he made his way to Bury to join the Parliament there. His intention was to stay the night in some lodging in the North Spital of St Saviours on the Thetford Road. It was eleven o'clock in the morning as he came through Southgate.

Rumours had been in circulation that he was gathering an army to come against the King and Suffolk. It was said that he had gone to Wales to raise this army. It was a story set about by his enemies. He had no heart for such a project. He had finished with ambition from the moment he realized where Eleanor's had sent her.

No, his one thought now was to make peace with the King and get Eleanor released. Then they would make a new life together.

A messenger was riding towards him and he could see from his livery that he came from the King.

'Orders, my lord Duke,' cried the messenger.

'Orders for me?'

'From the King, my lord. You are to proceed without delay to your lodging and there you shall stay until made aware of the King's pleasure.'

Gloucester had no alternative but to obey and accordingly went straight to his lodgings.

A meal was awaiting him and as he ate he wondered what his enemies had in mind for him.

One or two of his friends were with him. There were not many of them left and he contemplated how friends fell away from a man in times of disaster.

They talked of the King and the Queen who seemed to be gaining a great influence over her weak lord; and of Suffolk who with Beaufort seemed now to be ruling the country. Not for long. The Queen was showing her mettle. She was a forthright young lady although as yet but seventeen years old.

'I shall see the King,' said Gloucester, 'and ask him to release my wife. Then I shall be ready to relieve myself of the trappings of office and cosset myself a little.'

'You will soon recover your health then, my lord.'

He wondered. He had felt less well since he had arrived at the inn.

Sometimes he was nauseated and could not bear to eat the food they put before him.

Why did they keep him a prisoner here? Why could he not go to the Parliament and state his desire to hand over his power, to retire into obscurity with a wife who, if she had ever indulged in plots, had learned her lesson now?

His manservant had alarming news for him.

'My lord,' he said, 'members of your household have been arrested. Your enemies are saying that they conspired to kill the King and place you on the throne.'

'It is nonsense,' he cried, and he thought: Oh Eleanor, how could you? See what doubts and suspicions you have set in motion!

'Your son Arthur has been taken.'

'No ... no ... He did nothing. His only fault is that he is my son.'

'They will prove nothing against him.'

'They will tell the world they have proved what they wish to prove.'

He rose from the dinner table. He could not eat. He

wanted to be alone to think. This sudden illness was robbing him of all will to live. He, great Gloucester, brother to one King, uncle to another was a prisoner in this lodging house. They were going to condemn him; they were going to call him traitor. What would they do to him? Cut off his head as they had those of some of his ancestors? And if they decided to they would do it quickly so that there could be no outcry to save him.

He saw it all clearly. He had too many powerful enemies. The Cardinal was benign compared with Suffolk. He had tried to influence the King ... but others had done better than that and ever since Eleanor's trial he had been suspect.

He made his way to his sleeping apartments. He felt so weak that he must die.

He was ill ... close to death perhaps. There were times when he felt like it.

He lay still. Footsteps outside the room. Someone was coming. He felt too ill to care.

The door opened slowly. Someone was standing there.

*   *   *

They said that his health, ruined by the life he had led, had suddenly given way. He had been ailing for some time.

Yet there were still some to say that his death was very sudden.

The lords and knights of the Parliament were gathered close by and many of them came to look at his body.

They reported to the King that there were no signs of violence. He must remember that the Duke had not been in good health for some time now.

It was ordered that he should be put into a leaden coffin. He had already had a beautiful vault made for himself in St Albans. Let him be taken there and buried with the ceremony which it was proper to perform at the burial of a royal Duke.

Eleanor was stunned by the news. She knew now that she would be a prisoner until the end of her life.

She had been taken from Kenilworth to the Isle of Man, and as she looked out on the seething waters she would gaze with longing towards the mainland and think of all that she had lost.

They had murdered her husband, she was sure. She should

have been with him to protect him. She was deeply touched to hear that he had been on his way to the Parliament to try to secure a pardon for her.

Sometimes at night she fancied she heard the screams of Margery Jourdemayne and the moans of agony which must have come from Roger Bolingbroke in his last moments.

And Humphrey ... the mystery of his death would haunt her for the rest of her life, and she would ask herself as many people throughout the country were asking and would continue to ask for years to come: Did he die naturally? He had been ill; he was prematurely aged though he had lived fifty-six years and often riotously. Or did some assassin steal into his room on that fateful day?

She could not be sure. Only his murderers—if murderers there had been—would know.

All she could do was look ahead to the weary years which awaited her, and to contemplate how different her life might have been if she had been contented with what she had and had not attempted to stretch out to snatch a golden crown.

BIBLIOGRAPHY

Aubrey, William Hickman Smith	*National and Domestic History of England*
Costain, Thomas B.	*The Last Plantagenets*
	The Pageant of England 1377–1485
Fabre, Lucien	
Translated by Gerard Hopkins	*Joan of Arc*
France, Anatole	
Translated by Winifred Stephens	*The Life of Joan of Arc*
Green, John Richard	*History of England*
Guizot, M.	
Translated by Robert Black	*History of France*
Hume, David	*History of England from the Invasion of Julius Caesar to the Revolution*
Lang, Andrew	*The Maid of France*
Lowell, Francis C.	*Joan of Arc*
Oman, Charles	*Political History of England*
Oman, Charles	*The History of the Art of War in the Middle Ages*
Paine, Albert Bigelow	*Joan of Arc, Maid of France*
Ramsay, Sir James H. of Bamff	*Genesis of Lancaster*
Stenton, D. M.	*English Society in the Middle Ages*
Stephen, Sir Leslie and Lee, Sir Sydney	*The Dictionary of National Biography*
Stolpe, Sven	
Translated by Eric Lewenhaupt	*The Maid of Orléans*
Strickland, Agnes	*The Lives of the Queens of England*
Timbs, John and Gunn, Alexander	*Abbeys, Castles and Ancient Halls of England and Wales*
Wade, John	*British History*
Waldman, Milton	*Joan of Arc*